Amanda Cinelli was raised in a large Irish/Italian family in the suburbs of Dublin, Ireland. Her love of romance was inspired after 'borrowing' one of her mother's beloved Mills & Boon novels at the age of twelve. Writing soon became a necessary outlet for her wildly over-active imagination.

Now married, with a daughter of her own, she splits her time between changing nappies, studying psychology and writing love stories.

Kate Hardy has always loved books, and could read before she went to school. She discovered Mills & Boon books when she was twelve, and decided that this was what she wanted to do. When she isn't writing Kate enjoys reading, cinema, ballroom dancing and the gym.

You can contact her via her website: www.katehardy.com.

Amanda Browning still lives in the Essex house where she was born. The third of four children—her sister being her twin—she enjoyed the rough and tumble of life with two brothers as much as she did reading books. Writing came naturally as an outlet for a fertile imagination. The love of books led her to a career in libraries, and being single allowed her to take the leap into writing for a living. Success is still something of a wonder, but allows her to indulge in hobbies as varied as embroidery and bird-watching.

Once a Playboy...

AMANDA CINELLI
KATE HARDY
AMANDA BROWNING

MILLS & BOON

First Published in Great Britain 2018
by Mills & Boon, an imprint of HarperCollins*Publishers*
1 London Bridge Street, London, SE1 9GF

ONCE A PLAYBOY... © 2018 Harlequin Books S. A.

Resisting the Sicilian Playboy © 2015 Amanda Cinelli
Her Playboy's Proposal © 2016 Pamela Brooks
The Playboy's Proposal © 2001 Amanda Browning

ISBN: 978-0-263-26869-0

05-0718

RESISTING THE SICILIAN PLAYBOY

AMANDA CINELLI

For my dear friend Kirsty.
This story would never have been finished without you.

For my mother, Audrey. For your unwavering belief in
me, even when I didn't believe in myself.

And for my father, Paolo. For showing me that with
hard work and determination you can achieve anything.

CHAPTER ONE

DARA DEVLIN HAD found herself in a few sticky situations in this job, but this had to be by far the worst.

A professional event planner should never gatecrash. It had to be written somewhere in the company handbook. Yet here she was, straddling the second-floor balcony ledge of Milan's most exclusive nightclub in four-inch designer heels.

All in the name of business, of course.

The heels had certainly slowed progress up the slippery emergency ladder, but leaving them in the alley below was unthinkable. A woman stood by her shoes, no matter how sticky the situation. And this situation most definitely qualified as *sticky*.

Handbag in one hand, she silently willed her skirt not to tear as she manoeuvred herself less than gracefully over the cold stone ledge, landing on hard marble tiles. Her watch showed it was just past ten. An unfashionably early time to be going clubbing in this part of the world, but dancing wasn't on her agenda tonight.

The city's premier celebrity hotspot, Platinum I, was celebrating its grand reopening this weekend and entry was strictly invitation only. No amount of her Irish charm would sway the arrogant hostess with her little black clipboard.

Nevertheless, Dara was determined to get into this party one way or another. She was only in town for the weekend before she had to head back south to her company's office in Syracuse. Failing this task just wasn't an option.

When her various contacts had said Leonardo Valente was untouchable, she had accepted the challenge with enthusiasm. She had the opportunity to plan the most high-profile wedding of her career—all she needed was one man's cooperation.

How hard could it be?

Even after three weeks of rejected emails and dead-end phone calls she had refused to give up. Armed with her tablet computer and her snazziest designer suit, she had foolishly believed she could just travel to his Milan office and demand to be seen.

The joke was on her. Because it seemed that Leonardo Valente's office didn't even exist. The address on his secretary's email had led her to a professional call-answering headquarters, where her enquiries had all been rejected point-blank.

It was just plain good luck that she had found out about tonight. The first club in the worldwide Platinum chain was turning ten years old and celebrating with a star-studded relaunch weekend.

Her grasp on the Italian language was far from perfect, but one thing was certain: Leonardo Valente was here tonight, inside these walls. All she had to do was find a way inside.

She looked around the empty terrace and felt her stomach tighten. She had hoped it would be some sort of outdoor seating area where she could just climb over the wall and melt into the crowd. She bit her lip. It was still some part of the club, and it was her only hope of getting inside.

The wall of the building was made almost entirely out of glass, each pane a deep glossy black, making it impossible to see what was inside. The thump of music had been deafening down on the ground, but on this terrace it was completely muffled.

She ignored the uncomfortable twitch in her stomach, putting it down to nerves. She was sneaking into an exclusive event, after all—nerves were to be expected. In life sometimes you had to break the rules to get ahead, but this pretty much went against every fibre of her goody-two-shoes nature.

Pushing a strand of blonde hair from her face, she placed one hand on the window. Her pale skin reflected brightly in the black glass, her steel-grey eyes calm and focused as she made her way slowly from pane to pane. She began pressing her fingertips along each narrow gap, searching for a hinge, a hook—something that hinted at an opening.

After she had exhausted every possible angle, she stepped back and surveyed the rest of the terrace with a frown. It made no sense. Surely there had to be a way to get inside.

She felt a sudden irrational urge to kick the glass and force her way in. But that would never do. Dara Devlin quite simply did not lose her cool—no matter how rough the situation was getting. It was the main reason brides from all over the world called her to plan their dream Sicilian weddings.

With a deep, calming breath, she forced herself to think. While climbing up here had definitely been worth a shot, unfortunately she was now two storeys up and not going anywhere fast. Her hands gripped the cold stone as she peered over the ledge. The street looked much further down from up here, and she was suddenly feeling a lot less brave.

'*Signorina*, is there a particular reason you are sneaking around out here in the darkness?'

The deep, sensual voice came suddenly from behind her, making her breath catch painfully in her throat.

Dara turned slowly, eyes widening when she saw that a pane of glass had somehow disappeared and a man now stood watching her.

How had she not heard someone coming? It was far too late to try and escape back down the ladder now. Her mind raced as she tried to find a way to spin this that wouldn't get her arrested.

'I'm waiting for an explanation.'

His face was slightly obscured in the shadows, but she could tell from his dark suit and crossed arms that he was definitely someone in charge—most likely Security. Damn and double damn. This was not going well.

Time to think, Devlin. Forcing her tone to keep light, she laughed breathlessly and spoke in fast-paced English. No one arrested a silly blonde in trouble.

'Well, finally someone's bothered to come out and help me.' She sighed for dramatic effect. 'I've been banging on the glass for twenty minutes, trying to get back inside.'

'You couldn't find the door, no?'

His perfect English surprised her, but the mocking tone said he wasn't buying it. She kept talking anyway.

'It's a safety hazard. I was looking to get some fresh air and someone said I could step out here for a moment—'

'So you decided to scale the building to get to it?' he said. It wasn't a question, more an amused statement. 'Do you make a habit of wearing heels to climb up buildings? It's quite a talent.'

Dara opened her mouth to protest, but thought against it.

'One-way glass.' He gestured over his shoulder. It was too dark to see his face, but there was a definite smirk in his silky voice as he spoke. 'The moment you realised you weren't getting inside was really quite entertaining. I was convinced you were about to throw a tantrum.'

Dara huffed out the breath she hadn't even realised she had been holding. Well, it was great that he found this situation so funny, because from where she was standing her mission had just been unceremoniously called to a halt. She would likely be hauled out of here by the collar of her crisp white shirt and maybe even charged with trespassing.

'I realise how this looks—' she began, trying to keep the panic out of her voice.

'Do you? Because from here it looks like you were trying to break into my private floor in what I can only assume is a naughty secretary outfit.'

Dara frowned at that. 'What? I am *not* a naughty—' Her brain froze, processing the first chunk of his accusations.

The man stepped forward into the light, revealing a face that she had seen countless times in the tabloids. Dara felt her entire body freeze as she realised just who she had been lying to.

'Oh, God, you're him.'

Her razor-sharp professional reflexes turned to mush as she took in all six-feet-plus of muscular Sicilian male.

'If by "him" you mean the owner of the building you just attempted to break into, then that's a yes.' The glow seemed to have left his eyes now, and had been replaced by a keen cynicism. 'I suppose you're going to want to come inside now? Start telling me about how this is all some crazy misunderstanding?'

Arms folded across an impressive chest, he stood waiting for her to dig her hole even deeper.

Hot embarrassment clawed up Dara's neck. He clearly thought this was a scheme to get him alone. She'd read the magazines. Women threw themselves at Leo Valente everywhere he went. And it wasn't just that he was mega-rich—although for some women that would be more than enough. With this man, the words they used were *mouth-watering*, *delicious* and *sinful*.

It had always made her laugh to hear of men described like desserts, but now, standing five feet away from him, she could kind of understand the madness.

He was a far cry from her usual type. His dark hair reached just under his collar and was a bit too untidy, his eyelashes were too long and his jaw overgrown with dark stubble. But even she couldn't argue that he was a sight to behold. And he had taken one look at her tidy blazer and blouse and presumed she was some groupie, here to play dress-up games.

She almost groaned with embarrassment. This was *not* the shining first impression she had banked on.

'Well, as much as I enjoy being stared at, I really don't have all night.'

Dara's heart gave an uncomfortable thump. 'I wasn't staring,' she said, rather too quickly. 'I was just…thinking.'

Oh, now this was just getting worse and worse. The moment she had been working towards for three weeks had finally presented itself and her mind had decided to go into sleep mode.

One dark eyebrow rose, mocking her. 'Were you thinking about this particular situation, or are there other criminal acts you've committed tonight?'

Criminal? Dara felt hot panic rise in her chest. 'Mr

Valente, I can assure you I was not attempting to commit a crime.'

'Relax. I won't call in the hounds just yet. But you failed to notice the security camera watching your every move.' He pointed to a tiny blinking red light above her head. 'My team was halfway up here when I told them to wait.'

'Why did you do that?' The question was out before she could stop herself.

He shrugged one shoulder. 'I was bored. You looked interesting.'

She thought for a moment, but could not come up with a single response to that comment. Perhaps if he found her so interesting she could captivate him long enough to make her proposal.

She cleared her throat. 'Just so we're clear: I'm not a criminal. I'm a wedding planner.' She watched as his eyes narrowed.

'Same thing, in my opinion.' He smirked. 'I liked my naughty secretary theory much better.'

And just like that Dara found herself the subject of Leonardo Valente's infamous smouldering gaze. She cleared her throat, trying to think of something—anything—to break the tension. The air was beginning to feel very thin up here on this darkened terrace, and it had nothing to do with the altitude.

'Your theory is incorrect. I'm not here for anything like…like that.'

'Such a pity. Nonetheless, you have my attention.' He turned abruptly to go inside, pausing when she didn't immediately follow behind him. 'Unless you plan on going back down that ladder again, I suggest you follow me.'

With that he was gone, leaving Dara with no choice but to obey.

The room on the other side of the glass was twice the size of her entire apartment. She saw him press a few buttons in a panel on the wall and suddenly soft light illuminated the room. It was not an office, but nor was it an apartment. It reminded her of the lobby of a very exclusive hotel, with modern cubic seating and an impressive glass fireplace.

Exactly why a nightclub needed a room like this she wasn't sure—maybe he used it to entertain private guests. That thought made her clutch her handbag a little tighter in front of her, and feeling the outline of her computer reminded her of why she was there.

He pressed another button on the panel and the clever door slid silently back into place behind him. She could see that it was indeed one-way glass, and her ears burned at the thought of him watching her for all that time.

He turned around to face her and for the first time she noticed the vivid colour of his eyes. They weren't dark, as she had thought from his photographs, but a unique shade of deep forest green. Dara shook her head. Why was she even looking at his eyes, for goodness' sake? This was a business meeting, not a school dance.

'So, do you have a name—or will I just call you Spiderwoman?' That smirk was still firmly in place as he took a couple of steps towards her.

Her inner professional was sharp enough to see a perfect moment. 'I actually have my card in here somewhere…if you'd just give me a second…' She began fishing in her bag—maybe she should launch into the entire presentation now, before he had a chance to shoot her down.

Without warning he was in front of her, taking the bag from her hand and placing it gently on the floor. 'I did not ask for a card. I asked for your name—from your lips, preferably.'

His gaze travelled down to her mouth and she felt her stomach flutter in response. She ignored the sensation, straightening her chin and meeting his gaze head-on. 'It's Dara Devlin.'

He nodded, as though she had answered correctly.

'So...Dara the wedding planner...' His deep voice purred her name, as though he was tasting it on his tongue. 'What gives me the pleasure of your company this evening?'

'I'm not here for pleasure.' She took a step back, wanting to put as much distance between them as possible. 'What I mean is, I came here to find you. To talk business.'

He raised one dark brow. 'Who comes to a nightclub to talk business?'

'Well, *you* do,' she said confidently. That earned her a puzzled look. 'I'm here to discuss a possible deal between you and a very high-profile client of mine. All I'm asking is just five minutes of your time.'

'I have a swarm of media vultures downstairs in the club. Every one of them is waiting for "just five minutes". Why should you get to skip the queue?'

'If they deserved the time they would have climbed up here by now.'

Without warning he threw his dark head back and laughed—a deep, rumbling laugh that seemed to resonate right to her core. The gesture shocked her for a moment, and her eyes moved down to take in the strong column of his throat, the dark hairs that disappeared into the casually open collar of his shirt.

Dara swallowed, her throat feeling strangely dry. She

looked up—only to be pinned by that mocking emerald gaze again.

'You know, despite the fact that you could have killed yourself climbing up here tonight, I admit that I'm impressed,' he said. 'You deserve those five minutes based on sheer nerve and creativity.'

Dara smiled with triumph and eagerly reached for the tablet computer in her bag. 'Wonderful. I've actually prepared a short pitch, if you want to take a seat?'

'No,' he said simply.

Her bag flopped back down to the ground as she took in his sudden change of tone. 'But you said that—'

'I said I'd give you your five minutes, Dara Devlin. I didn't say when.'

She felt a frown crease her forehead and quickly smoothed it down. This man was impossible. It was just five minutes, for goodness' sake. They had easily spent three times that up here already.

He gestured for her to move towards the door, closing a button on his tailored suit jacket in the process. 'You can arrange a time with my secretary. In the meantime, the party is just getting started downstairs.'

Dara felt her temper finally bubble up to the surface. 'I've been calling your secretary for three weeks—why do you think I pulled this stunt?'

'I just presumed you enjoyed a little espionage on a Friday night.' He smirked.

She fought the urge to stamp her foot in frustration. She needed to get to the subject of this meeting, but it had to be done just right or he would shoot her down— just like all the others who had approached him before her. Her presentation built up slowly, allowing her time to sway his thinking. He clearly wasn't going to give her that chance.

'Aren't you just a little curious about what made me climb up here?' she asked, desperate to stall him.

He moved forward so that they stood little more than a couple of steps apart in the silent room. 'It surprises me to find that I'm quite intrigued by you.' His eyes lowered to take in every inch of her body in one heated sweep.

Dara felt a rush of heat colour her cheeks. She might not have much experience with flirtation, but there was no mistaking the glitter in his eyes. This man was everything the tabloids made him out to be. Suave, sensual and utterly scandalous.

'You know, I can't remember the last time I made a woman blush.' He stepped closer, his voice deepening. 'Come have a drink with me, Dara. Let down that beautiful blonde hair of yours.'

'I don't think that would be appropriate, Mr Valente.' She pushed a tendril of hair behind her ear, feeling more than a little self-conscious under his gaze.

'Mr Valente was my father—you can call me Leo.' He smiled. 'What business could be so important that it can't wait until Monday morning?'

Dara spied her chance to turn the conversation. 'My condolences on your father's recent passing. I understand the funeral was held at your *castello* in Ragusa?'

'So I've been told.' He shrugged. 'People die every day, Miss Devlin. I prefer to focus on more enjoyable pursuits.'

Even after bringing up the subject of his father, the man was still flirting with her. He really was a complete playboy. She decided a more direct approach was definitely needed.

'The *castello* is a beautiful piece of history. It's such a shame that it lies dormant most of the time.'

'Why do I get the feeling this is more than idle chit-chat?' He narrowed his gaze, all trace of flirtation gone.

'Well, you see, it's part of the reason that I'm here.' Feeling a sense of foreboding, she powered on. 'I'm here to propose a deal for Castello Bellamo that I feel you will benefit greatly from.'

She blurted it out as confidently as she could and felt the swell of victory as he froze in place. The playful charmer seemed to disappear before her eyes, his expression taking on a detached hardness.

He met her eyes, a single muscle ticking on his jaw. When he spoke his voice was somehow deeper than before, his accent more pronounced. 'Well, it seems you have wasted both your time and mine tonight. I'll tell you the same thing that I have told every other vulture that has approached me since my father's death. The castle is not for sale.'

Dara shook her head, desperate for him to understand. 'I don't want to buy it—I want to hold a wedding there. I'm sure that we can come to some sort of—'

A flick of his hand cut her off mid-sentence. 'I don't care if you want to use it to house blind orphans. The matter is not open for discussion.'

'I understand that the *castello* has been left in disrepair for some time now—'

'It can stay that way, for all I care. Contrary to what people may think, these little games don't work for me—no matter how pretty the messenger is.' His eyes raked down to her heels, taking in every inch of her body with an exaggerated slowness before meeting her eyes once more.

'This conversation is over,' he gritted. 'I'll have someone sent up to escort you out. Now, if you'll excuse me, I've got a party to attend to.'

Without another word he strode from the room, leaving Dara to stare after him in disbelief.

That had been a rather dramatic turn of events. She knew his father had died recently, and it had been tactless of her to use it as part of her argument. But what other choice did she have? The most lucrative wedding contract of her career was within touching distance and she had personally promised the bride Castello Bellamo. If she failed to deliver she could say goodbye to her miraculous gateway into society weddings. Her name would be worthless.

She was not going to be ruined without a fight.

Leo slid in behind the bar of the empty upper mezzanine of the club and waved off the young barmaid with an impatient hand. Taking down a bottle of aged whisky, he poured himself a generous glass and let the amber liquid burn down his throat in one fluid movement.

Blondie had caught him by surprise—there was no doubting that. Beautiful women were not a rarity in his world—supermodels and socialites lined up to be seen on his arm—but there had been something about that determined grey gaze that had sparked his interest in a way no woman had for months now.

No one had dared speak to him of his father since his death had been worldwide news. But to start with that and then make a move for the castle… He took another swig of whisky, a harsh bark of laughter escaping his throat. She definitely had nerve—he'd give her that.

As his temper slowly calmed he realised he was no longer alone in the private bar. Miss Devlin had come to a stop on the other side of the counter.

'Just so we're clear: I am not a messenger and I don't play games. Ever.'

She was angry, and it was a sight to behold.

'Never? You keep shattering my fantasies tonight, Miss Devlin.' Leo took in the crisp white shirt she wore, the outline of a lacy white bra barely visible at the front. His knuckles tensed on the glass in his hand as heat rushed through his veins. Damn, it had been way too long if the sight of a bra was arousing him.

'Do you take anything seriously, Mr Valente?'

She rolled her eyes, checking the time on her watch in a gesture of boredom. But Leo could see the hint of a flush high on her cheekbones. She wasn't as unaffected by him as she pretended to be.

He stepped forward, bracing his hands on the bar between them. 'Believe me, there are certain things I can take *very* seriously.' He let his eyes linger on her lips for a moment and smiled when she self-consciously took a step back. 'Look around you, Miss Devlin. I opened this club ten years ago. I now own one in every major city in the world, so you can see that I take the business of pleasure very seriously.'

'I'm here to talk about my proposal—not about pleasure.' She shook her head.

'A pity. I can tell that we would communicate very well on that subject.' He watched as heat flushed across her chest.

She laid her bag down forcefully on the counter. 'Are you always this forward?' Her voice was somehow calm and furious at the same time.

Damn it, but she was right. He was behaving like a caveman. What was it about this woman that set his teeth on edge? She was prickly, and direct, and sexy as hell. But she was here to talk about the one thing he was determined to ignore.

'You seem to have caught me off guard. Having an

unarmed woman bypass a million-euro security system will do that to a man.'

'If I were a man would you be any less impressed, I wonder?' She stood tall, meeting his gaze evenly.

Leo laughed, offering her a glass of whisky. 'You are refreshing, Dara. Consider this a peace offering for my inappropriate behaviour.'

'Thank you.'

She took the glass with both hands, holding it close to breathe in the aroma. It was a ridiculously feminine gesture.

Leo watched her for a moment, downing the rest of his drink in one go. 'You know, considering your position, I wonder how *I* have come to be the one apologising.'

'I can be very persuasive.' She smiled and took a sip of whisky, making a delicate little hum of approval.

Leo felt his blood pump a little faster. 'Something we both have in common.'

He stepped out from behind the bar, taking in her polite business suit once more. She was a walking contradiction, this one. All delicate and businesslike on the outside, but with the guts to scale a building in a skirt and heels. He wondered why he hadn't thrown her out yet.

She placed her glass down, turning to face him head-on with calm determination in the set of her shoulders. 'I will be leaving for Sicily in the morning. I'm asking you please to just consider my proposal.'

'You just broke the law and you expect me to do business with you?'

'I am asking you to at least give me a chance.' Her voice remained steady, with not a trace of remorse for tonight's actions.

'Do you honestly expect me to let you use a seven-hundred-year-old castle for a glorified circus?'

'Firstly, it's a wedding. Secondly, from what I understand the castle has been mostly unoccupied for years. Many jobs were lost when your father closed it to the public. We both know that poverty is already an issue in Sicily.'

'I think you overestimate my ability to empathise.' He had heard the same argument before countless times.

'Maybe so, but a high-profile wedding like this would bring a lot of opportunity to a struggling town like Monterocca.'

Leo felt the skin behind his neck prickle at her mention of the name. There was no reason for him to feel anything for that place. The people of his home town meant nothing to him. And yet he felt an uncomfortable pull in his stomach at her words.

'It would bring a storm of paparazzi,' he countered.

'Naturally. But from what I hear that might not be such a bad thing.'

He raised a brow in surprise. 'Have you been reading the tabloids, Dara?'

'I have been told that you have something of a bad reputation among the people of Sicily.'

'My father's reputation. Not mine,' he corrected.

'Yes, but his reputation has stood in your way in the past. It doesn't go unnoticed that you don't own a single club in your native region.'

Leo fought the urge to snarl. That was a particular sore spot of his. Opting instead for a nonchalant shrug of his shoulder, he leaned in. 'If I didn't know better, I'd say you cared.'

She straightened immediately, her guard firmly in place. 'Thankfully we both know that caring isn't high on the agenda here.' She gestured to the empty tables around them. 'So, this is the big exclusive launch party?'

'It's just a pre-launch. The lower floors are open to a select few guests. Tomorrow is the official event.' Leo looked down to where the floor below was filled with a swarm of people.

She followed him over to the floor-to-ceiling window that overlooked the entire club.

'Do you only mingle with the little people at official events?' she asked.

'Well, I have been kept busy up here by a very persistent blonde security breach, it seems.'

She ignored that comment, her delicate features taking on a focused edge. 'Did you know that those water features are blocking off the lounge area from the rest of the club?' she asked.

Leo blinked, following her gaze to take in the scene below them.

She continued. 'Also, the spotlights are a little too strong on the dance floor. Softer red-hued lighting would soften the transition into the seated areas.'

He followed her gaze with interest. 'Is there anything else you'd like to point out?'

She opened her mouth briefly, then stopped as if rethinking her actions.

'Oh come now, you've already begun—don't hold back on my account.' He raised a brow in challenge, noting the delicate glow on her cheekbones as she nipped at the skin of her lower lip.

'It's just…your staff's uniforms. They don't fit the image at all. They're quite…sparkly and frivolous.'

'Platinum is the signature colour,' he argued. 'They don't *sparkle*—they shine.'

She shrugged. 'They look sparkly to me. I wasn't trying to insult your style.'

'I thought you were all about honesty?' he scolded, frowning.

'I'm just trying to prove to you that I know what I'm talking about. No matter what kind of event you're throwing, the principle is always the same. Make it memorable, and make a statement. You're dealing with an exclusive clientele here—people who expect one-of-a-kind events every time. And that just happens to be my area of expertise.'

'You could see all of that from up here?'

'I have a keen eye for detail. I may not be the star guest of the party, but I make it my business to know how to plan one.'

'And my club does not fit your usual standard?'

'I don't have a "usual standard". In my world there is perfection or failure.'

'Ah, so this would be a failure?' He waited patiently for her answer.

Dara remained silent.

He let out a low bark of laughter. 'I've honestly never had someone insult me in order to convince me to sign a contract.'

'I believe in honesty. And if you choose Devlin Events to represent the *castello*, honesty is what you will get.'

He looked down at the crowd for a moment. 'So your plan is to throw a fancy wedding and fix my public image all in one go, is it? I'd say you're a little out of your league.'

'My résumé speaks for itself. I've personally forged contracts with some of the major resort chains around the island—Santo, Lucchesi and Ottanta.'

'You've worked for the Lucchesi Group?'

'I'm a freelance consultant. They hired me on a few occasions. The most notable being Umberto and Gloria's golden wedding anniversary. It was just a small garden party at their family home, but—'

Leo's business mind perked up at that. 'You are on first-name terms with Umberto Lucchesi?'

'Yes. He did offer me a job, which I politely refused. I prefer to be my own boss.'

Leo walked to the glass wall and looked down across the packed club below the mezzanine. Well, this had just gone from interesting to downright serendipitous. He wondered if she realised the significance of what she had just divulged. Maybe it was all a fabrication—she had researched him, after all.

But he knew there was no record of his history with Lucchesi...their recent disagreements. Business was a private affair among Sicilian men, and while he hadn't set foot on Sicilian soil in more than eighteen years he was still *siciliano* through and through.

He cursed as his phone rang, and the call took less than ten seconds before he ended it.

'I'm needed downstairs. Certain guests are getting impatient.'

Her eyes fell, and defeat was evident in the droop of her shoulders. 'Well, thank you for your time, Mr Valente.' She held her hand out to him.

He ignored it. 'It's Leo. And you misunderstand me. This conversation isn't over.'

'It's not?'

'Not by a long shot.' He smiled. 'One hour. We'll discuss this further then.'

She moved uneasily. 'Shall I stay up here?'

'You deserve to relax after your little stunt tonight, Dara. Come down to the dark side—drink, dance. Practise using the stairs, perhaps.' He began walking away, back towards his private elevator.

'But how will I know where to meet you?' she called.

'Don't worry. I'll find you.'

Leo smiled to himself as the elevator doors closed slowly, her shapely silhouette disappearing from view. He would finish this interesting interlude, and that was a promise.

CHAPTER TWO

LEATHER BARSTOOLS REALLY were a girl's worst enemy.

Dara sighed and adjusted the hem of her pencil skirt for what felt like the hundredth time. Glamorous socialites and powerful businessmen lined the dance floor, each designer dress more chic than the last. She felt hopelessly mismatched in her black skirt suit. She tapped the email app on her phone, even though it had barely been five minutes since the last check.

With a dull flicker, her emails vanished before her eyes. The screen turned completely blank.

Of course—a dead battery. She stuffed the useless device back into her bag. Was there anything that hadn't gone wrong tonight?

She was not an impatient person, but the music in here was too loud and it was about a million degrees too warm. Add that to the fact that an extremely rude group of models had commented on her appearance the moment she'd sat down. Her designer suit might as well have been rags next to their glamorous cocktail dresses.

At events like this she was the one who usually stood on the sidelines, barking into her headset at her team. Sitting idly at a bar just made her feel on edge.

Out of habit she scanned the room, noticing details about the layout and decor. For such an elite event, the organisation was nowhere near as fine-tuned as she would expect. And, as she'd told Leo Valente, the staff's uniforms were nothing short of theatrical—gauche, shiny silver tunics intended to represent the brand name: Platinum.

The sooner she wrapped up this meeting, the better. She was restless when she wasn't doing something productive. Winter was low season, mostly taken up with administrative tasks. She already missed the hectic schedule of her summer wedding list.

She huffed out an agitated breath and craned her neck to scan the crowd for the object of her thoughts once more. Her stomach lurched as she spotted him.

He stood on the opposite side of the dance floor, surrounded by members of the media. From her vantage point she could see that he stood head and shoulders above the other men, his broad shoulders fitting his tailored suit jacket to perfection.

She shouldn't be noticing his shoulders. She should be furious that he seemed to have forgotten about his promise. That 'one hour' had been up twenty minutes ago.

She fanned herself with a beer mat and looked up just in time to see a silver-clad bartender place an elaborate drink in front of her.

'Sorry, I didn't order this.' She pushed it slowly back towards him, only for him to slide it right back.

'Compliments of Signor Valente. For his beautiful blonde companion.' He smiled politely.

Apparently he hadn't forgotten her after all, she thought. Maybe this was his apology for leaving her waiting? She stared at the drink. It was a frothy cream-coloured cocktail that smelled of rich liqueur.

'What is it?' she asked as she took a small sip.

The young bartender smirked, leaning in closer. 'I believe in English it is called a Screaming Orgasm.'

A screaming *what*?

Her breath fought with an unfortunate sip of the offending cocktail, making her splutter her outrage noisily onto the counter.

Dara felt her face turn bright red. The bartender moved away, but not before she caught a glimpse of him laughing to himself. Of all the most blatant disregards for propriety, this was just outrageous.

She looked around and sure enough the group of models were now eyeing her even more intently. One of them commented loudly that clearly Valente's standards must be dropping.

Dara felt her cheeks burn with embarrassment. Was this why he'd asked her to stay here? Did Leo Valente expect her to sleep with him in order to get her contract? The thought sent a shiver of something suspiciously close to excitement down her spine.

She shook the foreign sensation off with a frown. She needed his help—that was true. But not at the expense of her pride. She had been a fool to promise Castello Bellamo to Portia Palmer without researching its owner first. Her choice was to sit here and act as a billionaire's plaything for the night or leave and face the consequences.

Her business reputation might be salvaged, but her pride...that was another matter entirely.

Making her decision, she grabbed her bag and pushed her way through the crowd towards the exit. Her heels ached with each step and the music seemed to be getting louder and louder. When she finally emerged out into the cool night air she felt as if she had just escaped hell itself.

Damn Leo Valente and his perfect unobtainable castle. Standing out in the chilly October air, she remembered that her phone was dead. She stalked her way back towards the club and asked the hostess to call her a cab. The dark-haired woman looked as if she might refuse for a moment, but thankfully nodded and disappeared inside.

Dara stood at the edge of the pavement and hugged her blazer tighter around her shoulders. Was she overreacting here? Maybe she should go back inside and give it one last try. The alternative was admitting to Portia Palmer that she had lied about being able to make her dream wedding in Monterocca a reality. The actress famously blacklisted anyone who got on her bad side.

Promising a location that everyone had tried to get for years and then taking it away most definitely qualified as bad.

She didn't know what on earth had possessed her to make such a ridiculous claim. She usually played by the rules, and she always came out on top. Why couldn't she have got landed with a kindly old man to convince rather than a hot-blooded Sicilian with a cruel sense of humour?

The door of the club slammed and jolted her out of her reverie. Dara spun round and came face-to-face with the object of her thoughts.

'Do you always run away from business meetings or am I just an exception?' he said, coming to a stop in front of her on the pavement. He was breathing heavily, as though he had just run through the entire club.

'I would hardly call being sat at a bar and plied with obscenely named alcohol a business meeting.' She folded her arms across her chest.

'You looked like you needed to laugh. Perhaps it was in bad taste.' He shrugged.

'You really do have a twisted sense of humour.' Dara huffed out a breath. 'I'm not prepared to…to play any games in order to get what I want here.'

He raised a brow, obviously understanding her meaning. 'Sorry to disappoint, but I'm not in the habit of coercing women into my bed.'

Dara's cheeks burned with embarrassment. 'Either way, I would be waiting until hell freezes over for you to hire out your castle. You practically said it yourself.'

'Castello Bellamo is my bargaining chip. Prove yourself to me and I will consider the contract.'

'Prove myself to you *how*, exactly?'

'The grand launch event tomorrow night will be very high profile. You seem to have a lot of opinions—I'd like to see you in action.'

Dara frowned. 'I don't understand…are you trying to offer me a job?'

'I'm offering you an audition to convince me of why I should trust you. A temporary consulting position, of sorts. Impress me and I'll go through your proposal. It's more than anyone else has ever gotten.'

She ignored the silky tone in his voice. 'But why offer me a chance in the first place? What's your game?'

He made a clucking sound. 'So untrusting, Dara. I'm curious to see if you're as ruthlessly ambitious as you say you are.'

'So if I pass the test, then you'll trust me?'

'Perhaps… But what kind of a businessman would I be if I trusted every beautiful blonde who offered me a deal?' He extended a hand towards her. 'So, Dara Devlin, are you prepared to risk your perfect reputation for a crumbling old castle?'

'"Risk" implies that I stand to fail.'

She accepted his hand and felt a frisson of electricity as his gaze intensified. The heat of his body seemed to flow up her veins. All of a sudden he was closer, his scent bombarding her senses as he leaned his body towards her. He pressed his lips to one cheek, then slowly progressed to the other.

Dara stood frozen as he eased back from her. The kiss was customary—she had got used to the gesture soon after moving to this country—but being so close to him, feeling the heat from his body scant inches from hers... She cleared the surprise from her expression, finding him watching her closely.

'My driver will see that you get back to your hotel safely.' He gestured to the town car that had pulled up by them. 'Until tomorrow, Dara...'

One last look and he was gone, walking back into his den of sin.

Dara watched him go, the realisation of what she had just agreed to making her insides flutter. She had just got further with Castello Bellamo than anyone had ever come before. But she felt as though she had calmly agreed to swim in a tank full of hungry sharks. No, she corrected herself, not sharks plural. One shark in particular.

Leo Valente was a smooth-talking predator, and she had somehow managed to catch his interest. She wouldn't let this chance go to waste. First she would wow him with her event expertise—then present him with her proposal for the castle. She smiled as she thought of his arrogant confidence. Sometimes even sharks needed to be taught a lesson.

Dara's hotel wasn't particularly fancy, but for such short notice it was good value and it didn't have bugs in the beds. That was good enough for her.

She decided to take the stairs down to the lobby to use up some of the nervous energy she had accumulated since leaving the club last night. After lying awake since dawn, staring into the distance, she had sprung out of bed and begun typing some ideas she'd had for the event tonight. They were good ideas—maybe some were even great—but that didn't mean they would be heard. After getting dressed and pacing the room for an hour, she'd decided against it.

Whatever Leo Valente's plan was for her this evening, she doubted it had anything to do with her organisation skills. It was up to her to convince him to contract Castello Bellamo out to her by not giving him a chance to ignore her logic.

She decided that she might as well see the sights while she mentally tortured herself. Whatever it was that he had in store for her, she was going to give it her all.

The lobby of the hotel had a small tourist kiosk. She approached the guide behind the counter and asked for some basic tools to see the main sights of Milan in a few short hours. The girl quickly began gathering various maps and brochures for her to plan her journey. She would need tickets for the trams, she announced, and headed through a small door behind the desk.

Dara picked up an Italian tabloid magazine and began carelessly flipping through the pages while she waited. Her hands stopped on an image of a familiar tall, dark Sicilian nightclub owner on a page entitled 'The Lonely Hearts Club'.

Dara almost laughed at the thought of Leo Valente being lonely. The man had women falling at his feet wherever he went. In this particular candid shot he was pictured bare-chested, sitting by a pool, and the look on his face was one of absolute boredom rather than love-sickness. The small bubble printed next to his head indicated that 'poor Leo' was tired of a life of supermodel flings and was ready to settle down. *'Is there a lioness brave enough to tame him?'* the final line wondered.

She turned to the next page, refusing to look at him. A lion indeed—that suited him much better than a shark. She had read somewhere before that lions liked to play with their food before they ate it. If ever there was an apt description for Leo Valente, that was it.

Her mind flashed back to the way he had looked at her last night, and she ignored the shiver of awareness that coursed through her. Sure, he was an attractive man—she could hardly deny that. But she had spent the past five years ignoring countless attractive men and she wouldn't be stopping now. Her career plan didn't leave time for men, and she was quite happy to keep it that way.

'Brushing up on current events, Dara?'

She snapped up her head in surprise, only to be pinned by a familiar smirking emerald gaze.

Leo raised a brow in silent question. 'My "lonely heart" is apparently worthy of your attention this morning... I didn't take you as the type to read gossip.'

Dara looked down and realised she was still holding the trashy magazine. 'I don't.' She said it a little too quickly. 'I'm just browsing while I wait for some travel information.'

She shoved the offending publication hastily back into the stand, straightening up to push an errant tendril of hair behind her ear.

He seemed taller and more imposing than he had the night before, if that was even possible. Dark jeans and a brown leather jacket accentuated the rough casual air that seemed to surround him wherever he went.

How had he known she was staying here? She didn't remember mentioning the name of her hotel to him. And besides, his event wasn't scheduled for another eight hours. Was he here to tell her he had decided not to give her a chance after all? Last night she had been lucky. She had caught him off guard, piqued his interest. Maybe he had woken up this morning and realised that this was one impulse he could erase.

She reflected on her black skinny jeans and warm woollen sweater, wishing she had worn something more professional. She had decided to be sensible today, choosing flat patent pumps for her plan of walking around the city. Now, as he stood in front of her, she felt short for the first time in her life. She was tall at five foot eight—especially by Italian standards. But she barely reached his chin.

Just then the kiosk attendant returned from behind the counter and placed a small tram card on the counter next to her bundle of maps and brochures.

'She doesn't need these any more.' Leo pushed the items back towards the attendant with a polite nod. The poor girl was clearly starstruck, with her head bobbing up and down and two bright pink spots on either cheek.

Dara groaned. Was that what she had looked like last night? She needed to remind herself to think sad thoughts when her painfully pale Irish skin decided to play up.

'I was planning to use those.' She reached towards the documents on the counter. She didn't care who he was—she wasn't going to let him hijack her day on another of his whims.

'The last time I checked you were *mine* for today.' His eyes glittered as he leaned casually on the counter. 'Like you said last night, Dara, I'm an impulsive man. If you want to work with me so badly, you need to learn to live by my rules. If I decide to take you to lunch, you drop your plans.'

Dara felt a shiver run down the back of her neck. This was ridiculous. He was practically ordering her to obey. She tried to think of a witty retort—something to wipe away that confident lift of his brow. Nothing came. She was here to audition for a role, and therefore she had to play his game. If that meant dropping her plans at his request, then so be it.

'Consider them dropped.' She fitted her bag under her arm and tilted her chin in what she hoped was a confident expression. 'I'm entirely at your disposal.'

One corner of his mouth tilted upwards, 'Congratulations. You just passed the first test. But I don't intend to dispose of you, Dara—not just yet.'

Leo had never thought he would get such satisfaction in seeing a woman eat. The rooftop *trattoria* was a little gem he liked to visit when he was in Milan, but he couldn't remember ever being so transfixed by a female companion before. She ate so carefully, spinning each forkful of spaghetti until it was wound tight before sliding it into her mouth. She refused to speak with a full mouth, and looked positively horrified when he did so without thought.

She had chosen spaghetti with fresh mixed seafood after enquiring about the specialities. She hadn't asked for a menu, and had graciously accepted the waiter's recommendations for a mixed appetiser platter they could share. The silver-haired Tuscan had positively beamed with delight at her accent when she spoke. Such a polite blonde foreigner with a clear Sicilian dialect—she was quite the novelty.

He took a sip of his sparkling water, watching as she placed the last forkful into her mouth. She had been eating so delicately he had hardly noticed that she had demolished the entire dish.

'Food is another passion of yours, I see.' He smiled.

She dabbed the napkin lightly at her mouth. 'Since I moved here—definitely.'

He followed the neat little movement of her hands as she placed her fork across the plate. The waiter promptly came and cleared the table, offering them an array of desserts which they both politely declined.

She sighed and sat back unselfconsciously in her seat, satisfied by the large meal. He imagined that might be how she looked after other types of satisfaction, and his stomach clenched at the thought.

Distracting himself, he stirred sugar into his coffee. 'A woman who likes to eat is a rarity in my world.'

She turned her head to look out of the window, across the dull Milanese skyline. 'The women in your world must be very sad and hungry.'

Leo smiled. 'The *siciliani* must have thought they were dreaming to find such a beautiful woman in their company who finishes a full meal.' He took a sip of the coffee, feeling the familiar strength hit his tastebuds.

She ignored his compliment. 'Actually, when I first moved to Syracuse all I ate were ham sandwiches and spaghetti in tomato sauce.'

'That's punishable by law in this country,' he scolded.

She smiled, nodding her head. 'I found that out soon enough. I think I lasted about a week before a colleague dragged me to her grandmother's house and made me confess my crimes.'

'Italian grandmothers are not known to be forgiving—especially when it involves food. I'm surprised you survived.'

Leo thought of his own upbringing. The array of servants in the castle kitchen. The silent meals alone with his nanny. Surprising himself with the direction of his thoughts, he sat forward, focusing on Dara's smiling features.

'It wasn't a laughing matter. That woman cooked twelve different types of pasta in the space of one hour.' She shook her head. 'It was the most dramatic reaction to food I have ever encountered.'

'My countrymen are not known for their delicate sensibilities.' He finished his coffee, regarding her as she sat still looking pensively out of the window. 'Tell the truth: have you eaten a plain tomato sauce since then?'

That earned him a smile. 'Not if my life depended on it.'

'Then you've passed the second test,' he proclaimed.

He watched as her expression drifted, all trace of their playful conversation melting away.

'Exactly how many tests do you have in store for me?' she asked as she took a sip from her water.

He leaned back into his seat, casual and in control. 'I don't like to put a limit on progress, Dara. As a businesswoman I'm sure you can understand that.'

'I'm glad to hear that, actually. I was considering showing you some ideas that struck me for your event tonight.' She reached for her handbag, then paused. 'Unless that violates my role as your temporary consultant?' She raised a brow.

Leo sighed. The woman was hell-bent on annoying him.

'Make it quick.'

She busied herself taking out a sleek tablet computer and unfolding the case into a neat stand, so that it stood upright as an impromptu presentation screen. She launched into a flurry of rough outlines, pinpointing the areas in which she felt his current plan lacked variety.

'So, you see, if you split the evening into two parts

you will avoid alienating the business clientele,' she concluded, finally.

Leo sat back in his chair and tilted his head to one side. The flow chart on the screen was genius. She had just achieved in one brainstorming session what a team of seven event organisers had failed to.

The Milan relaunch had been heavily debated for weeks, due to the awkward combination of 'party hard' celebrity guests and the more staid businessmen and politicians. Finding an event structure that could keep all groups entertained had proved impossible, and yet Dara had seen the solution after simply looking down from an upper floor window.

'Could you achieve all of this before you attend the event tonight?'

'Without a doubt.' She nodded confidently, her grey eyes lighting up with determination.

'I'll call my team in and you can get to work.'

She looked surprised for a moment 'Would your team not resent having a newcomer treading on their toes?'

'I'm beginning to wonder if *I* should be the one resenting them.'

She visibly relaxed into her chair. 'I'm glad you're open to change.'

He laughed, taking a sip of his coffee. '"Change" is an understatement. Things clearly need a shake-up. They're paid so well they've lost their creativity.' He sat forward, flicking the screen of her computer across to look through the images once more. 'I'll have my management team on hand—anything you need, they are at your disposal.'

'You make me sound important.' Her eyes sparkled as she closed down the screen and placed it back into her bag.

'And what about the uniforms?' he enquired casually, and smiled when her expression turned rueful.

'I don't expect you to overhaul your branding after one little statement.'

'Ah, but I'm an impulsive man, Dara.' He waved a hand, signalling to the waiter for their coats. 'Your comments last night have wounded my overblown pride. I'll expect that to be remedied by this evening too.'

Her eyes widened, her delicate hands twisting in her lap as she absorbed his challenge. 'It take it that this is another test?'

'You say you've never lost a challenge. Consider it an experiment.'

She straightened her shoulders. 'You trust me to make changes to your event *and* overhaul your signature uniform in less than seven hours?'

'Are you telling me you can't do it?'

'I can do it,' she said, all confidence. 'I just don't understand why you're giving me this opportunity when you've refused so many others.'

He sat back in his chair, once again taken by her honest approach to business. He had invited her tonight because of his attraction to her. But now, after she had once again proved she was more brains than body, he felt tempted to tell her at least a half-truth.

'Ten years ago I commissioned those uniforms as a gimmick. We had only been open a few months, and it was the first New Year's Eve event we ever held. The party was in full swing when a notorious designer came staggering in. He was drunk, as usual, and he stood in the middle of a crowd of journalists and began to shout that he could see himself in one of the suits.'

Leo laughed as he remembered the night clearly.

'The man was absolutely trashed, and he was amazed

by his own reflection in the material.' He rolled his eyes. 'But that's not how everyone else saw it. Anyway—long story short: word soon spread and our temporary costumes became a brand statement. I found the whole situation hilarious.'

He took another sip of coffee.

'It was a publicity stunt that worked, and it seemed that I was the only person who could see how ridiculous the staff looked. Until you, of course.' He raised his coffee cup in mock salute.

'My attention to detail is what keeps me in business.'

'Well, I'd imagine being associated with a big brand like Lucchesi doesn't hurt.' Leo dropped the name casually, watching her reaction with hooded intent.

'I'm hardly "associated" with the brand. I've been contracted for a few events—one with the Lucchesi Foundation, their charity for the hospitals of Sicily.'

'You must have made quite an impression for a relative unknown to be trusted by such a family.'

'I happened to get talking to Gloria Lucchesi and her daughters while I was planning a wedding in Syracuse.' She shrugged. 'I wish it was more impressive, but it was rather coincidental.'

'Nonetheless, you are on first-name terms with a very powerful family. That in itself is an achievement.'

'I suppose it is.' She smiled.

Leo mulled over her connection to Umberto Lucchesi. Their recent disagreement had caused a large problem that he was fast losing time to resolve. Not that a wedding planner could pose any solution, but she might possibly be useful.

He watched as Dara sat back in her chair, casually glancing towards him as she folded her napkin into a neat square on the table, then did the same with his.

She looked up and noticed his look of amusement at her actions. 'Sorry, it's a force of habit. Organisation is a natural impulse for me. Hence my choice of occupation.'

'And what does my choice of occupation say about me, I wonder?'

She twisted her lips. 'I don't think it would be appropriate for me to say.'

'You know, not very many women can make me feel as if I'm under scrutiny. And yet it's as though everything I say or do offends you.'

'I'm not offended by you. I'm quite aware of the fact that your impulses are the only reason I'm sitting here.' She shrugged.

'Oh, I wouldn't say that's the only reason...' He let his voice deepen slightly as he leaned forward and met her eyes. Dark blonde eyelashes lowered for one split second and her pupils dilated, leaving only a rim of steel grey around them.

That one reflex was enough to tell him what he'd come here to find out. No matter how indifferent she claimed to be, she most definitely was not unaffected by this intense chemistry between them.

'You are here because I want you to be. I always get what I want.'

He smiled as her eyes darkened even more, but this time in anger. Oh, yes, she was just what he needed to break his little spell of restlessness. He would break down each of those polite little barriers one by one, until she couldn't think straight any more.

She responded by throwing him her most polite smile. 'I understand that you're a powerful man, Leo, and that you grew up in a certain way. But sooner or later you will find that not everyone bends to your will. No matter how much you push.'

He ignored her comment about his privileged past. He was used to people's ignorant presumptions. He most definitely *had* grown up a certain way—but not the way most people would expect.

He leaned across the table, raising one brow in challenge. 'Are you sure about that? I've been known to be quite persuasive.'

'Well, there's something we have in common.' She smiled, and for a second he caught a glimpse of the fire buried underneath all that ice. He was enjoying sitting here with her, enjoying their sparring. She was nothing like any woman who had sparked his interest before.

She stood up as the waiter approached with their items from the cloakroom. 'I came here with one goal, Leo. And I never find myself off track—no matter how distracting the scenery.'

'I would expect nothing less.' He nodded in agreement.

She paused. 'Good. Because I won't be playing any more of your games. I'm a professional, and I like to get things done quickly.'

'As do I, Dara,' he purred.

Always the gentleman, he held out her coat, helping her to fit it comfortably around her shoulders. One errant finger lightly grazed the sensitive skin of her neck and he felt her shiver in response. Smiling, he eased back as she turned to face him.

'*Allora*, I think we understand each other,' he said, shrugging on his own coat quickly.

She continued to watch him with a mixture of accusation and reluctant awareness as they made their way outside into the chilly autumn afternoon. He stopped when his chauffeur approached them, opening the door of the limo with polite efficiency.

'My driver will take you to the club. My team will be at your command.'

Leo fought the urge to slide in beside her on the seat. She felt every ounce of this tension between them—he had seen it in her eyes. She wanted him, but she wouldn't let herself have what she wanted. That was a lesson that only came after prolonged temptation. He would show her just what it meant to lose control—but first he'd have to take her out of that comfort zone of hers.

CHAPTER THREE

DARA STOOD ON the lower floor of the club and made a final sweep of her surroundings. Leo's team had been very responsive to her advice—in fact they'd seemed almost relieved to have the responsibility taken from their shoulders. None of them had seemed particularly overjoyed to be planning such a high-profile event. Maybe Leo was right: they were jaded by success and lacked any motivation to strive further.

Well, that suited her just fine. Being in close proximity to such high-profile guests was a networking dream come true. She would make a few new contacts, get her own event contract signed, and then fly straight home to set about planning the wedding of her career. Finally her strict business plan was yielding the kind of results she had dreamed of when she'd left her life in Dublin behind.

Unconsciously she chewed on her bottom lip, trying to supress the memories that her mind conjured up every time she thought of her past life. The well-meaning glances filled with pity...the hushed conversations. She would forever be known as poor Dara Devlin back home—it had been the main reason she left it all behind. It would have been impossible to forge a new life in a place filled with such painful memories.

She remembered sitting in the hospital, her dream of

ever having a child having just been taken away from her. Only to find herself watching her fiancé coldly walk away from her for the last time.

No. She shook off the thoughts before they could take hold. She had done enough wallowing in the weeks before she had decided to move to Italy. Her life was good now. She should thank Daniel, really. He had set her free to focus on what she really loved. Her career gave her more satisfaction than family life ever could have. She was happy now—she truly was—and now she had the chance to *really* make a name for herself.

Portia Palmer was the biggest movie star Ireland had produced in the past ten years, and she had chosen Dara to plan her huge weekend wedding. She liked to think that the actress had somehow heard a glowing report from one of her happy clients. But sadly it most likely had more to do with Dara being the only Irish planner on the island. Miss Palmer was all about patriotism and her Celtic heritage.

But that was fine with Dara. Publicity was publicity, and if she hoped for her name to gain status it couldn't hurt to have a world-famous Hollywood star in her little black book.

Now, after seeing tonight's guest list, she felt butterflies flapping around in her stomach with nerves and anticipation. Leo hadn't been lying when he'd said he had high-profile guests. One quick flip through the hostess's list had revealed several notable European politicians, at least three racing drivers, a world-renowned fashion designer and the entire cast of the Luscious Lingerie catalogue. People like that could open more than doors for her in her career. They could knock down walls.

The snooty hostess from the night before suddenly

appeared by her side. Dara closed the list with a snap, trying not to look guilty.

'Signor Valente has instructed me to give you this.' The woman sniffed, holding out a small business card. She seemed quite unimpressed to be running such lowly errands for her employer.

Dara took the card with muttered thanks. It was plain black, with the single line of an address printed on the front. Nothing to indicate what kind of business it was.

'Am I supposed to go there?' she asked quickly as the hostess began to walk away. 'Did he not tell you anything else?'

The woman turned back and shrugged one shoulder, thoroughly bored with the conversation. 'I am told to give you this and make sure you go to the address.'

The event was less than two hours away, so Dara wasted no time in grabbing her things and taking the sleek chauffeur-driven town car that Leo had provided. Whatever this errand was, she needed to get back to her hotel soon if she stood a chance of looking half decent.

The car came to a smooth stop on one of the most upmarket streets in Milan. Giants of Italian fashion stood shoulder to shoulder here, with shopfronts that screamed luxury. But the address on the black card led her down a narrow alleyway to a door of exactly the same deep, nondescript black.

Her hand was hovering uncertainly over the knocker when the door swung open to reveal a tall fair-haired man in a sleek pinstriped suit.

'*Mademoiselle*, we've been waiting for you,' he said, taking her by the hand and leading her inside.

'Excuse me? I don't even know—'

He continued to lead her along by the hand, 'Just follow me.'

He was definitely French, she thought as they made their way up a short staircase to a large open-plan loft with carpet so white it hurt her eyes. The walls were mirrored on one side, and a few long purple drapes lined the wall on the other. Dara took a moment to look around, feeling hopelessly confused by the situation. Was she here to collect something?

'I was sent here by Leo Valente...' she began uncertainly. 'He didn't mention why—'

The blond man hushed her with a sudden snap of his fingers.

'We don't have time to chat. My team and I need to begin.'

As if on cue, a small army of women in black smocks appeared from behind one of the purple curtains. Dara caught a glimpse of row upon row of clothing racks before the curtain swung back into place, blocking her view.

'Hold on a minute—what *is* all of this?'

She raised a hand to stop the pinstripe-wearing bully as he loomed near, measuring tape in hand. A tight knot of tension formed in her stomach as one of the women hung a silky red dress on a hook beside the mirror.

The Frenchman gave an impatient sigh. 'We are here to style you, darling. Everything from hairpins to nail polish.' He glanced down at her short practical nails and frowned.

Dara clenched her fists, a mixture of embarrassment and anger forcing her to bite her lip. How dared that arrogant Sicilian brute organise this little stunt? As though she was some sort of pauper, here to be dressed up like one of the beautiful people for the night.

Indignation bubbled in her chest and she grabbed her phone from her handbag, ready to launch into a verbal attack on a certain nightclub mogul, only to realize that she didn't even have his phone number.

The memory of his face at lunchtime swam into her mind—that devilish smirk when she had shivered under his touch. He'd said he wasn't playing games any more, but that had been a lie. This little manoeuvre was designed to throw her off balance, to put him back in control. He clearly didn't like it that she was proving of practical use in tonight's event.

Willing herself to calm down, she took a deep breath and looked back at the sultry red number mocking her from the corner of the room.

'Did Signor Valente choose this gown for me?' she asked in a deathly quiet whisper, watching with narrowed eyes as the blond man's bravado faltered.

'He picked it out himself this afternoon, *mademoiselle*.' He stood up straight to emphasise his point. 'It is one of a kind.'

Just like the man himself, she thought snidely. This was the same kind of stunt as the cocktail last night. No other man would be so obnoxious as to choose a gown for a woman he barely knew.

She walked across the room and ran her hand down the jewelled fabric. If Leo had sent her here to unsettle her…well, he had succeeded. The thought of wearing something so blatantly sexual was akin to tearing out her own fingernails. Dara did *not* do sexual—she didn't even do sex any more.

For the first time in five years she felt once again as if she wasn't good enough. As if she needed to change herself to fit the items on someone's list. And that just wouldn't do.

The blond man and his team of beauty assassins stood

silently, watching her, hairbrushes and make-up wands like weapons in their utility belts.

She turned to face them, her eyes blazing with determination. 'I will be choosing something for myself.'

The Frenchman shook his head. 'Monsieur Valente has made his wishes very clear to my team.'

'Tell me, honestly, does this dress look like something I could pull off?' Dara gestured to the gown.

He turned his head to one side, examining her from head to toe with agonising intensity. 'Truthfully, no. Your chest is too flat to wear such a low neckline. And the colour is far too rich for such a pale complexion. Nonetheless, I refuse to go against my client's wishes.'

Dara ignored such blunt description of her flaws, crossing the room to stand in front of him, hands on her hips. 'Let's make one thing clear. *I* am your client. What will it do to your business if you send me out in such an ill-thought-out ensemble? It will be such a high-profile event too…'

She let her voice trail off and watched as his eyes widened with horror.

'I'm glad we understand each other.'

She smiled with satisfaction as he turned to his team and began barking orders to bring more dresses.

Leo looked at his watch as the guests started to filter in for the champagne hour. He was beginning to think that Little Miss Proper had decided to chicken out. His limo had gone to collect her over an hour ago. Taking another sip of the whisky he'd been nursing, he passed his gaze lazily around the room that Dara and his team had spent the afternoon finalising.

His coveted glass water features now sat in each corner of the dance floor. The overall effect made the room seem wider and brought much more attention to the features themselves. Low sofas flanked the dance floor, now an ideal space for the younger celebrity scene. The open area of the club was filled with loud pumping music, and the dance floor glowed with sultry lighting, giving it an almost mystical appearance.

In the entrance lounge a ten-foot champagne tower had been placed centre stage, and a clever little mechanism was sending glittering liquid down in an endless waterfall. The guests met at this feature and spread out easily, making the overall vibe sleek and relaxed. The upper lounge area had been transformed into a cocktail bar for the social elite crowd, its lower ceiling and distance from the dance floor making the noise less obtrusive and ideal for hushed business deals.

All in all, he was impressed.

He wasn't entirely sure what had compelled him to offer her this little audition—probably a mixture of curiosity and a mild attraction. Okay, so maybe *mild* wasn't the word for it…

He stood at the bar in the lower lounge, watching the guests arrive one by one. The night was just getting started but he was in no mood to play host.

Usually he would be the one in the middle of the crowd, with people hanging onto his every word. They would beg to hear about each of the once-in-a-lifetime adventures he'd been on. The wild parties, the daredevil stunts that the tabloids loved to cover. He had created an image for himself and his brand that drew people to him. But lately he had become steadily more jaded by the repetition in his lifestyle.

Until last night.

Dara had awoken a spark in him, and he felt the familiar hum of attraction driving him for the first time in months. Women had been far from his agenda while he dealt with the aftermath of his father's passing. His usually insatiable sexual appetite had been non-existent as he threw himself into his work.

He thought of how she might have reacted, seeing that red dress today. He knew she would be unprepared for such a high-glamour event, but admittedly his intentions were not entirely innocent. He was on edge, waiting for the inevitable explosion when she arrived. He was even considering making a phone call to his driver when a hand touched his shoulder.

Leo turned and immediately grasped the hand of the grey-haired man standing in front of him. 'Gianni—you got the invitation.'

'Well, I was hardly going to refuse a chance to see what else you've done to my club, boy,' he rasped.

Leo fought the urge to smile. His old friend hadn't changed one bit. Gianni Marcello was a dragon, but he was the closest thing to a father Leo ever had.

'The last time I checked this was still *my* club,' he corrected.

The old man waved a hand. 'A technicality. You smart-talked me into selling—just like you smart-talked your way to where you are now.' He paused to bark an order for two glasses of grappa at a startled waiter. 'You came to my hotel today. Since when did you start hand-delivering invitations?'

Leo smiled. 'I thought you might appreciate the gesture.'

Gianni snorted, unaffected. 'I was under the impression that you had forgotten where I live after all this time.'

Leo shrugged one shoulder casually, but inside he felt hot shame creep up his neck. He'd known Gianni wouldn't make this reunion easy, but perhaps this wasn't the best of settings to hash out their differences. Leo contemplated walking away, under the pretext of having business responsibilities, but the old man knew him better than anyone.

Looking around the lounge, Gianni scoffed loudly. 'Do you have any damned chairs in this place, or do I have to build one myself?'

Leo laughed, leading the way up the mirrored steps to the upper lounge. He found them a quiet seat in the corner furthest from the crowd. A few business contacts from Paris sidetracked him, requiring the usual chit-chat before he could slide comfortably into the seat opposite Gianni at the low table.

Their drinks arrived promptly and Leo took a sip of the strong liquid, feeling it burn down his throat and warm his chest. Gianni remained silent for a moment, watching him over the rim of his glass. The old man had always liked an air of suspense.

'You have made some powerful friends, I can see.' He gestured to a group of well-known city officials, sipping champagne down on the lower floor.

'A wise man once told me never to call a politician a friend,' Leo corrected.

Gianni nodded his head once. 'You always listened to me, boy.' He downed the rest of his drink in one go, setting it down harshly on the dark tempered glass. 'Except when it came to one thing.'

Leo sat back in his seat. He knew what was to come next. Had known the moment he'd decided to invite his old mentor. 'Go ahead and say what you came here to say. I owe you enough to listen this time.'

'Is that an apology for walking away from me six months ago?'

Leo averted his gaze, feeling like an unruly child

being scolded for disobeying the rules. Gianni Marcello was the only man he had ever respected enough not to make jokes in a serious conversation.

'You should have come to the funeral.'

The accusation was quiet, and yet it hit Leo like a knife to the gut. He had known the words were coming, and yet he suddenly felt betrayed.

'I thought you above all people would understand.'

'I understand that you acted out of anger. And I taught you better than that.' Gianni sat forward across the table, dark eyes shrewd with accusation.

Leo felt his body tense until he was sure he would smash the glass in his hand. Willing himself to calm down, he took a deep breath and met the familiar eyes of the man he trusted with his deepest secrets. 'I assure you, Gianni, anger was the furthest thing from my mind. I made a decision not to pay empty respects to a man I hadn't seen or spoken to in years. I stopped losing my temper over my father a long time ago.'

'Is that why you sold off every share he left you?' Gianni spoke with deadly calm. 'Don't lie to me, boy. It was an act of cold-blooded revenge and we both know it.'

'He left me those shares hoping I'd be tempted to take my place as his rightful heir. He knew I'd never accept it.'

Gianni knew nothing of what his father was truly capable of. No one knew.

Gianni shook his head. 'I'm not telling you that you made the wrong decision. I'm saying that your motivation was out of character.'

Leo waited a moment before speaking. 'Did it disappoint you to find I am exactly like him after all?'

'If you were like him you wouldn't have walked away from an inheritance worth billions twelve years ago and then have the nerve to do it all again the first chance you got. Vittorio Valente would turn in his grave, knowing his entire corporation is in pieces.'

'My father made his choices and died with the consequences.'

Beautiful green eyes flashed into Leo's mind, along with a face filled with youth and vitality—his mother's face...a face he hadn't thought of in twelve years. He brushed it away, refusing to let the memory surface.

Gianni frowned. 'Don't let the memory of a ghost haunt you for ever. You are a good man, Leo, but you're heading down a lonely path.'

'Have you been reading those gossip magazines?' He chuckled. 'I'm perfectly content to work hard and play harder for the time being.' He leaned back in his seat, stretching his neck muscles in an effort to relieve the painful ache in his temples.

'I was married for thirty-five years. And look at me now. A lonely widower, living in my own hotel suites like a damned salesman.' Gianni took another slug of grappa, his eyes twinkling suspiciously. 'But my wife gave me three sons. A man should always have his own sons to carry on his legacy.'

'Some day, maybe.' Leo shrugged.

The thought of settling down wasn't unappealing. He just wasn't cut out for that kind of lifestyle. He could be needed anywhere around the world from one day to the next. He never stayed in one place long enough to set down roots. And besides, roots held you down, trapped you in one place. If there was one thing he couldn't stand it was feeling trapped.

He shook off the unwelcome thought, watching as Gianni visibly ogled a passing brunette.

'Maybe I should follow your lead and find myself

some of those supermodels.' Gianni chuckled under his breath.

'Ah, they don't eat enough,' Leo jibed, and the sudden memory of Dara and her delicious lips as she ate stormed his thoughts.

'You never drank like a true Sicilian. Whisky is for Westerners.'

'You're still as politically incorrect as I remember.' Leo smiled.

The old man looked away for a moment. His expression was filled with sadness. 'You should have come to me, Leonardo. You always came to me.'

He looked confused, making him look every inch his seventy years. For the very first time Leo realised that the great dragon wasn't going to live for ever. The thought left an uncomfortable knot in his stomach.

He glanced across the lounge, wanting to end this conversation. Raking up the past did nothing for his temper.

A flurry of movement drew his eyes towards the edge of the lounge just as the loudest politician stopped speaking mid-sentence and pointed towards the tall blonde gracefully ascending the stairs.

She wasn't wearing the red dress. He almost wished she was. The dress he had chosen for her was deliberately risqué and playful—an attempt to take her out of her comfort zone. What she wore in its place was temptation personified.

A second skin of shimmering jewelled gold.

It fitted each curve so tightly it might as well have been painted on. He felt heat rush through his veins as he stood slowly, and their eyes met as she came to a stop by the bar. Raising one eyebrow, she made it clear he was going to have to come to her.

Gianni followed his gaze with interest. 'That one could

freeze hell with those eyes. Finally you've found a real woman, eh?'

Leo heard Gianni chuckle loudly behind him, but he was already across the lounge in a few long strides.

She smiled sweetly as he came to a stop in front of her. 'My apologies for being late. It seemed to take quite a long time to make me look presentable.'

'You changed the dress.'

She tilted her head to one side. 'Is there something wrong with this one?'

He resisted the urge to run his gaze down her wicked curves again. The dress wasn't indecent, by any means, in fact by some standards it was almost modest. Small delicate sleeves stopped just at the shoulder and the neckline swooped gracefully along her collarbone. It was just that it hugged every delicious curve of her body—a body he was trying very hard to ignore at this moment.

'I decided your choice wasn't appropriate for this evening.'

She turned slightly and his throat went dry. The dress was sinfully low-cut at the back, leaving the graceful curve of her spine completely bare for everyone to see.

He coughed, clearing his throat. 'It wasn't a request, Dara. I thought you would understand that.'

Dara stepped closer, her voice lowered to a dangerous whisper. 'I'm confused. At any point during our meeting this afternoon did I indicate that I have difficulty in choosing my own clothing?' She raised one sleek blonde brow.

'You were unprepared for the formal dress code tonight. I was ensuring that you'd fit the part of my event planner.'

'Temporary consultant,' she corrected. 'Out of interest, do you ensure that all of your potential business partners have the opportunity to bare their cleavage?'

Leo floundered at that question. This was not going to plan at all.

Just then a familiar voice came from behind his left shoulder.

'Leonardo, are you going to introduce me to this beautiful creature?'

He turned to see Gianni, his watery brown eyes twinkling with amusement.

Leo closed his mouth and turned to the man, a playful glint in his eye. 'I was planning to keep her away from you as a matter of fact.'

'She looks like she's planning to keep away from you too.' He chuckled, extending a hand. 'Gianni Marcello. I don't think we've met.'

Dara stepped forward and politely introduced herself, all trace of hostility gone from her face.

'Dara is my event planner,' Leo explained casually.

'Actually, I'm just here for tonight,' she corrected, with a swift glance in his direction. 'Leo is in the process of negotiating with my company.'

'A businesswoman!' Gianni exclaimed, clapping his hands together with glee. 'Thank goodness he's found someone who can actually hold a conversation in company.'

Dara had opened her mouth to correct him when they were suddenly interrupted by the club manager.

After a low murmured conversation with the man Leo turned back to them apologetically. 'It seems that it is time for the host to officiate,' he explained. 'Try not to bore her with your business talk.'

'He is quite the charmer, isn't he?'

Dara stopped watching Leo making his way across

the floor below and turned to find the older man, Gianni, watching her with interest.

'I gave him his first job, you know. Tending bar in my flagship hotel in Paris. Now look at him—drinking champagne with supermodels.' He chuckled.

'You own the Marcello Hotel chain?'

'I do.' He smiled. 'But as far as work goes, my children do that now. I'm just enjoying my golden years in the town that made me.'

'Were you born here in Milan?' she asked.

'I was born and raised in Bella Sicilia.' He smiled again, eyes twinkling. 'Business brought me to the industrial north. I opened my first hotel here forty-five years ago.'

'The Grand Marcello Milan was your first?'

'She was my crowning glory. Hence the reason my apartment is on the top floor there.'

She smiled back. 'I love the branding of your chain. "New city, old friends".'

'That tagline is probably the only part of my original work that still lives on.' He tutted. 'Young people want to make everything modern.'

Dara nodded in agreement. The old man was nice. He had a cantankerous warmth about him that made her feel instantly comfortable.

The champagne hour was going well, she thought as she looked down across the crowd of Milan's glittering elite. All here to be photographed for the society pages, no doubt. Soon the lights would dim and the official event would fade into the background, allowing them to use the club for its true purpose. Privacy, anonymity and sin.

The music was lowered and a tinkling sound resonated through the air. Dara looked down to see that Leo had moved up to the small stage erected in the middle of the dance floor. Gianni took her elbow and they made their way down to the lower floor as Leo began speaking.

He began to outline the concept of the club's renovation, explaining the fluid lines and mirrored backdrops. Gianni made a few more tutting noises beside her, commenting that it had been fine just the way it was.

Leo smiled brightly, ever the charismatic host, and he finished by thanking his team of staff in detail for their support.

'Finally, I have the greatest pleasure to introduce you all to a rising star in the industry—Miss Dara Devlin.'

To her horror he pointed her out in the crowd and she suddenly became the focus of three hundred curious stares.

What was he thinking? She was a nobody here. These people were looking at her as though expecting her to burst into song.

Leo smiled, oblivious to her horror. 'Miss Devlin is a recent discovery of mine, she is a rare creative talent in the industry. Such is her dedication to detail, she even gave the Platinum uniform a facelift to fit with our new theme.'

The crowd gave subdued applause, curious eyes glancing from the scarlet-faced event planner to the now very sleek waiters walking around all in black. Dara prayed for him to move on to another topic, breathing a sigh of relief when he began to wrap up the speech.

Gianni raised his brows beside her, seemingly quite entertained by the proceedings. 'He seems quite taken with you, *carina*.' He smiled.

Dara straightened her shoulders, trying in vain to dispel the heat from her cheeks. 'Mr Valente is a very successful man. I'm grateful to be working with him.' She took a sip from her cool soda water, feeling it hit her painfully dry throat.

'You are quite naive if you think he's just thinking about work.' His eyes twinkled.

Dara ignored the uncomfortable sensation in her stomach at his words. Leo *was* taking her seriously, now that she had proved her talent. There was a playful tension between them, of course, but she had no plans to act on it. Not at all.

She decided to ignore Gianni's comment, straightening her shoulders and saying, 'Actually, I'm negotiating an event contract for Castello Bellamo.'

The old man stilled, clearly taken by surprise with that information. Dara waited for him to speak, but he remained silent. Thinking it best to give him a moment, she looked out across the dance floor. Leo had just stepped down from the podium and began conversing with a group of men in sleek suits.

She looked down and saw that his eyes were trained on her even as he spoke. He was watching her intently, his green gaze seeming to reach across the dance floor to her. She should look away. She should restart her conversation with Gianni—something.

She turned back to see Gianni watching Leo with the most ferocious expression she had ever seen. 'Mr Marcello, is everything okay?' she asked tentatively.

'He's playing dangerous games. Excuse me for a moment.' His eyes darkened to furious points, and without another word the man began weaving forward through the crowd with a look of intent.

Dara followed suit, her heels forcing her to tread more carefully. 'I'm not sure what I said to bother you, but this is hardly the place to cause a scene.'

Gianni turned his head, still walking. 'You don't need to witness this.'

Leo saw them approach and instantly shooed away the group of people surrounding him. 'Gianni, you're looking a bit more colourful.' He smiled.

The old man jabbed a finger into Leo's chest, standing so close they were almost nose to nose. 'You say you're not playing games, boy? Then explain what kind of agreement you have with this young lady? Do you plan to sell off the only link you have left to your family?'

Leo looked genuinely shocked for a moment. 'Will you keep your voice down?'

Gianni shook his head, a harsh laugh escaping his lips. 'Always worried about your precious image, Leo. I thought you were hurting when you did what you did to Valente Enterprises, but this—' His voice cracked.

'I'm not selling the damned castle,' Leo spat harshly.

'He's not. I'm a wedding planner. We're discussing an event contract.'

'Stay out of this, Dara,' Leo warned.

'And I thought you were just entertaining the lady to charm her into bed,' said Gianni. 'It would be better if you sold it. Rather than make plans to exploit it like a cheap hotel.'

'Nothing is going to be planned in that damned castle—you hear me? It's staying there to rot.'

Dara felt the breath whoosh out of her lungs as she absorbed the reality of that statement. Neither man looked her way as they continued in their stand-off. Thankfully no one had noticed the little drama playing out in this quiet corner of the club.

'Then why is she here?' asked Gianni, voicing Dara's own question.

Leo was silent for a moment, his eyes moving to look

at her as if he had just remembered she was there. 'This is none of your business, Gianni.'

Dara watched as the old man's temper faded, to be replaced by a look of genuine hurt. Leo's eyes were so dark they looked almost black in the dim lighting.

Dara spoke up, straightening her shoulders. 'Well, it seems it's none of my business either.'

Refusing to meet Leo's eyes, she looked down.

'Thank you for shedding some light on the situation, Mr Marcello.'

With that, she turned on her heel and strode out of the club.

CHAPTER FOUR

STOPPING TO GRAB her coat and bag from the cloakroom, Dara willed herself to calm down. She could feel the tension inside her stretching to breaking point.

After devoting the entire day working herself to the bone to impress him…

After spending one hair-raisingly stressful hour on the phone to every major designer, looking for uniforms…

After letting him make her feel self-conscious…

She honestly thought that if he was to follow her she might wind up hitting someone for the first time in her life.

She stepped out into the chilly Milan night, the cool air making her shiver in earnest through the haze of cold anger.

He emerged through the doors behind her just as explosively as he had the night before. 'Dara, stop walking away and allow me to explain.'

'How long were you planning on stringing me along for?' She spun around to face him.

'Let's not do this on the street.' He looked to where the security guards stood like silent sentries inside the door.

'Oh, excuse me—I forgot all about your precious reputation. Please, do yourself a favour and go back to your adoring public.'

A long dark limo pulled up in front of them, the windows impenetrably black.

'You're not going to get anywhere by standing on the street. My car is right here. I don't want anything else on my conscience tonight.'

'Oh, I think we both know your conscience doesn't exist,' she scoffed.

Still, she frowned. She had forgotten about the trouble getting a taxi in Milan. If he was offering her his limo she would take it without a second thought. Anything to get her away from him as soon as possible.

'Well, it seems you are just as charitable as I thought you'd be, Mr Valente. My humble thanks for this consolation prize.' She opened the door and slid inside to the warm dark interior, her body still shaking with anger.

The door on the opposite side opened suddenly, and her eyes widened as Leo's tall frame slid easily onto the seat next to her.

'What are you doing?' she squeaked.

'I said I'd let you use the limo. I didn't say you would be going alone.' He shrugged one shoulder, banging his knuckles on the driver's window and setting the vehicle into swift motion.

He turned to face her, his voice deeply accented in the limo's quiet, dark interior. 'We are not finished yet, Dara.'

She felt his voice reach across the space between them, warm and seductive. Ignoring the pull, she remained silent and feigned indifference.

'You can ignore me if you like, but I have yet to fulfil my side of our bargain.' He waited for her to speak for a moment before continuing. 'Your work tonight was impressive. You've earned your chance to convince me.'

Indignation won out and she turned to face him. 'Excuse me if I'm suddenly disinclined to pitch to a brick wall.'

'You don't understand the situation with Gianni Marcello.'

He shook his head. That small movement incensed her more than anything else.

'I think I understand perfectly well. The bored playboy decided he'd have some fun while he was in town. An added bonus was the free event consultation. Too bad your friend ruined things before you tried your hand at the final prize, eh?' She crossed her arms defensively around herself.

'What you achieved tonight is unheard of. I wasn't lying when I said you have great talent. You achieved more in seven hours than my team could pull off in three months.'

'That means nothing to me. The only reason I did any of it was to get my contract.'

'My relationship with Gianni is complex. He does not understand some of the choices that I have made. I said what I had to in order to avoid a scene. The truth is I have been considering your proposal.'

Dara watched him silently. This change in tactics was making her head spin.

He sat back in his seat, stretching long muscular legs in front of him with casual ease. 'I'm offering you a chance to convince me. It won't be offered again.'

Dara deliberated for a moment. He had made a fool of her, but he still held the upper hand here. If there was a chance to salvage this wedding contract she had to take it. Much as it irked her to be played with in his little game… much as it wounded her pride.

'The wedding is for a high-profile actress—moderate numbers. Media would be limited to one magazine team.

It would be maybe three days from set-up to clean-up, with accommodation required for guests.'

She outlined the finer details of her pitch as clearly and effectively as she could, considering her lack of sleep and the intimate environment. Not to mention the large relaxed male sitting beside her, watching her every movement with interest.

'Sounds like you've thought of everything.' He ran a hand across the stubble on his jaw. 'And it sounds like a mutually beneficial arrangement.'

Dara felt unease prickle at the back of her mind. He had been deathly against any conversation about the castle last night—why the sudden easy consideration of her plans? She *had* done a fantastic job today—that much she could admit. But she wasn't naive enough to overlook the fact that something had to have sparked this sudden change of heart.

'What exactly has changed to make you think twice about rejecting my event?' she asked, watching as he raised his brows a fraction of an inch, narrowing his gaze.

'Maybe I'm hoping to leave you with a better impression of me than the one you have got so far.'

'Somehow I don't think that you care very much about anyone's impression of you.'

He shrugged. 'Depends on the person in question. But nonetheless you are correct that I have an ulterior motive. I was merely giving you a chance to lay out your proposal beforehand.'

Leo sat forward in his seat, green eyes intently holding her gaze.

'You need my help, Dara. And you have proved just how far you are willing to go in order to get it. I am asking you to go just a little further.'

He laid a hand on the dark leather between them, still

holding her gaze. It was a gesture of domination, designed to make her feel trapped, surely? She fought the urge to move back further in her seat.

'How much further are we talking, here?' Dara shook off the mildly indecent thoughts her mind conjured.

Leo seemed to deliberate for a moment, looking out at the passing streets before speaking.

'Do you know much about the newest Lucchesi development?'

Dara thought for a moment, the change in pace addling her already tired mind. 'The island he owns near Lampedone? He's turning it into some sort of self-contained luxury resort, I've heard.'

Leo nodded. 'Despite what you've heard or read, thus far I have made no attempt to expand my empire to Sicily. There is virtually no market for an exclusive brand like mine in any of the larger cities. That was until this Isola project came to light.' He sat forward, gesturing with his hands as he spoke. 'The island will be a hub of exclusive hotels, boutique restaurants. Every inch of real estate will be dedicated to five-star luxury. It's one of a kind.'

'I don't see what your interest in a new real estate development has to do with my wedding contract.' Dara spoke quietly, trying to make sense of his words.

'Umberto Lucchesi is head of the board of directors. He has the final word on all potential investment opportunities. I have made no secret of the fact that I want in on the project, and frankly they need my expertise and influence. That was made clear when the entire board approved my investment. All except Lucchesi.'

She shook her head. 'I'm sorry, but I don't think my small connection with him would help you to secure a major business deal.'

'All I would need is your presence, Dara. He is notoriously private and only holds meetings in his home or with the board of directors. There is an opera fundraiser at the Teatro Massimo in Palermo tomorrow night. Lucchesi and his wife will be hosting.'

Palermo? Tomorrow night? Dara fought the urge to laugh in disbelief. This was ridiculous. She had flown to Milan for a simple task and now here she was being asked to accompany a notorious playboy to the opera.

'Why exactly would my presence benefit the situation?' she asked rather breathlessly.

'I understand that this is rather unconventional. But I believe meeting with him in a cordial setting, with a familiar face by my side, might make him look upon me more favourably. He sees me as my father's son—a frivolous playboy with no morals. He clearly approves of you if he has worked with you on more than one occasion. Having you on my arm would be greatly beneficial.'

'Are you asking me to pose as your *date*?'

'What other reason would we have for being in Palermo together? It's the most believable scenario.'

Maybe it was tiredness after the past twenty-four hours catching up with her, but Dara felt a wave of hysterical laughter threatening to bubble up to the surface. The thought that anyone would believe a man like Leo Valente was dating a plain Irish nobody like her was absolutely ludicrous.

He continued, oblivious to her stunned reaction. 'You would leave the business talk to me. All I'd need is for you to act as a buffer of sorts. To play on your history with his family. Someone with a personal connection to smooth the way.'

'A buffer? Well that just sounds so flattering...' she muttered.

'You would get all the benefits of being my companion, being a guest at such an exclusive event. It would be an enjoyable evening.'

'Umberto Lucchesi is a powerful man. He must have good reason not to trust you,' she mused. 'I'm not quite sure I can risk my reputation.'

'I'm a powerful man, Dara. You climbed up a building to get a meeting with me. I'm offering you an opportunity to get exactly what you want. It's up to you if you take it or not.'

The limo came to a stop. Dara looked out at the hotel's dull grey exterior, trying desperately to get a handle on the situation. He was essentially offering her the *castello* on a silver platter. All she had to do was play a part until he got his meeting and she would be done.

'What happens if you're wrong? If having a buffer makes no difference?'

'Let me worry about that. My offer is simple. Come with me to Palermo and I will sign your event contract.'

She thought about the risk of trusting him. He hadn't given her any reason to trust him so far. But what other possible reason could he have for asking her to go with him?

A man like him could have any woman he wanted, so this wasn't simply about the chemistry between them. She was sure of that.

He must want in on the Lucchesi deal very badly if it had prompted him to consider her event. His initial reaction had been a complete contrast, his blatant refusal so clear. It was a risk to lie to a man like Umberto Lucchesi, but on the scale of things it was more of a white lie. And the alternative meant losing the contract. Losing everything she had worked for.

'If I go with you—' she said it quickly, before she could change her mind '—I want a contract for the *castello* up front.'

Leo felt triumph course through him as he felt Dara's shift towards accepting his offer. He'd seen the uncertainty on her face, knew the difficult position he was placing her in.

'You don't trust me, Dara?'

'Not even a little bit.'

'I would expect nothing less. I will have a contract drawn up by tomorrow. And I promise to return you to your office bright and early on Monday morning.'

'We would be staying in Palermo overnight?'

She asked the question innocently, but he'd seen the telltale movement of her hands in her lap. She was not as unaware of the tension as she made it seem.

'The suite will have more than one bedroom.'

'I want your word that there will be no more of your games. This is a professional arrangement.'

'Are you asking me to behave myself? To ignore the intense attraction between us?' he asked silkily.

'Yes. That's exactly what I'm asking.'

'This is a business arrangement, Dara. You may be posing as my date for the evening, but I can assure you I am capable of separating the two. Whatever impression you might have of me, I can assure you that I am a man of my word when it comes to business.'

Leo rapped the driver's window and the man got out and held the door of the limousine open for her to exit.

'My plane will leave at noon, so you have plenty of time to get some beauty sleep.'

He watched until she'd disappeared through the doors of the basic hotel. He hadn't lied when he'd said he was capable of separating business from pleasure. He was quite capable of it, usually. But his attraction to her was something that had caught him off guard.

After months of no interest in the opposite sex, this sudden acute awareness was almost painful. And she felt it too—he was quite sure of that. She would prove very useful tomorrow in cornering Lucchesi. But if he was being honest that was not his only objective. He wasn't quite ready to walk away from the challenge she presented just yet.

Maybe it was boredom…maybe his pride was bruised. But something drew him to Dara Devlin more than to any woman he had ever met. She intrigued him and maybe that was why he had insisted on provoking her with those little stunts at the club. He was a grown man not a teenager, for goodness' sake.

If he wanted to impress her then he had to get on her good side. It was his nature to be rebellious and provocative, but maybe a more subtle approach was needed. Either way, he always got what he wanted. And he was determined to show Dara exactly what she could have if she gave in to temptation.

The car turned sharply onto another narrow backstreet and Dara felt her stomach lurch. She sat bolt upright in the Porsche's deep suede seat, one hand clutching her phone like a talisman, the other holding onto the door for dear life. Leo drove as if he was on the Nürburgring, not the tiny cobbled streets of Palermo.

Rounding the last corner, he pulled the powerful vehicle to a smooth stop. She was out of the car in an instant, straightening her skirt and trying to regain her composure.

'You didn't enjoy the drive?'

Leo handed his keys to the valet and fell into step beside her as she powered up the pathway to the facade of the ancient building they had arrived at.

'I generally prefer to travel at a less ferocious pace.'

She stared up at the historical *palazzo*, amazed that she should be staying in such a place. They walked up marble steps and entered into a bright, ornate lobby. Dara felt her breath catch at the veritable feast of opulent decor.

'I always knew that some of these old palaces had been converted into luxury suites, but I never thought I would see inside one.'

She craned her neck to look up at the ornate ceiling artwork. Most of the original features had been preserved, and it was like stepping through a doorway into the eighteenth century.

The interior of the apartment was just as flamboyant as the lobby. Decorated in traditional Baroque fashion, it had high ceilings and large ornate chandeliers, with a sizeable balcony overlooking the terracotta rooftops of the city.

Leo guided her through the living area to a set of floor-to-ceiling double doors. 'Your room is through here. Your bag should have been brought up by now.'

'Already?' She raised her brows with surprise as he opened the double doors and, sure enough, her small black case was at the foot of the bed.

'I expect efficiency wherever I go.' He shrugged.

Dara took in the gigantic four-poster bed, draped with deep red velvet hangings and a gold-embroidered coverlet. It was the kind of bed that demanded lovemaking and romance. Too bad it would be getting neither tonight.

It suddenly dawned on her that in a few hours she would be posing as Leo Valente's date. And sleeping under the same roof as him. The insane urge to run screaming from the building was tempting, but she stood her ground. *Remember the goal here, Devlin.* One white lie and the *castello* was hers.

'We leave for the opera house at seven. Will you find something to wear in time?'

'I once sourced seven bridesmaids' dresses the day before a wedding I was planning. In mint green, might I add,' she professed proudly.

He didn't respond with his usual snark, instead taking a quick look at the screen of his phone. 'I have some business to attend to, but feel free to indulge yourself. Shoes, jewellery. Whatever you desire.'

He took a sleek silver card from his wallet and held it out to her.

'I can pay for my own clothes, but I appreciate the gesture.' She pushed the card back towards him.

Leo scowled at her. 'Fine. I will have the car collect us at seven.'

He left, closing the doors of the bedroom behind him.

Dara wondered at the change in his playful demeanour. Perhaps he was edgy about the significance of tonight.

She would need to get a start on shopping, but first things first… She kicked off her shoes and threw herself back onto the bed with a contented sigh of appreciation. It was like sinking into a cloud. She briefly imagined what it might be like not to be alone in this bed. To have a warm body next to her, touching her in all the right places.

What on earth was happening to her? She was going to have to keep her guard up around him. Her usually controlled libido seemed to be coming out of its enforced hibernation.

He wasn't even her usual type.

She thought of her ex-fiancé and his neat brown hair, his perfectly ironed shirts and slacks. Dan would never have looked at her the way Leo did. As though she was the most attractive woman in the room. Even before he'd found out she was as barren as the desert.

The ugly phrase jarred her momentarily. It was the phrase she had heard Daniel use to her father in a conversation she had never been meant to hear.

Thoughts of her past pressed through her control, filling her chest with emotion. The news that she would never have children had shaken her to her core. She had always prided herself on not being needy in her relationships, unlike most of her girlfriends. Dan was the only man she had ever slept with. Their sex life had been nothing spectacular, but she'd told herself that their mental connection was worth much more than the lack of wow factor in the bedroom. Apparently he hadn't felt the same.

Dara shook off the irritation that always followed thoughts about their break-up. Moving to stand in front of the floor-length mirror by the bed, she frowned at her reflection. She wasn't sexy—she knew that. But once upon a time she had felt moderately attractive...she had accepted male attention graciously.

She was by no means vain. She knew that she had a slim figure and long legs, but her features were plain and her chest far too small. Why a man like Leo would ever be attracted to her, she didn't know. Perhaps it was the simple fact that she had made it clear that nothing would happen between them.

But the problem was the longer they were together, the more she *wanted* something to happen.

She walked away from the mirror, trying her best not to groan. What was it about this man that made her second guess herself? Leo Valente was trouble with a capital T, and she needed to keep her own attraction under control if she had any hope of keeping his at bay.

Leo grabbed two flutes of champagne from a passing waiter and returned to his seat in the private box.

He'd seen that Dara had taken out her phone and was busily tapping away.

'The tech-junkie look isn't exactly what I want in a date,' he scolded.

'Just give me a minute and I'll be done.' She tapped a few more times on the screen.

'You're on my time tonight, Dara.' He took the phone swiftly from her grasp, putting it in his inner pocket. 'You can have it back after the opera if you behave.'

She stared at him. 'That is a very high-handed approach to regaining my attention.'

'You don't find it charming?' He placed a flute of champagne in her hand.

'Not even a little bit.' She straightened, sipping her champagne and looking pointedly away from him down towards the crowds swarming below them in the theatre.

Leo felt more than a little irked at her dismissal. He had spent all afternoon on conference calls so he could free up some time. Only to be coolly ignored by her from the moment he'd collected her from the *palazzo*.

She looked spectacular, with her blonde hair swept back from her face in a neat chignon, revealing delicate diamond-drop earrings. Her gown was elegant and refined—a swathe of pale silver that formed a seductive heart shape at the front, showing just enough skin to leave a little mystery.

He moved closer to her, speaking quietly. 'I would imagine you prefer a very docile man. One you can organise and control, perhaps?'

'I don't really have a preference.' She shrugged one delicate shoulder. 'I have a very busy career that fulfils me. Dating is not high on my agenda.'

'Again with the agenda, Dara? You seem to have it all figured out into neat little boxes. It sounds so perfectly perfect.'

'You're mocking me, but there is a lot to be said for having a plan.'

'When building a nightclub empire, definitely. But everything else is free fall to me. I enjoy surprises. If it weren't for surprises we wouldn't be here tonight.'

'Back to the point: when will I be expected to sidetrack the Lucchesi's?'

'Not until the first interlude. Follow my lead and don't go off script.'

Dara fought the urge to make a snappy retort, instead relaxing as the music started up. The ancient opera house was beautiful, with its iconic gold architecture and deep red velvet curtains. She had promised herself years ago that she would see a show at the Teatro Massimo—it was on her list of tourist-type things to do while she was living here. A list that she never seemed to get to with her workload...

As the curtain came down for the first interlude she felt butterflies in her stomach. Leo gestured for her to follow him out into the crowd mingling outside the doorway. This was it. The moment of truth. He laid one hand at the small of her back as they walked down the corridors towards the royal box, where the Lucchesi family was seated. The heat from his palm seared into her skin, making those butterflies flap even faster.

A group of people were gathered around the entrance, talking loudly about the performance. One woman stood out, her opulent diamond jewellery outshone only by what had to be the most eye-blurringly white fur stole that Dara had ever seen.

Leo caught Dara's eye, gesturing for her to step forward and intercept the woman's attention.

Dara pasted on her most brilliant smile as Gloria Lucchesi came out of the crowd, embracing her warmly. She tried not to look at Leo, noting the smug expression on his face.

'Dara, darling—what are you doing out in public without your headset?' The older woman joked.

Dara laughed obligingly at the jibe, feeling unease as Leo stepped right up to her side, sliding his hand around her waist possessively.

'I'm here with my…my date, Leo Valente.'

Her voice stumbled over the words, her heart hammering in her chest. Whether it was the effect of lying so brazenly, or the result of being touched so intimately, Dara felt as if her heart was about to leap out of her chest.

Her skittishness evaporated once she noticed that Gloria Lucchesi had quite literally frozen in place, her hand clutching at her necklace in a gesture that was much more than simple surprise. Dara felt a sense of foreboding as Umberto Lucchesi came to stand beside his wife, his features ruddy with barely leashed anger.

Gloria placed a hand on her husband's arm before speaking to Dara directly. 'Miss Devlin, can you please explain what you are doing here with my husband's nephew?'

Umberto Lucchesi looked like a man ready to pounce.

Leo continued to stare, unblinking. 'How nice to see you, Uncle.'

'How dare you ambush me at a charity function?' the

older man practically hissed under his breath, looking around the hall to see they were not being overheard.

'I bought a ticket—just like everyone else here.'

True to form, Aunt Gloria stepped forward to calm the situation. 'Umberto, please stop being so dramatic,' she chastised. Her tone was one of calm confidence. 'My husband forgets that he is in the middle of the Teatro Massimo, not shouting in a boardroom.'

Gloria placed a friendly hand on Dara's arm. Leo noted Dara's polite smile, her gentle tone as she defused the situation with questions about Gloria's daughters.

Umberto remained silent and continued to stare at him across the narrow hallway.

'We will not do this here, Valente,' he hissed.

'Most certainly not,' Gloria interjected. 'It's high time you ridiculous men quit this feud and showed each other a little forgiveness. Leonardo, I want to welcome you home to Sicily, darling. I have missed you.'

'Thank you, Zia, I'm afraid your husband doesn't quite feel the same.'

'That's an understatement,' Umberto scoffed.

Gloria spoke directly to him. 'Come to our villa to-morrow evening for dinner. You can talk business then. For now, let us all enjoy the rest of the evening.' She guided her husband into the throng of people, looking back to wink at Dara.

Leo smiled at Dara. That had gone just the way he'd planned it. A private meeting attained, on Lucchesi's home turf. But Dara frowned, turning back towards the box. Leo followed, confused at her sudden change in mood.

Dara waited until they were back in the box before turning to him. She pressed one accusatory finger into his shoulder. The gesture made his eyes widen.

'You could have warned me that I was walking into an episode of a *soap opera*, for goodness' sake.'

'I didn't think it would benefit the situation if you were aware of my history with Umberto.'

'No, you didn't think it would benefit *you*.' She turned away, fuming. 'How did I not know that you were related? How is it not common knowledge?'

'He is my mother's younger brother. He made a point of removing himself from any connection to the Valente name when my mother passed away.' He spoke matter-of-factly, anger evident in the hard set of his jaw.

Dara felt her anger deflate, taken by surprise by his candid statement. 'That must have been very difficult.'

'My mother died quite suddenly—she was only thirty-eight. The funeral was an ugly affair, and her family blamed my father. And me.'

'Goodness, she was very young. Life can be cruel sometimes.'

Leo waved off her gentle comments. 'I am merely divulging the facts to you—not looking for sympathy. I've had twelve years to get over it.'

He shoved his hands into the pockets of his designer tuxedo, a sardonic tilt to his brow. This was a man who kept his true feelings buried. She couldn't imagine revealing her own painful memories in such a matter-of-fact fashion.

Dara thought of the way the two men had just stood toe to toe, eyes spitting fire at one another, in the glamorous gilded hallway of the *teatro*.

'Leo, I've helped you to get your meeting. I've fulfilled my part of our bargain. We agreed that I would act as your date for tonight only.'

'I can't go alone to dinner. You will accompany me

to keep up the pretence that we are an item. Gloria likes you, and she is the key to keeping the peace.'

Dara shifted uneasily on her feet, smoothing a hand over the smooth pearl satin of her gown. She had felt like a princess earlier, walking down the steps of the *palazzo* to find Leo leaning against the door of the limo, dressed in a perfectly tailored black tuxedo. He looked sinfully handsome and powerful, and it was doing all kinds of strange things to her breathing every time he held her arm or looked at her with that smouldering dark gaze.

She needed to cut her losses before she did something stupid. One more night with Leo was a risk she couldn't take.

He was watching her intently. 'What is it that worries you, *carina*? That they won't believe we are a couple? Because that won't be a problem.'

'It's too risky. We know nothing about each other. What if they ask questions?' she argued.

'They won't need to.' He stepped closer. 'Dara, we practically crackle every time we are alone together. The chemistry between us is quite obvious.'

'It is?' Dara felt a little dazed under his scrutiny.

'Oh, yes.' He lowered his voice. 'We naturally react to each other. That's not something that can be feigned easily and we can use it to our advantage.'

'I don't see how arguing with each other will make it seem that we are a couple.'

She turned away, fighting against herself. She was enjoying this little charade they had embarked upon. It was beginning to feel like an alternative reality to her hectic and rather solitary life in Syracuse.

'Tension can be interpreted in many ways.'

Leo stepped behind her, close enough that she could feel his breath below her ear.

'Physical signs are the first things that people notice. Unconscious displays of intimacy.' He reached for her hand, lacing his fingers through hers.

Dara's breath caught in her chest at the effect of the innocent yet explosive contact on her already heightened senses.

'So we hold hands and everything will be okay?'

'There is no need to go over the top when subtlety will work much better. I might rest a hand on the small of your back while we talk. Display possession.'

Dara tried to focus on his words, but all she could think about was how hard and warm his hand felt surrounding hers. It had been so long since she'd had her hand held.

She shook off that warm fuzzy thought. She tried to seem blasé, barely noticing his movement until she felt his hand slide sensually low on her spine.

'What are you doing?' she squeaked.

'Dara, no one will believe this if your voice rises an entire octave every time I touch you,' he whispered in her ear as they were rejoined by the other guests in their box.

She took the opportunity to retake her seat and study the programme while she calmed her erratic breathing. The music started and Leo sat beside her. Very close beside her.

'Let's try this again,' he whispered softly.

His hand came to rest upon hers in her lap, his fingers massaging the back of her palm idly, just as a lover's might. He looked straight ahead, focusing on the beautiful performance, completely unaffected by their contact.

She was suddenly very aware of her breathing as she tried to concentrate on the stage below.

His fingers laced through hers as his head tilted and he whispered in her ear. 'Much better, Dara, a perfect balance between quiet disdain and shivering anticipation.'

'I did not shiver,' she hissed, turning to find his eyes filled with mirth.

The couple next to them tutted with disapproval.

'You're being deliberately disruptive.' She shook her head, focusing on the show below.

'I can't help it.' He tilted his head again, his attention now completely focused on her.

'Well, try harder,' she scolded, folding her hands in her lap tightly. 'This isn't the place to teach me how to lie effectively. I haven't even agreed to continue this little charade.'

'You're right.' He stood up, grabbing her by the hand and speaking quietly to the couple behind them. 'Excuse us—my beautiful companion isn't quite feeling herself.' He pulled her up from her seat easily and motioned for her to precede him out through the door of the box.

Dara exited into the corridor, turning to face him as he closed the door behind him. 'I didn't mean that we had to leave,' she said, exasperated.

'My attention wasn't exactly on the show.' He stepped closer. 'Something occurred to me in there.'

Dara watched as he took another step, bringing him so close they were almost chest to chest. His eyes didn't leave hers as he leaned closer, his gaze sweeping over her lips with clear intent. The thought occurred to her that she was going to let him kiss her. Even worse—she wanted him to.

'What occurred to you?' she whispered, her tongue sneaking out to dampen her lips before she could stop herself.

He followed the movement eagerly. 'You have no reason to help me after tonight.'

'I suppose you're right.' She shook off the feeling of disappointment at his words. He was correct. After tonight they had no reason to continue to work together except for maybe exchanging emails about the *castello*.

'What if I offered you more than a contract for your celebrity wedding?' he asked quietly.

Dara felt her pulse quicken at the word *more*.

'I've been thinking... The castle is virtually abandoned, with no purpose. Your vision for this wedding will bring vitality to it again. It might even help bring some revenue to Monterocca. God knows they need it, being so far from the busier tourist resorts.'

'I'm flattered you paid so much attention to my slideshow.' She smiled.

'I can offer you exclusive rights to hold a small amount of select weddings at the *castello*. I will hire you to oversee the renovations and ensure it is fit for purpose again.'

'Leo, that would be...amazing...' she breathed.

'I want nothing more to do with the place once this deal is finalised. So it's not a selfless act. I trust that you will do a good job, Dara?'

'I assure you that you will have nothing to worry about,' she gushed, the excitement of his revelation taking her completely by surprise.

'You will accompany me tomorrow evening, then?' he said plainly.

Dara laughed. 'I suppose I'll have to now.'

'It will be the last thing I ask of you.'

His expression was earnest as they made their way down the corridor to the grand hallway and out towards the waiting car.

The thought of spending another evening as the focus

of his attention, of having him touch her and speak to her like a lover, made her feel uneasy.

She stayed silent on the drive back to the apartment, her thoughts still frazzled from their encounter in the opera box. He had barely touched her and she'd been on the verge of throwing herself at him. She had been so sure he was about to kiss her in the corridor.

The fear of being branded a liar by Umberto Lucchesi was nothing compared to the fear of being kissed by Leo Valente. He hadn't kissed her yet, but with an entire evening planned in his company tomorrow, surely it was inevitable that he would.

It had been so long since she had kissed anyone she was afraid she'd forgotten how to do it. Maybe it was best to treat it as a task. She never went into tasks unprepared. She would treat it like pulling off a sticking plaster. Quick and painless. After all, the fear of the unknown was usually worse than the act itself.

When they entered the apartment Leo pulled off his bow tie in one movement, throwing it on a side table and moving towards the door of his bedroom.

'Wait.' She spoke as confidently as she could muster. 'I just want to try something first.'

On steady feet she walked to him, seeing his eyes widen as she stepped close. Her lips touched his—hesitantly at first, then fully. He smelled amazing this close, and his lips were hard and hot under hers. She stepped back before she could get too comfortable, feeling her legs tremble just a little bit as she put some distance between them once more.

'There—that's the awkward first kiss over and done with.' She smiled, proud of herself for finding a logical way to deal with an uncomfortable situation.

Leo stayed silent for a moment, his expression entirely unreadable. Then he took a step, closing the space between them. 'If you wanted to try it out, all you had to do was ask, Dara.'

'It was just a practice run. For tomorrow.' She felt her body react as he closed in once more. As if her skin remembered him, was begging him to step closer again. What on earth had come over her?

'In that case I think we need another try.'

His lips were on hers before she could formulate a reply. But this kiss was not simple and exploratory, as hers had been. His mouth was hard on hers, his lips pressing with an urgency she had never felt before. She felt it too. It was as though the entire world had fallen away and all that mattered was this. Feeling his mouth on hers, his hands wrapping around her waist.

His wicked tongue traced a trail of fire across her lips, demanding access. She tried to think straight. This was all wrong. It had started as a simple kiss and now suddenly she was being ravished.

She tilted her head back and he took advantage. His hands moved from her waist down to her bottom, holding her to him. She had never felt awareness like this before. The feel of his hard chest against her own made her nipples peak with need. Her breasts felt heavy, aching with the demand to be in the open air. She felt wanton and free and prayed her sanity wouldn't return any time soon. She let her own tongue move against his, following the rhythm and feeling the hard weight of his arousal press against her.

He began kissing a passionate trail of fire down the soft skin of her neck. Dara moaned at the sensation, shocked at the sensation of molten heat building between her thighs.

She wanted him more than she had ever wanted any

man before. His smell, his touch was driving her so wild she could barely think. All she could hear was the sound of her heart beating loud in her ears. His breath was equally as ragged as he nibbled her earlobe and pulled the neckline of her dress down so that it rested high on her waist.

Dara felt her body react reflexively, softening to him, unconsciously offering more. Cohesive thought left her as she gave in to the warmth of his hard muscular body surrounding her. He pushed against her shoulders until she was lying on the plush sofa in the living room. His mouth lowered to the sensitive skin of her breasts and the last remnant of her resolve seemed to melt away. All she could feel was him and the wild, primal movements of his lips and teeth as they tasted and teased her.

His tongue circled one tip as his thumb and forefinger slowly tortured the other. She writhed under his touch, her hips arching up to meet the hard ridge below his abdomen.

He raised his head to kiss her once more, his lips softer this time as he continued to tease one nipple with his fingers. His hand moved lower, tracing a path down her stomach to her lower thigh. He pulled the silken material of her dress up so that it bunched around her hips. His fingers were stroking up the skin of her thigh as his lips continued to demand brutal response from her own. She grabbed a fistful of thick dark hair, feeling a wave of triumph as he growled and kissed her harder.

His hand caressed her, higher still, cupping her over the thin lace of her underwear. She felt her stomach clench in response and raised her hips to meet him, feeling his fingers press against that sensitive part of her through the gauzy material. She needed his skin on hers—needed the release that she could feel building.

He growled low in his throat as she put her hand over his, guiding him towards the edge of the French lace, begging him to reach inside. His hands were everywhere... his lips were in her ear murmuring something incomprehensible in Italian.

He stilled momentarily, his hips pressed hard against her as she lay spread underneath him on the sofa. '*Dio*, you make me forget myself,' he breathed harshly. 'We have to slow down for a moment... I need to get some protection from the bedroom.' He traced a trail down her neck, licking the hollow of her throat.

Dara felt as though a bucket of ice had been thrown over her as she realised just what had been about to happen. She barely knew him and she had been about to have wild, unprotected sex with him on a sofa. Where was her self-control now?

Clambering out from underneath his powerful frame, she fought against the emotion building in her chest.

'What's wrong?'

He held on to her, his powerful bare chest still burning against her skin. She pushed more forcefully this time, noting his expression turn quickly to confusion as he moved, letting her struggle to her feet.

'I can't do this,' she breathed, tugging at her wrinkled dress to cover her exposed flesh. She felt completely bared, mortified at her own behaviour.

Leo stood up, then remained deathly still, his breathing laboured and heat high on his cheekbones. 'You're the one who walked over to *me*, Dara.'

'I didn't kiss you like—like that,' she stammered, trying desperately to get her ragged breathing under control.

'Are you angry because I kissed you or because you liked it a little too much?'

'We barely know each other. I don't do things like this.'

It wasn't a lie. The thought of casual sex was an entirely foreign concept to her. But right now her panic had nothing to do with morals and more to do with the thought of getting close to any man again.

'I make you lose control, Dara. That's what you don't like. I don't know why you're so afraid of letting yourself have pleasure.'

'Don't assume that you know me—or how I feel.' She shook her head.

He didn't know what it was like to have your life plan taken away without warning. To have a man you trusted shatter your entire self-worth to pieces. She could very easily use sex with Leo to unwind and forget about the memories bubbling to the surface. But she wouldn't, and that was her choice to deal with.

Leo shrugged with finality, clearly done with arguing over the matter. 'Fair enough. Let me know when you change your mind.'

She walked to her bedroom door, looking back one more time to where he stood like a Greek god in the middle of the ornate living room.

'I won't.'

'It's so nice to have our Leo back—isn't it, girls?'

The Lucchesi family sat together in the formal sitting room of their historic Palermo villa. Umberto Lucchesi was known for collecting what he perceived to be pieces amongst his country's greatest treasures. His love of historic architecture was inherited from his aristocratic lineage.

Gloria smiled indulgently as her two teenaged daughters nodded politely in unison, and Leo laid his hand on top of Dara's, feeling her tense slightly. Her face belied her discomfort but she smiled at him—a warm smile no doubt intended to display affection.

He could see the confusion in her eyes, sense how distant she had become since last night. His night had consisted of a very cold shower and a much needed glass of whisky.

She had enjoyed kissing him, and what had followed afterwards, much more than she'd intended to. He remembered the way the soft curves of her breasts had felt beneath his palms. She was a well of heat under all that ice. But now, knowing how good her skin tasted, it made it even more difficult to sit close to her without throwing her over his shoulder like a caveman and finding the nearest bed.

The only problem now was that he wondered if he would ever get enough. She was intoxicating. Since they had arrived at dinner he'd found himself touching her at every excuse. He had no doubt that she would come to him before the night was through—he could see it in the sultry way she kept regarding him every time she thought he wasn't looking. She was at war with her precious rules, but he had a feeling he knew who would win out.

She shot him another glance as he laid his hand against the warmth of her back.

His uncle interrupted his erotic thoughts. 'Leo, let's take a cigar outside and let the women chat.' Umberto gestured for him to follow him out onto the back terrace.

Leo regretfully closed the door behind them, leaving Dara inside to talk with his aunt and cousins. It was clear that his uncle knew why he was here. He had gotten him alone...now all he needed to do was appeal to the man's logic and speed up this deal. Then he could focus on Dara.

'So, nephew. You've played your hand well.' Umberto lit a cigar, letting the smoke billow in the air between them. He offered one to Leo.

Leo refused with a wave of his hand.

Umberto huffed out a cloud of smoke, looking up at the darkening evening sky. 'So, tell me, is using the blonde a vital part of your plan or just a little extra fun while you're here?'

'Dara and I have been seeing each other for a while now.'

'Spare me the lies, Valente. You know I don't take well to them.' The older man scowled. 'She's too good for a low life like you. She's got character.'

Leo felt a prickle of unease at the back of his neck. 'Umberto, whatever happened between my father and you is history. I am the furthest thing from him there is.'

'I can tell by your reputation that you have no value for family. That was Valente's worst trait. A Sicilian man puts his family first.'

'My choice of lifestyle is irrelevant. I am the most obvious choice for your development. It's clear to everyone around you and yet you refuse to cut me in. I have the expertise and the resources.'

'I'm not talking about the womanising. Although I do prefer to do business with family men who know the true meaning of responsibility.' Umberto narrowed his eyes, glowering at Leo with a look of unbridled anger. 'You want to know why I'm blocking this deal? I refuse to do business with someone who treats their own flesh and blood like dirt.'

Leo felt the comment cut him deep. He knew Umberto was alluding to his mother. To the way she had been treated by his father—and by Leo, to a certain extent.

'Your father sent my sister into an early grave. The

Valente name means nothing to me but selfishness and betrayal.'

'My mother put herself into that grave, Uncle. She committed suicide. She was not the woman you think she was.'

'She was not perfect, no. But she deserved better than to be locked away like a dirty little secret.'

Leo felt the pain of his uncle's words cut to his core. His mother *had* deserved better—they both had. The only person to blame for the life they'd led was his father. But he refused to argue over a bunch of ghosts when his goal was within touching distance. Memories belonged in the past, where they couldn't hurt anybody.

'I'm not here to talk about ancient history. I'm here to talk about the Isola project. I thought that by coming here peacefully, healing the rift between us, we could finally see each other as equals.'

'We will never be equals as long as a Valente owns Lucchesi land.'

Leo thought of the *castello* in Monterocca. His mother's family had owned Castello Bellamo for hundreds of years until she'd married a Valente and signed it away.

He spoke quietly, aware of Umberto's unbridled anger at what he perceived to be yet another slight on his family name. 'I am half-Lucchesi, remember?'

Umberto shook his head.

'My mother would not be happy to know her brother was treating her son this way, Zio.'

Umberto raised one silvery brow. 'Don't play on my sentimentality. It doesn't exist.'

Leo was exasperated. The man was just throwing block after block at him, leaving no room to negotiate. 'What must I do to prove myself?'

'You know what I want. The same thing I told your father I wanted the day he put my sister in the ground.'

Leo ran a hand down his face. He'd had a feeling it might come to this. 'The *castello* is my birthright.'

'It was built with Lucchesi blood. My family have far more right to Bellamo.'

'You're asking me to part with the place I called home for most of my childhood.'

'If it holds such sentimental value for you why have you left it to rot? You want in on the Isola project? You know what *I* want.'

The older man walked back inside, leaving Leo alone on the terrace with nothing but the sound of the waves rushing against the rocks in the gulf.

Too much quiet made him irritable, and he was grateful when Dara came to find him moments later.

'How did it go?' she enquired.

'As well as I imagined it would.' He shrugged. 'He has made it clear what it will take to let me in on the deal.'

'Is it something you can do?' she asked innocently, handing him a glass of wine.

'It would complicate a lot of things. Upset some people.'

He thought of Dara's face when he told her of his plan for the *castello*. He had heard her on the phone to her client, confirming their contract details. He had offered Dara a complete solution to her problems—a chance to further her business to the next level and avoid ruin. How was he going to tell her that he had to take it all away?

Their contract had loopholes in his favour—he had made sure of that in case it came to this. He had known there was a possibility that Umberto was using the Isola deal to leverage him into signing over the castle, but he hadn't planned on caring about who it might affect.

Dara looked at him thoughtfully. 'You want that deal badly enough to have accepted my event pitch. I don't see what can be so important that you would consider walking away from it now?'

Leo knew she had no idea what she was talking about, but she was right. They didn't know each other well enough for him to take her feelings into account. He had no reason to feel guilty. The loss of the venue might cause her trouble, but he would pay her off. Make sure he lessened the financial blow.

He wouldn't tell her straight away. He would wait at least until he had made his decision.

Dara noticed the stern set of Leo's jaw as they got into the limo. It had been a long evening of polite conversation. The kind of conversation that arose when there was a lot of tension in the air. She noticed that the air of mischief that normally surrounded him had evaporated, to be replaced with a brooding distance.

She found herself wondering at his change in mood, willing him to say something inappropriate and break the silence. She had spent the entire night arguing all the reasons why she shouldn't just cross the hall and slip into his bed. It had been sheer torture, with every fibre in her body urging her to give in to the way he made her feel.

'You keep looking at me,' he said darkly. 'Something to say?'

Dara raised her brows at his tone. 'I was just wondering why you were sitting there like a petulant child all of a sudden.'

'I'm not in the mood for this right now,' he warned.

'It's okay for you to be a jerk, but when it's given back you get annoyed?' She laughed, trying to lighten the mood.

'I was told not to be playful, if I remember correctly. Once the show was over. Or do you forget last night already?'

Dara felt heat creep into her cheeks. How could she ever forget last night? The memory of his mouth devouring hers, his hand sliding between her thighs, had kept her awake most of the night. She had been unable to sleep, knowing he was so near, confused at the sudden longing consuming her. It was *not* how she usually reacted to men—not since she had made the decision never to be with a man again.

She was unable to think around him and unable to resist the temptation he offered.

'Like I said, I'm in no mood to play games.' He stared out of the window, oblivious to the nature of her thoughts.

'What if I'm not playing games any more?' She spoke quietly, not quite knowing what she'd been about to say until it had already left her lips. 'What if I've changed my mind, Leo?'

Leo watched her for a moment, moving his hand to rest it casually on her thigh. 'I think that maybe you need to spell it out for me, *carina*. In case I am getting the wrong idea.'

With shaky fingers she rested her hand on top of his. Anchoring him there. This was madness. She was supposed to move away, to make a snarky comment or give him the cold shoulder. Not hold his hand like a wanton.

That was the problem, though. She *felt* wanton.

She felt more sexually charged than she had ever felt in her entire relationship with her ex-fiancé. With Dan it had been mutual respect, puppy love.

This was raw lust.

He was completely still, watching intently for her

reaction. She could feel his gaze burning through her. She stopped thinking, grabbed the front of his shirt and pressed her lips hard to his.

CHAPTER FIVE

LEO FELT THE LAST remnant of his restraint disappear in a haze of heat, as he ran his hands up her sides, his mouth devouring hers. All the pent-up frustration came pouring out of them both as her hands found his hair and she ran her fingers through it, anchoring his head close as he leaned down to kiss her neck.

He began to undo the top few buttons on her blouse and felt her hesitate.

He raised a brow in silent question.

She answered by pulling his head back up and kissing him again. He growled low in his throat, lifting her off the seat and onto his lap. He moulded her curves to him, bunching her skirt up high on her hips and running his palms down the length of her thighs.

'God, you are perfect.'

He groaned, cupping both breasts in his hands and kneading gently. He tilted his hips upwards, moulding their bodies together in a way that made her gasp. He could feel the moisture between her thighs already. She was hot and burning for him.

'We shouldn't be doing this back here,' she breathed. 'The driver might see.'

He ignored her whisper and moved against her again, smiling when she groaned even louder.

'I think you're enjoying the risk.'

'Yes…' she murmured, her eyes closing in a sensual haze as he moved against her in a steady rhythm.

Leo felt victorious as he watched her lose control and give in to the pleasure he was giving her. He pulled her bra down part way, exposing her nipples to him.

'Beautiful…' he murmured, taking one hardened peak into his mouth, then the other.

The limo drove onto rougher terrain and their bodies moved together with the vibrations as he feasted on her as if she was a dessert. His erection moved against her core, torturing them both with the delicious friction.

He vaguely heard Dara curse, felt her body grow tense as he bit down gently on her nipple. Her sudden shuddering release took them both completely by surprise, making her collapse on top of him in a daze of ragged breathing.

'*Dio*, that was the most erotic thing I have ever seen,' he murmured, kissing a trail down her neck.

Dara sat astride him, with her hands still clasped behind his neck. He shifted under her, painfully aware of his rock-hard erection still pressing insistently against her moistened underwear.

She shifted back on his lap, her cheeks rosy from the effects of her orgasm. Her shy smile was breathtaking as she reached down, placing her hand on the hard ridge of his jeans and biting her lower lip as he groaned in response.

Seeing, once again, how much he affected her was more than he could handle. It was like a drug. Now that he had tried it, he just wanted more. The thought of taking her here on the back seat of the limo, in the darkness, almost made him come on the spot.

With extreme restraint Leo placed his hand on top of Dara's, just as she began to lower the zip of his jeans.

She froze, confused as to why they were stopping.

'We are just about to arrive back at the *palazzo*,' he said, smiling at her evident disappointment.

He had succeeded in his efforts to seduce her. She was now his for the taking. And yet he felt the unfamiliar tug of his conscience, threatening to rain down on his lust.

Dara slid off his lap and began closing the buttons of her white blouse with shaky fingers. Her hair was in a tangle around her shoulders…her skirt had twisted around her waist. He had ravished her in the back seat of a moving vehicle and now, in true Valente fashion, he was planning on taking what he wanted before casting her aside.

She would want nothing more to do with him if he took his uncle's deal. Umberto's words repeated in his mind: he was just like his father. The thought gave the same effect as if he had just doused himself with ice water.

She smiled seductively at him as they walked side by side up the marble steps of the *palazzo*.

Leo hesitated just inside the doorway. 'I think… that you should make your own way up from here.' He avoided her eyes.

'You're not coming upstairs?' she asked, confused at his sudden coldness. She'd clearly presumed they would continue their encounter, after what had just occurred in the limo.

She didn't realise that it was taking every fibre of his self-control not to carry her up to that ridiculously erotic bed of hers and make love to her all night long. Her lips were rosy from his kisses, her hair deliciously mussed.

And once again that lacy bra was taunting him through her crisp white shirt.

'I have some things to get done before we head down to Ragusa tomorrow.'

He avoided her gaze, motioning to the valet, who handed him the keys to his Porsche. A drive might clear his head of this ridiculous guilt. And rid him of the ghosts that taunted his every thought.

'Will you be gone long?' she asked.

Leo continued to walk away, refusing to turn around in case he changed his mind. 'I'll see you at breakfast tomorrow, Dara. Sleep well.'

Their drive to the province of Ragusa was made mostly in silence, except for a brief stop for lunch at a roadside café. In less than three hours they reached the shores of the Ionian sea, and a further twenty minutes saw them make their way up the long stretch of coastal road and enter the small sleepy town of Monterocca.

They continued around the winding road to where the cliffs began to lower to sandy beaches and small fishing docks. As they turned the final bend around the headland Dara took a deep intake of breath. It was spectacular.

The castle stood high on a rocky promontory, dominating the surrounding landscape with its high turrets and imposing boundary walls. As they drove through the stone pillared entry Dara felt suddenly dwarfed by the enormity of the place.

She had only seen pictures before now, and photographs were nothing when confronted with the real thing. The stone walls seemed to glow pink in some places, with medieval turrets providing the highest points. The long straight avenue from the main road was rough and untamed. Wild foliage seemed to sweep in and engulf the car entirely at some points. Finally they reached a wide cobbled courtyard with a circular fountain set in the middle. Crumbling statues stood haphazardly all around, some missing their heads, some missing entire limbs.

Dara stepped out of the car and craned her neck to look up at the majestic stonework that decorated the entrance. This close, she could see the complete disrepair the castle had been left in. Chunks of stone had fallen down from the walls in some places. The windows seemed black with dust, and grime and weeds grew from every crevice. All the same, it was a powerful feeling to be surrounded by so much history.

'This place is *breathtaking*.' She sighed, busy taking in every tiny detail of the facade. She pointed to a wing that stretched out at an unusual angle from the main square tower. 'This part isn't medieval, is it?' she asked curiously. Her knowledge of architecture was pretty basic— she generally left historical details to the experts.

He rounded the car to stand next to her, crossing his arms over his chest and leaning casually against the door. 'The whole place is just one big patchwork of various eras. I never thought it was particularly beautiful.'

She shook her head with disbelief. 'How can you say that? It's the imperfections that make it so eye-catching.'

He was wearing sunglasses, but she could still see the sardonic tilt of his brow as he turned to face her. 'So your Hollywood actress is booking it based on all its eye-catching imperfections, is that right?'

'Actually, I think she wants it because her first film was about a Sicilian prince. They filmed in Palermo, but that particular castle was demolished. This one is apparently quite similar.' She shrugged. 'Either way, I don't argue with good publicity.'

He made a grunting sound of accord and took a set of

keys from his pocket. He didn't speak another word, still in the same distracted mood as the night before.

They made their way inside the main entryway to a great hall with a ceiling that had to be at least three storeys high. The windows were so filthy, barely any light could get in.

Leo had told her that the housekeeping team consisted of a local woman, Maria, and her husband, who took care of basic tasks. From what she could tell they had just done their best to stop the grounds from being overrun with weeds and keep the dust as minimal as possible with the castle closed up for so long.

'Right, let's get this over with,' Leo said roughly.

Dara took out the clipboard she had brought with her to take notes, shrugging when he looked at her curiously. 'I thought I might as well jot down my ideas as we go.'

'Always so efficient.' He sighed. 'Don't fall behind. Believe me, you *will* get lost.'

Their voices echoed loudly off the high stone walls as he showed her around the lower level of the main wing. The place was huge, and already she knew she really would be lost in a moment if she didn't follow closely behind him.

She ran her finger along a dusty sideboard, looking upon a row of small framed photographs of a young Leo. He was curly-haired, with emerald-green eyes, smiling mischievously into the camera.

Dara couldn't help but smile down at the photos. 'I cannot believe you lived in a place like this as a child. It must have been one big adventure, day after day.'

He followed her gaze, his eyes narrowing on the photos of his childhood self. 'It wasn't anything like you would expect.'

He carried on down the hallway, naming each room in a bored monotone as they passed through.

They made their way up the sweeping staircase and Dara began to amble down the corridors more slowly behind her grumpy guide. She wanted to look at the place properly—not just power through at lightning speed.

She stopped as they passed right by a set of large double doors. She knew from the rest of the castle that it would lead to yet another private wing.

'You never said what's through this way,' she called to him as he continued to stride down the hall ahead of her.

'That one is off-limits. Keep moving.' He stopped at the top of the hall impatiently.

She frowned. They were supposed to be inspecting the entire castle in order for her to arrange the renovations. How could any area be off-limits?

'This is beginning to sound like a scene from a really lame fairy tale. Is that where the beast lives?' She chuckled, hoping to lighten the mood.

She could see his silhouette, unmoving at the end of the hall, one hand resting on a side table as he waited for her to follow him. She felt frustration bubble to the surface. He had been extremely irritable all morning, and since arriving at the castle he had stopped interacting with her completely. He clearly wasn't up to doing this job properly, but that didn't mean she wouldn't get it done.

'I need to get a look at the whole place. No exceptions.'

She turned the handle of the door to the wing slowly, watching to see his reaction. He didn't budge as the sound of the hinges creaking open echoed through the hall.

Well, he could suit himself, then, she thought stubbornly. He could stay out here in his bad mood all he wanted.

Clutching her clipboard, she threw the doors wide and continued through to the mysterious forbidden wing.

Leo stood frozen in the hallway, listening as Dara's footsteps echoed through his past. He'd told her not to go there. Of course she hadn't listened. She was hell-bent on dredging up every memory this godforsaken place had to offer.

His initial view of the castle hadn't bothered him as much as he had thought it would. After twelve years he still remembered every window, every crack in the facade. He had vowed to remain emotionless and logical. It was a building—not a demon. He would show her around in a practical fashion, get the building work arranged and then make an effort to apologise for last night.

After his meeting with Umberto, and all their talk of this place, he had found himself momentarily regretting his pursuit of Dara. His uncle's deal was tempting, but agreeing to it meant lying and double-crossing.

He shouldn't care about hurting her. He should have just taken what she had clearly been ready to offer. But something in him had stalled, and he had spent the night driving furiously up a myriad of coastal roads, then returning to the *palazzo* once he'd been sure she had gone to bed.

He turned back towards the doors she had disappeared through. He wasn't going down there. There was only so much he could take in one day. This castle housed more than just his own cold childhood memories.

A loud bang came from down the corridor, and a woman's scream. *Damn it, Dara*, he thought angrily as he took off through to the largest wing of the castle, down the long carpeted corridor and into the grand master bedroom where his parents had once slept.

Dara stood on one of the ghostly covered chairs, her eyes darting around the floor wildly. 'Sorry, there were rats on the bed!' she squeaked, holding her battered clipboard like a shield in front of her. 'Bloody huge ones.' She shuddered.

Leo's eyes swept across to the large bed that dominated the room. A high majestic canopy flowed down from the ceiling to rest on the four-poster. His mother had imported it from Paris. He remembered her boasting about it to one of her friends. It had belonged to a queen. That had been his mother, she had always been fascinated by royalty.

The weight of long-suppressed memories was beginning to crush his self-restraint. He needed to get out of this castle now...before he lost his mind.

'I told you not to come in here,' he growled, watching as her eyes went wide. 'Get down from the damned chair. There are no rats.'

Dara lowered one foot to the floor, still anxiously scanning the perimeter of the dark room.

'There were at least three of them. They scurried off when I dropped my clipboard...' she said, her knuckles white as chalk as she held up the makeshift shield.

'I don't give a damn about rats. The place is likely infested with all kinds of vermin.'

He pinched the bridge of his nose, trying to ignore the memories threatening to engulf him. Lifeless brown eyes, staring into nothing...

'I will need to make sure that all the rooms have been cleared before we can consult the restoration contractor,' she rambled on beside him, unaware of his inner turmoil. 'Leo, are you even listening to me? We need to note all the details—'

She stepped closer and he turned to her without warning.

'Just stop with your details for once and get the *hell* out of this room.' His voice was harsh and he watched her eyes widen with shock.

'Leo… I'm sorry if I've said something to bother you.'

'I'm fine,' he gritted. 'I need to go find the house-keeper. You can finish the rest of the tour by yourself.'

He turned on his heel and strode from the room. It took all his strength not to run as if he was being chased by the ghosts that plagued his memory.

He should never have come back to this place. It made him feel things he'd vowed never to feel again. But it wasn't Dara's fault that he was on edge, and he made a mental note to make it up to her once he'd got his temper under control.

After three hours spent cataloguing every room of the *castello* Dara needed a shower. Badly. Out of the entire estate only three bedrooms were kept open and maintained, along with the kitchen, one of the dining rooms and a downstairs salon. Every other room was closed up, its furniture sheathed in ghostly white dust covers.

Still, it was rather magical, being the only person wandering around a place filled with so much character. Leo had left the castle entirely, leaving a message with the housekeeper to tell her that they would be having dinner at six. His desertion didn't faze her. She'd enjoyed her time alone with her work. The thought of all of the possibilities that this place held made her giddy as she chose a bedroom with an en-suite bathroom and set about having a hot shower to wash off all the dust.

Weddings could be held here in any season, she mused as she towel-dried her hair into soft waves at the gilt dressing table by the bed. Outdoor summer ceremonies overlooking the cliffs…candlelit winter feasts in the ballroom. She really did adore her job, and she knew she could make this *castello* beautiful again—bring it back to life. Not only would she be known for planning the wedding of the year, but she would also have exclusive rights to one of the most sought-after venues in the country.

Once she had dressed, in a simple black wrap dress and her trusty heels, she made her way down to the dining room for dinner.

Leo stood at the fireplace, stepping forward as she entered the room.

'Glad to see you've returned.' She breezed past him, determined not to show how his continued coldness was affecting her.

Leo helped her into one of the chairs at the end of a ridiculously long banquet table. 'I hope you're hungry? Maria has outdone herself.'

Their place settings were side by side—much more convenient than having to shout across the room to one another along the length of the table.

'This is quite intimate for a simple meal.' She poured herself a glass of wine, noticing that each of the antique candelabra had been lit around the room. The overall effect was beautiful, and strangely romantic. 'All we're missing is a violinist and I'd feel like a real aristocrat,' she joked.

'I'll make a note of that.' He smiled as Maria began serving an array of delicately prepared seafood.

The smell of lemon-drizzled prawns filled the air, to be followed by *pesce spada* and oven-roasted vegetables. Swordfish was her personal favourite since moving to Sicily.

They spoke of Dara's thoughts on the renovations, and Leo listened intently to her excited plans. By the time the housekeeper cleared their plates Dara's hunger had been well and truly satisfied.

Leo finished off his glass of wine, thanking Maria for her service and refusing dessert. They were both in favour of allowing the older woman to go home for the night after such a spectacular meal.

Leo sat forward in his seat once they were alone, his green eyes darker than usual in the muted lighting. 'I wanted to apologise for my behaviour, Dara.'

'You have no need to apologise for anything. We are both entitled to change our minds.'

'Is that what you think happened?' He shook his head. 'Dara, look at me. I haven't changed my mind about anything. Not one bit. I just felt I had coerced you into this. Had been heavy-handed.'

She felt something lift inside her, knowing he hadn't rejected her. Not that it made his treatment of her any less harsh. 'I'm a grown woman who can make her own choices, you know. I wouldn't have been willing to—you know...if it wasn't something I wanted.'

Leo laughed. 'It seems I've made a complete mess of this.'

He held her gaze for a moment before standing up.

'I want to show you the beach before it gets dark— would you walk with me?'

Dara hesitated, looking down at her shoes. 'It's October...'

'We can take ten minutes to enjoy the sunset—you won't freeze. Don't deny yourself the little pleasures in life. It's not always about the bigger picture.'

Dara followed Leo through the kitchens and down some stone steps at the back of the castle. The courtyard was growing darker by the minute as they traversed the gardens towards the cliff face.

Leo removed his shoes, leaving them at the top of the stone steps. He turned back to her, looking to where she stood poised on the top step.

'Come on, do something spontaneous for once.'

'I'm not as rigid as you seem to believe I am,' she said, and slid off her delicate heels.

Dara took his arm as they descended the stone steps to the beach below the cliffs. She felt slight terror at the height, but Leo gripped her hand tight until they set foot on the sand.

'My tutor brought me down here sometimes for science lessons.' He picked up a small stone, throwing it across to land in the water with a splash. 'He was the most uninteresting man I have ever known.'

Dara was intrigued at his sudden willingness to talk about his childhood. 'You didn't go to school?'

'The schools around here were too common for my father. He believed himself and his family far too important. I had many tutors. All in the castle.'

'That sounds rather lonely.'

'I never knew any different.' He shrugged. 'It was just the way things were.'

Dara imagined the young boy she had seen in the photographs all alone, wandering the castle grounds. 'Did your mother approve of your isolation?'

Leo walked further down the beach towards a small marina nestled into the cliff face. 'My mother didn't really have an opinion on very much.'

Dara followed closely behind him. 'You seemed quite angry when I went into her bedroom today.'

'Family history is not my favourite topic,' he said, surveying the small dock.

'I understand that.' Dara understood all too well.

She watched as Leo stepped forward onto the rickety

wooden pier. There was one boat tied up to a post. Wood rotten and black in some parts, it was amazing it hadn't succumbed to the ocean already. She would imagine the weather could get pretty rough here during high tide.

Leo cleared a place on the dock so that they could sit and watch the sun sinking down into the sea.

'What about you, Dara? Any skeletons in your perfectly organised little closet?'

She shrugged. 'I suppose everyone has some event or relationship in their past that shapes their future.'

'That was a very polite way of deflecting my question.'

'I don't have some sort of deep, dark secret, if that's what you mean. My childhood was quite normal. No sob stories, no traumatic events.'

He turned to look at her briefly. 'Well, then, what made you move away from such a perfect happy life?'

'My career brought me here and I decided to stay.'

'And yet you have never replaced Mr Ex-Fiancé? Did it end badly?'

'Very few relationships end calmly and logically.' She toyed with the hem of her dress, feeling uncomfortable at the turn this conversation had taken.

'So what was it that made you decide you weren't going to marry him?' Leo asked.

She sighed, shrugging one shoulder. Clearly he wasn't going to give up on this line of questioning any time soon, so she might as well give him something. 'Dan was a very successful doctor—a highly regarded surgeon. Top of his field. He made it clear that he wanted the professional family set-up. You know...loving wife with dinner on the table, two darling children to kiss goodnight. He had all the details planned—including the name of the golden retriever we would have.'

'Sounds very detailed. A match made in heaven, I would think.'

'On paper, I suppose it was. I thought it was what I wanted. Thought it would make us both happy. But in the end I just didn't tick all of the boxes.'

'You couldn't give him the golden retriever?' Leo asked playfully.

Dara felt her breath catch in her throat, the memory of that day in the hospital crashing down on her.

'I couldn't give him children.'

Leo's smile faded. 'And that was a problem for him?'

She nodded. 'I found out when we had been engaged for a little over a year. Three months before our wedding was planned. I had been feeling ill and I went into hospital for some tests. The doctors were beginning to worry that there was something sinister going on.'

Dara remembered her fear when nobody had been able to give her any answers for her strange symptoms. She'd been twenty-three. The doctors had never even considered that premature menopause might be the cause for her chronic headaches, insomnia, hot flushes. The day her doctor had sat her down and told her she was becoming infertile and there was no cure...

'When I told Dan he was very understanding at first. The medical mind in him made him want to know all the details and consult some colleagues. We tried to salvage what few eggs I might have left, but it was too late.'

Leo laid a hand over hers and she fought the urge to pull away. He would pity her now—just as her entire family did. Poor barren Dara and her useless body. The old self-loathing threatened to overpower her.

She stood up quickly, shaking the sand off her dress in quick sharp movements.

'What happened with your fiancé?' Leo stood too,

looking at her warily, as though afraid she would run away at any moment.

'Isn't it obvious?' Dara shook her head, a harsh laugh escaping her lips. 'He wanted a wife who could procreate. It was a pretty straightforward situation.'

'He left you because of your condition? What a heartless bastard.' Leo looked furious.

Dara sighed, looking out at the red-tinged sky. Leo didn't understand how difficult things had been in the months leading up to her diagnosis. She had been ill with headaches every day, and deathly tired. And sex had been so painful they had stopped having any at all. It had felt as if every single trace of her femininity had died in the hospital that day, along with her hopes of ever being a mother.

Lying in her hospital bed, she had overheard her father speaking with Dan in hushed tones in the hallway outside. The two men who were both supposed to have loved her, talking about how she was 'barren as the desert' and what a shame it was as she was so beautiful—as if it had stained her in some way.

Leo looked appalled. 'Did this Dan treat every woman like a prize mare or was it just you?'

'He had a very clear plan for his life. We both did. I decided to offer him a chance to reconsider our relationship. It wasn't easy for him to be with me all those months. I was irritable all the time, and I had virtually no interest in sex. If he'd stayed with me he would never have fathered a child the normal way.'

'Like I said— he was heartless,' Leo said plainly, looking her straight in the eyes. 'It's not your fault that nature did this to you. You should never have been made to feel inferior.'

'I was never very family orientated, but I suppose I always just presumed I would have children one day. Now that the choice has been taken from me I'm actually quite happy to focus on my career.'

She had her arms wrapped around herself. Leo felt the urge to embrace her, but decided against it. He now understood why she was so ambitious, so driven and serious. She had immersed herself in her career, moved to a new country—all in an effort to outrun her painful past. In a way they were quite similar.

This conversation had got far too deep for two people who had only met a few short days ago.

Dara looked at him, her expression one of quiet contemplation. 'I'm sorry, I should never have allowed this to get so personal.'

'Never apologise to me, Dara.' He stepped closer. 'Not for this. Don't ever let anyone think that you are less of a woman because of your condition.'

'With the way things were with Dan, I thought I was destined to live a life of celibacy. And then you came along and all of a sudden I feel…sexual again. I almost feel normal.'

'In my experience, what we feel when we touch is far from "normal".' Leo felt arousal thrum in his veins as she nipped her teeth along her lower lip. 'I want nothing more right now than to drag you up to the nearest bed and bury myself deep inside you until you can't think.'

'Oh…' she breathed, her voice husky with desire. 'I should be appalled at such a primitive statement…'

'You're not, though—are you?' He stepped closer, moulding his body against her soft warmth. Holding her to him so that she could feel just how badly he wanted her.

'No. I want you to take me right here on this beach,' she said plainly, a smile playing on her sensual mouth.

Leo claimed her mouth in a hard kiss, any thought of gentle seduction gone from his mind. He kissed her until their breath was ragged, her lips swollen and pink.

Grabbing her by the hand, he began powering across the sand to the stone steps.

'What happened to doing it right here?' she asked breathlessly, colour high on her cheeks as they practically ran up the beach.

'I think I can manage to get you to a bed at least once. I won't have you thinking I'm a complete barbarian.'

He winked, gathering her up into his arms swiftly before she could protest.

'Nope, not a barbarian at all.' She laughed as he carried her up the steps two at a time.

CHAPTER SIX

Leo set her down in the middle of his bedroom, his breathing only slightly laboured from the exertion. 'There will be no stopping tonight,' he warned, as he pulled off his shirt.

She began unwrapping the tie of her dress, her hands trembling with excitement as she watched him unzip his jeans. Watching him undress, she let her hands still in their progress. Her mouth felt completely dry as she took in his smooth, muscular abs, the dusting of dark hair on his chest that trailed down his stomach in a perfect line.

'Are you just going to watch me or take off some clothes yourself?' he challenged.

'Shut up and kiss me,' she growled, throwing her hands around his neck and glorying in the feeling of having his mouth on hers again.

It wasn't enough. She moaned, running her fingertips along his shoulders, feeling the muscles bunch under her touch.

Suddenly his hands were everywhere, caressing her neck, cupping her breasts. He pulled her tight and pressed her hard against the door behind her. She felt herself held between its hard surface and his hard body and moaned again.

He undid the tie of her dress, pulling the material

down her shoulders and letting it pool on the floor. She stood there, in her plain white bra and lacy thong, and gloried in the look of appreciation on his face.

Removing her bra to free her breasts, he kissed each tip briefly before running his hands down her abdomen slowly. Without warning he sank to his knees in front of her.

Dara felt her body freeze momentarily as his lips touched against the material of her underwear. She had tried this once in the past, but hadn't liked the sense of exposure it gave her. She debated pulling him up to kiss him again, only to feel his hands pulling the material swiftly to one side.

His mouth pressed against her sex—hard and hot. His tongue darted slowly between her folds, stroking against her in a rhythm so slow and firm she thought she might melt. The sensation of being kissed and licked so intimately by him was far removed from anything she had ever felt before. She didn't feel exposed…she felt worshipped.

Her orgasm built slowly, every inch of her body tightening to an almost painful peak before exploding in a spectacular release. She let herself give in to this gift he was giving her, murmuring with satisfaction as the tremors subsided.

That little noise seemed to drive him wild. He stood and twined his fingers in her hair, held her while his tongue plundered her mouth. He was greedy, his tongue like fire against her own. She could taste herself on his lips, and the erotic thought turned her on even more as she scraped her fingertips down his back.

She needed him now—before she burst into flames. He seemed to understand her urgency. One sharp tug and her underwear was on the ground, in a pool around her feet.

His eyes closed and a deep growl sounded from his throat as she reached down to pull at his briefs. He was rock solid, so large she was amazed he didn't tear the fabric through. As her fingers closed around him she heard his deep intake of breath, a low moan. They were both breathing frantically, urgency taking them over. He removed his briefs and raised one of her thighs to wrap it around his waist.

She needed him inside her now. No more waiting. Her hips arched up to meet his, and she felt the long hard heat of his erection enter her in one deliberately slow thrust. His lips nuzzled into her neck as he retreated, then thrust again, the sensation making her shudder. He quickened the pace, grabbing her other thigh so that she was fully wrapped around him.

She understood the frantic movement of his hips. She felt the same raw greed that was consuming him. She needed more…so much more.

Her back was flattened hard against the wall as he worked magic between her thighs, and she felt the toe-curling pressure rise within her once again. His breath was heavy against her neck, his tongue tasting her and nipping her skin as she twisted her hands greedily in his hair.

All of a sudden she was pulled from the wall and carried a few steps. Expecting to be thrown down on the bed, she bit her lip as her back came in contact with the smooth surface of a wooden desk, the intimate contact between them unbroken. His eyes darkened at the look of surprise on her face as he moved within her again, this time with his hands on her breasts, his fingers on the tight peaks driving her even wilder.

'That's it…come for me again,' he purred, his eyes watching her as she writhed with every thrust.

She shook her head. It was right within her reach… she was at breaking point…she just couldn't seem to get high enough. As though reading her thoughts, he slipped one finger between their bodies, caressing her where the fire burned hottest.

Light exploded behind her eyelids as release crashed upon her. His thrusts came faster and harder, his mouth lowering to her breasts, devouring them as he sought his own release. She shattered into a million pieces just as he groaned, his hands gripping her hips as his orgasm took over.

His thrusts slowed, her own spasms eased off, and she vaguely felt the weight of his head resting upon her bare breasts. Neither of them made a sound for a moment, letting their breathing return to normal. She felt as though her body would collapse if she tried to move any time soon.

He moved to drop a kiss between her breasts before raising up to look at her. Deep green eyes seared into hers with a heat so intense it might have burnt through metal.

'I thought we might have at least made it to a bed this time,' he breathed, running his fingers slowly from her breasts to her stomach as he stood up straight. She shivered in response and he smiled. A slow, predatory smile of complete satisfaction.

Despite the molten heat still thrumming in her veins, she felt suddenly aware that she was *very* naked. She sat up on the desk and slid herself down to her feet, feeling the heat of his body press up against her. This was insane—they had barely finished and he was kissing her again, running his hands up and down her body. She had never been savoured like this before…as if her skin was irresistible.

'I can't think straight,' he growled, leaning down and pressing his forehead to hers. 'I can't stop touching you.'

They stood still for a moment, just looking at each other. Leo grabbed her by the hand and led her slowly into the en-suite bathroom. They stood in the shower stall and he turned the water on full blast, fumbling with the nozzle until the temperature adjusted from chilly to pleasantly warm.

He pulled her into his arms in one movement, the warm water cascading down over them, and Dara sighed and moulded her body to his. The sensation of their hot wet skin fused together was sinfully erotic.

He grabbed a bottle of shampoo and massaged it first into his own hair, then hers. His fingers loosened her already relaxed muscles. She hadn't thought his touch could get any more amazing. She had been wrong. His soapy hands moved over every inch of her skin, his fingers leaving a trail of fire in their wake.

His hands tilted her head back into the spray and the water rinsed the soap from her hair and body as he continued to trail soft kisses down her neck. She moved against him, feeling the smooth hot thrust of his erection slide against her stomach.

'You know, there's something I've never done…' She tried to keep her voice steady and confident as the image of what she was about to suggest flooded her senses.

'Mmm…? And what might that be?' He continued to kiss her neck, strong fingers kneading the soft flesh of her bottom as they ground against each other under the spray.

She broke the contact between them, releasing herself from his hold and meeting his eyes intensely. 'Sit down,' she commanded, gesturing to the long seat that lined the shower wall.

His brows rose but he obeyed, lowering his tall lean frame onto the seat with ease. She looked down at him and thought this had to be the single most erotic image she had ever seen. His dark wet skin was in sharp contrast with the white tiles of the shower wall. His hair was wet and curled dangerously around his features. She towered over him in this position, and felt strangely aroused by the sensation of sensual power she held over such a man.

Getting down on her knees, she moved between his legs and watched his eyes widen in surprise. She placed her hands on his thighs and felt the muscles bunch in response. She wrapped her fingers around the long hard length of him and took a moment to simply slide her hand up over the smooth silky skin.

She'd never been allowed to do this before. And the sensation felt strangely forbidden. As his breathing quickened she leaned forward and tasted him with the tip of her tongue. He arched his back in response and made a sharp hissing sound.

'Is this good for you?' she asked uncertainly.

His laugh was half choked. 'Oh, it's more than good.'

He twined his fingers through her hair, applying pressure to the back of her head as she took him in deeper. He moaned in response and she moved a little faster, rejoicing when he groaned louder.

His arms reached down and pulled her up suddenly, lifting her until she slid onto his lap with ease. She twined her fingers around his neck and felt him enter her quickly.

'Do you see what you do to me?' he groaned as she began to move over him.

Being on top gave her the same sensation of being completely in power, completely in control of their pleasure. This alone was enough to topple her over the edge. She moved her hips forward and back, moaning when he grabbed her hips greedily and began to urge her on even faster.

'Don't stop,' he murmured, running his hands over her bottom and up her back, kissing a fevered path along her neck with lips that seemed to be made of molten lava.

Dara felt her orgasm building once more, and she felt the frantic beating of his heart that signalled his own. She slowed her pace, feeling him starting to lose control. One final sweep of her hips had them both tumbling over the edge and she collapsed on top of him as the tremors racked her body.

Dara woke to an unknown sound intruding on her dreams. It took her a moment to take in her unfamiliar surroundings, and then she looked to find she was alone in the large bed.

The sheets were tangled from the events of the night before. They had made love countless times throughout the night. Leo's appetite was insatiable. The gauze curtains around the queen-size bed swayed in the breeze— she could smell oranges and salt from the surf.

She felt wickedly satisfied and smiled, giving her hips a little wiggle as she got out of bed to look out of the windows at the waves crashing against the cliffs below the castle turrets. She wouldn't let herself regret last night. She felt happy and attractive and sensual again, and that was nothing to be ashamed of. He had given her a wonderful gift without even realising it.

As she opened the bedroom door the smell of acrid smoke burnt her nostrils and she instinctively launched into a run, bare feet clipping down the marble tiles. She reached the kitchen just in time to see Leo drop a steaming pot of coffee into the sink with a guttural oath.

'Is everything okay?' she asked, taking in the coffee grounds spilled across the counter and down onto the floor. It was as though a small child had decided to play chef.

'No, everything is *not* okay. This is the second time it's burnt,' he growled. 'Apparently Maria doesn't work until noon. What's the point in hiring a housekeeper if she's not here for breakfast?'

His brow furrowed as he emptied the contents of the pot down the drain and peered inside the lid.

Dara stepped up beside him and peered in herself. The bottom of the steel pot was coated with a layer of thick burnt coffee grounds. He had put the coffee and the water in the wrong compartments.

'Have you ever made your own coffee?'

His frown deepened. 'It can't be that difficult, surely?'

'You really are a pampered playboy.' She chuckled, taking the ruined pot and setting it to steep in cold water.

'You seem very well rested this morning.' He smiled, stepping behind her.

'I don't see how. We didn't sleep very much.'

She tried to remain casual, unsure of what the protocol was this morning. Would he expect her to leave straight away after breakfast? There was no real need for her to stay any longer—she could arrange the renovations over the phone easily.

She felt very insecure all of a sudden.

'I've never been accused of being pampered before.' He laughed, turning her around and kissing her mouth deeply. He moaned in approval, running his hands past her waist to caress her bottom. 'Good morning...' He smiled.

'Good morning to you too.' Dara felt a little less tense, but was still unsure of her place here.

She watched as he moved to sit down lazily at the breakfast bar.

'I wouldn't get too comfortable there—I'm going to show you how to make coffee. I'm not doing it for you.'

She showed him step by step how to fill the base of the pot with fresh water and pack the coffee tight into the basket above. With a look of thoroughly male triumph he breathed in the aroma as dark liquid began to rise into the top chamber.

Dara busied herself readying a tray of food and plates to take out onto the terrace, where they sat at the outdoor breakfast table, a large canopy shielding them from the morning sun.

Leo set down two cups of steaming coffee onto the table.

'Congratulations. You have just become self-sufficient.' She feigned applause as he stacked his plate with some of the delicious brioche.

'I have always been self-sufficient,' he argued, taking a bite of his food. 'I simply prefer to pay people to serve me my morning coffee.'

'Paying people to care for you is not the same thing as being self-sufficient. You just wind up relying on your lifestyle to keep you afloat.'

He stopped eating and leaned forward, regarding her over the rim of his coffee cup. 'What about you, Dara? Who do you rely on?'

She thought for a moment then shrugged. 'Honestly? No one. I like to feel independent, so I do most things for myself.'

'Does your family support your choice to live so far away?'

Dara took a bite of grapefruit, taking the chance to

mull over his question in her mind. Her family was the most unsupportive unit she had ever known, but she wasn't about to bare her soul to him about that. She thought of her father and his stoic chauvinistic logic. If it was up to him she would be cooking breakfast for a husband and children right now, not advancing her career.

A vision of small dark-haired children at a table suddenly came to her mind. Their father was looking on indulgently. A father with suspiciously familiar green eyes. She shook her head, chasing away the thoughts. Family was not important to her. Not any more. She preferred not to dwell on things she would never have.

She looked up from her fruit and realised he was still waiting for her to answer. 'My family aren't particularly close. Maybe that's a bad thing to some people—the great Italian family mindset and all. But it fulfils me to focus on my career. My parents send a card at Christmas and birthdays. I do the same. It works for us.' She shrugged.

'I'm not judging you, believe me. I'm the last person to lecture anyone about family values. I don't even own a home.'

'Oh? I presumed you had a collection of luxury penthouse apartments dotted across the world.'

'I own plenty of real estate, of course. Paris, Barcelona, New York—you name it. Luxury apartments, mostly. But that's not the same as having somewhere you can call home.'

He sat back comfortably in his seat, looking out at the view of the ocean below them.

She was suddenly quite curious. 'If you don't own a home, then where do you live?'

'I don't live anywhere in particular. I stay wherever my work takes me. It's practical.' He finished the last of his coffee, setting the cup down on the table and sitting back again in the chair.

Dara shrugged, also looking out across the view. She sensed the matter ran a little deeper than that. A man didn't live in hotel rooms all year round just because it was 'practical'.

Leo stood up, deciding to deflect the conversation by gathering Dara into his arms.

She placed a hand on his chest, holding him away from her lips.

'Leo, what are we doing here?' she asked quietly.

'We are two adults who are about to go back upstairs to have fantastic sex for the rest of the afternoon,' he said confidently, moving the strap of her nightgown down her shoulder smoothly.

'I mean, what am *I* doing here? I have a job in Syracuse…I have clients. And you have your own company to run. This is madness.'

It *was* madness—they both knew it. But he had never felt so enthralled by an affair before. He was wealthy enough to have people run his affairs for a few days with minimum fuss while he indulged in a little leisure time. And Dara had already said that she could run her business remotely during low season.

After last night, the prospect of selling the *castello* and hurting Dara felt even more uncomfortable. But this wasn't about feelings—it was about sex, and they both knew that.

'I think we both know what we want, Dara. And I for one am prepared to take a few days away from reality to have it.'

'You want me to stay here? With you?'

'I want you in my bed for as many nights as it takes for us to tire of each other.'

He leaned down to kiss her neck, feeling his groin tighten as she moaned in response.

'I think that can be arranged,' she said breathlessly.

'I think this is my favourite deal of all.'

Leo smiled seductively, taking her by the hand and leading her back to the bedroom.

CHAPTER SEVEN

THE NEXT COUPLE of days passed in a haze of sexual fog. Most of their time was spent in the bedroom—they ventured out only for nourishment and a bout of fresh air.

The fresh air had consisted of a late-night walk on the beach, when he'd proceeded to make love to her slowly on the old wooden dock, with the sea water lapping around them.

Naturally Dara still found time to arrange some inspections for the structural work that needed to be done. And a removal team was organised for that morning, to ensure none of the antique furniture would be damaged during the building work.

Mountains of furniture now sat in the grand hall, cluttering up the space. Leo came to a stop in the hall just as a group of workmen finished carrying an elegant cherrywood vanity table down the stairs.

'What do you think you're doing with that?' he bellowed, feeling hot rage course through him at the sight of their filthy grease-smeared hands.

The men had been laughing at some private joke, but at the sound of his voice they faltered, letting one side of the table fall to the tiles with a sharp thud. Leo watched with horror as a long crack snaked through the precious glass mirror.

He felt fear grip his throat and moved with lightning-fast speed, squaring up to one of the workmen dangerously. 'Do you realise what you've done?' he shouted.

A memory clawed at his mind... Her eyes were black as night and filled with rage as she towered over him...

He barely registered Dara's hands on his shirtsleeve, pulling him back from the cowering man.

'Leo. He's just doing his job,' she pleaded, her eyes wide with worry.

He towered over her. '*Nothing* is to be moved from the master rooms—you hear me? Leave it the way it is or this whole thing is over.'

She stood back from him, confusion and hurt clouding her eyes. 'But the work covers the whole castle, Leo. All this furniture has been ruined with water damage... it's worthless now.'

It had always been worthless to him, he thought harshly, remembering his mother's reflection in the shiny glass. Everything about that room was toxic.

But it needed to be left alone or it would seep out and drag him under all over again.

'Just put it back,' he gritted, turning on his heel and stalking out through the door.

His breath came in deep bursts as he strode away from the courtyard. The cypress trees shielded him from the sun as he followed the stone path down the side of the hill. This whole place was one big black spot in his memory—a black hole of loneliness and despair. Dara thought he hated it because of the memory of death. She didn't understand that the memories of life could be far worse.

He didn't know where he was going until he heard the crunch of stone disappear and realised he was heading across the formal gardens to the large stone family crypt. The structure was an original part of the castle, restored by his grandfather in an effort to make some sort of tradition for his family. He needed to go in—needed to remind himself of who he was. He wasn't that lonely boy any more.

His feet echoed on the marble steps as he reached the tall black iron-clad door. It was never locked, always open for mourners to come and pay their respects. Resting his fingers on the cold metal, he took a deep breath and pushed.

The door swung forward easily, cold air rushing forward like the fingers of death on his face. And just like that he was engulfed by the dark damp smell of his childhood.

'Leonardo, you must learn to be silent,' she had commanded him, pushing her soft hand against his head until he was inside the darkness of the bad place.

He'd looked up at his mother's beautiful face, at green eyes just like his own, thick dark curls bathed in light from the outside world. She'd leaned down to kiss him on the forehead lightly, her fingers still clutching his shirt collar, reminding him of her power. He'd begged her to forgive him, told her he hadn't meant to come into her room, hadn't meant to speak out loud. He had forgotten Mamma's rule again.

She'd shaken her head, pushing him back. 'Silence, *piccolo mio*. When you learn to be silent Mamma will let you come out.'

The door had closed with a bang, the echo bouncing off the marble tombs that lined the walls. He'd smacked his hands over his ears until the vibrations had stopped. Then there had been nothing. Only darkness so thick and black it had been as if light had never existed.

He'd sat down against the cold stone graves where his

ancestors' dead bodies nestled until the cold had seeped into his bones...

The breath returned to his lungs with a shuddering gasp and he felt a warm hand on his shoulder. He looked up to see Dara, the sun glowing in her blonde hair through the open doorway of the crypt. He became aware that he was hunched, sitting against the tomb nearest the door. How long had he sat here? And how much had she seen?

He stood up, wiping the dust from his jeans with quick sharp smacks, avoiding her eyes as he tried to get his heartbeat back under control.

'Are you okay?' She looked concerned, her brow marred by a thin line of worry.

'I'm fine,' he gritted.

'You're sweating.' She reached a hand out to touch his forehead.

'Damn it, Dara, I said I'm fine.'

He grabbed her hand, holding on to the warm skin and feeling its silky heat seep into him. Touching her skin seemed to remind him that his words were true. He was a grown man, and ghosts had no power over him.

He grasped her hand tightly and steered her out of his nightmare and into the light of the gardens.

'Where are we going?' she asked breathlessly as they powered through the overgrown gardens towards the low stone wall of the castle perimeter.

'I want to show you something.'

He led them down 'his' path—the path he had always taken as a young boy. The smell of the sea filled his nostrils, loosening the tight pain in his chest. The rocks were tall and smooth as they descended the swift decline from the castle to the sea. His footsteps were steady and he held her hand tight, gripping her waist at times so she wouldn't fall. The afternoon wind whipped around them as the weather took an unseasonably stormy turn.

The last of the smooth rocks ended sharply and he jumped down onto the sand of the beach, holding her by the waist and lowering her safely. His fortress still lay nestled in the rocks. A safe, sturdy structure made from stone and mortar. He pushed the door, feeling the hinges creak and groan as they gave way. The roof and walls were still intact—the water hadn't yet claimed his little haven.

'What *is* this place?' Dara asked, her voice breathless from their climb down, her blonde hair wild around her face.

The small square room had stone floors and tiny latticed windows. He vaguely remembered the walls had been painted a dull white, but now years of damp had rendered them almost black in some places.

'It was used as a boathouse at one time, back when my father still lived here. One day I was running away and I found it. It became my own little castle.' He smiled at the memory.

'Did you run away very often?' She frowned.

'Oh, all the time. I would plan my escape in detail, pack a suitcase and food and take off.'

He walked across to the small grimy window, looking out at the wild stormy sea outside.

'I used to imagine I was a pirate, waiting for my ship to come and rescue me from a desert island. It varied, really, the mind of a boy is fickle. One day a pirate, the next day a dragon-slayer. I never could choose just one.'

She smiled, wrapping her arms around herself in the chill. 'That sounds very exciting. Did you always return home after these little adventures?'

'A boy runs out of food very quickly when he's slaying dragons, Dara.'

'Didn't your mother ever wonder where you were?'

'No. Never. I rarely saw her, you see. This was my castle, and her bedroom was hers. Our paths rarely crossed.' He pushed away the memories.

'Is that why you don't want her room disturbed? Because it was her place?'

Leo crossed back to where Dara stood, shivering in the doorway.

'I don't want to talk about ghosts any more.' He smiled, sliding his hands up and down her soft skin, warming her. 'In my castle we play games until we're forced to go back for food.'

She raised an eyebrow. 'Adults don't play games, Leo.'

'Ah, my poor, serious Dara, I beg to differ.' He leaned in, biting softly into the sensitive skin of her earlobe.

'You can't mean…?' She gasped. 'In here? But it's freezing cold.'

'I promise we can find ways to keep warm.'

Dara lay boneless and relaxed, listening to the sound of Leo's breathing return to normal. His eyes were closed but she could feel the tension slowly returning to his body as he came down from the glow of their lovemaking.

This time seemed to have been more intense than before, with a pile of nets and blankets providing a makeshift bed for their heated bodies. As attentive and sensual as he had been, he hadn't been able to shake the shadows from his eyes. It was as though some unknown force was still there and he was running, using the intense pleasure between them to get away from it.

She sat up on her elbows, looking down at his tousled

curls against her bare stomach. 'Tell me what happened back there?' she asked gently.

His voice rumbled against her skin. 'You mean when I lay you down and told you I would be the dragon this time?'

'Be serious for once, would you? You were sitting in that crypt with a look of terror on your face, Leo. It scared me.'

'I'm a grown man, Dara—' He protested, sitting up on the makeshift bed and grabbing his jeans from the crumpled pile of clothes on the dusty stone floor.

She sat up too, placing a hand on his shoulder, stopping him from moving away from her. 'Even grown men have nightmares.'

He laughed. 'Nightmares would have made my childhood a little more entertaining. As you can see, I suffered from boredom.'

'Children don't run away from home because they're bored.'

He sighed. Standing up, he walked over to a small chest of trinkets, his jeans draped low on his hips.

'My mother liked silence.' He spoke in a monotone, tracing his finger along the silver lid of the box. 'She would fly into a rage whenever her peace was disturbed. I imagine it had something to do with the multitude of medication she took daily. Anyway, on occasion a young boy likes to make noise. When I got too loud she would send me there for quiet time.'

'To the crypt?' Dara felt shock pour into her veins. She remembered how pale and terrified he had looked, pushed tight against the marble wall.

'I don't know when I realised there was something wrong with her,' he continued. 'She would be fine some days, and then others…she just wasn't. I was maybe five or six when she first put me in there. I lost my first tooth and I ran to her room to tell her. I forgot myself. It seemed like I was in that place for hours before she let me out.'

Dara felt tears choke her throat. How could a mother be so cruel to her own son? His reaction when the men had dropped the table suddenly made sense—he was used to being punished for touching anything in that room. He was used to being kept out. She sat up, forcing herself not to cry for fear he would stop.

He kept talking in that monotone, turning the trinkets over in his hands one by one.

'When I was twelve she came to find me one day. It had been months since the last episode. I had learned not to speak to her or provoke her. I had learned to be silent. She was in a blind rage—kept calling me Vittorio. Apparently I was beginning to resemble my father a little too strongly. I wouldn't go to the crypt that time. She never physically hurt me so I knew she couldn't make me go. I just remained silent until she walked away.'

'It sounds like you were forced to grow up much too soon.'

'I thought I had learned how to keep myself safe. How to keep her happy. But I woke up that night and she was trying to set my bedroom on fire.'

Dara gasped, her breath stilling in her throat.

He turned to face her, his eyes grim and lined. 'Nobody was hurt. The housekeeper had been awake and she heard my shouts. She and her husband put out the fire before it could spread too far. It was finally enough for my father to fly home from his business to take me and put me in a boarding school in Sienna.'

'What did he do with your mother?'

'She stayed here. The housekeeper knew how to keep it quiet. Father ordered more medication to help her sleep.

He said she suffered with her nerves. I didn't see her for six months after that night.'

Leo shook his head. Running his fingers through his hair, he walked across to the window, staring out into the distance.

'She continued in her cycle of madness for years after that. I'd spend Christmas and summer with my father. He would bring me to see her occasionally, but she never spoke to me. I sometimes wondered why we even bothered. Boarding school changed me—I became rebellious and loud, and going back to the castle would make me feel like I was suffocating. Home became a distant nightmare. A few weeks before my eighteenth birthday I got accepted into Oxford in England. My father was determined his future CEO would get the best education. I don't know what possessed me to travel down to see her. I felt like maybe if she knew I was leaving the country I might get some sort of reaction. When I got here the castle was empty. I'll never forget the silence.'

Dara could tell by his posture that this was difficult for him. She wanted to tell him that it was fine, that he didn't have to tell her any more.

'I went to her room and she was lying on the bed wearing her best dress. I remember thinking she looked like Sleeping Beauty. I didn't touch her. I just knew. There is a certain heaviness to the air when you're in the presence of death.'

Dara covered her mouth with her hands, tears welling up in her eyes.

'She had been there for more than a day—just lying there on the bed. A week's worth of sleeping pills in her stomach. All of the staff had been sent away in one of her rages. They'd tried to call my father but he was on a yacht somewhere with one of his mistresses.'

Dara stood up and walked over to him, touching his shoulder to find he was deathly cold. 'There was nothing you could have done. Mental illness is not something that can be cured by a son's love.'

'I don't remember feeling anything towards my mother other than fear. From six years old I knew that she was ill. I'd learned to adapt. And the day of her funeral, standing there and watching them slide her casket into the tomb...' He turned to look at her, genuine anguish hardening his features. 'I honestly felt like a dead weight had been lifted from my shoulders. There was always a fear in me—even after I went away to school. I always feared she would come back for me. She truly hated me. And as I looked into my father's eyes I saw that exact same relief and I knew she had been right. I was exactly like him.'

'Leo, your mother was ill. People in that kind of mental state can see things very differently to reality.'

'When the ceremony was over I watched him finish off his cigar and mash it into the ground outside the crypt. I felt something bubble up inside of me like never before. I had always strived to be the best, to get his approval. I'd always wanted him to notice me. *He* wasn't ill—he didn't have any excuse for his behaviour. I walked up to him and asked him why he never did anything to help her. He shook his head and said he couldn't control her personality. She was weak and had brought shame on our family name. By keeping it secret he'd spared her a lot of embarrassment. So I punched him square in the jaw and walked away. I decided that I might *look* like him but I would never be as heartless as he was.'

'So that's why you sold his company? Revenge?'

'Childish, maybe.' He shrugged, sitting down behind her and pulling her back against his chest.

'It wasn't childish. He didn't deserve your respect, Leo.'

Dara felt his warmth against her back, this marvellous man who had opened her eyes to so many things. He lived life to the fullest and disregarded the rules in order to escape all of this. Underneath the charming bad boy was someone who just wanted to be cared about.

The thought was almost too much to bear. She was beginning to care for him too much, and the feeling scared her. Knowing that he was just as damaged as she was made it harder to think of their relationship as it was. This new closeness between them was complicating things, tangling up her emotions in knots.

Leo held Dara in his arms and attempted to process the feelings trying to burst through his chest. He was thirty years old and this was the first time he had ever spoken about his upbringing to anybody. What was it about this woman that had made him want to lay himself bare?

His past was something that had always been buried in a deep crevice of his mind, filled with shame and confusion. But now, after saying it all out loud and hearing her say he was normal... He felt lighter than he had in years. The memories of fear were suddenly just that— old memories.

For the first time he felt entirely present in the moment, in this boathouse, with this woman in his arms. He felt as if he could stay still with her and not feel afraid. As if this was a safe place to stay for a little while— maybe even longer.

Later that night Leo stood in the doorway of the master bedroom while Dara slept soundly. When the call from his Paris club had awoken him he had debated on whether to wake her. But after another night of marathon lovemaking he'd decided to let her sleep. She had been working hard on the *castello* by day and spending each night in his bed. She deserved some quality sleep.

The Platinum club in Paris had got into some legal difficulty with licensing, and he was required there before midday to meet with his team of advisers. The jet was ready and he needed to leave as soon as possible. The realisation that he didn't want to leave made him all the more intent to go. He needed some head space to process the events of the past few weeks.

For so long he had been someone who avoided emotional entanglements and kept his affairs at a distance. He had bared far too much to her yesterday. She had every right to call time on whatever it was that they were doing. She hadn't signed up for a no-strings fling with an emotional wreck.

Dara's eyes fluttered open just as he moved to walk out through the door.

'Leo—where are you going?'

'Paris. I have some business to attend to.'

He fought the urge to climb back into bed with her. The thought of a morning on a plane followed by an afternoon in a courthouse was hardly a fair trade.

'Will you be gone long?' She moved the covers teasingly close to her nipples, smiling like the wicked temptress she had become.

'I'll be back as soon as my business is done. You have work to complete here too.'

Leo paused, considering his words carefully as she sat up on the bed.

'It's time we started wrapping up this deal,' he said finally, seeing the look of confusion on her face.

'Is there something wrong?' she asked.

'I'm a very busy man, Dara.' He moved towards the door. 'We'll talk when I return.'

* * *

Dara watched as Leo's car disappeared down the drive and felt her heart sink in her chest. This wasn't meant to happen. She sat down on the veranda, watching as the sun started to rise over the waves, orange and red mixing in with the mirror-like calmness of the water. He'd said this was just fun—two adults enjoying themselves and burning out an attraction.

When had it become more than that?

He knew she couldn't give him any sort of future. She had told him she was a lost cause. It would be just like her to get the idea into her head that he felt something more just because they had shared their life histories. She had spent the past five years convincing herself that she was happy alone, and she had almost begun to believe it. Now, after only a week with Leo, she knew just what she had been denying herself.

Angrily, she stood up and got dressed.

Perhaps he pitied her because of her condition. Maybe it was out of some misplaced sense of chivalry that he had stayed so long. She didn't truly want more, did she? He would never be happy with her. He was a Sicilian—it was in his blood to want children. Hc had never said otherwise. Sure, he lived a bachelor lifestyle now, but some time in the future he would settle down and start a family of his own. At least he had the choice.

The thought of him with another woman made her throat well up with emotion. When had she begun thinking of him as hers?

She spent the morning busily inspecting the repair work in the dining hall. All traces of water damage were gone, and the walls had been painted a burnished orange, true to the original style. She gazed up at the newly polished wooden beams on the ceiling, remembering how they had looked when they'd first arrived.

It was hard to believe it had been little more than a week since she had been thrown into Leo's world. She missed him already, and he had only been gone a few short hours.

Her thoughts were interrupted by the sound of a car coming up the driveway. He couldn't have made it all the way to Paris and back already. She got to the door just as an unfamiliar silver sports car came to a stop in the courtyard.

Umberto Lucchesi stepped out of his car, a warm smile on his face as he embraced her. 'Dara, so nice to see you again.'

'Leo isn't here, I'm afraid. He's been called away for the day on urgent matters.'

'Actually, I'm here to see you.' He smiled, stepping back to look up at the facade of the ancient *castello*. 'Don't look so worried. I simply wanted to come here and explain myself to you.'

Dara frowned. 'Explain yourself? About what?'

'Well, I presume Leo has told you he will soon be selling the castle to me?'

Dara felt the betrayal hit her like a gunshot. Her hands dropped to her sides as she took in Umberto's words.

'No, he hasn't mentioned it.' She spoke as steadily as she could.

'Yes, the deal was made in Palermo. I'm sure you know that the *castello* originally belonged to my family?'

Dara nodded, trying to follow his words, but the knowledge that the deal had been done in Palermo cut her even deeper. He had known for days. He had known that he was going to tear her life apart and yet he'd still gone ahead and seduced her anyway.

Hot tears threatened to overflow in her eyes. A lump of emotion was forming in her chest.

'Did he send you here to tell me?' she asked quietly, trying and failing to conceal the tremor in her voice.

Umberto shook his head. 'Look, I don't want to get in between whatever is going on with you and my nephew. I just want to make sure that you know that the Lucchesi Group will be happy to fulfil this contract of yours with Miss Palmer once the *castello* is under our brand.'

'With all due respect, I've just found out that my contract is null and void. I don't think I'll be handing it over to you.'

'I'm not suggesting that. I can see you've been caught off guard, here, so I will leave you to gather your thoughts. Come and have lunch at the resort tomorrow and we can talk further.'

Dara barely registered the older man getting into his car and leaving. She sat down on one of the marble benches at the edge of the courtyard, feeling her control finally tearing to shreds around her. Tears flowed down her cheeks onto her lap.

CHAPTER EIGHT

LEO WALKED INTO the main lobby of his uncle's Syracuse resort. The old man had been very cryptic about meeting him there.

After spending two full days in Paris, thinking, he had made a decision to end his business with his uncle before returning to Monterocca.

Dara was the only reason he had gone back to his childhood home. It was because of her that he had faced his demons and let go of the darkness he'd carried around with him since his mother's death. His feelings for her were intense and new, but what they had uncovered at the *castello* together was worth ten times more than any deal.

Umberto descended the main stairs and Leo raised his hand to greet his uncle—but froze as he noted the beautiful blonde step out from behind him. As he watched, Dara shook hands with Umberto, her face a polite mask of professional gratitude.

She turned and saw him just as he reached the foot of the staircase. Her features tightened and she turned away, thanking Umberto again before walking in the opposite direction.

Leo felt as though a train had just run him over. He froze in place, watching her walk away, before his brain caught up.

Umberto clapped him hard on the back, taking his hand in greeting.

'Glad to see you could make time for me, boy,' he said. 'We've had a slight change of plan with the resort, so I'm pushing the contracts through today.'

Leo moved to follow Dara across the lobby—only to have his uncle stop him.

'I won't have a scene here, Valente,' he warned.

'What is she doing here?' Leo gritted.

'Miss Devlin has accepted my offer of employment.'

'You callous bastard,' Leo breathed, seeing red haze his vision. 'You did this to convince me to sell the *castello*?'

'You have been dodging my phone calls all week. I felt like you needed some incentive. But apart from that the girl has a contract with Portia Palmer. A household name at my newest boutique hotel is an opportunity too good to miss. I wanted to make sure we were all on the same page.'

'You wanted to remove any potential roadblocks!'

Umberto shrugged. 'Leo, this is how real business is conducted. If you want in on my development then you've got to grow a thicker skin.'

'I'd much rather have a conscience.'

Leo turned and strode across the lobby in pursuit of Dara. He caught up with her just as she turned down the hallway to the business suites.

She turned to face him and he noted the telltale smudges under her eyes. She looked as if she hadn't slept or eaten in days. Like a woman who had been betrayed.

'There's nothing left to say, Leo.'

'Oh, I think there's plenty left to say.'

He spoke calmly, belying the anger coursing through

him. He opened the door of an empty conference room, motioning for her to step inside.

Dara moved away from him to the head of the conference table, her hands resting on a high-backed leather chair.

Leo shut the door, turning to stare down at her. 'You have made a monumental leap of faith, trusting that snake without speaking to me first.'

'He told me that he was going to allow your investment deal in return for the sale of the *castello*—was that a lie?' She crossed her arms, hurt evident in the shiny brightness of her eyes.

Leo felt hot shame course through him at being the cause of her anger. 'I did not agree to anything.'

'But you were going to.' She was so certain in her statement.

Would she believe him if he said he'd come here today to say no to the deal? That he wanted to keep the castle?

He no longer associated Castello Bellamo with darkness and fear. Now it was filled with memories of warm soft skin and hot passion.

Dara continued, making a show of closing the clasp on her small handbag. 'I mean, why would you walk away from a million-euro deal for a small-time wedding planner you're just having a fling with? We're both adults here, Leo. We knew what this was. And to be honest I don't blame you. It's better this way. Lucchesi has promised me my own division here, so I'll be my own boss. My company would have been ruined anyway. This way I'll still get to plan the Palmer wedding. I'll be fine.'

'I came here today to tell my uncle that I was backing out of the deal. That I wanted to keep the *castello* after all.'

'Why on earth would you do that?'

'Because for the past week I've been more honest and real than I've ever been before. You crashed into my life and forced me to revisit a past I never wanted to think about again. Do you have any idea what that feels like for someone like me?' He shook his head, pacing to the end of the room. 'And now you're telling me that Umberto just had to tell you I was selling the castle and you jumped ship?'

'In light of your sudden change in behaviour, it wasn't so hard to believe. Taking a position here is a secure logical move for me.'

'Screw logic!' he bellowed, turning back towards her and slamming his hand down on the conference table. 'You're so willing to just hand over that wedding contract? To give it up without a fight? What happened to the woman who climbed up a building to fight for her career?'

'I have no other choice.'

'You *always* have a choice, Dara. No one has a gun to your head. You want to know what I think? I think you're scared. You feel it too—whatever this thing is between us. And running away at the first sign of danger is easier than staying around to risk getting hurt.'

Dara stared at the man standing before her. She took a deep breath, trying to calm the chaotic thump of her heart.

Leo walked around the table to stand before her. 'You can keep pushing me away with logic and business but I know that's all a front.'

He leisurely brushed a wisp of hair from her face, making her shiver in response.

Dara stiffened, taking a quick step back from him. 'Leo...this was just sex.' Her voice was almost a whisper, the emotion in her throat making it hard for her to form words. 'Nothing more.'

She shook her head, looking out of the window to the bay below. How could she look at him when he had just offered her more and she was throwing it back in his face? She was showing her love for him by making this decision. By letting him see that this was just a week of madness. He would never be happy with a woman like her. He deserved someone whole. Someone better.

Leo stood up straight, taking a step away from her. 'Well, it's clear you've made your choice.'

Dara remained silent as he walked towards the door, pausing to look back at her. For a moment she thought he might say something else. She didn't know if she could take much more before she broke down completely. To her relief he turned and walked away without another word.

She waited until she heard his footsteps disappear before she let the tears come. The emotion of the past twenty minutes had left her gutted inside. She felt physically ill. He would be back to his old lifestyle by tomorrow. She had no doubt. Men like Leo Valente didn't brood over women. They moved swiftly on to the next willing partner.

She remembered that day in the boathouse—him laying his past out in front of her. She had seen through the playboy facade to the man underneath. Did she honestly think he was capable of such deceit or had she jumped the gun in leaving the *castello* so quickly to escape her own feelings? Maybe things would have been different if she had waited for him to explain first.

Wiping the tears from her face, she shook her head with finality. What was done was done.

She wasn't sure she would ever recover from Leo Valente. She wasn't sure she even wanted to.

Dara had thought the week since their last encounter had been difficult. But nothing compared to knowing that Leo would be in the building today, to finalise the contract for his investment in his uncle's development. She half expected to look up from her desk and see him in her doorway, all charming smiles and smooth talk. She almost hoped to see him.

Her decision to hand over the planning of Umberto's celebration dinner tonight had been made out of self-preservation. She couldn't stand to see the hurt in Leo's eyes one more time. Or, worse, to see that he had brought some leggy beauty as his date. Even the thought made her knuckles clench.

She mentally chastised herself. That was ridiculous. She had no claim on him now. She'd never even had one to begin with. And she had forfeited any rights she might have had when she'd walked away from him.

The memory of his words sent a fresh knot of emotion to her throat. *'You always have a choice, Dara.'*

'What are you doing up here? The dinner starts in twenty minutes.'

Umberto Lucchesi stood in the doorway of Dara's office, a glass of champagne in his hand.

'I don't think it would be appropriate for me to attend this evening. Considering my recent history with Mr Valente.'

'Leo won't be here this evening. Tonight is a good time for me to introduce you to the Lucchesi Group family. To celebrate the deal of the century.'

'I thought he was signing the contract today?'

'He has postponed it once again. Said he was otherwise engaged. It is merely a technicality,' the older man scoffed.

Dara felt her lips tighten at the thought of what *otherwise engaged* might mean. 'If the deal is not completely signed, why are you celebrating?'

'Among Sicilian businessmen a spoken agreement is taken just as seriously as a written contract. I will have the contract sent over to the *castello* tomorrow—he can sign it then. Tonight we celebrate.'

Then knowledge that Leo was still in Monterocca had caught her off-guard. She'd thought he would be back to jet-setting around the world by now. Knowing he was in the castle…in the place where they had shared so much… She wondered if his reluctance to leave was about business or of a more sentimental nature.

The older man continued to ramble on. 'No one is truly surprised that the castle is to be mine once more. It's just as it should always have been. Out of the hands of those traitors.' He spoke almost to himself.

'It was never yours,' Dara said quietly, and watched the man freeze and regard her through narrowed eyes.

'That *castello* belonged to my mother—and all the land that goes with it. It is mine by blood. It does not belong to some disrespectful Valente.'

Dara stood up, feeling her temper snap. 'Don't you *dare* speak about the man I love that way.'

'You forget your place here, Dara. You are my employee now, not his. Your loyalty is to me.'

'I'm beginning to realise that I've made a mistake. You are a spiteful, mean old man.'

Venom spat from every hard line on his ravaged face as he stared her down. 'Portia Palmer's wedding is contracted to me now. You walk away and you lose your client and all of your hard work for nothing.'

'It wasn't for nothing.'

Dara smiled to herself. It wasn't for nothing at all. It was for the biggest something she had ever experienced.

She grabbed her coat and bag, sidestepping Umberto Lucchesi in the doorway. Even if Leo turned her away—even if she had missed her chance—she still had to try.

Dara pulled up outside Castello Bellamo and breathed in the familiar scent of sea and oranges.

The front door opened and Maria came running out.

'I thought it was you!' She embraced her in a warm hug. 'I told him you would come back—I told him—'

'Is he here?' Dara interrupted, the urgent need to speak with Leo overtaking her good manners.

'He's been down at the pier all day.' She smiled, warmth in her eyes. 'He needs a woman like you, Dara. You are a kind soul.'

Dara felt her eyes well up. She had probably done too much damage to expect forgiveness, but she had to at least try.

The stone steps down to the beach gave her just enough time to plan a speech in her head. But all of that went to mush when she was only a few steps away.

He had his back to her, his attention focused on a piece of wood he was repairing on the pier. He wore jeans low on his hips...his white T-shirt was torn and covered with dirt.

He turned and saw her, their eyes meeting across the short expanse of sand between them. Dara steeled her reserve and walked closer to the small wooden pier, aware of his gaze on her the whole time.

'I didn't realise you were so handy,' she said, taking in the array of tools set out alongside him.

'Hello to you too, Dara.' His face was guarded, his expression unreadable as he stepped down from his perch and wiped his hands on a nearby towel. 'My uncle sent you, I suppose?'

'Nobody sent me. I'm here because I want to be.'

'I'm honoured.' He laughed, kicking a few rocks off the polished wood with a thump.

'Please, no jokes.' Dara felt queasy with nerves, and it must have shown on her face because his expression suddenly turned deathly serious.

'Is something wrong? Is he treating you badly?'

He walked towards her.

'No, nothing dramatic like that.'

'What, then?' He met her gaze intently.

'I've missed you,' she whispered, softly placing one hand against his chest.

He looked down at her, and for a split second she imagined he might kiss her. But then he stepped away, putting distance between them. She felt her heart thump uncomfortably.

'I suppose I deserve that,' she said quietly.

'You travelled all this way just to tell me that?'

'No. I came to tell you not to sell the *castello* to Umberto Lucchesi. I've realised that I made a mistake. That you were only selling it for me now. And I'd be the reason that such a beautiful place gets exploited by that man.'

'You decided all that today—when the contract is as good as signed? Again, your timing is impeccable, Dara. What does your new boss have to say about all this?'

'It doesn't matter because I quit.'

Leo's eyes narrowed. 'Dara, please tell me that you retained your rights to the Palmer contract?'

'I didn't. The contract goes to Lucchesi. But the *castello* doesn't have to.' She took a deep breath, stepping closer to him. 'What you said about finding your home here… That means so much more to me than some celebrity wedding. I want you to be happy. I want you to have this beautiful castle and a family of your own. You deserve happiness.'

'It sounds suspiciously like you care about me…'

'I *do* care about you. I love you for sacrificing your happiness for mine, but I just couldn't live with myself if I'd let you do it.'

'Dara…' He stepped closer, reaching for her, but she held back, knowing that if he touched her she would just implode completely.

'I have never felt happier than during the time I spent here with you,' she whispered. 'I'll treasure the memory, but it's best that we both draw a line under it and carry on with our separate lives. You see, someone like me—'

'I'm going to stop you there.'

His mouth was soft on hers, his lips tasting her slowly and deliberately. She reached up and drew him closer, unable to control the raw emotion sweeping through her. This might be the last time she ever kissed him, so she needed to savour every moment.

She felt his shock as she deepened the kiss, controlling it with an urgency she had never felt before. She pressed close, so that their bodies were completely in contact. She could feel his heart beating frantically against her hand.

He was the one to break the kiss. He held her at arm's length, a slow smile spreading across his face.

'I forget what I was saying…' she mumbled, pressing a hand to her swollen lips.

'You were about to tell me that you're no good for me because you can't give me children and I deserve a complete woman. Or something else ridiculous along those lines, I imagine.'

'Right. Well, now you've taken the power out of my argument by pre-empting me.' She laughed weakly.

'There was no power there to begin with, because that's a load of lies and you know it.'

Dara began to argue but he stepped closer, wrapping his arm tighter around her waist.

'Do I have to kiss you again?' he warned. 'I love you for who you are—not how many children you can bear for me. I want to build a life with you, Dara. For us to laugh together and travel together and come home together after a hard day's work and argue over who does the dishes.'

'You are far too pampered to *ever* wash your own dishes.'

'That's true.' He laughed.

'I'm sorry I almost ruined this. I'm so used to feeling like I'm not enough. The thought that you could ever be content with just me is terrifying. And even more terrifying is that when you call me perfect... I almost start to believe it myself.'

'I will call you perfect every day until you believe it. Because that's what you are.'

'I love you,' she whispered.

'*Dio*, it took you long enough to realise it.'

He laughed into her neck, nuzzling the skin gently.

EPILOGUE

LEO WAITED IMPATIENTLY by the entrance of the *castello*. The final toasts had just been made in the marquee and the wedding guests were settling in for a night of dancing and celebrations. The June sun had been strong all day, leaving the night air balmy and the sea calm.

It had all gone off without a hitch—Dara had made sure of that. He spied her finally exiting the tent, still not a blonde hair out of place. Seeing her in action today, planning the pivotal wedding of her career, made the past eight months of stress worthwhile.

Portia Palmer had proved a much more demanding bride than the Lucchesi Group could manage, so when the *castello* sale had been cancelled Umberto had been more than happy to pass the actress on to a more capable wedding planner.

Dara had risen to the challenge with gusto, and once word had got out that she was Portia's wedding planner the requests had starting pouring in. She already had the next year booked solid, and the summer so far had included events for politicians, television personalities and minor British royalty. She was a sensation.

But, as much as their careers had kept them busy, they still found time for each other. This weekend marked the start of a two-week vacation he had been planning for weeks. It began tonight.

'There you are.' She breezed up to him, planting a kiss on his lips. 'You disappeared after dinner.'

'I have a surprise. Can I steal you away now, or are you still on headset duty?'

She touched the small black device that was clipped to her earlobe. 'I'm officially off the clock. The team have it from here.'

'Excellent.' He unclipped the earpiece and unceremoniously threw it over her shoulder.

'Leo! That thing cost money, you know. My company's not exactly hitting the billion-euro mark just yet.'

He laughed, pulling her by the hand inside the castle and up to the master suite.

'You know, if you were that eager to take me to bed you should have just asked.' She smiled seductively, pulling at his tie.

'Not yet—first the surprise.'

'So mysterious...' she mused, following him out onto the balcony.

On cue, the sky was filled with an eruption of colour. Bursts of red and blue reflected in the bay.

'Oh, Leo, it's beautiful,' she mused. 'Portia will be so pleased. What a wonderful way to end the night.'

'I wanted to make this magical for *you*. This moment. It's been something I've been waiting to do for quite a while now.'

Dara gasped as he pulled out a small box from his pocket, knowing what was inside.

'You say I'm impulsive, but I bought this ring the day I went to Paris. I knew even then.'

He opened the box to reveal a spectacular vintage

sapphire, handpicked by himself. Something with history and class.

'You were so sure I would say yes?' she teased.

'Well, I suppose I could always take it back...' He closed the box, putting it back in his pocket.

Dara placed one hand on her hip. 'You see, I was planning on asking *you* to marry *me*. You've totally ruined the surprise now.' She tried not to smile, but failed, grinning widely.

Leo placed the ring on her left finger—a perfect fit.

'I can't wait to call you my husband. How would you like to elope to somewhere exotic?'

'No big white wedding? I thought you would want to plan a festival of extravagance for your own.'

Dara shook her head, gazing up at him with tears in her eyes. 'It doesn't matter where or when, as long as I become your wife. All I will ever want is right here in front of me.'

He leaned down and captured her mouth in a kiss that promised for ever. His perfect Dara...his home.

* * * * *

HER PLAYBOY'S PROPOSAL

KATE HARDY

To my fellow Medical authors—because you're a really lovely bunch and I'm proud to be one of you. xxx

CHAPTER ONE

ISLA TOOK A deep breath outside the staffroom door. Today was her second day at the emergency department of the London Victoria Hospital, and she was still finding her place in the team. She'd liked the colleagues she'd met yesterday, and hopefully today would go just as well—with new people who didn't know her past and wouldn't judge her. She pushed the door open, then smiled at the nurse who was checking the roster on the pinboard. 'Morning, Lorraine.'

'Morning, Isla. You're on cubicles with Josie and Harry the Heartbreaker this morning,' Lorraine said.

'Harry the Heartbreaker?' Isla asked.

Lorraine wrinkled her nose. 'I guess that's a bit of a mean nickname—Harry's a good doctor and he's great with patients. He listens to them and gives them a chance to talk.'

'So he's very charming, but he's a bit careless with women?' Isla knew the type. Only too well.

'Harry dates a lot,' Lorraine said. 'He doesn't lead his girlfriends on, exactly, but hardly anyone makes it past a third date with him.'

And lots of women saw him as a challenge and tried to be the exception to his rule, Isla guessed. 'Uh-huh,' she said. She certainly wouldn't be one of them. After what had happened with Stewart, she had no intention of dating anyone ever again. She was better off on her own.

'OK, so he'd be a nightmare to date,' Lorraine said with a wry smile, 'but he's a good colleague. I'm sure you'll get on well with him.'

So professionally their relationship would be just fine; but it would be safer to keep Harry the Heartbreaker at a distance on a personal level. Isla appreciated the heads-up. 'Everyone else in the department has been lovely so far,' she said, smiling back. 'I'm sure it will be fine.'

Though she hadn't been prepared for quite how gorgeous Harry the Heartbreaker was when she actually saw him. The expression 'tall, dark and handsome' didn't even begin to do him justice. He would've been perfectly cast as one of the brooding heroes of a television costume drama, with dark curly hair that was a little too long and flopped over his forehead, dark eyes, a strong jaw and the most sensual mouth she'd ever seen. On horseback, wearing a white shirt, breeches and tailcoat, he'd be irresistible.

Harry the Heart-throb.

Harry the *Heartbreaker*, she reminded herself.

Luckily Josie had already triaged the first patient and was ready to assist Harry, which meant that Isla had enough time to compose herself and see the next patient on the list.

Harry was a colleague and that was all. Isla had no intention of getting involved with anyone again, no matter how gorgeous the man looked. Stewart had destroyed her trust completely, and that wasn't something she'd be able to put behind her easily.

* * *

Harry finished writing up his notes and walked into the corridor to call the next patient through. He knew that Josie had gone to triage her next patient, so he'd be working with the newest member of the team, Isla McKenna. He'd been on leave yesterday when she'd started at the London Victoria and knew nothing about her, other than that she was a senior nurse.

He eyed the nurse in the corridor with interest. Even without the double giveaways of her name and her accent, he would've guessed that Isla McKenna was a Scot. She had that fine porcelain skin, a dusting of freckles across her nose, sharp blue eyes and, beneath her white nurse's cap, dark red hair that he'd just bet looked amazing in the sunlight. Pure Celt. It was a long time since he'd found someone so instantly attractive. Not that he was going to act on it. For all he knew, she could already be involved with someone; the lack of a ring on her left hand meant nothing. 'Isla McKenna, I presume?' he asked.

She nodded.

'Harry Gardiner. Nice to meet you. How are you settling in to the ward?' he asked as they walked down to the cubicles together.

'Fine, thanks. The team seems very nice.'

'They're a good bunch,' he said. 'So where were you before you moved here?'

'Scotland,' she said, her face suddenly shuttering.

Clearly she thought he was prying and she'd given him as vague an answer as she could without being openly rude. 'Uh-huh,' he said, lightly. 'Just making polite conversation—as you would with any new colleague.'

She blushed, and her skin clashed spectacularly with her hair. 'Sorry. I didn't mean to be rude,' she muttered.

'Then let's pretend we've never spoken and start again.' He held out his hand. 'Harry Gardiner, special reg. Nice to meet you, and welcome to the London Victoria.'

'Isla McKenna, sister. Thank you, and nice to meet you, too,' she said.

Her handshake was firm, and Harry was surprised to discover that his skin actually tingled where it touched hers.

Not good.

He normally tried not to date colleagues within his own department. It made things less complicated if his date turned out to have greater expectations than he wanted to fulfil—which they usually did. And instant attraction to the newest member of their team definitely wasn't a good idea.

'So who's next?' he asked. Hopefully focussing on work would get his common sense back to where it should be—firmly in control of his libido.

'Arthur Kemp, aged seventy-three, suspected stroke,' Isla said, filling him in. 'The paramedics did a FAST assessment—' the Face Arm Speech Test was used in cases of suspected stroke to check whether the patient's face seemed to fall on one side or if they could smile, whether they could hold both arms above their head, or if their speech was slurred '—and they gave him some aspirin on the way here. I've done an initial assessment.'

'ROSIER?' Harry asked. Recognition of Stroke in the Emergency Room was a standard protocol.

She nodded. 'His score pretty much confirms it's a stroke. I checked ABCD2 as well, and the good news is that his score is nil on the D—he's not diabetic. His blood sugar is fine.'

Harry picked up immediately what she was telling him—there was only one section of the test with a nil score. 'So the rest of it's a full house?'

'I'm afraid so,' she said. 'He's over sixty, he has high blood pressure and residual weakness on his left side, and the incident happened over an hour ago now.'

'Which puts him at higher risk of having a second stroke in the next two days,' Harry said. 'OK. Does he live on his own, or is he in any kind of residential care?'

'He has a flat where there's a warden on duty three days a week, and a care team comes in three times a day to sort out his meals and medication,' Isla told him. 'They're the ones who called the ambulance for him this morning.'

'So if he did have a second stroke and the warden wasn't on duty or it happened between the care team's visits, the chances are he wouldn't be found for a few hours, or maybe not even overnight.' Harry wrinkled his nose. 'I'm really not happy with that. I think we need to admit him to the acute unit for the next couple of days, so we can keep an eye on him.'

'I agree with you. His speech is a little bit slurred and I'm not happy about his ability to swallow,' Isla added. 'He said he was thirsty and I gave him a couple of sips of water, but I'd recommend putting him on a drip to prevent dehydration, and keep him nil by mouth for the next two or three hours. Nobody's going to be able to sit with him while he drinks and then for a few minutes afterwards to make sure he's OK—there just won't be the time.'

'Good points, and noted.'

Mr Kemp was sitting on a bed, waiting to be seen.

Isla introduced him quickly. 'Mr Kemp, this is Dr Gardiner.'

'Everyone calls me Harry,' Harry said with a smile. 'So can you tell me about what happened this morning, Mr Kemp?'

'I had a bit of a headache, then I tripped and fell and I couldn't get up again,' Mr Kemp said. 'My carer found me when she came in to give me my tablets and my breakfast.'

Isla noticed that Harry sat on the chair and held the old man's hand, encouraging him to talk. He was kind and waited for an answer, rather than rushing the patient or pressuring him to stop rambling and hurry up. Lorraine had been spot on about his skills as a doctor, she thought. 'Can you remember, either before or after you fell, did you black out at all?' Harry asked. 'Or did you hit your head?'

Arthur looked confused. 'I'm not sure. I don't think I blacked out and I don't remember hitting my head. It's hard to say.' He grimaced. 'Sorry, Doctor. I'm not much use. My daughter's husband says I'm an old fool.'

So there were family tensions, too. The chances were, if they suggested that he went to stay with his family for a few days, the answer would be no—even if they had the room to let the old man stay. 'Don't worry, it's fine,' Harry reassured him. 'I'm just going to do a couple of checks now to see how you're doing. Is that OK?'

'Yes, Doctor. And I'm sorry I'm such a nuisance.'

Either the old man was used to being made to feel as if he was a problem, or he was habitually anxious. Or maybe a bit of both, Harry thought. He checked Mr Kemp's visual fields and encouraged him to raise his arms; the residual weakness on Mr Kemp's left side that

Isla had mentioned early was very clear. And there was a walking frame next to the bed, he noticed. 'Do you normally walk with a frame?'

'Yes, though I hate the wretched thing.' Arthur grimaced. 'It always trips me up. It did that this morning. That's why I fell. Useless thing.'

Harry guessed that Mr Kemp did what a lot of elderly people did with a walking frame—he lifted it and carried it a couple of centimetres above the ground, rather than leaving the feet on the floor and pushing it along and letting it support him. Maybe he could arrange some support to help the old man use the frame properly, so it helped him rather than hindered him.

'Can you see if you can walk a little bit with me?' he asked.

He helped Mr Kemp to his feet, then walked into the corridor with him, encouraged him to turn round and then walk back to the cubicle. Harry noticed that his patient was shuffling. He was also leaning slightly to the left—the same as when he was sitting up—and leaning back slightly when he walked. Harry would need to put that on Mr Kemp's notes to be passed on to any carers, so they could help guide him with a hand resting just behind his back, and stop him as soon as he started shuffling and encourage him to take bigger steps.

Once Mr Kemp was seated safely again, Harry said, 'I'm going to send you for an MRI scan, because you had a headache and I want to rule out anything nasty, but I think Sister McKenna here is right and you've had a small stroke.'

'A stroke?' Arthur looked as if he couldn't quite take it in. 'How could I have had a stroke?'

'The most likely cause is a blood clot that stopped the blood supply to your brain for a little while,' Harry explained. 'It should be cleared by now because you're able to walk and talk and move your arms, but I'm going to admit you to the acute medical unit so we can keep an eye on you for a day or two.' He decided not to tell Mr Kemp that his risk of a second stroke was higher over the next day or two; there was no point in worrying the poor man sick. Though his family would definitely need to know. 'Has anyone been in touch with your family?'

'Sharon, my carer—she should have rung my daughter, but Becky'll be at work and won't be able to come right away.' He grimaced. 'I feel bad about taking her away from her job. Her work is so important.'

'And I bet she'll think her dad is just as important as her job,' Isla said reassuringly.

'Too right,' Harry said. Even though he didn't quite feel that about his own father. Then again, Bertie Gardiner was more than capable of looking after himself—that, or his wife-to-be Trixie, who was a couple of years younger than Harry, could look out for him.

He shook himself. Not now. He wasn't going to think about the upcoming wedding. Or the fact that his father was still trying to talk him into being his best man, and Harry had done that job twice already—did he really need to do it all over again for his father's *seventh* wedding? 'We'll have had your scan done by the time your daughter comes to see you,' Harry said, 'and we'll be able to give her a better idea of your treatment plan.'

'Treatment?' Mr Kemp asked.

'The stroke has affected your left side, so you'll need a little bit of help from a physiotherapist to get you back to how you were before the stroke,' Harry said. 'I'm also going to write you up for some medication which you can take after your scan.'

'Is there anything you'd like to ask us?' Isla asked.

'Well, I'd really like a nice cup of tea,' Mr Kemp said wistfully. 'If it wouldn't be too much trouble.'

'We can sort that out in a few minutes, after you've had your scan,' Isla said. 'At the moment you're finding it hard to swallow and I don't want you to choke or burn yourself on a hot drink, but we'll try again in half an hour and you might be able to swallow better by then. And I'll make sure you get your cup of tea, even if I have to make it myself.'

'Seconded,' Harry said, 'though I'll admit my tea isn't the best and you'd be better off with coffee if I'm the one who ends up making it.' He smiled at the old man. 'We'll get things sorted out and make sure your daughter finds you.' He shook the old man's hand and stood up. 'Try not to worry. We'll make sure you get looked after properly.'

'I'll be back with you in a second, Mr Kemp,' Isla said, and followed Harry out of the cubicles.

'Can you organise a scan and then transfer him to the acute unit?' he asked quietly when they were outside the cubicle.

She smiled at him. 'Sure, no problem.'

Her smile transformed her face completely. Harry felt the lick of desire deep inside his gut and had to remind himself that his new colleague might be gorgeous, but she was also off limits. 'Thanks,' he said. 'I'll write everything up.'

It was a busy morning, with the usual falls and sprains and strains, and a six-month-old baby with a temperature that wouldn't go down and had then started having a fit. The baby's mother had panicked and asked a neighbour to drive them in rather than waiting for an ambulance, and the triage team had rushed her straight into the department.

The baby's jaws were clenched firmly together, so Harry looked at Isla and said quietly, 'Naso-pharyngeal, I think.'

Almost as soon as he'd finished talking, she had an appropriately sized tube in her hand and was lubricating the end. Between them, they secured the baby's airway and gave her oxygen, and Isla was already drawing up a phial of diazepam.

Clearly she'd come across convulsions in babies before.

Between them, they checked the baby's blood glucose and temperature.

'Pyrexia,' Harry said softly. 'I'm pretty sure this is a febrile convulsion.'

'So we need to cool her down and check for infection,' Isla said. At his nod, Isla deftly took off the baby's sleep-suit and sponged her skin with tepid water while Harry checked with the baby's distraught mother when she'd last given the baby liquid paracetamol. Once the fit had stopped and the baby's temperature spike had cooled, Isla prepared everything for an infection screen.

'I've never seen anything like that before. Is Erin going to be all right?' the baby's mother asked.

'She's in the best place and you did the right thing to bring her in,' Harry reassured her. 'I think the fit was caused by her high temperature, but we need to find out what's causing that—if it's a virus or a bacterial infection—and then we can treat her properly.'

'Will she have any more fits?' Erin's mother asked.

'Very possibly,' Isla said, 'but that doesn't mean that she'll develop epilepsy. Having a high temperature is the most common cause of fits in children between

Erin's age and school age. We see this sort of thing a lot, so try not to worry.'

Worry, Harry thought. Parents always worried themselves sick over small children. And so did their older siblings—especially when they were supposed to be taking care of them and things went badly wrong.

He pushed the thought away. It was years ago, now, and he was older and wiser. Plus nowadays Tasha would give him very short shrift if he fussed over her too much; she was fiercely independent. And you couldn't change the past; all you could do was learn from it. Harry had most definitely learned. He never, ever wanted to be responsible for a child in that way again.

'I'm going to admit her,' Harry said, 'purely because she's so young and it's the first time she's had a fit. Plus I want to find out what's causing the infection. We'll keep an eye on her in case she has more convulsions. But you can stay with her.'

'I'll take you both up to the ward and introduce you to the team,' Isla said.

'And she's going to be all right?' the baby's mother asked again.

'Yes,' Harry said, and patted her arm. 'I know it's scary, but try not to worry.'

Ha. And what a hypocrite he was. He knew that panicky feeling all too well. *Would the baby be all right?* The overwhelming relief when you knew that the baby would survive. And then the guilt later on when you discovered that, actually, there was a problem after all… Harry's mistake had come back to haunt him big time.

'Is there anyone we can call for you?' Isla asked.

'My mum.' Erin's mother dragged in a breath. 'My husband's working away.'

'OK. As soon as Erin's settled on the ward, we'll get in touch with your mum,' Isla promised.

Harry worked with Isla on most of his list of patients that morning, and he liked the fact that his new colleague was incredibly calm, had a sharp eye, and her quiet and gentle manner stopped patients or their parents panicking. The perfect emergency nurse. He had no idea where she'd trained or where she'd worked before—Scotland was a pretty big area—but he'd just bet that she was sorely missed. She'd certainly be appreciated at the London Victoria.

They hadn't had time for a coffee break all morning and Harry was thirsty and ravenous by the time he took his lunch break—late, and he knew he'd end up grabbing something fast in the canteen so he could be back on the ward in time. When he walked into the staffroom, Isla was there.

'Hi, there. Do you want to come and grab some lunch with me?' he asked.

She gave him a cool smile. 'Thanks, but I don't think so.'

He frowned. 'Why not?'

Her expression said quite clearly, *do you really have to ask?* But she was polite as she said, 'It's nice of you to ask me, but I don't think we're each other's type.'

He blinked, not quite following. 'What?'

She looked uncomfortable. 'I, um, might be new here, but that doesn't make me an instant addition to a little black book.'

Then the penny dropped. She thought he was asking her out? Some of the other staff teased him about being a heartbreaker and a serial dater, but that was far from true. He always made sure that whoever he dated knew it was for fun, not for ever. And he hadn't been asking her out on a date anyway. Obviously someone had been gossiping about him and she'd listened to the tittle-tattle rather than waiting to see for herself. 'Actually,' he said quietly, 'as you're new to the team, I was guessing that you hadn't had time to find your way around the hospital that well yet and you might not have anyone to sit with at lunchtime, that's all.'

Her face flamed, clashing with that spectacular hair. 'I—um—sorry. I'd just heard…' She broke off. 'Sorry. I'm putting my foot in it even more.'

'Heard what?' The words were out before he could stop them.

'You have, um, a bit of a reputation for, um, dating a lot.'

He sighed. 'Honestly, where the hospital grapevine's concerned, you can't win. If you don't date, then either you're gay or you've got some tragic past; and if you do date but make it clear you're not looking for a serious relationship, then you're at the mercy of everyone who wants to be the exception to the rule and you get called a heartbreaker. Not everyone's desperate to pair off and settle down.'

'I know.' She bit her lip. 'Sorry.'

But he noticed that she still hadn't accepted his invitation to join him for lunch. Which stung. Was his reputation really that bad?

Pushing down his exasperation at the hospital grapevine, Harry gave Isla his sweetest smile. 'OK, but I give you fair warning—if you try and eat a sandwich in here, you'll be lucky to finish half of it before someone calls you to help out with something.'

'I guess it's all part of working in a hospital environment,' she said lightly.

OK. He could take a hint. 'See you later,' he said.

In the canteen, Harry saw a crowd he recognised from the maternity ward and joined them. But all the while he was thinking about Isla. Why had their new nurse been so guarded? Was it just because of whatever nonsense she'd heard about him on the hospital grapevine? Or was she like that with everyone?

Just as Harry had predicted, Isla was halfway through her sandwich when someone came into the rest room and asked her to help out.

She didn't mind—it was all part and parcel of being part of a team on the busiest department in the hospital.

But she did feel bad about the way she'd reacted to Harry the Heartbreaker. Especially after he'd explained why he'd asked her to lunch; it was just what she would've done herself if a new team member had joined the practice where she'd worked on the island. She'd been unfair to him. And, even though she'd apologised, she'd felt too awkward to join him and ended up making things worse. He probably thought she was standoffish and rude. But how could she explain without telling him about the past she was trying to put well and truly behind her?

It didn't help that she found him so attractive.

Common sense told Isla that she needed to keep her distance. Apart from the fact that she'd seen a few working relationships turn really awkward and sour after the personal relationship had ended, she wasn't in the market for a relationship anyway. Particularly with someone who had the reputation of being a charmer.

Professional only, she reminded herself. She'd apologise again for the sake for their working relationship. And that would be that.

* * *

Isla was rostered on cubicles again with Josie and Harry in the afternoon. Harry had just finished with a patient who'd been brought in with a degloving injury; when he came out of the cubicle, she asked quietly, 'Can we have a quick word?'

'Sure.'

Isla took a deep breath. 'I wanted to apologise about earlier.'

He looked blank. 'About what?'

'I was rude and standoffish when you asked me to go to lunch with you.'

His eyes crinkled at the corners. 'Oh, that. Don't worry about it. Blame it on the hospital grapevine blowing everything out of proportion.'

She felt the betraying colour seep into her face. This would be the easy option because there was some truth in it, but he'd been kind and he didn't deserve it. 'Should've known better because hospital gossip likes to embroider things,' she said. Not just hospitals: any small community. Like an island off the coast of Scotland where everybody knew practically everything about everyone. And she of all people knew how it felt to be gossiped about unfairly. 'I was rude. And I apologise. And maybe I can buy you a cup of tea later to make up for being so horrible.'

'You weren't horrible, just a bit…well, offish. Apology and offer of tea accepted. We can have Mr Kemp as our chaperone, if you like,' he suggested.

How could he be so good-natured about it? It made her feel even more guilty. 'I guess it's a good excuse to see how he's getting on.'

'Great. It's a non-date,' Harry said.

And oh, that smile. It could light up a room. He really was gorgeous. And nice with it. And he had a sense of humour.

It would be all too easy to let Harry Gardiner tempt her.

But this nurse wasn't for tempting.

They spent their afternoon break in the Acute Medical Unit with Mr Kemp.

'Thank you for the tea,' he said.

'Our pleasure,' Isla told him with a smile.

'You won't get into trouble for being here, will you?' he checked.

This time, Harry smiled. 'It's our afternoon break. We're allowed to take it outside our own ward if we want to.'

'I'm such a trouble to you,' Mr Kemp said.

'It's fine,' Isla reassured him. 'Has your daughter been able to visit, yet?'

'She's coming straight after work. I do feel bad about it. She's had to get someone to pick up the kids.'

'All the working mums I know are great at juggling,' Harry said. 'I bet you she's picked up her friend's children before now. It won't be a problem. Everyone mucks in to help their friends. How are you feeling?'

'Well enough to go home,' Mr Kemp said. 'If I was home, I wouldn't be a burden to everyone.'

He was able to swallow again, Isla thought, but he definitely wasn't quite ready to go home. And he'd be far more of a worry to his family if he was on his own in his flat. 'I'm sure the team here will sort things out for you,' she said brightly.

And she discovered that Lorraine had been absolutely on the ball about Harry being great with patients, because he somehow managed to find out that Mr Kemp loved dogs and got him chatting about that, distracting him from his worries about being a burden.

'You were brilliant with Mr Kemp,' she said on their way back to the Emergency Department.

Harry gave a dismissive wave of his hand. 'Just chatting. And I noticed you were watching him drinking and assessing him.'

She nodded. 'I'm happier with his swallowing, but I think he'll be in for a couple more days yet. They'll want to assess him for a water infection or a chest infection, in case that contributed to the fall as well as the stroke. And they'll need to get social services in to look at his care plan as well as talk to his family. I'm guessing that he's not so good with accepting help, and from what he said to us earlier it sounded as if his son-in-law doesn't have much patience.'

'Very true.' Harry gave her a sidelong look. 'Though I know a few people caught between caring for their kids and caring for their elderly parents. It can be hard to juggle, and—well, not all parents are easy.'

'And some are brilliant.' Isla's own parents had been wonderful—they'd never believed Andrew's accusations right from the start, and they'd encouraged her to retrain in Glasgow and then move to London and start again.

'Yes, some are brilliant.' Harry was looking curiously at her.

'It takes all sorts to make a world,' she said brightly. Why on earth hadn't she moved him away from the subject of parents? Why had she had to open her mouth? 'And we have patients to see.'

'Yes, we do. Well, Sister McKenna.' He opened the door for her. 'Shall we?'

CHAPTER TWO

'Is ISLA NOT coming tonight?' Harry asked Lorraine at the bowling alley, keeping his tone casual.

'No.'

Lorraine wasn't forthcoming with a reason and Harry knew better than to ask, because it would be the quickest way to fuel gossip. Not that Lorraine was one to promote the hospital rumour mill, but she might let slip to Isla that she thought Harry might be interested in her, and that would make things awkward between them at work. She'd already got the wrong idea about him.

All the same, this was the third team night out in a fortnight that Isla had missed. On the ward, she was an excellent colleague; she was good with patients and relatives, quick to offer sensible suggestions to clinical problems, and she got on well with everyone. The fact that she didn't come to any of the team nights out seemed odd, especially as she was new to the department and going out with the team would be a good chance for her to get to know her colleagues better.

Maybe Isla was a single parent or caring for an elderly relative, and it was difficult for her to arrange someone to sit with her child or whoever in the evenings. But he could hardly ask her about it without it seeming as if he was prying.

And he wasn't; though he was intrigued by her. Then again, if it turned out that she was a single parent, that'd be a deal-breaker for him. He really didn't want to be back in the position of having parental type responsibilities for a child. OK, so lightning rarely struck twice—but he didn't want to take the risk.

'Shame,' he said lightly, and switched the conversation round to who was going to be in which team.

Two days later, it was one of the worst days in the department Harry had had in months. He, Isla and Josie were in Resus together, trying to save a motorcyclist who'd been involved in a head-on crash—but the man's injuries were just too severe. Just when Harry had thought they were getting somewhere and the outcome might be bearable after all, the man had arrested and they just hadn't been able to get him back.

'I'm calling it,' Harry said when his last attempt with the defibrillator produced no change. 'It's been twenty minutes now. He's not responding. Is everyone agreed that we should stop?'

Isla and Josie both looked miserable, but voiced their agreement.

'OK. Time of death, one fifty-three,' he said softly, and pulled the sheet up to cover their patient's face. 'Thank you, team. You all worked really well.'

But it hadn't been enough, and they all knew it.

'OK. Once we've moved him out of Resus and cleaned him up, I'll go and find out if Reception managed to get hold of a next of kin and if anyone's here,' he said.

'If they have, I'll come with you, if you like,' Isla offered.

'Thank you.' He hated breaking bad news. Having

someone there would make it a little easier. And maybe she'd know what to say when he ran out of words.

The motorcyclist, Jonathan Pryor, was only twenty-seven, and his next of kin were his parents. The receptionist had already sent a message to Resus that Jonathan's mum was waiting in the relatives' room.

'I hate this bit so much,' he said softly as he and Isla walked towards the relatives' room.

'We did everything we possibly could,' she reminded him.

'I know.' It didn't make him feel any better. But the sympathy in her blue, blue eyes made his heart feel just a fraction less empty.

Mrs Pryor looked up hopefully as they knocked on the door and walked in. 'Jonathan? He's all right? He's out of Theatre or whatever and I can go and see him?'

Harry could see the very second that she realised the horrible truth—that her son was very far from being all right—and her face crumpled.

'I'm so sorry, Mrs Pryor,' he said softly, taking her hand. 'We did everything we could to save him, but he arrested on the table—he had a heart attack, and we just couldn't get him back.'

Sobs racked her body. 'I always hated him riding that wretched motorcycle. I worried myself sick every time he went out on it because I *knew* that something like this would happen. I can't bear it.' Her voice was a wail of distress. 'And now I'll never see him again. My boy. My little boy.'

Harry knew there was nothing he could do or say to make this better. He just sat down next to Mrs Pryor and kept holding her hand, letting her talk about her son.

Isla went to the vending machine. Harry knew without having to ask that she was making a cup of hot, sweet tea for Mrs Pryor. He could've done with one himself, but he wasn't going to be that selfish. The only thing he could do now for his patient was to comfort his grieving mother.

'Thank you, but I don't want it,' Mrs Pryor said when Isla offered her the paper cup. 'It won't bring my son back.'

'I know,' Isla said gently, 'but you've just had a horrible shock and this will help. Just a little bit, but it will help.'

Mrs Pryor looked as if she didn't believe the nurse, but she took the paper cup and sipped from it.

'Is there anyone we can call for you?' Harry asked.

'My—my husband.' She shook her head blankly. 'Oh, God. How am I going to tell him?'

'I can do that for you,' Harry said gently. 'It might be easier on both of you if I tell him.' Even though he hated breaking bad news.

Mrs Pryor dragged in a breath. 'All right—thank you.'

'And you can come and see Jonathan whenever you feel ready,' Isla said. 'I'll come with you, and you can spend some time alone with him, too. I can call the hospital chaplain to come and see you, if you'd like me to.'

Mrs Pryor shook her head. 'I've never been the religious type. Talking to the chaplain's not going to help. It's not going to bring Jonathan back, is it?''

'I understand,' Isla said, 'but if you change your mind just tell me. Anything we can do to help, we will.'

'He was only twenty-seven. That's way too young to die.' Mrs Pryor shut her eyes very tightly. 'And that's a stupid thing to say. I know children younger than that get killed in accidents every day.'

Yeah, Harry thought. Or, if not killed, left with life-changing injuries, even if they weren't picked up at first. His own little sister was proof of that. He pushed the thought and the guilt away. *Not now.* He needed to concentrate on his patient's bereaved mother.

'It's just...you never think it's going to happen to your own. You hope and you pray it never will.' She sighed. 'I know he was a grown man, but he'll always be my little boy.'

Harry went out to his office to call Mr Pryor to break the bad news, while Isla took over his job of holding Mrs Pryor's hand and letting her talk. On the way to his office, Harry asked one of the team to clean Jonathan's face and prepare him so his parents wouldn't have to see the full damage caused to their son by the crash. And then he went back to the relatives' room to join Isla and Mrs Pryor, staying there until Mr Pryor arrived, twenty minutes later. The Pryors clung together in their grief, clearly having trouble taking it all in. But finally, Mr Pryor asked brokenly, 'Can we see him?'

'Of course,' Harry said.

He and Isla took the Pryors through to the side room where Jonathan's body had been taken so they could see their son in private. They stayed for a few minutes in case the Pryors had any questions; then Isla caught Harry's eye and he gave the tiniest nod of agreement, knowing what she was going to say.

Then Isla said gently to the Pryors, 'We'll be just outside if you need us for anything.'

'Thank you,' Mrs Pryor said, her voice full of tears.

Outside the side room, Isla said to Harry, 'I'll finish up here—you'll be needed back in Resus.'

'Are you sure?' he asked. He was needed back in Resus; but at the same time he didn't think it was fair to leave Isla to deal with grieving parents all on her own.

She nodded. 'I'm sure.'

He reached out and squeezed her hand, trying to ignore the tingle that spread through his skin at her touch—now really wasn't an appropriate time. 'Thank you. You were brilliant. And even though I know you're more than capable of answering any questions the Pryors might have, if you need backup or want me to come and talk to them about anything, you know where to find me.'

'Yes. Those poor people,' she said softly.

'This is the bit of our job I really wish didn't exist,' Harry said.

'I know. But it does, and we have to do our best.' She squeezed his hand back, and loosened it. 'Off you go.'

He wrote up the paperwork, and headed back to Resus. To his relief, the next case was one that he could actually fix. The patient had collapsed, and all the tests showed Harry that it was a case of undiagnosed diabetes. The patient was in diabetic ketoacidosis; Harry was able to start treatment, and then explain to the patient's very relieved wife that her husband would be fine but they'd need to see a specialist about diabetes and learn how to monitor his blood sugar, plus in future they'd have to keep an eye on his diet to suit his medical condition.

Mid-afternoon, Harry actually had a chance to take his break. He hadn't seen Isla back in Resus since leaving her with the Pryors, so he went in search of her; he discovered that she was doing paperwork.

'Hey. I'm pulling rank,' he said.

She looked up. 'What?'

'Right now, I really need some cake. And I think, after the day you've had, so do you. So I prescribe the hospital canteen for both of us.'

'What about Josie?'

Harry smiled. 'She's already had her break and is in cubicles right now, but I'm going to bring her some cake back. You can help me pick what she'd like.'

For a moment, he thought Isla was going to balk at being alone with him; then she smiled. 'Thanks. I'd like that.'

'Let's go,' he said. 'We have fifteen minutes. Which is just about enough time to walk to the canteen, grab cake, and chuck back a mug of coffee.'

She rolled her eyes, but stood up to join him.

'How were the Pryors?' he asked softly when they were sitting at the table in the canteen with a massive slice of carrot cake and a mug of good, strong coffee each.

'Devastated,' she said. 'But they got to spend time with their son and I explained that he didn't suffer in Resus—that the end was quick.'

'Yeah,' he said with a sigh. 'I hate cases like that. The guy still had his whole life before him.' And something else had been bugging him. 'He was only five years younger than I am.' The exact same age as one of his siblings. And he'd had to fight the urge to text every single one of his siblings who was old enough to drive to say that they were never, ever, *ever* to ride a motorbike.

'He was three years younger than me,' Isla said.

It was first time she'd offered any personal information, and it encouraged him enough to say, 'You were brilliant with the Pryors and I really appreciate it. I assume you had a fair bit of experience with bereaved relatives when you worked in your last emergency department?'

'Actually, no.'

He blinked at her. 'How come?'

'I wasn't in an emergency department, as such—I was a nurse practitioner in a GP surgery. I retrained in Glasgow and then came here,' she said.

Something else he hadn't known about her. 'You retrained to give you better opportunities for promotion?' he asked.

'Something like that.'

She was clearly regretting sharing as much as she had, and he could tell that she was giving him back-off signals. OK. He'd take the hint. He smiled at her. 'Sorry. We're a nosey bunch at the London Victoria—and I talk way too much. Blame it on the sugar rush from the cake.'

'And on having a rough day,' she added. 'So you've always worked in the emergency department?'

'Pretty much. I trained in London; I did my foundation years here, with stints in Paediatrics and Gastro-enterology.' Because of what had happened to Tasha, his first choice had been Paediatrics. He'd been so sure that it was his future. 'But, as soon as I started in the Emergency Department, I knew I'd found the right place for me. So I stayed and I worked my way up,' he said.

'Thirty-two's not that old for a special reg,' she said thoughtfully. 'Though I've already seen for myself that you're good at what you do.'

Funny how much her words warmed him. He inclined his head briefly. 'Thank you, kind madam.'

'It wasn't meant to be a compliment. It was a statement of fact,' she said crisply.

He grinned. 'I like you, Isla. You're good for my ego. Keeping it in check.'

She actually smiled back, and his heart missed a beat. When she smiled, she really was beautiful.

'I've known worse egos in my time,' she said.

'And you gave them just as short shrift?'

'Something like that.'

He looked at her. 'Can I ask you something?'

'That depends,' she said.

'Why haven't you come to any of the departmental nights out?'

'Because they're not really my thing,' she said.

'So you don't like ten-pin bowling, pub quizzes or pizza.' He paused. 'What kind of things do you like, Isla?'

'Why?'

'Because you've only been at the London Victoria for a couple of weeks, you've told me that you retrained to come here, and I'm assuming that you don't really know anyone around here. It must be a bit lonely.'

Yes, she was lonely. She still missed her family and her friends in the Western Isles hugely. And, even though she was trying to put her past behind her, part of her worried about socialising with her new colleagues. It would be too easy to let something slip. And then their reaction to her might change. Some would pity her; others would think there was no smoke without fire. And neither reaction was one she wanted to face.

She didn't think Harry was asking her out—he'd already made it clear he thought his reputation wasn't deserved—but it wouldn't hurt to make things clear. 'You're right—I don't know many people in London,' she said softly. 'And I could use a friend. *Just* a friend,' she added. 'Because I'm concentrating on my career right now.'

'That works for me,' Harry said. 'So can we be friends?'

'I'd like that,' she said. Even if his smile did make

her weak at the knees. Friendship was all she was prepared to offer.

'Friends,' he said, and reached over to shake her
hand.

And Isla really had to ignore the tingle that went
through her at the touch of his skin. Nothing was going
to happen between them. They were colleagues—about
to be friends—and that was all.

CHAPTER THREE

WHEN ISLA WENT into the staffroom that morning for a mug of tea, Harry was the only one there. He was staring into his mug of coffee as if he was trying to lose himself in it. She knew that feeling well—she'd been there herself only a few months ago, when her life had turned into a living nightmare—and her heart went out to him.

'Tough shift so far?' she asked, gently placing her hand on his arm for a moment.

'No—yes,' he admitted. Then he grimaced. 'Never mind. Forget I said anything.'

It wasn't like Harry Gardiner to be brusque. The doctor she'd got to know over the last month was full of smiles, always seeing the good in the world.

He also hadn't quite lived up to his heartbreaker reputation, because since Isla had known Harry he hadn't actually dated anyone. He'd even turned down a couple of offers, which was hardly the act of the Lothario that the hospital rumour mill made him out to be. Maybe he'd told her the truth when he'd said he wasn't a heartbreaker.

Right now, something had clearly upset him. Though she understood about keeping things to yourself. Since the day that Andrew Gillespie had made that awful accusation and her fiancé had actually believed him, she'd done the same. Keeping your feelings to yourself was the safest way. 'OK,' she said. 'But if you want to talk, you know where I am.'

'Thanks.' But Harry still seemed sunk in the depths of gloom. He was still serious when he was working in minors with her, not even summoning up his store of terrible jokes to distract a little boy whose knee he had to suture after Isla had cleaned up the bad cut.

By mid-afternoon, she was really worried about him. To the point of being bossy. 'Right. I'm pulling rank,' she said. 'You need cake, so I'm dragging you off to the canteen.'

'Yes, Sister McKenna,' he said. But his eyes were dull rather than gleaming with amusement. And that worried her even more.

Once they were sitting in the canteen—where she'd insisted on buying lemon cake for him—she asked, 'So are you going to tell me what's wrong?'

He said nothing; but she waited, knowing that if you gave someone enough space and time they'd start talking.

Except he didn't.

'Harry, either you've suddenly become a monk and taken a vow of silence as well as chastity, or something's wrong.'

He looked at her. 'How do you know I'm chaste?'

She met his gaze. 'According to the hospital rumour mill, you haven't dated in a month and everyone thinks you must be ill.'

'They ought to mind their own business.' He scowled. 'I'm not ill. I just don't want to date.'

Fair enough. She could understand that; it was how she felt, too.

'And the silence?' she asked.

He sighed. 'I don't want to talk about it here.'

So there *was* something wrong. And she liked Harry. She hated to think of him being miserable. And maybe talking to her would help him. 'After work, then? Somewhere else, somewhere that people from round here aren't likely to be hanging round to overhear what you're saying?'

There was a gleam of interest in his eyes. 'Are you asking me on a date, Sister McKenna?'

'That I'm most definitely not,' she said crisply. But then she softened. 'We're friends, Harry, and friends support each other. You look upset about something and you've been a bit serious at work lately, so something's obviously wrong. If you want to go for a drink with me after work or something and talk, then the offer's there.'

'I could use a friend,' he said. 'But you never socialise outside work, Isla. And isn't someone waiting at home for you?'

'I'm single, as well you know.'

He wrinkled his nose. 'I didn't mean that.'

'I don't follow.'

'Maybe you have a child,' he explained, 'or a relative you're caring for.'

'Is that what people are saying about me? That because I don't go on team nights out, I must be a single parent with babysitting problems?'

He winced. 'People get curious. But I haven't been gossiping about you.'

Given what he'd said about the hospital rumour mill, she believed him. 'Just for the record, I don't have a child, and I don't look after anyone. There's just me. And that's fine.'

'Not even a goldfish or a cat?'

'No.' She would've loved a dog, but it wouldn't be fair to leave a dog alone all day. Hospital shifts and pets didn't mix that well, unless you were in a family where you could share the care. Not to mention the clause in the lease of her flat saying that she couldn't have pets. 'You know what the old song says about not being able to take a goldfish for a walk.'

'I guess.' He paused. 'Thank you, Isla. I'll think of somewhere and text you. Shall we meet there?'

She knew exactly what he wasn't saying. Because, if they travelled to the pub or café together, someone was likely to see them and start speculating about whether they were seeing each other. Harry obviously didn't want to be the centre of gossip, and neither did she. 'Deal,' she said.

After his shift finished, Harry texted Isla the address of the wine bar and directions on how to find it.

Funny, she was the last person he'd expected to take him under her wing. She didn't date, whereas he had the not-quite-deserved reputation of dating hundreds of women and breaking their hearts. He'd been at the London Victoria for years and she'd been working there for just under a month. And yet she'd been the only one in the department who'd picked up his dark mood; and she'd been the only one who'd offered him a listening ear.

Harry didn't tend to talk about his family.

But maybe talking to someone who didn't know him that well—and most certainly didn't know any of the other people involved—might help. A fresh pair of eyes to help him see the right course of action. Because this wedding was really getting under his skin and Harry didn't have a clue why it was upsetting him so much.

It wasn't as if his father hadn't got remarried before. So why, why, *why* had it got to him so much this time?

Harry was already halfway through his glass of Merlot when Isla walked into the wine bar, looked round and came over to his table. 'Hi.'

'Hi. You look lovely. I've never seen you wearing normal clothes instead of your nurse's uniform.' The words were out before he could stop them and he grimaced. 'Sorry. I wasn't hitting on you.'

Much.

Because he had to admit that he was attracted to Isla McKenna. That gorgeous creamy skin, her dark red hair, the curve of her mouth that made her look like the proverbial princess just waiting to be woken from her sleep by love's first kiss...

He shook himself mentally.

Not now.

If he told Isla what was going through his head right now, she'd walk straight out of the bar. And it would take God knew how long to get their easy working relationship back in place. He didn't want that to happen.

'You look odd without a white coat, too,' she said, to his relief; clearly she hadn't picked up on his attraction to her and was just responding to his words at face value.

'Let me get you a drink. What would you like?' he asked.

'I'll join you in whatever you're having.' She gestured to his glass.

'Australian Merlot. OK. Back in a tick.'

Ordering a drink gave him enough time to compose himself. He bought her a glass of wine and walked back to their table, where she looked as if she was checking messages on her phone. 'Everything OK?' he asked.

'Yes.' She smiled at him. 'I'm just texting my mum, my sister and my brother to tell them I've had a good day.'

'You miss your family?' he asked.

She nodded. 'Sometimes the islands feel as far away as Australia.'

'The islands?' he asked, not sure what she meant.

'The Western Isles,' she said.

So she was from the Outer Hebrides? You couldn't get much more different from London, he thought: mountains, pretty little villages and the sea, compared to the capital's urban sprawl and the constant noise of traffic.

'It isn't that bad really,' she said. 'I can fly from here to Glasgow and then get a flight to Lewis, or get the train from Glasgow to Oban and catch the ferry home.'

But the wistfulness in her tone told him how much she missed her family. Something he couldn't quite get his head round, because he often felt so disconnected from his own. And how ironic that was, considering the size of his family. Eight siblings, with another one on the way. OK, so he didn't have much in common with his two youngest half-brothers; but he wasn't that close to the ones nearest his own age, either. And he always seemed to clash with his middle sister. Guilt made him overprotective, and she ended up rowing with him.

'But we're not talking about me,' she said before he could ask anything else. 'What's wrong?'

'You're very direct,' he said, playing for time.

'I find direct is the best way.'

He sighed. 'Considering how much you clearly miss your family, if I tell you what's bugging me you're going to think I'm the most selfish person in the universe.'

She smiled. 'Apart from the fact that there are usually two sides to every story, I very much doubt you're the most selfish person I've ever met.'

There was a tiny flicker in her expression, as if she was remembering something truly painful. And that made Harry feel bad about bringing those memories back to her.

'I'm sorry,' he said. 'Look, never mind. Let's just have a drink and talk about—oh, I dunno, the weather.' Something very English, and very safe.

She laughed. 'Nice try. Iain—my brother—squirms just like you do if we talk about anything remotely personal.'

'I guess it's a guy thing,' he said, trying to make light of it and wishing he hadn't started this.

'But sometimes,' she said gently, 'it's better out than in. A problem shared is a problem halved. And—' she wrinkled her nose. 'No, I can't think of any more clichés right now. Over to you.'

Despite his dark mood, Harry found himself smiling. He liked this woman. Really, really liked her. Which was another reason why he had to suppress his attraction to her. He wanted to keep her in his life instead of having to put up barriers, the way he normally did. 'I can't, either.' He blew out a breath. 'I hate talking about emotional stuff. And it's easier to talk when you're stuffed with carbs. They do fantastic pies here, and the butteriest, loveliest mashed potato in the world. Can we talk over dinner?'

'Pie and mash.' She groaned. 'Don't tell me you're planning to make me eat jellied eels or mushy peas as well.'

'Traditional London fare?' He laughed. 'No. For vegetables here I'd recommend the spinach. It's gloriously garlicky.'

'Provided we go halves,' she said, 'then yes. Let's have dinner. As friends, not as a date.'

Why was she so adamant about not dating? He guessed that maybe someone had hurt her. But he also had the strongest feeling that if he tried to focus on her or asked about her past, she'd shut the conversation down. 'Deal.'

Ordering food gave him a little more wriggle room.

But, once their food had been served and she'd agreed with him that the pie was to die for, he was back on the spot.

Eventually, he gave in and told her. Because hadn't that been the point of meeting her this evening, anyway? 'My dad's getting remarried,' he said.

'Uh-huh. And it's a problem why exactly?'

'Speaking like that makes you sound like Yoda.'

She gave him a narrow-eyed look. 'Don't try to change the subject.'

'You're a bossy lot, north of the border,' he muttered.

'And you Sassenachs have no staying power,' she said with a grin. 'Seriously, Harry, what's wrong? Don't you like his new wife-to-be?'

Harry shrugged. 'I don't really know her that well.'

'So what is it?'

'This is going to stay with you?' he checked.

She rolled her eyes. 'Of course it is.'

'Sorry. I didn't mean to accuse you of being a gossip. I know you're not. I don't...' He blew out a breath. 'Well, I don't tend to talk about my personal life.'

'And I appreciate that you're talking to me about it now,' she said softly.

He sighed. 'Dad wants me to be his best man.'

'And you don't want to do it?'

'No. It'd be for the third time,' Harry said. 'And I

really don't see the point of making such a big song and dance about the wedding, considering that in five years' time we'll be going through the exactly same thing all over again.'

She said nothing, just waited for him to finish.

He sighed again. 'My father—I don't know. Maybe it's a triumph of hope over experience. But this will be his seventh marriage, and this time his fiancée is younger than I am.'

His father's seventh marriage? Seeing that many rela- tionships go wrong would make anyone wary of settling down, Isla thought. 'Maybe,' she said softly, 'your father hasn't found the right woman for him yet.'

'So this will be seventh time lucky? That'd go down really well in my best man's speech. Not.' He blew out a breath. 'Sorry. I didn't mean to be rude to you or take it out on you.' He grimaced. 'My father's charming—that is, he can be when it suits him. He can be great com- pany. But he has a seriously low boredom threshold. And I can't understand why none of his wives has ever been able to see the pattern before she actually mar- ried him. Well, obviously not my mum, because she was the first. But every single one after that. Get mar- ried, have a baby, get bored, have an affair, move on. Nothing lasts for Dad for more than five years—well, his last one was almost seven years, but I think Julie was the one to end it instead of Dad. Or maybe he's slowing down a bit now he's in his mid-fifties.' Harry sighed. 'I really liked Fliss, his third wife. Considering she had to deal with me as a teenager...' He shrugged. 'She was really patient.'

'Did you live with your dad when you were grow- ing up?' Isla asked.

Harry shook his head. 'I stayed with him for the occasional weekends, plus a week or so in the long school holidays. I lived with my mum and my three half-sisters. My mum also has a marriage habit, though at least she's kept husband number four.' He paused. 'Maybe that's it. Dad only has sons—six of us. Maybe he's hoping that his new wife is carrying his daughter.'

Isla added it up swiftly. Harry was one of nine children, soon about to be ten? And he'd said something about his mum being his father's first wife. 'I take it you're the oldest?'

He nodded. 'Don't get me wrong. I like my brothers and sisters well enough, but there's a whole generation between me and the littlest ones, so we have absolutely nothing in common. I feel more like an uncle than a brother.' He gave her a thin smile. 'And let's just say the best contraception ever is to get a teenager babysitting for their younger siblings. I definitely don't want kids of my own. Ever.'

'Remind me to tell my brother Iain how lucky he is that he only had me and Mags tagging around after him,' she said.

'You're the baby of the family?' he asked.

'Yes, and I'm thoroughly spoiled.'

He scoffed. 'You're far too sensible to be spoiled.'

'Thank you. I think.' She paused. 'Right. So you don't want to be the best man and you don't want to go to the wedding. I'm assuming you're trying not to hurt anyone's feelings, so you could always say you can't make the wedding due to pressure of work. That we're really short-staffed and you just can't get the time off.'

'I've already tried that one,' Harry said. 'Dad says my annual leave is part of my contract—he's a lawyer, by the way, so I can't flannel him—and he says they can always find a locum or call in an agency worker to fill in for me. Plus he gave me enough notice that I should've been able to swap off-duty with someone months ago to make sure I could be there.'

'How about a last-minute illness? Say we had noro-virus on the ward and you came down with it?' she suggested.

'Norovirus in the middle of summer?' He wrinkled his nose. 'Nope. That one's not going to fly.'

'You have other medics in your family, then?' she asked.

'One of my sisters is a trainee audiologist. But every-one knows that norovirus tends to be at its worst in the winter. All the newspapers make a big song and dance about emergency departments being on black alert at the peak of the winter vomiting virus season.' He sighed. 'I've thought about practically nothing else for weeks, and there just isn't a nice way to let everyone down.'

'So the kind approach isn't going to work. Have you tried telling any of your brothers that you don't want to go?'

He nodded. 'Jack—he's the next one down from me.'

'What did he say?'

'He thinks I should be there to support the old man. So does Fin—he's the next one down from Jack.'

'And how old are they?'

'Dad's kids are all spaced five years apart. So Jack and Fin are twenty-seven and twenty-two, respectively,' he explained. 'The odd one out will be the new baby, who'll be seven years younger than Evan—he's the youngest.'

'OK. So you have to go to the wedding. But what about this best man business? Isn't there anyone else who could do it? Does your dad have a best friend, a brother—or, hey, he could always be different and have a woman as his best man if he has a sister,' she suggested.

To her relief, that actually made Harry crack a smile. 'Best woman? I can't see Auntie Val agreeing to that. She says Dad's the male equivalent of a serial Bridezilla.' He took another sip of Merlot. 'Uncle Jeff—Dad's brother—has done the duty twice, and so has Marty, his best friend.'

'So if the three of you have all done it twice, what about your next brother down? Or the youngest one? Could it be their turn?'

'I could suggest it.' He paused. 'But even if I can be just a normal wedding guest instead of the best man, it still means running the gauntlet of everyone asking me how come I'm not married yet, and saying how I ought to get a move on and settle down because I'm ten years older now than Dad was when he got married the first time, and that means I'm totally on the shelf.'

'Apart from the fact that men are never described as being on the shelf, you would still've been a student medic at twenty-two,' Isla pointed out. 'And, with the crazy hours that junior doctors work, you wouldn't have had the time to get married or even spend that much time with your new wife back then.'

'But I'm not a student or a junior doctor now. In their view, I have no excuses not to settle down.'

'Maybe you could take a date to the wedding?' she suggested.

That would be Harry's worst nightmare. Taking a date to a family wedding implied that you were serious about taking the relationship further; then, when it was clear you didn't want to do that, someone would get hurt. But

Isla clearly meant well. 'I guess it would be a start—but it wouldn't stop the questions for long. They'd want to know how we met, how long we'd been dating, how serious it was, when we were planning to get engaged...' He rolled his eyes. 'They never stop.'

'So what would stop the questions?' she asked. 'What if you told them you're gay?'

'Nope. They'd still want to meet my partner. It's not the gender of my partner that's the issue—it's the non-existence.' He sighed. 'What would stop them? A hurricane, if it started raining fishes and frogs... No, that still wouldn't stop the questions for more than five minutes.' He blew out a breath. 'Or maybe I could invent a fiancée. And she isn't coming to the wedding with me because...' He wrinkled his nose. 'Why wouldn't she be with me?'

'She's working?' Isla suggested.

He shook his head. 'They'd never believe it. Same as the norovirus idea. The only way they'd believe I was engaged was if I turned up with my fiancée in tow.'

'And I'm assuming that you don't have anyone in your life who's even close to being a fiancée?'

No.

But, now he thought of it, that wasn't such a bad idea. If there was someone he could convince to go with him. Someone safe. Someone who wouldn't get the wrong idea. Someone *sensible*.

'That's a good point,' he said. 'She wouldn't have to be a real fiancée.' He smiled as he warmed to his theme. 'Just someone who'd go to the wedding with me and stop all the endless questions. Enough to keep everyone happy and nobody gets hurt.'

'Lying is never a good idea,' Isla said, grimacing.

'Hey—you suggested it.'

'Forget it. I was being flippant. It's a stupid idea.'

'Actually, I think it's a great one. And it won't be a lie. Just a teensy, tiny fib to shut everyone up. Not even a fib, really: it'd be more of an exaggeration,' Harry said. 'And if anyone asks me afterwards about setting a date, I can say that my fiancée and I realised we were making a mistake, had a long talk about it and agreed to call it all off.' He smiled. 'And my fake fiancée will know all this up front, so it'll be just fine. She won't be expecting me to marry her.'

'Do you have someone in mind?'

Someone safe. Who wouldn't get the wrong idea. Who didn't have a partner to make things complicated. And the person who ticked all those boxes just so happened to be sitting right opposite him.

Would she do it?

There was only one way to find out.

He looked straight at her. 'What are you doing, the weekend after next?'

CHAPTER FOUR

'LET ME GET this straight.' Isla's eyes were the most piercing shade of blue Harry had ever seen. 'You want me to go to this wedding with you—as your fake fiancée?'

It was the perfect solution to his problem. And she'd sort of suggested it in the first place. 'Yes.'

'No.'

'Why not? Because you're on duty and it'd be awkward to swap shifts with someone without explaining why and setting the hospital rumour mill going?'

'No, actually, I'm off duty that weekend.'

'Then what's the problem?' He frowned. 'You're exactly the right person to ask.'

'How?' she scoffed.

'Because if I ask anyone else to come to the wedding and meet my family, they'll have expectations,' he explained. 'They'll think that meeting my family means that I want a relationship with them. But you—you're different. You don't date. So you'll understand that I'm only asking you to come with me to the wedding to take the heat off me and stop my family nagging me to death about settling down, not because I'm secretly in love with you and want to spend the rest of my life with you.'

'That's crazy, Harry.' She shook her head. 'As I said, I was being flippant when I suggested it. You can't possibly go to a wedding and pretend you're with someone when you're not.'

'Why not?'

'Because you'll be lying to your family.'

'No, I'll just be distracting them a little,' he corrected. 'Isla, I'm asking you because I'm desperate.'

'Did you hear what you just said?' Her voice was so soft; and yet at the same time there was an edge to it.

And he could see why. He could've phrased it a lot better. He winced. 'I don't mean desperate as in…' He shook his head to clear it. 'I'm digging myself an even deeper hole, here. What I mean, Isla, is that I need a friend to support me through a day I'm really not looking forward to. A friend I can trust not to misinterpret my intentions.'

'We barely know each other,' she pointed out. 'For all you know, I could be a psychopath.'

'Ah, now that I *am* clear about,' he said. 'I've spent a month working with you. I've seen you with patients. You're kind—you're tough when you need to be and you don't shy away from difficult situations, but overall you're kind and you're sensible and you're…' He floundered for the right word. 'Well, you're nice.'

'Nice.' She sounded as if he'd just insulted her.

'I like you. Enormously. Which is why I'm asking you—because I can trust you,' he said. 'You're safe.'

'We'd still be lying to your family.'

'A white lie. Something to keep them all happy, so their attention stays on the wedding instead of on me.'

'Nobody's ever going to believe I'm your fiancée.'

'Of course they are. If we keep the story to as near the truth as possible, it'll be convincing. We work together—

and as far as they're concerned I fell in love with you as soon as I met you. You're a…what's the Scottish equivalent of an English rose?'

'I have no idea. A thistle?'

Hmm. She definitely sounded prickly right now.

'They won't buy it.' She rolled her eyes. 'I bet you normally date glamorous women. And I'm hardly the type who'd be scouted for a modelling agency.'

'You're a bit too short to be a model,' he agreed. 'But if you were six inches taller, you could be.'

She scoffed. 'It's not just my height. I'm not thin enough, either.'

'You're not fat by any stretch of the imagination. You have curves. Which isn't a bad thing.' Apart from the fact that now he was wondering what it would be like to touch said curves. How soft her skin would be under his fingertips. And she was strictly off limits, so he couldn't allow himself to think about that. 'Any of my family would take one look at you and think, yes, she's exactly the type Harry would fall for. Beautiful hair, beautiful skin, beautiful eyes, a kissable mouth.'

And now he'd said way too much. She was looking thoroughly insulted.

'It's not just about looks,' he said, guessing that was the problem—he knew his sisters hated being judged on what they looked like rather than who they were. 'As soon as they talked to you they'd think, yes, she's bright and sparky and not afraid to speak her mind, so she's perfect for Harry. He's not going to get bored with her. You've got the whole package, so it's totally believable that I'd fall for you.'

She lifted her chin. 'I'm not looking for a relationship.'

'I know, and neither am I. What I'm looking for right

now is a friend who'll help me out of a hole and humour my family for a weekend.'

'So it's suddenly gone from a day to a weekend?' she asked, sounding horrified.

'It's in Cornwall, which means it's a five-hour drive from here—and that's provided we don't get any hold-ups on the motorway. The wedding's on Saturday after-noon. We can drive up first thing in the morning, stay overnight in the hotel, and then drive back on Sunday at our leisure. Which is far better than spending at least ten hours stuck in a car, as well as going to a wedding.' He blew out a breath. 'And I know it's a bit of a cheek, asking you for two days of your precious off-duty. I wouldn't ask unless I was…'

'Desperate?' Her voice was very crisp and her ac-cent was pronounced.

'Unless I could think of any other way out of it,' he corrected. 'Or if I could think of someone else who was single but who wouldn't misunderstand my mo-tivation for asking her to be my plus-one for the wed-ding.' He sighed. 'Look, forget I asked. I don't want to ruin our working relationship. I like you and respect you too much for that, and I haven't meant to insult you. This whole thing about the wedding has temporar-ily scrambled my brains. You're right. It's crazy. Let's pretend we never had this conversation.' He gave her a grim smile. 'I'll just man up, go to the wedding, and do what I always do about the nagging—ignore it.' He looked away. 'My next brother down is married, and the brother below him is engaged. Maybe that'll be enough to distract them all.' Though, more likely, it would give everyone more ammunition. If Jack and Fin could find someone and settle down, why couldn't he?

Though he knew the answer to that. He didn't believe

in love. Not with the number of divorces he'd seen. The first one had been his parents, when he was five; then two more for his mum, and five more for his dad. That was all the proof Harry needed that marriage and settling down didn't work out for his family.

Isla looked at Harry. He'd said he didn't want to go to his father's wedding. Was it really that unreasonable of him to want someone to go with him—someone who wouldn't give him a hard time about his marital status? And to ask someone who he knew wouldn't misinterpret the request as his way of suggesting a serious relationship?

Then again, he was asking her to lie. Something she really didn't agree with. But she hadn't told Harry why she had such a thing about lying. About what had happened on the island: that her fiancé's stepfather ruined her life. He'd made a totally untrue complaint about her to her boss, which of course had been investigated. Any complaint against a member of the practice—even if it wasn't true—had to be considered seriously.

Even though she'd been completely exonerated of any wrong-doing, half the island had still believed that it must've been a cover-up. Andrew Gillespie was charming, popular, and employed a lot of people locally. What possible reason would he have had to lie?

She knew the answer to that. And if she'd told the full truth it would've blown his life apart—and there would've been collateral damage, too. People she really cared about would've been badly hurt. The gossip would have spread like wildfire, and done just as much damage.

But what had really hurt her was that Stewart had believed Andrew's lie. The one man she'd expected to be on her side... And he'd let her down. He hadn't backed her. At all.

She took a deep breath. 'Let me think about it.'

Harry's face brightened. 'You'll do it?'

'I said I'll *think* about it,' she corrected. And maybe she could find a compromise. Something that meant Harry could have her company at the wedding but without lying about it.

'Thank you. I appreciate it. And, if you do decide to go with me, I'd be more than happy to buy you a dress or whatever.'

'That's nice of you,' she said, 'but it really won't be necessary. Apart from the fact that I can afford to buy my own clothes, thank you very much, my wardrobe consists of a wee bit more than just my uniform and jeans.'

He laughed. 'That's what I like about you. You always tell it straight.'

'There's no point in doing otherwise.'

He smiled. 'Agreed.'

'So now can we change the subject?'

Isla thought about it late into the evening when she got home to her flat. She liked Harry's company; and weddings usually meant good food, good company and dancing, all of which she enjoyed. She was seriously tempted to go with him.

And that was exactly the reason why she should say no.

It would be all too easy to get involved with Harry, and she didn't want a relationship. Neither did he. And she really felt for him. Why did his family put so much pressure on him to settle down? Why couldn't they see him for who he was—a gifted doctor who was fantastic with patients?

Her own family had always supported her and valued her. They'd stuck up for her and done their best to squash the rumours that Andrew Gillespie had started. And, when it was clear that the whispers weren't going to go away and she was going to have to leave, they'd backed her. So Isla found it hard to understand why Harry's family didn't support him.

Or was it that he didn't let them close enough to support him? Had his determination to avoid his parents' mistakes and string of broken marriages made him push them away?

She decided to sleep on it.

And she was still mulling it over on her way to work, the next morning.

Not that she had a chance to discuss it with Harry during the day. He was rostered on cubicles while she was busy in Resus, spending the morning helping to stabilise a teenage girl who'd been knocked over crossing the road while she was so busy texting her boyfriend that she didn't see the car coming. The girl had a broken pelvis, her left leg and arm were broken in several places, she had internal bleeding, and the team had to fight hard to control it before she was able to go up to the operating theatre and have the bones fixed by the orthopaedics team. The afternoon was equally busy, with two heart attacks and a suspected stroke, though Isla was really glad that in all three cases there was a positive outcome and the patients were all admitted to the wards to recover.

By the time her shift was over, Harry had already left the hospital, though he'd also left a text message on her phone asking her to call him or text him when she'd come to a decision.

If she said no, she'd feel guilty about tossing him to the wolves.

If she said yes, she'd be lying. Something she didn't want to do. Someone else's lies had wrecked her engagement, and then she'd ended up leaving the job she loved and moving hundreds of miles away to make a new start.

But Harry was trying to keep his family happy, not trying to get his own way and prove how much power he had. Which was a very different category of lying from Andrew Gillespie's. It still wasn't good, but it wasn't meant maliciously. It meant Harry could let his family down gently.

Or maybe just having someone go with him to the wedding would be enough. They didn't necessarily have to pretend to be a couple, did they?

She picked up her phone and called him.

The line rang once, twice, three times—and then the voicemail message kicked in. Not even a personalised one, she noticed: Harry had left it as the standard bland recorded message saying that his number was unavailable right now, so please leave a message or send a text.

'It's Isla,' she said. 'Call me when you're free.'

It was another hour and a half before he returned the call.

'Hi. Sorry I didn't pick up—I was playing squash,' he said. 'How was Resus today?'

She liked the fact that he'd thought enough to ask her about her day rather than going straight in to asking whether she'd made a decision. 'Full-on,' she said, 'but all my patients survived, so it was a good day. How was cubicles?'

'Good, thanks.' He paused. 'I take it you were calling about my message?'

'Yes.' She took a deep breath. 'I've thought about it. A lot. I don't like lying, Harry. I can't go to the wedding with you as your fiancée.'

'Uh-huh.' His tone was perfectly composed and so bland that she didn't have a clue what he was thinking. 'I understand. And thank you for at least considering it. I appreciate that.'

Then she realised he thought she was turning him down. 'No, I'll go with you, Harry,' she said.

'So you've just changed your mind?' He sounded confused.

'No. I mean I'll go to the wedding with you, but as your friend—not as your fiancée.' She paused. 'That'll be enough to keep the heat off you, without us having to lie.'

'You'll actually go with me? Really?' He sounded faintly shocked, and then thrilled. 'Isla—thank you. I really appreciate it. And if there's ever a favour you want from me in return, just name it and it's yours.'

'It's fine,' she said.

'And I meant what I said about buying you an outfit for the wedding.'

'Really, there's no need. Though I could do with knowing the dress code.'

'The usual wedding stuff,' he said. 'It's a civil do. Just wear something pretty. Oh, and comfortable shoes.'

'Comfortable shoes don't normally go with pretty dresses,' she pointed out.

'They need to, in this case. The reception involves a barn dance.'

'A barn dance?'

'Don't worry if you've never done that kind of thing

before—they have a guy who calls out the steps. Actually, it's a good idea because it makes everyone mix, and you get to dance with absolutely everyone in the room.'

Did he really think she'd never been to that sort of thing before? 'I'm Scottish,' she reminded him with a smile. 'In the village where I lived back on the island, we used to have a ceilidh every third Friday of the month.'

'That,' he said, 'sounds like enormous fun.'

'It was.' And she'd missed it. But the last couple she'd gone to had been miserable, with people staring at her and whispering. In the end she'd made excuses not to go. 'Is there anything else I need to know? What about a wedding present?'

'I've already got that sorted,' he said. 'So I guess it's just timing. I thought we could wear something comfortable for the journey—just in case we get stuck in traffic, with it being a summer Saturday—and get changed at the hotel.'

And that was another issue. If he'd been expecting to take her to the wedding as his fake fiancée, did that mean he expected her to share a room with him? 'Won't all the rooms already be booked? So I might have to stay at a different hotel.'

'Dad block-booked the hotel. You'll have your own room,' he said.

'Thank you.' So at least there wouldn't be any misunderstandings there. That was a relief. She'd had enough misunderstandings to last her a lifetime.

'All I need now is your address, so I know where to pick you up,' he said.

She gave him the address to her flat.

'Excellent. And thank you for coming with me, Isla. I really appreciate it,' he said.

The next evening, just as Isla got home from work, her neighbour's door opened.

'There was a delivery for you while you were at work,' she said, handing Isla the most gorgeous bouquet. 'Is it your birthday or a special occasion?'

Isla smiled and shook her head. 'They're probably from my family in Scotland.'

'Because you've been in London for over a month now and they're missing you? I know how they feel.' The neighbour smiled ruefully. 'I really miss my daughter, now she's moved to Oxford. I send her a parcel every week so she knows I'm thinking of her. She works so hard and it's nice to be able to spoil her, even if it is at a distance.'

'And I bet she appreciates it just as much as I appreciate these,' Isla said. 'Thanks for taking them in for me.'

'Any time, love.' The neighbour smiled at her and went back to her own flat.

Once Isla had unlocked the door and put the flowers on the table, she looked at the card. The flowers weren't from her family; they were from Harry. His message was short, to the point, and written in handwriting she didn't recognise, so clearly he'd ordered them online or by phone.

I just wanted to say thank you for helping me. H x.

How lovely. She couldn't even remember the last time she'd had flowers delivered to her. And these were utterly beautiful—roses, gerberas, irises and gypsophila.

She called him. 'Thank you for the flowers, Harry.

They're lovely. You didn't need to do that, but they're gorgeous.'

'My pleasure. I hope it was OK to send them to your flat? I didn't want to give them to you at work in case it started any gossip.'

Which was really thoughtful of him. 'It's fine. My neighbour took them in for me.'

'And thank you about the best man stuff, too,' he said. 'I spoke to Dad at lunchtime and he loves the idea of Evan being his best man. Julie—Evan's mum—called me to say she thinks it's a good idea, too. It makes him feel important and that his dad isn't going to forget him, even though he no longer lives with him and Julie.'

'That's good. I'm glad.' She paused. 'That sounds like personal experience.'

'I guess it is,' he said. 'I was a bit younger than Evan when my parents split up, but I can still remember worrying that Dad would forget me if he didn't live with me, because he'd have a new family to look after.' He gave a wry chuckle. 'To Dad's credit, though, he tried to keep seeing us. Even when he was going through the screaming row stage of his marriages, Saturday mornings were reserved for his boys.'

'All of you? Or did you take turns?' she asked.

'All of us, until we'd pretty much flown the nest and were off at uni somewhere.' He gave a small huff of laughter. 'Though when I look back I was always in charge of getting us all to play football at the park, because Dad would be busy flirting with someone on the sidelines. That's how he is. Be warned, he'll probably flirt with you at the wedding.'

A cold shiver ran down Isla's spine. Andrew had flirted with her, too.

Almost as if Harry was reading her thoughts—which

was ridiculous, because of course he couldn't do that—
he added, 'Just take it with a pinch of salt. He doesn't
mean any harm by it. He just likes flirting.'

'Right.'

'Anyway. Thanks again,' Harry said. 'See you tomorrow.'

'See you tomorrow,' she said.

CHAPTER FIVE

THE NEXT WEEK and a bit flew by. At the crack of dawn on Saturday morning, Isla packed a small overnight case; she was glad she'd kept her packing to a minimum when Harry arrived, because she discovered that there wasn't much room for luggage in his bright red sports car.

'Do they know about this car on the ward?' she asked.

'Oh, yes.' He grinned. 'And they're torn between teasing me about it and pure envy because it's such a beautiful car.' He paused. 'Do you drive?'

'Yes, though I don't have a car in London because there's no point, not with the Tube being so good.'

His grin broadened. 'I'd never drive this to work because it's much more sensible to use the Tube, but on days off... Sometimes it's nice just to go wherever the mood takes you without having to worry about changing Tube lines or how far away the train station is from wherever you want to go.' He indicated the car. 'Do you want to drive?'

'Me?' She was faintly shocked. Weren't men usually possessive about their cars? And Stewart had always hated being driven by anyone else, so she'd always been the passenger when she'd been in the car with him.

'If you'd rather not drive through London, I'll do the first bit; but, if you'd like to get behind the wheel at any point, all you have to do is tell me,' Harry said. 'She's a dream to drive.'

'You're a walking cliché, Harry Gardiner,' she said, laughing. 'The hospital heartbreaker with his little red sports car.'

He just laughed back. 'Wait until you've driven her and then tell me I'm a cliché. Come on, let's go.'

The car was surprisingly comfortable. And Isla was highly amused to discover that the stereo system in the car was voice controlled. 'Boys and their toys,' she teased.

'It's so much better than faffing around trying to find what you want to listen to, or sitting through songs you're not in the mood for,' he said. 'By the way, if you'd rather connect your phone to the stereo and play something you prefer, that's fine by me.'

'Actually, I quite like this sort of stuff,' she admitted.

'Classic rock you can sing along to.' He gave her a sidelong glance. 'Now, Sister McKenna, that begs a question—can you sing?'

'You'd never get me doing karaoke,' she prevaricated.

'I won't tell anyone at work if you sing out of key,' he promised with a grin. 'Let's do it.'

'Seriously?'

'It'll take my mind off the wedding,' he said.

'So you're still dreading it?'

'A bit,' he admitted. 'Though I guess it'll be nice to see all my brothers. We don't get together that often nowadays.' He shrugged. 'Obviously the girls won't be there, because they're not Dad's, so you'll be saved from Maisie interrogating you.'

'Maisie?'

'My oldest sister,' he explained. 'Then there's Tasha and Bibi.' He gave her a wry smile. 'There are rather a lot of us, altogether.'

'It's nice that you all get on.'

'The siblings do, though the ex-wives are all a bit wary with each other,' he said. 'Obviously there have been some seriously sticky patches around all the divorces, but things settled down again after a while. The only one of his ex-wives coming to the wedding is Julie, and that's only because Evan's too little to come on his own.'

'Uh-huh,' she said. 'OK. Put on something we can sing to.'

'A girl after my own heart,' he said with a smile, and did exactly that.

Isla thoroughly enjoyed the journey; and, after they'd stopped for a rest break at a motorway service station, she actually drove his car for a while.

'Well?' he asked when they'd stopped and he'd taken the wheel again for the final bit of the journey.

'It's great,' she said. 'I can see why you love it.'

'Told you so,' he said with a grin.

Though he stopped singing along to the music as they drew nearer to the hotel where the wedding was being held. By the time he parked the car, he looked positively grim.

She reached over and squeezed his hand. 'Hey. It's going to be fine. The sun's shining and it's going to be better than you think.'

'Uh-huh.' He didn't sound convinced, but he returned the squeeze of her hand and gave her a half-smile. 'Thank you, Isla.'

'That's what friends are for. You'd do the same for me.' And she tried to ignore the fact that her skin was tingling where it touched his. It was a completely inappropriate reaction. Even if she wanted to start a relationship with someone—which she didn't—this definitely wasn't the place or the time. 'Let's do this,' she said.

He nodded, climbed out of the car, and insisted on carrying her luggage into the hotel as well as his own.

When they reached the desk to book in, the receptionist smiled at them. 'Dr Harry Gardiner? Welcome to Pentremain Hotel. Here's your key. You're in room 217. Second floor, then turn left when you get out of the lift.'

'There should be two rooms,' Harry said. 'Harry Gardiner and Isla McKenna.'

'I'm afraid there's only one room booked,' the receptionist said. 'But it *is* a double.'

'There must be a mistake,' Harry said. 'Dad definitely said we had two rooms.'

'I'm afraid there's only one.' The receptionist bit her lip. 'I'm so sorry. We're fully booked, so I can't offer you an alternative.'

'It's fine,' Isla said, seeing how awkward the receptionist looked and not wanting to make a fuss. 'We can sort this out later. Thank you for your help.' She forced a smile she didn't feel.

Going to the wedding with Harry was one thing; sharing a room with him was quite another. And he didn't look exactly thrilled about the situation, either.

They went to the lift and found their room in silence.

'I'm so sorry about this. I did say that we were just friends and we needed two rooms. I hope my father isn't making assumptions,' Harry said. 'Look, I'll ring round and see if I can find myself a room somewhere nearby.'

'Harry, this is your family. You ought to be the one to stay here,' Isla pointed out.

'I'm really sorry about this. Dad definitely said we

had two rooms. Give me a moment and I'll find an alternative,' he said, grabbing his phone to check the Internet for numbers of nearby hotels and guest houses.

Several phone calls later, he'd established that there were no rooms available anywhere near. 'Absolutely everywhere is fully booked with holidaymakers. Which I guess you'd expect on a weekend at this time of year.' He sighed. 'OK. I'll sleep in the car.'

'You can't possibly do that!' Isla frowned at him. 'Look, it's just for one night. We can share the room.'

'In that case, I'll take the couch.'

'You're too tall, your back will feel like murder tomorrow morning.' She took a deep breath. 'Look, we're adults. We can share a bed without...' She stopped before she said the words. Even thinking them made a slow burn start at the base of her spine. *Making love. With Harry.*

Any woman with a pulse would find Harry Gardiner attractive, and of course it would cross her mind to wonder what it would be like to be in his arms. She'd just have to make sure she didn't act on that impulse. 'Well,' she finished lamely.

'You're right. It's not as if we're teenagers,' he said. And at least he hadn't seemed to pick up on what was going through her head.

'Exactly. Now, we need to get changed,' she said briskly. 'Do you want to change in here or in the bathroom?'

'You pick,' he said.

'Bathroom,' she said, and escaped there with her dress and make-up bag.

Sharing a room with Isla McKenna.

It was the sensible solution, Harry knew.

The problem was, he didn't feel sensible. He was already on edge about the wedding, and if they shared a bed it would be all too easy to seek comfort in her.

She's your colleague, he reminded himself. Off limits. She wants a relationship just as little as you do. Keep your distance.

He'd just about got himself under control by the time he'd changed into the tailcoat, wing-collared shirt and cravat his father had asked him to wear. He left the top hat on the bed for the time being, took a deep breath and knocked on the bathroom door. 'Isla, I'm ready whenever you are,' he said, 'but don't take that as me rushing you. There's plenty of time. I just didn't want you to feel that you had to be stuck in there while I was faffing about in the other room.'

She opened the door. 'I'm ready,' she said softly.

Harry had never seen Isla dressed up before. He'd seen her wearing jeans and a T-shirt, and he'd seen her in her uniform at the hospital. On every occasion she'd worn her hair pinned back and no make-up, not even a touch of lipstick.

Today, she was wearing a simple blue dress that emphasised the colour of her eyes, a touch of mascara, the lightest shimmer of lipstick—and she looked stunning. Desire rushed through him, taking his breath away. How had he ever thought that Isla would be *safe*? He needed to get himself under control. Now.

'You look lovely,' he said, hearing the slight croak in his voice and feeling cross with himself for letting his emotions show.

'Thank you. You don't scrub up so badly yourself, Dr Gardiner,' she said.

Exactly the right words to help him keep his burgeoning feelings under control, and he was grateful for them. 'Shall we?' he asked and gestured to the door.

'Sure.' She gave him a cheeky grin. 'Don't forget your hat.'

'No.' He glanced at her high-heeled shoes and did a double-take. 'Isla, are you going to be able to dance in those?'

'I'm Scottish. Of course I can.' She grinned. 'And if I can't I'll just take them off.'

He really, really wished she hadn't said those words. Because now there was a picture on his head that he couldn't shift. Isla, all barefoot and beguiling, standing before him and looking up with her eyes full of laughter. And himself taking off every piece of her clothing, one by one...

Get a grip, Harry Gardiner, and keep your hands and your eyes to yourself, he warned himself. He pinned his best smile to his face, and opened the door.

'Isla, this is my father, Robert Gardiner,' Harry said formally when they joined the wedding party in the hotel gardens. 'Dad, this is my friend Isla McKenna.'

Isla could see the family resemblance. Although Bertie's hair was liberally streaked with grey, clearly once it had been as dark as Harry's, and if it hadn't been cut so short it would've been as curly as Harry's, too. Bertie had the same dark eyes and same sweet smile as his son, though Harry hadn't inherited his dimples.

'It's lovely to meet you, Mr Gardiner,' she said.

'Everyone calls me Bertie,' he corrected with a smile. 'It's lovely to meet you, too, Isla—I can call you Isla?'

'Yes, of course.'

'Good.' His eyes twinkled at her. 'I believe I have

you to thank for persuading Harry to be here at all, and I hear it was your idea for Evan to be my best man.'

She winced. 'Sorry, that sounds horribly like interference on my part.'

He smiled and clapped her shoulder. 'Sweetheart, it was an inspired suggestion, and you talked Harry into coming so I most definitely owe you champagne.'

For a moment, she froze. Andrew Gillespie had been just as charming and flirtatious, but he'd hidden a serpent under the smile. Then she remembered Harry's warning that his father would flirt with her but meant nothing by it. And he was right. There was nothing remotely assessing in the way Bertie looked at her. No hidden agendas. He wasn't a carbon copy of Andrew.

'Now, has my boy here introduced you to everyone?' Bertie asked.

'We've hardly had time, Dad—remember, we drove up this morning from London and we had to get changed.'

'You could've come last night and had dinner with us,' Bertie pointed out. 'But you said you were on a late shift and couldn't get anyone to swap with you.'

'Exactly.' Harry gave him a tight smile. 'I happen to work in the busiest department at the hospital, you know.'

'Hmm.' Bertie rolled his eyes. 'Come with me, sweetheart, and I'll introduce you.'

'Where's Trixie?' Harry asked.

Bertie smiled. 'Now, son, you've been to enough of my weddings to know that it's bad luck for the groom to see the bride before the ceremony.'

And then Isla finally relaxed, liking the way Harry's father was able to poke fun at himself.

The next thing she knew, she'd been introduced to a dozen or more of Harry's family, including most of his brothers. The twelve-year-old looked as if he'd rather not be there and she made a mental note to go and chat to him later; the seventeen-year-old looked a little awkward. The two oldest, Jack and Fin, seemed to be assessing her suitability for Harry.

'Sorry about that,' Harry said softly as soon as they were alone again. 'Clearly they were under instructions from Maisie. Jack's only a year and a bit older than her, and they see things pretty much the same way.'

'It's fine,' Isla said with a smile.

The wedding ceremony was held under a canopy on the clifftop, and the views were breathtaking. And seeing the sea made Isla feel suddenly homesick.

'Are you OK?' Harry asked.

'Sure. It's just been a while since I've seen the sea properly.'

'Before we go back to London,' he promised, 'we'll go for a walk on the beach.'

'I'll hold you to that. It's the one thing I regret about London—there's no sea. And I miss walking by the waves.'

'There's a beach of sorts on the Thames. I'll show you some time, if you like.'

'Thank you.'

The wedding itself was lovely. Harry's youngest brother was indeed the best man, and he handed the rings to Bertie at the altar.

Trixie and Bertie's vows were very simple and heartfelt. Isla guessed that Harry was going to find this bit the hardest, so she slipped her hand into his and squeezed his fingers. He squeezed back and then didn't let her hand go.

* * *

After the wedding, the photographer had everyone clustering together in groups. Isla particularly liked the one of Bertie with his six sons, all of them wearing top hats and then a second shot with them all throwing their hats into the air. She took a couple of snaps on her phone for posterity.

And then the photographer called her and Harry over. 'Now, you two. Stand together here.' He posed them, then shook his head. 'I want you closer than that,' he said.

Oh, help. He was clearly under the misapprehension that she and Harry were a proper couple. Just as she had a nasty feeling that Harry's family thought that, too—even though Harry had made it clear they were just friends.

'That's it. Arms round each other,' the photographer said.

They'd have to go along with it. Making a fuss now would make everything awkward and embarrassing.

'Look into each other's eyes,' the photographer said. 'That's it. I want to see the love. As if you're just about to kiss each other.'

Isla's mouth went dry.

Kissing Harry.

The worst thing was, she could just imagine it. Putting her hand up to stroke his cheek, then sliding her hand round his neck and drawing his head down to hers. Parting her lips. Seeing his pupils widen with desire. Feeling his lips brush against hers, all light and teasing and promising; and then he'd pull her closer, jam his mouth properly against hers and deepen the kiss…

'That's *exactly* what I'm talking about!' the photographer crowed.

Isla focussed again and saw the shock in Harry's eyes.

Had she given herself away? Or was he shocked because the same feelings had been coursing through him?

She didn't dare ask, but she made some excuse to dive back into the crowd. And please, please, let her libido be back under control before Harry could guess what she'd been thinking.

Trixie—who turned out to be a primary school teacher—clearly understood how bored the younger members of the family would find things, so she'd arranged a duck race on the stream running through the hotel grounds for them. Evan insisted on making a team with Harry, and made their duck into a pirate.

Harry was such a sweetheart, Isla thought; he was as patient with all the children here as he was in the emergency department. And yet he'd been so adamant about not wanting children of his own. She couldn't quite work it out.

'He's very good with children,' Bertie said, joining her.

'They love him at work—he has this stock of terrible jokes to distract them,' Isla said with a smile.

'I can imagine. Half of them come from his brothers.' Bertie paused. 'So you met when you started working together?'

Isla had half expected an inquisition. And the best way to stop the misconception being uncovered and making things really awkward would be to stick as closely to the truth as possible. 'Yes—a couple of months ago.'

'And you're a doctor, too?'

'No, I'm a nurse,' Isla said.

'Senior nurse, actually.' Harry came up and slung one arm casually around Isla's shoulders, clearly having worked out what was going on. 'Let's have the inquisition over now, please, Dad.'

'If you actually told me things, Harry,' Bertie grumbled good-naturedly, 'then I wouldn't have to pump other people for information, would I?'

'I'm a doctor. I'm used to keeping things confidential,' Harry said with a grin.

'You're impossible,' Bertie said with a sigh.

'Like father, like son,' Harry said with a broad wink. 'Isla's my friend. End of story. Come on, Isla—it's time for food and I'm starving,' he added, and shepherded her into the large marquee on the lawn.

The food was wonderful: Cornish crab terrine followed by roast beef and all the trimmings, then a rich pavlova with clotted cream and raspberries, and finally a selection of traditional Cornish cheeses and crackers.

The waiters topped up everyone's glasses with champagne, ready for the speeches.

The father of the bride gave the first speech. Sticking with tradition, he welcomed the guests, thanked everyone for coming, spoke a little bit about Bertie and Trixie, and then toasted the bride and groom.

Harry murmured in her ear, 'Excuse me—I'm going to have to leave you for a minute or two.'

She realised why when little Evan stood up on his chair, with Harry crouched beside him.

'I'm Evan and I'm my daddy's best man,' Evan said proudly. 'My big brother Harry says my speech has to be funny, so I'm going to tell you my favourite joke. What did the banana say to the monkey?' He waited for a moment before delivering the punchline. 'Nothing—bananas can't talk!'

Everyone laughed.

'Harry says the speech has got to be short as well as funny, so I'll stop now. Happy wedding day, Daddy and Trixie.'

Everyone echoed, 'Bertie and Trixie.'

Harry whispered something in Evan's ear and the little boy's eyes went wide. 'Harry, I forgot!'

Harry smiled at him and patted his shoulder, and mouthed, 'Go on.'

'Um, I'm sorry, everyone, I forgot the other bit. The bridesmaids look really pretty and they did a good job. You have to drink to the bridesmaids now.'

There were amused and indulgent laughs, and everyone chorused, 'The bridesmaids.'

Bertie stood up last. 'And I must say thank you to my best man, who did a fabulous job.'

'And Harry,' Evan chipped in.

Bertie grinned. 'I gather it was a bit of a team effort between my youngest and my oldest sons. But that's what family's all about. Pitching in together.' He raised his glass. 'I'd like to make a toast to my beautiful bride, Trixie, and to my wonderful family—thank you all for coming here to celebrate with us.'

Harry quietly came back to join their table at that point. Isla reached for his hand under the table and squeezed it.

After the speeches, it was time to cut the cake. 'The middle layer is chocolate,' Trixie said, 'so that should make all the men in my new family happy.'

'As sweet as you are,' Bertie said, and kissed her. 'And I believe the band is ready for us. Perhaps we could all move in to the other marquee?'

The band was set up at one end, and there were chairs lining the edges of the floor. For the first dance, the band played a slow dance; Bertie and Trixie started things off, followed by the bride and groom's parents, and then the bridesmaids and best man.

Isla wondered if Harry was going to suggest dancing with her, but at the end of the song the singer announced, 'And now it's time for you all you to dance off that cake—I want everybody up on the floor, and there's no excuse for not dancing because we're going to call the steps for you.'

There were protests from the younger members of the wedding party, but they were roundly ignored—and, by the middle of the first dance, everyone was laughing and thoroughly enjoying themselves. Isla knew most of the steps from the ceilidhs she'd been to back on the island. Her own wedding reception would've been just like this. But she pushed away the sadness; now wasn't the time or place, and she wasn't going to let the shadow of Andrew Gillespie spoil this weekend.

Harry watched Isla dancing while he was on the other side of the room. Her glorious hair flew out behind her, and she'd been telling the truth about being able to dance in high heels. Before today, he hadn't had a clue how well his colleague could dance. If the rest of the staff could see their quiet, capable, almost shy senior nurse right now...

She was sparkling, and she fitted in well with everyone. And he noticed that Isla had even managed to get his two middle brothers to join in the dancing, rather than sitting on the edge of the room, mired in teenage awkwardness. She'd actually got them laughing as they danced together. Harry already knew from working with her that she had great people skills, but this was something else. She wasn't just coping with his extended family, she was actually joining in with them.

He had a nasty feeling that Isla McKenna was the one woman who could tempt him to break his 'no serious relationships' rule. So much for asking her to come here with him because she was safe: she was nothing of the kind. And he would need to be careful, especially as they were sharing a room tonight.

And almost everyone in his family had something to say about her to him. Fin said it was about time he found someone like her; Jack pointed out how well she was getting on with everyone and how nice she was with the teenagers; Julie came over to say how much little Evan liked her and so did she.

If his family had their way, they'd be getting married next week, Harry thought moodily. And he hoped Isla wouldn't take any of it to heart. He'd told them the truth. They just didn't want to believe it, and wanted him to have the happy-ever-after.

Marriage wasn't an option he would ever seriously consider. In his world, the happiness from marriage was brief and the heartache lasted an awful lot longer.

The band had a break when the canapés and sandwiches appeared, and he managed to snatch some time with Isla.

'Oh, look at this—miniature Cornish pasties, and miniature scones with clotted cream and strawberry jam!' she exclaimed in delight. She tried a scone. 'Oh, you really have to try this, Harry,' she said, and popped a bite of scone into his mouth.

His lips tingled where her fingers had touched them.

Oh, help. He was going to have to keep himself under strict control. It would be all too easy to do something stupid—like catch her hand and kiss the back of her fingers, and then turn her hand over so his mouth could linger over the pulse at her wrist.

'This is one of the nicest weddings I've been to,' she said.

Harry pulled himself together with an effort. 'I guess it's better than I thought it would be.' The real reason that it was better for him was because she was there, but he was wary of telling her that because he didn't want her to take it the wrong way. Especially as he had a nasty feeling that it meant more to him than just the support of a friend—and, despite the fact they'd just celebrated a wedding, he knew this wouldn't last. It never did.

But he pushed the thoughts away and forced himself to smile and be sociable.

After the break, the band switched from the barn dance to more traditional wedding music. Isla danced with his two oldest brothers and Bertie, and then Harry reclaimed her.

Just as the band segued into a slow dance.

It was too late to back out now, because she was already in his arms.

Now he knew what it was like to hold her close. She was warm and soft and sweet. And it scared him, how right this felt—like the perfect fit.

He could see his father smiling approval at him. His brothers did likewise.

Oh, help. They all thought that he and Isla had been fibbing about their relationship and were a real couple—and, even though he'd originally intended that they believe that, he realised now that Isla had been right and it made things way too complicated.

They really ought to sit out the next dance. Go and talk to other people. Distract his family.

But he couldn't let her go. The next song was another slow dance, and he ended up drawing her closer and dancing cheek to cheek with her instead. He could smell her perfume, all soft and beguiling—much like Isla herself. He closed his eyes. All he had to do was turn his head towards her, just the tiniest fraction, and he'd be able to kiss the corner of her mouth. And then he'd find out if her lips were as sweet as the rest of her.

He felt almost giddy with need. It had been a long time since he'd wanted to kiss someone as much as he wanted to kiss Isla McKenna.

Giddy was about right. The mood of the wedding had clearly got to him and he needed to start being sensible, and that meant right now, before he did something they'd both regret.

He pulled away from her slightly.

'Are you OK?' she asked, her blue eyes dark with concern.

He nodded. 'I just need some fresh air.'

'I'll come with you if you like.'

He ought to say no. He really, really ought to make an excuse to put some distance between them. Not walk outside with her in the gardens under the light of a full moon.

But, despite his best intentions, he found himself saying yes, holding her hand and walking out of the marquee with her.

CHAPTER SIX

THE SKY WAS darkening and the first stars were appearing; they were so much brighter out here in the countryside than they were in London. Harry could hear the gentle, regular swish of the waves against the sand at the bottom of the cliffs and it was hypnotic, soothing his soul. He sat down on the grass next to Isla, looking out at the sea, and slid his arm round her shoulders. For a moment he felt the tiniest bit of resistance from her; then she leaned into him and slid her arm round his waist.

Funny how right it felt. Not that he was going to let himself think about that. Because he didn't do serious relationships and he valued Isla too much to mess things up between them.

They sat in companionable silence together for a while. Eventually, she was the one to break it. 'So are you really OK, Harry?' she asked softly.

'Yeah. I'm OK.' He blew out a breath. 'It's just… This whole wedding thing. It's good to see my brothers, but when I look at them I can't help remembering the times they've cried on my shoulder, convinced it was the end of the world because their mum and dad were fighting all the time, or had just split up and they had to move house and start at a new school. Every divorce caused so much damage. It uprooted the kids and made them so miserable.'

'They all seem pretty well adjusted now.'

Except him, perhaps. Not that he intended to discuss that. 'But they've still been hurt.' He sighed. 'Ten marriages between my parents. It's a bit excessive.'

'Your dad seems happy.'

'For the moment—but you can see the pattern, Isla. It's meant to be a seven-year itch, but Dad only seems to make it to four or five years before he's had enough and misses the thrill of the chase.' He shook his head. 'And I don't want to be like that, Isla. If I'm like my parents and I can't settle down... I don't want to hurt anyone.'

'And that's why you isolate yourself?' she asked.

He'd never thought about it in that way. He'd always thought about it as saving others from him repeating his parents' mistakes. 'I guess.'

She rubbed her thumb in a comforting movement against his back. 'You're pretty hard on yourself, Harry. From what I've seen today, your family loves you. Your brothers all look up to you.'

He gave her a wry smile. 'Maybe.'

She twisted her head to kiss his cheek, and heat zinged through him at the touch of her mouth against his skin. Just as much as it had when the photographer had suggested they should look in love with each other, as if they were just about to kiss.

Right at that moment he'd really wanted to kiss Isla, to see if her mouth was as soft and as sweet as it looked. Her eyes had been wide and dark, and it would've been oh, so easy to lean forward and do it. Just as he wanted to kiss her, right now.

This was a bad idea.

He knew he ought to take his arm from her shoulders, move away from her, and suggest that they go back to the marquee and join the dancing.

But he couldn't move. It felt as if they were held together by some magnetic force. Something he couldn't break—and, if he was honest with himself, something he didn't want to break.

'You're a good man, Harry Gardiner,' Isla said. 'I can understand why you avoid connecting with anyone—but you're really not being fair to yourself. You're loyal and you're kind, and I think you more than have the capacity within you to make a relationship work. To really love someone.'

He groaned. 'You sound like my mother. And my sisters.'

'If that's what they say, then I agree with them,' she said.

'Can we change the subject?' he asked plaintively.

'Because you're too chicken?'

Yes. 'No, because the sky's beautiful and I don't want to talk about something that makes me antsy.'

'Fair enough,' she said.

'You looked as if you were enjoying the dancing earlier.'

'The barn dance? Yes—it's very similar to the ceilidhs we had on the island. That's what we were going to have for our wedding.'

Wedding?

Isla had been going to get married?

The fact that she was single—and had made it clear she intended to stay that way—meant that something must have gone badly wrong. Was that the reason that had made her leave the island? And why she'd reacted so badly to the idea of being a fake fiancée—because she'd once been a real one?

'Were?' he asked softly.

She shook her head. 'Don't worry about it. It's a long story.'

'Right now I have all the time in the world.' His arm tightened round her shoulders. 'It's not going any further than me—you've kept my confidence and I'll keep yours. Plus someone very wise once told me it's good to talk because it's better out than in. A problem shared is a problem halved, and all that.'

'Before I ran out of clichés, you mean?' she asked wryly, clearly remembering that conversation.

'What happened? Your fiancé died?' he asked quietly. It was the only reason he could think of why Isla hadn't got married.

'Stewart? No. He's still alive and perfectly healthy, as far as I know.' She blew out a breath. 'We'd known each other since we were children. I guess it all goes with the territory of living in a small community. You end up settling down with someone you've known for ever.'

He waited, giving her the space to talk.

'We started dating a couple of years ago. He asked me to marry him and I said yes. My family liked him and I thought his liked me.'

So that had been the problem? Her ex's family hadn't liked her? And yet she'd still been prepared to meet his own family today. His respect for her went up another notch.

'But then Stewart's mum asked me for a favour,' she said softly. 'According to Bridie, Andrew—Stewart's stepfather—had bit of a drink problem. She wanted me to talk to him and see if I could persuade him to get some help to stop drinking, before he ended up with cirrhosis of the liver.' She looked away. 'I was trying to help.'

'And he didn't like you interfering?'

'Partly, but Andrew got the wrong end of the stick
when I asked to talk to him privately. He assumed I
was interested in him and he made a pass at me.' She
sighed. 'I should've handled it better. I just hadn't expected him to react in that way. I always thought his
marriage to Bridie was rock-solid and he would never
even think about looking at another woman.'

'It wasn't your fault, Isla. Besides, any decent man
understands that if a woman says no, it means no.'
Harry had a nasty feeling where this might be going.
'So he wouldn't take no for an answer?'

'Oh, he did,' she said grimly. 'But Andrew Gillespie
was used to getting his own way. He really didn't like
the fact that I'd said no to him. So he called the head of
the practice and said that I'd behaved unprofessionally.
He claimed that I'd asked to see him privately under
the guise of talking about his health, and then made a
pass at him.'

'What? That's appalling. I hope your boss sent him
away with a flea in his ear.'

'My boss,' she said, 'had to investigate. Exactly as he
was bound to do if any patient made a complaint about
any of the staff at the practice.'

'But it obviously wasn't true.'

'And I was exonerated.' She blew out a breath. 'But
you know all the clichés. There's no smoke without
fire. Mud sticks.'

He blinked. 'Other people believed him?'

She nodded. 'I lived in a village. Everyone knew me;
but everyone also knew Andrew. He was popular with
the locals—partly because he employed a lot of them,
and partly because he could be very charming indeed.'

'But surely your fiancé and his mum knew the truth?'

'Andrew could be persuasive as well as charming.'

Harry really didn't get this. 'But his wife asked you to have a quiet word with him and help him with his drinking problem. She knew there was more to him than met the eye. Surely she must've known that he wasn't telling the truth?'

'And there's another cliché for you: stand by your man. Even if it means upholding a lie.'

'That's...that's...' He didn't have the words. 'I don't know what to say.' But there was one thing he could do. He shifted her on to his lap and held her close. 'Best I can do right now is give you a hug.'

'Gratefully accepted.'

And, oh, he wanted to kiss her. Except that would be totally inappropriate. He couldn't suggest that they lose their worries in each other. Much as he felt that it might help them both tonight, tomorrow they'd have to face up to their actions and it would all get way too messy. So he just held her. 'I'm really sorry that you had to go through something so horrible. And I don't see how anyone who'd known you for more than ten minutes could believe that you'd ever be unprofessional, much less try it on with your fiancé's stepfather.'

'Thank you for the vote of confidence,' she said.

'I still can't get over the fact that people you'd lived with and worked with and treated thought that you were capable of that kind of behaviour. Much less your ex. And right now I don't know what to say,' he said. 'Other than wanting to punch this Andrew Gillespie guy very hard—and I know exactly where to hit him to do the most damage—and wanting to shake your ex until his teeth rattle for being such an idiot and not seeing straight away that you weren't the one telling lies.'

'Violence doesn't solve anything,' she pointed out.

'Look at all the drunks we have to patch up on a Friday and Saturday night.'

'I know, but it would make me feel better,' he said.

She smiled. 'You're not a caveman, Harry.'

'Right now I'd quite like to be. Being civilised can be overrated.'

She stroked his cheek. 'Thank you for taking my part.'

'Isla, anybody who knows you would realise the truth without having to be told. You're honest, dependable and sincere.'

'Thank you. Though I wasn't fishing for compliments.'

'I know. I'm just telling you, that's all. And I'm sorry that you had to go through such a horrible situation. Though I'm glad you chose to work at the London Victoria. And I'm also very glad you're here with me right now.' And he really understood now why she wasn't in the market for a relationship—why she'd been wary even of joining in with the team outside work. She'd been let down so badly. It would be hard to take the risk of trusting someone again.

If anyone had told Isla a month ago that she'd be sitting on Harry's lap with their arms wrapped round each other, she would've scoffed.

And yet here they were. Doing exactly that.

And she'd just spilled her heart out to him.

Odd that Stewart had known her for years and years, and yet he'd got her totally wrong; whereas Harry had known her only a few weeks and he knew her for exactly who she was. *Honest, dependable and sincere.* It warmed her heart to know that was what he thought of her.

'I'm glad I'm here, too,' she said. And, even though she knew she was skating on very thin ice indeed, she gave in to the impulse to lean forward and kiss his cheek. 'Thank you for believing in me.'

His eyes went even darker. 'Isla.' He was looking at her mouth.

Just as she was looking at his.

Was he wondering the same as she was, right now? What it would be like if their lips actually touched? Did his mouth tingle with longing, the same way that hers did—the same way she'd felt when the photographer had posed them, except this time it was just the two of them in the starlight, and it felt so much more intense?

Clearly yes, because he leaned forward and touched his mouth to hers. And it felt as if the sky had lit up with a meteor shower. His mouth was warm and soft and sweet, promising and enticing rather than demanding, and she wanted more.

She slid her hands into his hair; his curls were silky under her fingertips. And he drew her closer so he could deepen the kiss.

'We wondered if you two lovebirds would be out here,' a voice said, and they broke apart.

She felt colour flare through her cheeks as she looked up at Harry's father and new stepmother. What on earth did she think she was doing, kissing Harry like that in the middle of the garden where anyone could see them?

'Don't say a single word,' Harry said, dragging a hand through his hair and looking as guilty as Isla felt.

'It's my wedding day and it's Cornwall, so it's meant to be romantic,' Bertie said. 'Though you weren't quite telling the truth about being just friends, were you?'

Harry groaned. 'Dad. Not now.'

'We came out to find you because Evan is supposed

to be going to bed and he refuses to go without saying goodnight to you—and that's both of you, actually,' Trixie said, including Isla. She grinned. 'He likes you. We all do, Isla.'

'OK, OK, we're coming,' Harry said, and exchanged a glance with Isla. She climbed off his lap and they headed in to the marquee to say goodnight to Evan. The little boy did his best to persuade them to read him a couple of stories each, but Julie whisked him away with a promise of 'later'.

'You're a natural with kids, Isla,' Harry remarked when Evan had gone.

'Because of my job,' she said. 'And so are you.'

He laughed. 'It's my job—and probably because I have so many siblings.'

'And yet you say you don't want kids of your own, even though you're so good with them. I don't get it.'

'I just don't,' Harry said. 'And I'd rather not talk about it.'

'Fair enough.' And she hadn't told him everything about Stewart, so she was hardly in a position to nag about keeping secrets.

'Come on—they're playing your song,' Harry said as the band started playing Abba's 'Dancing Queen'.

It was a deliberate distraction, and Isla knew it, but at the same time she didn't want to push him. He'd looked as if he'd had enough soul-baring for today.

'I'm a little bit older than seventeen, you know.'

'You can still dance,' he said, and led her onto the floor.

What else could she do but join in? Especially as this part of the band's set was cover versions of all the kind of songs that got everyone on the floor at weddings, from the youngest to the oldest.

Though Harry avoided the slow dances that were played every so often to change the mood and the tempo, she noticed. Which was probably just as well, given what had happened outside in the garden. If they'd been in each other's arms again, holding each other close, the temptation to repeat that kiss might've been too much for both of them.

At the end of the evening, they headed for their room.

'I really ought to take the couch,' Harry said.

'Because we kissed in the garden?' She took a deep breath. 'Let's blame it on the moonlight and Cornwall being romantic.'

'I guess.'

'Harry, we're adults. We've got a long drive back to London tomorrow. We both need sleep. It's not as if I'm planning to pounce on you.' Even though part of her really wanted to.

'Of course. And you're right.' He gave her a smile, but she could see that he had to make the effort. 'Do you want to use the bathroom first?'

'Thank you.'

She lingered as long as she dared, hoping to give herself a little time to calm down. Once she'd cleaned her teeth and changed into her pyjamas, she went back into the bedroom. Harry was still dressed. 'Do you have a preferred side of the bed?' she asked.

'Whichever you don't want,' he said.

'Thanks. I like to sleep by the window,' she said. 'See you in a bit.'

When Harry came out of the bathroom, he was wearing pyjamas and Isla was in bed. It was all very civilised and proper, but underneath everything there was an undercurrent. Her mouth was still tingling in memory of that kiss. Plus this was the first time she'd shared a bed with anyone since she'd broken up with Stewart. Even though they'd both made it clear that this was going to be completely chaste, it still felt unnerving.

Particularly as part of her didn't want this to be chaste at all. And, from the way Harry had kissed her under the stars, she had a feeling that it was the same for him. Wanting the ultimate closeness—but scared it would all go wrong, and not wanting to have to deal with the resultant carnage.

'Goodnight,' he said, climbed in beside her and turned his back.

Which was the most sensible way of dealing with it, she thought. Keeping temptation well at bay. 'Goodnight,' she echoed, and turned her own back.

Isla was very aware of his closeness and it took her a while before she could relax enough to sleep. She woke briefly in the night to discover that Harry was spooned against her, one arm wrapped round her waist and holding her close. She'd really missed this kind of closeness. It would be oh, so easy to turn round and kiss him awake; but that would change everything and it wouldn't be fair to either of them. She knew he didn't want a relationship; she didn't want one either.

Even if Harry Gardiner did kiss like an angel.

She'd just have to put it out of her mind. They were colleagues and friends, and that was that.

The next morning, Harry woke to find himself spooned against Isla, with his arm wrapped round her. Her hand was resting lightly over his, as if she welcomed the closeness.

He could tell from her slow, even breathing that she was still asleep.

Oh, help.

She was all warm and soft and sweet. It would be so easy to brush that glorious hair away from her shoulder and kiss the nape of her neck, his mouth brushing against her bare skin until she woke.

And he knew she'd respond to him, the way she'd responded to his kiss in the garden last night. If his father hadn't interrupted them, he had a nasty feeling that he might've carried Isla to the bed they shared right now and taken things a whole lot further.

As in all the way further.

He took a deep breath. She'd told him about what had happened to her in Scotland, though he had a feeling that she'd left a fair bit out. Why on earth hadn't her fiancé believed in her? Surely he'd realised that his stepfather hadn't been telling the truth? Although Isla hadn't said which of them had broken off the engagement, Harry knew it had shattered her faith in relationships.

So he needed to ignore his body's urging. He had to do the right thing.

Carefully, he disentangled himself from her without waking her, took a shower and dressed. It was still relatively early for a Sunday morning after a wedding reception, but they had a long way to drive and it would be sensible to leave earlier rather than later. He made them both a cup of tea from the hospitality tray on the dresser, set hers on the table next to her side of the bed, and touched her shoulder. 'Isla.'

Her eyes fluttered open. For a moment, she looked confused, as if she wasn't sure where she was or why someone was sharing her bedroom. Then her eyes widened. 'Oh. Harry.'

'Good morning. I made you a cup of tea.'

'Thank you,' she said, sounding almost shy. 'What time is it?'

'Eight. I know it's a bit early.'

'But we have a long drive.'

He was relieved that she understood. 'I thought I might go for a walk before breakfast. It'll give you a chance to shower and get changed.'

She looked grateful. 'I appreciate that.'

'See you in half an hour?'

'I'll be ready and packed,' she promised.

'Yeah.' He smiled at her. So there wasn't any collateral damage from last night, then—either from the kiss or from her telling him about her past. She still looked a little shy with him, but he knew she'd won her trust. Just as she'd won his.

And, back in London, everything would be just fine.

CHAPTER SEVEN

AT BREAKFAST, LITTLE Evan was there and insisted that they join him and his mother. Isla was amused to note that he copied Harry exactly in everything he ate; clearly the little boy had a serious case of hero-worship where his big brother was concerned.

When they'd finished, they said goodbye to Harry's family, then drove back to London. It was much quieter on the way back; there wasn't quite an awkward silence between them, but this time Harry was playing classical music rather than something they could both sing along to, and Isla didn't really know what to say. They probably ought to discuss what had happened yesterday and reset the ground rules, but she had the distinct impression that Harry didn't want to discuss it and would change the subject if she raised it.

Although they stopped for lunch, Harry suggested that they grabbed a burger at the motorway service station—and she noticed that this time he didn't offer to let her drive.

She'd always been good with people, but the way Harry was stonewalling her was unlike anything she'd ever known.

'Are you OK?' she asked.

'Sure. Just thinking about work.'

And there wasn't really an answer to that.

'Do you want to come in for coffee?' she asked when he parked outside her flat, even though she was pretty sure he'd say no.

'Thanks, but I've already taken up enough of your time this weekend,' he said, equally politely.

Isla felt as if somehow she'd done something wrong; but, if she tried to clear the air, would it make things even worse between them?

She was beginning to see what the hospital grapevine meant about Harry the Heartbreaker. He was already withdrawing from her and they'd gone to the wedding just as friends, not as part of a date. Was he really that wary of emotional involvement?

'Thank you for coming with me this weekend,' he said.

'Hey, that's what friends are for,' she said lightly. Though she had a nasty feeling that their burgeoning friendship had just hit an iceberg, one that could totally sink it.

Harry was still in scrupulously polite mode as he took her bag from the car and saw her to her door. 'See you at work tomorrow, then,' he said.

'Yes, see you tomorrow.'

And he really couldn't escape fast enough, she noticed. Back inside her flat, she kept herself busy by catching up with her chores, but it wasn't quite enough to occupy her full attention. She couldn't help wondering if what had almost happened between them in the moonlit garden would affect their relationship at work. Tomorrow, would Harry be his usual self with her, or would he have withdrawn even further?

She had no answer the next morning, because they

weren't rostered on together; he was in Resus and she was on triage duty.

But, in the middle of the morning, a woman came in carrying a toddler who rested limply against her. She sounded utterly distraught as she begged, 'Please help me—it's my grandson. I think he's dying!'

Isla signalled to the receptionist that she'd take the case.

She swiftly introduced herself. 'I can see that you're worried, but I need you to take a deep breath and answer some questions for me so I can help your grandson,' she said gently. 'What's his name and how old is he?'

The woman's voice was quavery but her answers were clear. 'Peter Jacobs, and he's two.'

'Can you tell me what's happened, Mrs Jacobs?'

'He started being sick and his vomit was a weird colour, a kind of greyish-black. And he's drowsy—at this time of the morning he's usually really lively. I called the ambulance, but they said they'd be a while before they could get to us, so I asked my neighbour to drive us in.'

Greyish-black vomit. It flagged up alarm signals in Isla's brain. 'Do you know if he's eaten anything he shouldn't have?' she asked.

'He said something about sweeties and tasting nasty. I couldn't think what he might have eaten, at first—I always keep any tablets in the medicine cabinet on the wall in the bathroom, and it has a child lock on it even though he can't reach it yet—but my husband's been taking iron tablets. He has arthritis in his hands so he can't use a childproof cap on his tablets. I didn't realise he'd left them in our bedroom instead of putting them back in the medicine cabinet. It has to be those—Peter hasn't been in the garden, so I can't think of anything else.'

'Do you have any idea how many tablets he might have eaten?'

Mrs Jacobs shook her head, and rummaged in her bag to produce a packet of iron supplement tablets. 'I brought these in case they'd help you. My husband can't remember how many he's taken, but it wasn't completely full. Please help us.' Her face was anguished. 'My son's never going to forgive me if anything happens to Peter.' She swallowed hard. 'If he—if he dies. I can't…'

'He's not going to die,' Isla soothed, though she knew that iron poisoning could be fatal in children. 'You did the right thing by bringing him straight here. Do you have any idea how long ago he might have taken the tablets?'

'It must have been in the last hour or two.' She bit her lip. 'Lee dropped him off just before he went to work. My daughter-in-law's away on business and Lee had to go in. I was only supposed to be minding Peter for the morning. And now…' She broke off, shuddering.

Isla squeezed her hand. 'Try not to worry. Let's go in to the department now because I need to discuss something very quickly with the doctor and then we'll treat your grandson.' She took Mrs Jacobs into Resus and beckoned Harry over.

'This is Mrs Jacobs and her grandson Peter, who's two and we think he might have accidentally eaten some iron tablets,' she said. 'Mrs Jacobs, would you like to sit here and give Peter a cuddle while I fill Dr Gardiner in on all the details?'

Mrs Jacobs looked grey with anxiety, but she did as Isla directed and sat on the bed with Peter on her lap.

'Mrs Jacobs doesn't know how many tablets he took, but she thinks it happened in the last couple of hours. The symptoms sound like iron poisoning.' She gave him a rundown of what Mrs Jacobs had told her.

'I agree—it sounds like iron poisoning.' Harry said. 'OK, we need serum iron, full blood count and glucose. Iron tablets are radio-opaque, so let's do an X-ray to find out how many tablets he took, and then we'll do gastric lavage or even whole bowel irrigation.'

Isla knew that activated charcoal couldn't absorb iron, so bowel irrigation was the most effective treatment, but it was going to be an unpleasant experience for the little boy and even worse for his grandmother. 'I know she's going to be worried about her grandson, but I think we should advise her to stay in the relatives' room while we treat him.'

'Agreed. Let her go with you to the X-ray,' Harry said, 'but then it's hot sweet tea and wait for us to finish.'

They went over to the bed where Mrs Jacobs was sitting with her grandson. 'Peter, I'm Dr Harry and I'm going to try and make you better,' Harry said.

The little boy clearly felt too ill to smile, let alone respond verbally.

Harry turned to the boy's grandmother. 'Mrs Jacobs, we're going to run some blood tests and give him an X-ray to see if we can get a better idea of how many iron tablets he's taken; then we'll be able to treat him. I know this is going to be hard for you, but while we're treating him I'd like you to wait in the relatives' room.'

'Why can't I stay with him? He doesn't know anyone here and he'll be frightened,' Mrs Jacobs said.

'It'll upset you more to see the treatment than it'll upset Peter to be with us, especially as he's quite groggy,'

Harry explained. 'I promise we'll do our best for him, and we'll come and get you so you can be with him again as soon as he's stable.'

She looked distraught. 'My son's never going to forgive me.'

Forgiveness. Yeah. Harry knew all about that. His mother and Tasha had forgiven him for that awful afternoon, but he'd never been able to forgive himself. Even now he still woke up in a cold sweat, having relived the whole thing in his dreams. Seeing his little sister tumble all the way down the stairs, and everything felt as if it was in super-slow motion—and, whatever he did, he just couldn't stop it happening. And then she lay there on the floor, not moving...

Except his dream was always that bit worse than real life. The worst and ultimate might-have-been. In his dream, Tasha never woke up. In real life, thank God, she had.

Mrs Jacobs bit her lip. 'I thought I'd been so careful. I've got cupboard locks and those things you put on the door to stop it slamming on their little fingers. I never thought he'd go into our bedroom and take those tablets.'

Just as Harry had never thought that Tasha would follow him up the stairs. He gave her a rueful smile. 'You can never predict anything with toddlers—and I'm sure your son will forgive you. You'd be surprised what children will forgive their parents.' *And their brothers*.

Mrs Jacobs didn't look convinced.

'You made a mistake, and you'll know in future to keep everything locked away,' Isla said. 'We'll do our best to make sure he's going to be absolutely fine. Do you want someone in the department to call your son for you?'

Mrs Jacobs shook her head. 'No, that wouldn't be fair on him. I'll do it.'

'OK,' Harry said, and squeezed her hand. 'Try not to worry too much, and this will take a while.'

'You can come with me to the X-ray department, so he won't be scared,' Isla said, 'and then I'll show you to the waiting room. Peter, sweetheart, I'm Nurse Isla, and I'm going to help Dr Harry look after you and make you better.'

She took Peter and Mrs Jacobs to the X-ray department, then showed the older woman where to wait. By the time Isla came back to Resus, Harry already had the X-ray up on his screen.

'There seem to be a dozen tablets,' he said. 'So we'll need to do a whole bowel irrigation.'

It was an unpleasant and lengthy procedure, but between them they managed to get rid of the iron tablets and stabilise Peter's condition.

'Shall I go and fetch his grandmother now?' Isla asked as they transferred the little boy to the recovery room.

'Good idea,' Harry said. 'The poor woman must be worried sick.'

Isla went into the relatives' room to see Mrs Jacobs. There was a man with her who bore enough family resemblance for Isla to guess that he was Peter's father.

They both looked up as she walked in. 'Is he all right?' they asked in unison.

'He's going to be absolutely fine,' Isla said, 'and you can come in to the recovery room to see him and have a word with Dr Gardiner.' She looked at the man. 'I assume you're Peter's father?'

'Yes. I couldn't believe it when Mum called me.'

'I'm sorry,' Mrs Jacobs said. 'And I promise you

nothing like this will ever happen again while I'm looking after him.'

'He could've *died*,' Mr Jacobs said, his voice cracking.

'But he didn't,' Isla said gently, resting her hand on his arm for a moment in sympathy, 'and accidents happen. The most important thing is that Peter's all right—and the scariest part is over now.'

She took them through to the recovery room, where Mr Jacobs put his arms round his son and held him tightly. The little boy was still groggy, but mumbled, 'Daddy, Peter got poorly tummy.'

'I know, baby. I love you,' Mr Jacobs said, 'and you're going to be all right.'

'Want Mummy,' Peter said tearfully.

'Mummy will be home soon,' Mr Jacobs said, 'and I'm not going to leave you until she's back. You're safe.'

The little boy snuggled against his father. And oh, how Harry never wanted to be in that position again. Worried sick about a small child whose injuries could've been fatal.

'Mr Jacobs, this is Dr Gardiner,' Isla said.

'Peter's going to be fine,' Harry said. 'I assume your mum already told you that he accidentally ate some iron tablets.'

'Dad should never have left his tablets where Peter could see them,' Mr Jacobs said, his voice tight. 'I can't believe he was so stupid.'

'Peter isn't the first toddler who's eaten tablets thinking that they were sweets and he won't be the last,' Harry said calmly. 'No matter how careful you are, accidents happen, and your mother did exactly the right thing in getting Peter straight here.'

What a hypocrite he was, telling this man that accidents happened and to forgive his mother. Because Harry had never been able to forgive himself for Tash's accident. Not after they discovered that the damage was more permanent than concussion and a broken arm. 'We irrigated his bowel to get rid of the tablets.'

'Oh, my God—that sounds horrific!' Mr Jacobs said, looking shocked.

'It's more effective at getting rid of the tablets than giving him an emetic, and it's also less risky,' Isla said.

'But he'll have nightmares about it.' Mr Jacobs bit his lip. 'My poor boy, having to go through all that.'

'He probably won't remember any of it. He's very young and was quite groggy when he came in,' Harry reassured him.

'So can I take him home now?' Mr Jacobs asked.

'No—because he's so young we want to admit him to the children's ward for the next twenty-four hours, so we can keep an eye on him,' Isla explained.

'So he could get worse?' Mrs Jacobs asked, her face full of fear.

'The early symptoms have settled now, but they sometimes come back the day after, so we always play it safe with young children and keep an eye on them,' Harry said. 'We can take you up to the children's ward and introduce you to the team, and they have facilities for parents or grandparents to stay overnight.'

'I can't believe…' Mr Jacobs shook his head as if to clear it. 'Oh, my God. If I'd lost him…'

'He's going to be fine,' Isla reassured him. 'I know it's easy for me to say, but try not to worry.'

Harry was glad she'd been the one to say it. Those particular words always felt like ashes in his mouth when the patient was a child.

She took the Jacobs family up to the children's ward

and helped them settle in, then headed back down to the Emergency Department. She'd missed her lunch break, so she grabbed a coffee in the staff kitchen and topped it up with cold water so she could drink it more quickly. She knew she could grab a chocolate bar from the vending machine on the way back to the triage team, and that would keep her going to the end of her shift.

Isla was halfway through her coffee when Harry walked in, holding two packets of sandwiches and two cans of fizzy drink. 'I guessed you wouldn't have time for lunch, either, so I nipped out to the sandwich stall by the hospital shop and grabbed these for us. They didn't have a huge choice but there's tuna mayo or chicken salad. You get first pick.'

'Thank you,' she said, feeling a huge surge of relief. Harry was behaving just as he had before they'd gone to Cornwall—which meant that the weekend hadn't damaged their working relationship after all. She hadn't realised quite how worried she'd been about it until she felt the weight leaving her shoulders. 'Why don't we split them and have one of each?'

'Sounds good to me,' he said.

'The kettle's hot. Do you want a coffee?'

He indicated the drinks. 'I'll get a quicker caffeine hit from this. I bet you put cold water in that coffee, didn't you?'

'Yes,' she admitted.

He grimaced. 'I prefer my coffee hot, thanks all the same. Do you want one of these cold drinks?'

'I'll stick with my half-cold coffee, but thanks for thinking of me,' she said. 'How much do I owe you for the sandwich?'

He flapped a dismissive hand. 'It's your shout, next time. That was a good call with young Peter.'

'I feel for his grandmother,' Isla said. 'She was trying her best, and accidents happen. Her son was so angry with her.'

'His dad probably feels guilty because he wasn't there to stop it happening, and that's why he was so angry,' Harry said. He blew out a breath. 'And that's another reason why I don't ever want to settle down and have children. You can't do a job like this and give enough attention to your kids.'

Plenty of other hospital staff managed it, Isla thought. Harry was letting his family background colour his judgement. But it wasn't her place to argue with him. 'Mmm,' she said noncommittally, and ate her sandwich. 'I'd better get back to the triage team.'

'And me to Resus. See you later.'

'Yeah.' She smiled at him. 'Thanks again for the sandwich.'

It was a busy week in the department. Isla wasn't looking forward to being rostered on cubicles on Saturday night; she hated having to pacify the more aggressive drunks, who seemed to take the hospital's zero tolerance policy personally and it made them even more aggressive with the staff.

She knew that having to deal with aggressive patients was par for the course for the shift, but her heart sank when she saw her patient at one o'clock in the morning; the guy had clearly been in a fight. As well as the black eye and lacerations to his face, there was what looked like a bite on his hand; either he'd hit the other man very hard on the mouth, in which case there might well be a tooth embedded within the bite, or the other guy had just bitten him anyway.

Damping down her dismay, she reminded herself that she was a professional.

'How long ago did this happen, Mr Bourne?' she asked.

'I've been waiting here for hours, so you tell me,' he asked, curling his lip.

Great. Drunk and aggressive, and not in the mood for giving information. She suppressed a sigh.

'I thought you lot had to see us within a certain time?'

'We have targets,' she said, 'but we have to treat the more urgent cases first. That's why we explain to patients that they might have to wait, and someone who came in after them might be seen first because their condition is more urgent.'

'Huh.' He swore enough to make his opinions about that very clear.

'I need to examine your hand, Mr Bourne. May I?'

He held his hand out for her to take a look. Thankfully, she couldn't see any foreign bodies in the wound. 'The good news is your hand isn't broken,' she said when she'd finished examining his hand, 'and there doesn't seem to be any joint involvement. As it's a puncture wound, there's more risk of it developing a bacterial infection, so I need to clean it thoroughly before you go. But it won't hurt because I'll do it under local anaesthetic. Can you remember the last time you had a tetanus injection?'

He shrugged and pulled a face. 'Dunno. Maybe when I was at school.'

'OK. I'll play it safe and give you a tetanus shot as well.'

He took one look at the needle before she anaesthetised his hand and was promptly sick.

''S not the drink. 'M not good with needles,' he slurred.

'It's OK,' she said. 'I'll clean it up when I've finished treating you.' She numbed the skin around the bite, irrigated it thoroughly, and had just turned away to get scalpel from the trolley to debride the ragged edges of the wound when she felt her bottom being roughly squeezed.

Unbelievable.

She turned round and glared at him. 'That's not appropriate behaviour, Mr Bourne. Don't do it again. And may I remind you that we have a zero tolerance policy here?'

'Oh, come on, love.' He leered at her. 'Everyone knows what you naughty nurses are like beneath that starched uniform.'

'You're here as my patient,' she said firmly, 'and nothing else. Just to make it very clear, Mr Bourne, I'm not interested, and I don't want you to touch me like that again. Got it?'

'You don't mean that. You know you want—'

But the man broke off his blustering when the curtain suddenly swished open.

Harry stood there, his arms folded and his face grim. 'Problem, Sister McKenna?'

She just nodded towards the patient.

'There's no problem, Doc,' Mr Bourne slurred. 'She's just being a tease, that's all. Playing hard to get.'

Isla had been here before, thanks to Andrew Gillespie. Another drunk, though he'd had more of a civilised veneer. Anger flashed through her; she was half tempted to be totally unprofessional and smack the guy over the head with one of the stainless steel bowls on the trolley.

But then she went ice cold. She'd told Harry some of what had happened with Andrew back on the island. And this case was oh, so similar. Would he think that Isla had been lying to him, and her two accusers were telling the truth after all? That she was a tease and she'd asked for it? Would he, like Stewart, refuse to back her?

'Playing hard to get? Absolutely not,' Harry said, his voice filled with contempt. 'That's complete and utter rubbish.'

Relief flooded through her. It wasn't going to be like before, then. Harry was going to back her. And she was shocked by how much she'd wanted him to believe her.

'We have a zero tolerance policy in this department,' Harry said, 'and that includes both verbal and physical abuse of the staff. Sister McKenna is here to treat you—and if you continue abusing her and touching her without her consent, then you'll leave the hospital without any treatment.'

Mr Bourne clenched his fists. 'And you'll make me, will you?'

'You're drunk,' Harry said. 'You've thrown up everywhere and you're barely capable of standing, so it wouldn't be hard for security to escort you out.'

'Too scared to do it yourself?' Mr Bourne taunted.

'No, too busy tending to people who need help,' Harry said. 'Don't try and play the tough nut, because I'm not interested. I'm here to do a job, not to bolster your ego. By the look of your hand, if we don't treat you, it'll be infected by the morning and it's going to hurt like hell—so it's your choice. You can apologise and let us do our job, or you can leave now and risk a serious infection. Your call.'

'I could sue you.'

'You could try,' Harry said, 'but who is a judge going to believe? Two professional medics, or someone who's too drunk to use his judgement?'

This could escalate very quickly, Isla thought. And if that comment about needles had been the truth rather than bravado, maybe there was a quick way of stopping Mr Bourne in his tracks. 'You'll need antibiotics,' she said, and took the largest syringe from the trolley.

The drunk went white when he saw it.

She quickly put a bowl into his hands. 'If you're going to throw up again, please try and aim for this. If you're sick over your hand, I'll have to clean it out again.'

He retched, but thankfully the bowl remained empty.

'Is there something you'd like to say to Sister McKenna?' Harry asked coolly.

'Sorry,' Mr Bourne mumbled.

'Good. And I don't want another word out of you unless it's to answer a question.' Harry turned to Isla. 'Sister McKenna, I'll stay with you to make sure this man doesn't make a nuisance of himself.'

'Thank you,' she said. 'And now I can get on with my job.' She finished debriding the wound. 'Because this is a bite wound, Mr Bourne,' she said, 'I can't put stitches in it straight away as there's a greater risk of infection. You'll need to go and see your family doctor or come back here in three or four days and we'll stitch it—then.' She put a sterile non-sticky dressing over it and looked at Harry. 'Given that it's a hand wound involving a human bite, should we use prophylactic antibiotics?'

'Good idea,' he said. 'I'll prepare the syringe for you.'

'And a tetanus shot, please,' she said.

'But you're the doctor,' the drunk man mumbled, staring at Harry as he drew up the medication. 'Not supposed to take orders from a nurse.'

'I told you I didn't want another word out of you,' Harry reminded him, 'and for your information Sister McKenna is a senior nurse and is more than qualified to do all of this. I'm only here as a chaperone because you were behaving like an idiot. I suggest you treat the staff here with the respect they deserve.'

'Sharp scratch,' Isla said cheerfully, and administered the tetanus shot.

Mr Bourne whimpered.

'And another,' she said, and gave him the antibiotics. 'I don't expect you'll remember what I say to you right now,' she said, 'so I'll give you a leaflet to back it up. Go to your family doctor or come back here in three or four days to have that wound stitched. If the skin around the wound goes red, swollen and tender, or you get a temperature, then you need to see someone straight away as it means you have an infection. But hopefully the antibiotics should prevent that happening in the first place.' She handed him the leaflet. 'Is anyone waiting for you outside?'

'Nah. The mate who brought me here will've gone home by now or his missis'll be in a snit with him, snotty cow that she is.'

'Then I'll leave you to make your own way out of the department,' she said.

He grimaced, got to his feet and lumbered off.

'I'm pulling rank,' Harry said. 'Staff kitchen, right now.'

Isla shook her head. 'I need to clean this place up first.'

'Then I'll help you,' he said, and did exactly as he promised.

When all the vomit had been cleaned up and the cubicle was fit for use again, he said softly, 'No more arguments. Staff kitchen.'

She nodded and went with him in silence.

He put the kettle on. 'I'm making you some hot, sweet tea. Are you all right?' he asked.

'Thanks, but I really don't need tea. I'm fine.'

'Sure? Apart from the fact that his behaviour was totally unacceptable, that must've brought back—'

'I'm fine,' she cut in, not wanting to hear the rest of it. Memories. Yeah. It had brought them back. But she wasn't going to let it throw her. 'And thank you for coming to the rescue.'

'Which any of us would do if any colleague was dealing with a difficult patient. You don't have to put up with behaviour like that.'

'Not just that,' she said softly, 'you believed me. You backed me.'

He smiled. 'Isla, apart from the fact that I know you well enough to be absolutely sure you'd never do anything unprofessional or encourage patients to grope you, the guy stank of stale booze and vomit—not exactly female fantasy material, was he?'

'I guess.'

Harry grimaced. 'And his attitude to women stank even more.'

She nodded. 'Just a bit.'

'Are you really sure you're OK?' he asked.

'Yes. But thank you for asking.'

He patted her shoulder. 'Any time.'

Heat zinged through her at his touch; and how inappropriate was that? Especially given that he'd just had to rescue her, and he'd said that she would never do anything unprofessional.

She could do with a cold shower.

Or an injection of common sense.

'I really don't need any tea, and it's heaving out there. We'd better get back to work. See you later,' she said. And she walked away before she said something needy or stupid. Harry Gardiner had made it very clear that he was off limits, and she'd promised herself she wouldn't get involved with anyone again.

And that was non-negotiable.

CHAPTER EIGHT

HARRY WAS WAITING for Isla when she came off duty after the handover.

'I'm seeing you home,' he said.

'Thank you, but there's no need,' she said.

'Actually, there is. You had a rotten shift.' He paused. 'And I'd just feel a bit happier if I saw you home and made you a bacon sandwich.'

'Tough. I don't have any bacon.'

'Then we'll do plan B,' he said. 'I know a very nice café not far from here where they do the best bacon sandwiches ever. And a bacon sandwich with a mug of tea is the best answer to a rubbish shift.'

'You're not going to give up, are you?' she asked.

He smiled. 'Nope.'

'A bacon sandwich would be nice,' she admitted, 'but I'm buying. To say thanks for rescuing me earlier.'

'Am I allowed to buy us a mug of tea, then?'

'I guess so.' She smiled at him.

They walked to the café together, where they ordered bacon sandwiches and a large pot of tea with two mugs.

'Thanks again for rescuing me,' she said.

'I'd do the same for any colleague who was being hassled by a patient,' he said.

'I don't mean just that—we'd all step in—but the fact that you believed me.'

'Of course I did,' he said softly. 'But that's why I wanted to have breakfast with you this morning. Because I don't want the behaviour of a stupid, thoughtless patient ripping open some fairly recent scars.'

'It did, a bit,' she admitted. 'It made me remember the look on Andrew's face when I turned him down, and then how my life suddenly went into quicksand mode.' And it was still her biggest fear: that someone would make another false accusation against her, that even though she was exonerated people would still think she'd done something wrong, and she'd have to pick up the wreckage of her life all over again.

Harry reached across the table and squeezed her hand. 'I know you had a tough time on the island, but that's not going to be repeated here,' he reassured her. 'Apart from the fact that every single person in our department knows you're totally professional, the guy was drunk and obnoxious.' He paused. 'There's more to it than that, isn't there?'

She sighed, suddenly too tired to hold it in any more. 'I was so scared you wouldn't back me.'

'Of course I'd back you! You're my colleague and my friend.' He frowned, as if remembering something. 'But you said your ex didn't back you when his step-father lied about you. Why not?'

She sighed. 'I guess for him there were only two possibilities. One was that I was a faithless liar who was trying to cheat on him with his stepfather and was lying even more about it to save my own skin when I'd been found out. The other was that I was telling the truth, and the man who'd brought him up since he was two and treated him as if Stewart was his biological son rather than his adopted son was capable of cheating on Stewart's mother.'

'But surely he knew you well enough to know that you'd never cheat on him—that you weren't the liar?'

'That's what I'd hoped, but I was wrong,' she said sadly. 'I suppose he went for the lesser of two evils. For him, it was better to think that he'd made a mistake and picked the wrong person than to think that his mother had made a bad choice and could end up being hurt. Bridie had already had enough unhappiness in her life, with Stewart's dad being killed at sea when Stewart was only six months old. Andrew had made everything all right again. Stewart needed to believe that it was still going to be all right.'

'Even though that meant not believing you?'

'As I said, it was the lesser of two evils.' She bit her lip. 'I had hoped that, once he'd got over the shock, he'd see I was telling the truth and we'd work it out. But it was obvious he didn't want to see it. Then again, even if he had seen it, I'm not sure I would ever have managed to get past the feelings of being betrayed. How could I spend the rest of my life with someone who didn't believe me? What would happen the next time we had a difference of opinion—would he take my part, or would he assume that I was lying?' She looked away. 'So I broke it off.'

'Did Stewart know that Andrew had a drink problem?'

'I don't know. I guess Andrew could be very plausible and, if Bridie was colluding with him to keep the situation from everyone...' She sighed. 'Probably not.

'And you didn't tell Stewart the truth?'

'How could I? Breaching patient confidentiality is totally unprofessional—and doing that would've meant that Andrew's accusations were true, at least in part. Plus Bridie and Andrew could've denied that he had a drink problem. And that in turn would make Stewart and everyone else think that either I was lying to save myself, or that I was perfectly happy to gossip about something that a patient had told me in strictest confidence.'

'So whatever you did, you couldn't fix the situation—someone would end up being hurt. That's a horrible situation to be in.'

'It wasn't much fun at the time,' she said wryly. 'At least my family and close friends believed me.'

'But the gossip still drove you away from the island?'

'I was going to tough it out. But every day I had to face the same kind of speculation. Every day I had patients who didn't want to see me because they'd lost their trust in me. Every day I found I couldn't do my job properly because all the lies and the gossip were getting in the way. After three months of it, I wasn't sleeping or eating properly because I was so miserable. Which is when my parents, my brother and my sister sat me down, told me they loved me and they believed in me. They said basically I could stay on the island and let my soul wither away a little more every day, or I could leave and retrain and recapture the joy in what I did for a living.'

'And that's why you chose to work in the emergency department? Because you'd still be helping people, but they wouldn't know you and you wouldn't know them, and there wouldn't be any cradle-to-the-grave stuff?'

'Which is ironically why I became a nurse practitioner in the first place,' she said. 'But yes. And I like my job in the emergency department. I do.'

'But you miss your family.'

'I'm a big girl. I'll cope. And,' she added sadly, 'you might want to have it all, but in the end I guess you have to make some sacrifices and learn to compromise. That's life.'

'I guess,' he said. 'But in your shoes I'd be really angry about it.'

'I was,' she said, 'but I'm pretty much over the anger now. I'm just sad it worked out that way.'

'And then some idiot who's drunk out of their mind starts behaving in the same way towards you.'

'There is that,' she admitted.

'And because the guy had beer goggles on, he clearly assumed everyone else did, too.'

'Beer goggles?' She wasn't with him.

'When you've drunk enough beer to think that who- ever you see is more attractive than they are. Except in this case he was right about you and wrong about him- self,' Harry explained.

'Even sober and not covered in his own vomit, he wouldn't have been my type,' Isla said with a grimace.

'That's a cue to ask what your type is,' Harry said, 'except I wouldn't quite dare.'

'And I wouldn't answer,' Isla said crisply. Because she wouldn't dare tell Harry Gardiner that he was ex- actly her type. Not just because he was easy on the eyes, but because he was a genuinely nice guy and she liked the way he treated other people. She just wished he'd be a bit kinder to himself.

He laughed. 'And that's my cue to top up our mugs of tea.' He released her hand. 'Seriously, though, I was worried about you. We all have things in our career that make us flinch when we come across a similar case later on.' He always hated dealing with toddler falls. Especially serious ones. Not that he planned to tell Isla about that. Instead, he said, 'For me, it's a ruptured abdominal aortic aneurysm.'

'You lost the patient?' she asked.

'Yup. On my very first day in the emergency department. It was very nearly my last,' Harry said. 'I mean, I know statistically we lose more patients in our department than any other, simply because of the nature of the job. But I wasn't prepared to lose someone on my first day. She was the same age as my grandmother—in fact, she even looked like my grandmother. Masses of fluffy grey curls, carrying a little bit too much weight. She came in with back pain.' He blew out a breath. 'She was sweating, tachycardic and hypotensive. I thought it might be a ruptured abdominal aortic aneurysm, but she didn't have any mottled skin on her lower body and, because she was overweight, when I examined her I couldn't be sure that there was a pulsatile abdominal mass. I went to see my special reg to ask for a second opinion and some advice on what I should do next, but by the time we got back to my patient she'd collapsed and the nurse was calling for the crash team. And then we lost her. I went home after my shift and cried my eyes out, then I rang my grandmother and begged her to get herself checked out properly and go on a diet.'

'Oh, Harry.' Her sympathy showed in her expression, too.

'Going in to work the next day was awful. How did I know I wouldn't kill off any more patients?' He shrugged. 'I seriously thought about giving up medicine.'

'Harry, you didn't kill your patient. You were young and inexperienced, and you did the right thing—you knew you were in over your head and you went to get help rather than blundering on.'

'I still should've thought harder about what I was doing. I should've had a much lower threshold of suspicion and got the portable ultrasound.'

'Even then, you probably couldn't have saved her,' Isla pointed out. 'You know as well as I do that a ruptured aortic aneurysm has a really high mortality rate and a lot of patients don't even make it to hospital.'

'I knew that with my head,' Harry said, 'but my heart told me otherwise.'

'But you got through your next shift?'

'Yes. Actually, the senior sister on the ward was a real sweetheart. She gave me a hug when I came in, told me that I'd been unlucky to have such a bad first day in the department, and that I was to put it out of my head. And then she said I was rostered in Resus.' He blew out a breath. 'I was terrified that I'd kill another patient. But I saved someone. A toddler who'd had a severe allergic reaction to eggs. The paramedics had already given her adrenaline, but she got worse on the way to the emergency department and I had to intubate her and stabilise her. And that's when I realised what our job was all about. You do your very best to save someone. Sometimes you can't, and some patients are very difficult to help—but as long as you know you've done your very best then that's enough.'

That was true. But he hadn't done his best with Tasha, had he? He'd left the stair gate open and assumed she wouldn't follow him. And he wasn't going to put himself back in a situation where so much would be at risk—not ever, ever again.

When they'd finished their breakfast, Harry insisted on walking Isla home.

She paused at her front door. 'I guess that bacon

sandwich revived me a bit. Would you like to come in for a coffee?'

Part of Harry wanted to back away. After all, he'd told Isla some pretty personal stuff in the café. Plus he had a nasty feeling that this thing between them was drawing nearer and nearer towards a proper relationship, the one thing he'd always sworn to avoid—and actually going in to her flat was another step towards that.

But his mouth clearly wasn't working in sync with his brain, because he found himself saying, 'Thanks, I'd like that.'

'Come and sit down and I'll put the kettle on. Decaf?'

'If I'm to get any sleep this morning, then yes please,' he said with a smile.

She ushered him into her living room and bustled off to the kitchen. Her flat was neat and tidy, just as he'd expected.

The mantelpiece in her living room was full of framed photographs. There was one of Isla on her graduation day with two people who were obviously her parents, as he could see the resemblance to both of them; a couple of weddings that he guessed were her older sister and her brother, given that Isla was the bridesmaid and again he could see a resemblance; and others which were obviously christening photographs.

And the look of sheer love on her face as she was holding the babies told him everything: Isla was the sort who wanted to settle down and have a family. Right now she was still getting over the way her ex had let her down, but Harry thought that these photos were a warning sign that he really shouldn't start anything with her because they wanted completely different things out of life. Things that weren't compatible.

They'd talked about compromising, but this was one

area where he just couldn't compromise. He didn't want to be responsible for a child. Given his genes, if he tried to make a go of it with Isla and actually got married, there was a fair chance they'd end up divorced—and if they'd had a child, that would mean shattering another life. He didn't want to put a child through the kind of hurt he'd been through when he was smaller. And he didn't want to hurt Isla, either.

So he needed to back off.

Right now.

Which was exactly what he'd been doing since the wedding…until that drunk had groped Isla and claimed that she'd started it. Harry really couldn't have left her to deal with that on her own, especially because he knew it had happened to her before. And he'd been thinking with his heart rather than his head when he'd taken her for breakfast and seen her safely back here.

He was just about to stand up, go to the kitchen and make some excuse to leave when Isla came through with two mugs of coffee and a tin of biscuits, which she put down on the small coffee table in the centre of the room.

Too late.

He'd have to stay long enough to drink his coffee, or it'd be rude and he'd upset her. And he wanted to let her down *gently*.

Small talk. That was what would save the situation. 'Nice flat,' he said.

'I like it,' she said. 'It's light and airy, and although it's a bit on the small side it's convenient for work.'

He managed to keep the small talk going for just long enough to let him gulp down his coffee. Then he yawned and said, 'I really ought to leave and let you get some sleep. I need some myself or I'll be nodding off all through my shift tonight.'

'I know what you mean,' she said with a smile. 'See you later. And thanks again.'

'No problem,' he said.

And when he left her flat, he gave himself a pep talk all the way home. Back off. Keep your distance. And stop wanting something you definitely can't have.

CHAPTER NINE

HARRY WAS DISTANT with Isla that night at work; she would've put it down to them both being busy, but he didn't ask her to eat with him or have coffee together at their break.

They didn't see each other while they were off duty on Monday and Tuesday, but he was distant with her for the next couple shifts they worked together.

Something had obviously happened, but Isla couldn't work out what she'd said or done to upset him. He'd been so lovely with her when the drunk had upset her; he'd backed her on the ward, and then he'd made her feel safe and secure by having breakfast with her and walking her home. But, now she thought about it, he'd started going distant on her when she'd made him a mug of coffee, back at her flat.

She really needed to clear the air and find out what she'd done so she didn't repeat it. She valued him as a friend and a colleague and she didn't want anything spoiling that.

Was it the shadow of Andrew Gillespie? Harry had said he believed her, but was he having second thoughts now, the way so many people on the island had back then?

At the end of their shift on Friday, Isla waited to

catch Harry. 'Hey. I was thinking, maybe we could go for a drink somewhere.'

'Sorry, I can't.' He gave her an apologetic smile. 'I'm supposed to be playing squash. League match.'

Why did that feel like a made-up excuse? she wondered. 'Harry, I think we need to talk,' she said quietly. 'I've obviously done something to upset you and I'd like to clear the air. Can we meet after your squash game, maybe?'

He didn't look her in the eye and his tone was a little too breezy for her liking when he said, 'You haven't upset me at all.'

'So why have you been keeping as much distance as you can between us, this last week?' she asked.

Harry looked away. 'Have I?'

She sighed. He still couldn't look her in the eye? Oh, this was bad. 'Yes, and we both know it. I thought we were friends.'

'We are.'

'So what's happening?' she asked.

He shrugged. 'I've no idea what you mean.'

'Then come round for a drink when you've finished your squash match.'

'Sorry, I can't. We're all going out for a pizza afterwards.'

She gave up. 'OK, have it your way. Clearly I'm making a massive fuss over nothing. Enjoy your squash match.'

Harry watched her walk away, feeling guilty. After all, she was right: he had been lying to her. He wasn't playing squash at all this evening, much less going out for a meal afterwards with friends.

He lasted another two hours before the guilt got the better of him and he texted her. Isla, are you at home?

It was a while before she replied. Why? I thought you were playing squash. League match, you said.

He squirmed, practically hearing the tones of Scottish disdain and knowing he deserved it. But she had been right earlier: they did need to clear the air. Is that offer of a drink still open?

For a nasty five minutes, he thought she was going to say no. And he'd deserve that, too.

Then his phone pinged. Sure.

Relief flooded through him. See you in an hour?

He stopped off at the supermarket and bought an armful of the nicest flowers he could find, a mix of sweet-smelling white and lilac stocks. By the time he stood on her doorstep after ringing the bell, he felt ridiculously nervous.

'For you,' he said, thrusting the flowers at her when she opened the door.

'Thank you—that's very kind of you. But what's the occasion?' she asked.

She deserved the truth. 'No occasion. It's guilt and an apology,' he said.

She looked puzzled. 'I'm not with you, but come in. Do you prefer red or white wine?'

'Whatever you've got open.'

'There's a bottle of pinot grigio in the fridge. Perhaps you'd like to open it for me while I put these gorgeous flowers in water,' she suggested. 'The glasses are in the cupboard above the kettle.'

He found the glasses and the wine, opened the bottle, and poured them both a drink while she arranged the flowers in a vase, then put the bottle back in the fridge.

She ushered him through to the living room and he put the glasses down on the coffee table.

'So what's all this about, Harry?'

'You're right,' he said, 'about all of it. I *have* been avoiding you all week.'

'Why?'

He took a deep breath. 'Because we're supposed to be friends.'

She frowned. 'I thought we were.'

'We are.'

'Then...' Her frown deepened. 'Harry, you're not making any sense at all.'

'I know,' he said miserably. 'You were supposed to be safe.'

'And I'm not?'

'Far from it,' he said.

'Why?'

He sighed. 'Because I kissed you in Cornwall. Every time I see you, I want to do it again. And I know I'm rubbish at relationships and you've been hurt before, so the only thing I could do was stay out of your way,' he finished. 'Give me a few more days to get my head straight, and then hopefully I can look at you again without wanting to...' His mouth went dry as his imagination supplied the rest of it. Without wanting to pick her up, carry her to bed, and make love with her until they both saw stars.

'Without wanting to what, Harry?' she persisted.

'It doesn't matter,' he said, 'and I'm not going to make a nuisance of myself. But I thought you deserved an explanation and an apology.'

'Thank you.' She paused. 'But just supposing,' she asked softly, 'I've been thinking about Cornwall, too?'

'Then you're as crazy as I am,' he said, equally softly,

'because we can't do this. You've been badly hurt, and the last thing you need is to get mixed up with someone like me.'

'And how would you define someone like you?'

'You know what they call me at the hospital.' He shrugged. 'Harry the Heartbreaker. The man who won't date you more than three or four times because he doesn't do commitment.'

'That isn't the man I see,' she said. 'The man I see is kind, decent and caring. He notices the little things and he does his best to make everything right without making a huge song and dance about it all.'

'They're right about one thing. I don't do commitment,' he repeated. 'Come on, Isla. You've met my family.'

'And they're lovely.'

'They're lovely,' he agreed, 'but they're no good at commitment. My parents have ten marriages between them, including the one to each other. *Ten*. So it's in my genes to make a mess of things.'

'Or maybe,' she said, 'you could learn from your parents' mistakes.'

'I already have,' he said, 'and for me that means not getting involved in a serious relationship.' He looked at the glass of wine he hadn't even touched. 'I'd better go.'

'Why?'

'You know why, Isla. Because I don't want to give in to temptation and do something that'll hurt us both.'

'You curled around me in your sleep,' she said.

Yeah. He knew. He'd woken with her in his arms, all warm and soft and sweet. It had taken every single bit of his strength to climb out of that bed instead of waking her with a kiss. 'So?' he asked, trying his best to drawl the word and sound totally uninterested.

'So,' she said, 'maybe I woke before you did and I didn't move away.'

'Seriously?' That had never occurred to him. And now she'd said it, he could hardly breathe.

'Seriously,' she said. 'And maybe I've been thinking about it every single morning since when I've woken up. And maybe the bed's felt way too big.'

He went very still. 'Are you saying…?' He couldn't get the words out. Couldn't think straight. Was this really possible? Could they…?

'Maybe,' she said, 'I've been remembering how it felt when you kissed me.' She paused. 'And maybe I'd like you to do that again.'

'You'd actually risk a relationship with me?' he asked, wanting to make it clear.

'My head says no, that I should be sensible.'

'Fair enough.' He agreed with her completely.

'But there's another bit of me that thinks, maybe I shouldn't let what happened with Stewart wreck the rest of my life. Maybe it's time I was brave and took the risk.'

He could hardly breathe. She was choosing him? 'With me? But I'm about as high-risk as you could get.'

'I like you, Harry,' she said softly, 'and I think you like me, too. And I don't mean just as friends.'

'But what if it all goes wrong?' he asked. 'I can't promise you that this is going to work out. I can't promise you for ever.'

'I'm not expecting for ever. We're both adults. If it doesn't work out, then we'll be sensible about it and put our patients and the team first at work, just as we do now,' she said. 'But consider this, Harry—what if it goes right?'

His mouth went dry at the thought.

Risking a relationship with Isla McKenna.

Dating her.

Kissing her.

Making love with her.

He knew she'd been hurt. But if she was prepared to take the risk, then he'd have to step up to the plate and be brave, too.

'We need to set some ground rules,' he said.

She nodded. 'Ground rules sound fine to me.'

'Firstly, this is between you and me—as far as work is concerned, we're just colleagues.'

'That's sensible,' she said. 'Agreed.'

'Secondly, we're honest with each other—if we're uncomfortable with anything, then we say so.'

'Again, I don't have a problem with that.'

'Thirdly...' He couldn't think of anything else because his brain had turned to mush.

'Thirdly,' she said softly, 'why don't you just shut up and kiss me, Harry?'

Something he'd been aching to do ever since Cornwall—ever since he'd first found out how sweet and soft her mouth was.

'That,' he said, 'is the best idea I've heard all day.' He took her hand and drew it to his lips.

He could feel the shiver run through her as he kissed the back of each finger in turn, keeping his gaze firmly fixed on hers. Yeah. Me, too, he thought. He ached with wanting her. He turned her hand over and brushed his mouth against her wrist, and she shivered again. Still keeping eye contact, he found her pulse point with his lips; he could feel it beating strong and hard.

And then he drew her into his arms and kissed her properly.

And it felt as if the sun had just come out and made everything shimmery and sparkling.

He ended up sitting on her sofa, with Isla on his lap, her head pillowed against his shoulder and their arms wrapped round each other.

'OK?' he asked softly.

'Very OK,' she said, stroked his face.

'I'm on an early shift tomorrow. You?'

'Same,' she said.

'Are you busy afterwards? Or can I see you?'

'I'm not busy. I'd like to see you,' she said.

'Dinner,' he said. 'And dress up. Because we're actually going to go on a proper date.'

She laughed. 'Why does that make me feel as if I'm eighteen years old again?'

'Me, too. Which is crazy.' He kissed her lightly. 'Right now I want to do all kinds of things, but I'm going to keep myself in check because I think we need to take this slowly. Get used to the idea.' He stole another kiss. 'I don't date. But for you I'm going to try to change. I don't know if I can,' he warned, 'but I'm going to try. That's the best I can promise.'

'And that's enough for me,' she said.

'Hmm.' He kissed her again. 'I'll see you at work tomorrow. And then I'll meet you here at seven.'

'Sounds perfect.' She wriggled off his lap, letting him stand up, then walked him to the door and stole a kiss. 'Good night, Harry. Sweet dreams.'

'They will be,' he said softly. 'You, too.'

Isla managed to concentrate on her patients for the whole of Saturday—it helped that she and Harry were rostered on different sections of the departments and their breaks didn't coincide—but anticipation prickled through her once she was back at her flat.

A proper date.

And he wanted her to dress up.

So it ought to be a little black dress.

She dug out her favourite dress from her wardrobe, and took time with her hair and make-up. Her efforts were rewarded when she opened the door to Harry and his eyes widened.

'You look stunning,' he said.

'Thank you. And so do you.' She'd seen him wearing a suit before, but she was so used to seeing him in a white coat at work that she'd forgotten how sexy he looked in formal dress.

He reached out to twirl the end of her hair round one forefinger. 'Your hair is glorious,' he said, his voice catching.

'Thank you.' She smiled. 'It gets in the way at work. That's why I wear it pinned back.'

'I like it both ways—when you're being a starchy matron and when you're being a siren.'

She laughed. 'I'm not a matron—and I am so not starchy.'

'No, but you don't put up with any nonsense. Which is a good thing.'

'And I'm not a siren.'

'I beg to differ,' he said. 'You're the walking definition of sexy.'

She laughed again. 'Flatterer.'

'Nope. Statement of fact. And I can't wait to take you to dinner, Ms McKenna.' He glanced at her high heels. 'Can you walk in those?'

She rolled her eyes. 'I'm a nurse. I walk miles every day.'

'In flats.'

She took pity on him. 'Yes.'

'Good. Because it's a nice evening and I wanted to stroll hand in hand with you.'

'Works for me,' she said with a smile, and locked the door behind her.

They walked hand in hand to the tube station. Harry didn't say where they were going, but she also noted that he didn't have to stop and look up directions. Was it because he usually took his dates to wherever he'd booked a table, or did he just know London really well?

'This might be a bit cheesy,' he warned when they got to the West End. 'I've never been to this place before, but it's always on the list of the most romantic restaurants in London and the reviews are good. And I wanted to take you somewhere a bit special for our first date.'

So there she had her answers: he knew London well, and he'd never taken anyone else to this particular restaurant. Warmth spread through her and she found herself relaxing. And she fell in love with the restaurant on sight: the ceiling had been made into a canopy covered in white blossom and fairy lights, there were tealight candles on the tables casting a soft glow, the seats were all covered in red velvet, and the tablecloths were pure white damask.

'I can see exactly why this place tops the list,' she said. 'It's lovely.'

And the menu was equally good; she couldn't resist the hand-dived Scottish scallops, then corn-fed spring chicken with potato gnocchi, green beans and baby carrots. Harry joined her; it tasted every bit as good as it sounded, and he insisted on sharing a bottle of champagne.

'This is fabulous,' she said, 'but remember we're going halves.'

'Absolutely not,' he told her, his dark eyes sincere.

'This is our first official date, so I am most definitely picking up the bill, but...'

Anticipation tightened in her stomach. Was he saying there were strings attached to dinner?

'If you want to buy me lunch tomorrow, I won't be offended,' he finished. 'Or just a chocolate brownie and some coffee in the hospital canteen, if you're working.'

'I'm off duty tomorrow. If you are, too, then it's a date for lunch,' she said.

'And a walk first,' he said. 'There's something I want to show you.'

'What?' she asked, intrigued.

'If I tell you now, it won't be a surprise tomorrow,' he said, tapping his nose and laughing.

She liked this side of Harry—the fun, charming, relaxed man.

And she enjoyed sharing a pudding with him, even if he did eat more of the chocolate mille-feuille than she did.

'I've had a really lovely evening,' she said when he walked her back to her front door. 'Thank you.'

'My pleasure.'

'Do you want to come in?'

He stole a kiss. 'Yes. But I'm not going to. We're going to take this slowly.'

So neither of them would get afraid and back away? 'Works for me,' she said softly, and kissed him goodnight. 'I'll see you tomorrow.'

CHAPTER TEN

ON SUNDAY MORNING Harry woke, smiling, because he knew he was seeing Isla. He texted her to let her know he was on the way to meet her.

'So where are we going?' she asked when they left her flat.

'I thought we'd have a wander through the city.'

She smiled. 'Sounds good.'

When they emerged from the Tube station, Isla looked around and said, 'Isn't that Big Ben? So we're doing the touristy places?'

'Not especially,' he said, 'though if you want me to take a picture of you with Big Ben or the statue of Boudicca in the background, we can go up to the bridge.'

'No, I'm happy to go wherever you had in mind.'

He took her along the south bank, then groaned when they stopped. 'Sorry, I should've checked the tides.'

'Tides?' she asked.

'The Thames is a tidal river, so sometimes you see the beach just here and I thought you might like that. I guess it's the nearest you'll get to the sea in London.'

'Maybe another time,' she said.

They walked over the Millennium Bridge to St Paul's; then Harry led her through little side streets and a park to a part of Clerkenwell that was full of upscale clothes shops, jewellers, art shops and cafés.

'I thought we could have lunch here,' he said.

'This is lovely.' Most of the cafés had tables outside with umbrellas to shield their patrons from the sun; it made the place feel almost Mediterranean. 'Do you recommend anywhere in particular?' she asked.

'I haven't been here before,' Harry admitted. 'So pick one that takes your fancy.'

They browsed the menus on the boards outside; Isla chose a café with a French influence and they ordered a croque monsieur with freshly squeezed orange juice, then shared a brownie.

'Good choice,' Harry said. 'The food's great here.'

'And it's really nice exploring London with someone who actually knows the place,' Isla said.

'I've lived in London since I was eighteen. Obviously I don't know every single street, but I know a few nice out-of-the-way places,' he said, 'and it's always good to find somewhere new. I saw a write-up of this area in a magazine.' And he couldn't think of anyone he wanted to share this with more.

Funny, now he'd actually made the decision to start a proper relationship, it felt easy. Natural. The wariness he usually felt when dating someone had gone.

Or maybe it was because he'd found the right person.

Not that he was going to pressure Isla by telling her that. It was way too soon even to be thinking about it. They'd keep this low-key and fun, and see where it took them both.

At work, Harry and Isla managed to be professional with each other and treated each other strictly as colleagues. They were careful never to leave the hospital together unless it was as part of a group. Harry had persuaded Isla to open up a little more and come to one of the team nights out. He noticed that she thoroughly enjoyed the ten pin bowling, and went pink when one of the others told her they were all glad she'd come along because it was nice to get to know her outside work.

Later that evening, she told him, 'I'm glad you made me go. I really feel part of the team now.'

'Good. Welcome to London,' he said, and kissed her.

He saw Isla most days after work; one of them would cook, or they'd grab a takeaway, or if they'd gone into the city they'd find some nice little bistro. He felt they were getting closer, more and more in tune; the more he got to know her, the more he discovered they had in common. He actually felt in tune with her. There wasn't that antsy feeling that she'd expect more than he could give and it would all go spectacularly wrong. With her, he could relax and be himself—something he'd never experienced before. At the end of the evening it was getting harder to kiss her goodbye on her doorstep.

And it was harder to keep everything to himself at work, too. Whenever he saw Isla, it made him feel as if the sun had just come out. He found himself making excuses just so that their paths would cross in the department. And surely someone at the hospital would notice that he smiled more when she was around and start asking questions?

One Wednesday night when he'd walked her home after the cinema, she said to him, 'How brave are you feeling?'

'Why?' he asked.

'As we've made it way past your proverbial fourth

date,' she said, 'I thought maybe we could, um, run a repeat of a certain garden in Cornwall. Except it won't be in a garden and we're not going to be interrupted. And this time we don't have to stop and be sensible.'

Heat rose through him. 'Are you saying…?'

'Yes.' She lifted her chin. 'I'm ready.'

The heat turned up a notch. 'Me, too,' he said softly. 'You have no idea how much I want you.'

'I think, Dr Gardiner, that might be mutual.' And the huskiness in her tone told him that she meant it.

Once she'd closed the front door behind them, he pulled her into his arms and kissed her. He nibbled her lower lip until she opened her mouth, letting him deepen the kiss. It was intoxicating; but it still wasn't enough. He needed the ultimate closeness.

He broke the kiss, whispering her name, and drew a trail of open-mouthed kisses all the way down her throat. She tipped her head back and gave a breathy little moan.

So she was as turned on as he was? Good—though he had no intention of stopping yet.

The thin strap of her top was no obstacle to him. He nuzzled along her shoulder, then along the line of her collarbones. 'I want you so much, Isla,' he whispered. 'Your skin's so soft, and I want to touch you. See you.'

'Do it,' she said, her voice shaky.

'Not here.' He picked her up.

'Troglodyte,' she teased.

'Yeah.' He stole another kiss. 'So where am I going?'

'Harry, my flat has four rooms and you've seen three of them. I hardly think you need directions or a map.'

He laughed. 'Sister McKenna, with her scathing Scottish common sense.' He carried her across the hallway to the one doorway he hadn't walked through. 'Are you sure about this, Isla?' he asked.

'Very sure.' She paused. 'Though do you have protection?'

'Yes.' He stole a kiss. 'And that's not because I'm taking you for granted or because I sleep around.'

'I know. You're being practical.'

'Exactly.' He wanted to make love with her but he didn't want to make a baby with her. He didn't want children. Ever. He'd already had that responsibility way too young in his life, and it had gone badly wrong. He wanted to keep life simple. *Safe*. None of that gut-wrenching fear.

He pushed the thoughts away, opened the door while balancing Isla in his arms, carried her over to the bed and then set her on her feet again. He let her slide down his body so she could feel how much she turned him on.

'Well, now, Dr Gardiner,' she said, but her voice was all breathy and her face was all pink and her eyes were all wide.

'Well, now, Sister McKenna,' he said, and his voice was as husky as hers. 'What next?'

'Your move,' she said.

'Good.' He slid his fingers under the hem of her top, stroked along the flat planes of her abdomen. 'May I?' he asked softly.

She nodded, and let him peel the soft jersey material over her head.

She was wearing a strapless bra; he traced the edges of the material with his fingertips, then slid one hand behind her back, stroked along her spine and unhooked her bra.

'You're beautiful,' he whispered as the garment fell to the floor.

Colour heated her face. 'And I feel very overdressed.'

'Your move,' he said.

She was almost shy in the way she undid his shirt and slid the soft cotton off his shoulders. 'Very nice pectorals, Dr Gardiner.' She smiled and slid her hands across his chest, then down over his abdomen. 'And that's a proper six-pack.'

'So we're touching as well as looking now, are we?' He cupped her breasts and rubbed the pad of his thumbs across her hardening nipples.

She shivered. 'Oh, yes, we're touching.'

'Touching isn't enough. I want to taste you, Isla. Explore you.' He dropped to his knees and took one nipple into his mouth. She slid her hands into his hair; he could feel the slight tremor in her hands as he teased her with his lips and his tongue.

She followed his lead, dropping to her knees and undoing the button of his jeans.

He did the same with hers, then leaned his forehead against her bare shoulder and chuckled.

'What's so funny?' she asked.

'We didn't think this through.' He gestured to their positions. 'Right now I'll be able to pull your jeans down as far as your knees, and that's about it.'

She looked at him. 'And we're on the floor, when there's a nice soft bed right next to us. How old are we, sixteen?'

He stole a kiss. 'You make me feel like a teenager. In a good way, though; there's none of the angst and fear that the first time's going to be a disaster instead of perfect.' He nibbled her earlobe. 'Because we're both old enough to know it's not going to be perfect or a disaster.'

'What is it going to be, then?' she asked.

'An exploration. Discovering what each other likes. Where and how we like to be touched. Kissed.' He punctuated his words with kisses, then got to his feet, took her hands and drew her to her feet beside him.

'Starting here,' he said, and finished undoing her jeans. He stooped to slide the denim down over her curves and helped her step out of them. 'Your move, I think.'

She did the same with him, then grinned. 'You're wearing odd socks.'

'It's a London thing. A trend. The ultimate in sophistication,' he said.

She laughed. 'Is it, hell.'

'Busted.' He kissed her. 'I wasn't paying attention last time I did my laundry. I was thinking of you. Fantasising.'

'Oh, yes?'

'Definitely yes.'

He got rid of the rest of their clothes, pushed the duvet to one side, then picked her up and laid her against the pillows. 'You look like a mermaid,' he said, kneeling down beside her.

'A mermaid?'

'With that glorious hair spread out like that—definitely a mermaid. Or maybe a Victorian model for some super-sultry goddess,' he mused.

'Compliment accepted.' She reached up to stroke his face. 'And you're as beautiful as a Michelangelo statue.'

'Why, thank you.' He leaned forward to steal a kiss. 'And your skin's like alabaster, except you're warm and you smell of peaches.'

He nuzzled his way down her sternum, then paid attention to the soft underside of her breasts. 'You're incredibly lovely,' he said.

'Just like you fantasised when you were doing your laundry?'

'Way better,' he said. He rocked back on his haunches. 'I want to explore you,' he said softly.

Colour bloomed again in her cheeks. 'I'm all yours.'

He started at the hollows of her anklebones, stroking and kissing his way up to the back of her knees. Her breathing had grown shallow by the time he parted her thighs, and she slid her hands into his hair to urge him on. She shivered when he drew his tongue along her sex, dragged in a breathy moan when he did it again, and when he started teasing her clitoris he heard her murmured 'oh' of pleasure.

Harry was really looking forward to watching Isla fall apart under his touch. He loved the idea that he could turn all that sharp common sense to mush, just for a little while.

Her body tensed, and he felt the moment that her climax hit.

'Harry,' she whispered, and he shifted up the bed so he could hold her tightly.

'OK?' he asked when she'd stopped shaking.

'Very OK—I wasn't expecting that,' she said. 'I thought you said this wasn't going to be perfect?'

He smiled and stroked her face. 'I'm not finished yet, not by a long way.'

'No—I think it's my turn to make you fall apart,' she said. Her hands were warm and sure as she explored him.

Harry loved the way she made him feel, the way his blood heated with desire as she stroked and caressed him. Then she dipped her head so that glorious hair brushed against his skin, and desire surged through him.

'Isla,' he said softly, 'I love what you're doing to me and you feel like heaven—but right now I really, *really* need to be inside you.'

'Your wish is my command,' she teased. 'Condom?'

'In my wallet—in my jeans pocket.'

She climbed off the bed, fished his wallet out of his jeans and threw it to him. He caught it and took out the condom. 'Are you really sure about this?'

'Really sure,' she said, her voice husky, and took the little foil packet from him. She opened it, rolled it over his shaft and leaned over him to kiss him. 'Do you have any idea how sexy you look, lying there on my bed?'

'Not as sexy as you'll look with your hair spread over the pillow like a mermaid,' he replied.

'Hmm, so the man has a thing about mermaids?'

He drew her down to him, shifted so that she was lying beneath him and knelt between her thighs. 'Yeah,' he said, and eased into her.

It was very far from the first time that he'd ever made love, but it was the first time that Harry had ever felt this kind of completeness, this kind of bond.

Which made Isla McKenna dangerous to his peace of mind.

But she drew him so much that he couldn't resist her. Didn't want to resist her.

She held him tightly as his climax burst through him.

CHAPTER ELEVEN

WHEN HARRY HAD floated back to earth, he moved carefully. 'Help yourself to anything you need in the bathroom,' Isla said. 'The linen cupboard's in there with fresh towels.'

'Thanks.'

Isla lay curled in bed while Harry was in the bathroom, feeling warm and comfortable and that all was right with the world. She didn't bother getting up and dressing; Harry hadn't taken his clothes with him to the bathroom, and she was pretty sure that he'd come back to bed with her. Like Cornwall all over again, except this time they wouldn't be falling asleep on opposite sides of the bed, trying to keep a careful distance between them. This time, they'd fall asleep in each other's arms.

When Harry came back, his skin was still damp from the shower and he looked utterly gorgeous.

'I'm afraid I smell of flowers,' he said. 'Your shower gel's a bit, um, girly.'

She laughed. 'Actually, in Regency times, there was very little difference between the scents men and women used. Lots of them were floral—based on rose, lavender or orange flower water.'

He looked intrigued. 'How do you know that?'

'I read a lot of Regency romances,' she said, 'and I

was interested in all the social history side of things. I looked up a few things on the Internet—according to one of the really long-established London perfume houses, Beau Brummell's favourite scent involved lavender.'

'Beau Brummell? Hmm. So you like Regency dandies, do you?'

'And Scottish lairds—and I dare you to say it's girly for a man to wear a kilt.'

He laughed. 'Can you imagine me in a kilt?'

'Oh yes—especially if you let your hair grow a bit.'

'My hair?'

'You know your mermaid thing? Well, that's me and period drama. It's the sort of thing I love watching on telly. And you'd be the perfect period drama hero,' she said. 'I can imagine you riding horseback and wearing a tricorn hat.'

'We could always play the lady and the highwayman,' he said with a grin. 'I think I'd like that. Hands up, my lady.'

'Now, you need a domino mask to do that properly, and maybe a white silk scarf over your face, otherwise I could tell the local magistrate what you look like and you'd get arrested.' She laughed. 'Come back to bed.'

He shook his head. 'Sorry, I really need to go. I'm on an early shift tomorrow.'

'I have an alarm clock.'

'Even so. I don't have a change of clothes or a toothbrush.'

'I can always put your stuff through the washing machine, and I'm pretty sure I have a spare toothbrush in the bathroom cabinet.'

But he wouldn't be swayed. And the carefree, laughing man who'd just teased her about her highwayman fantasy had suddenly gone distant on her.

He got dressed in about ten seconds flat.

And Isla felt wrong-footed, unsure what to do next. Should she get dressed and see him out? Or just grab her dressing gown?

But when she moved to get out of bed, he said, 'Stay there. You look comfortable. I'll see myself out.'

'OK.'

'See you tomorrow,' he said.

'Sure,' she said, masking the flood of hurt that he could walk away so easily. And she noticed that he didn't even kiss her goodbye before he left. How could he switch from being so sexy and dishevelled to so cool and dispassionate, so very fast?

She'd thought they were both ready for the next step, but had this been an intimacy too far? Was Harry having second thoughts about their relationship? And would he revert to being the heartbreaker that the hospital grapevine said he was? Was he right when he said he wasn't capable of committing to a relationship?

Bottom line: had she just made a really, really stupid mistake?

The questions went round and round in her head. And she had no answers at all.

Harry knew he'd behaved badly.

He'd seen the hurt in Isla's face, even though she'd masked it quickly.

And he'd bet right now that she was feeling used. That he'd basically had his way with her and walked away.

Ah, hell.

This was a mess.

Maybe he needed to be honest with her and tell her that he was running scared. Panicking. But that would mean admitting that his feelings about her were changing. That he thought he might be falling in love with her—her warmth, shot through with common sense and humour that he found irresistible.

He didn't get involved. He'd never wanted to get involved. He'd seen the carnage it left behind every time his parents divorced their current partner—and, even though everyone eventually managed to be civil for the children's sake, he knew from first-hand experience what it felt like in the early days. When your world crumbled round you and you thought it was your fault, that you'd done something bad that made it impossible for your parents to live together. When you didn't understand what was going on.

And so he'd always kept his relationships light. Walked away before things started getting serious.

Except this time it was too late. It was already serious between him and Isla. And he didn't know when or how that had happened. They'd started off as friends; then, little by little, he'd fallen in love with her. Everything from her dry, slightly scathing sense of humour through to the way she smiled. From the cool, capable way she handled every crisis at work through to her sensual delight in eating out.

The blood seemed to rush out of his head as it hit home: he was in love with her.

Which left him stuck between a rock and a hard place.

Either he walked away from Isla—which would hurt; or he let their relationship move forward, risking being hurt even more when it went wrong. Because it *would* go wrong: he'd learned that from his parents. Love didn't last.

Isla had said at his father's wedding that she thought he had the capacity to make a relationship work—that he was isolating himself, and it was wrong because he was loyal and kind and loving.

But he wasn't so sure. Did he really have that capacity?

He'd already hurt her. Guilt prickled at him. He knew she'd wanted him to stay, and yet he'd walked away. Rejected her. Let his own fears get in the way. He hadn't been fair to her. At all.

And he slept badly enough that night that he texted her first thing in the morning.

I'm sorry. I was an idiot last night.

Her reply was suitably crisp: Yes, you were.

I don't have any excuses.

But he wasn't quite ready to admit the truth—that he'd never felt like this about anyone before and it left him in a flat spin.

But can you forgive me?

It was a big ask, and he knew it.

I'll think about it, she replied. See you at work.

Would things have changed between them at work? It was the one constant in his life, the place where he was sure of himself and knew he belonged. He didn't want that to change. And he was antsy all the way to the hospital.

But Sister McKenna was as calm and professional as she always was, treating Harry just like she treated every other member of the team. It helped that they weren't rostered on together; and Harry was able to relax and sort out his patients' problems.

Isla didn't reply to his text suggesting dinner. She also hadn't said anything about any other arrangements, so he bought flowers and chocolates and headed over to her flat. If she wasn't in, then he'd leave his apology with a neighbour.

Thankfully, she was in.

And she frowned when she saw the flowers and chocolates. 'Harry, what is this?'

'An apology,' he said.

She raised an eyebrow. 'Would you be repeating your father's mistakes, by any chance?'

It had never occurred to him before: but, yes, he was. Now he thought about it, Bertie was always sending flowers or chocolates to apologise for behaving badly. 'Ah,' he said, and grimaced. 'I think the penny might just have dropped.'

'I don't want you to give me flowers or chocolates when we fall out,' she said.

No. He knew that she wanted something that would cost him far more. She wanted him to talk to her. To open his heart.

He blew out a breath. 'I'm really not good at this sort of stuff, Isla.'

'Would a mug of tea help?'

Even though he knew it had strings attached, he nodded. Because he knew she was making more of a concession than he deserved.

'Come in. And thank you for the flowers. Though

if you ever buy me flowers again,' she warned, 'then I might hit you over the head with them.'

'Noted. Though I guess at least they'd be soft,' he said, trying for humour.

To his relief, she laughed.

Taking heart from her reaction, he walked forward and put his arms round her. 'I'm sorry. It's just…'

'You don't do relationships, and I asked you to stay the night. Which is tantamount to proposing to you with a megaphone while standing on a table in the middle of the hospital canteen.'

'In a nutshell,' he agreed. 'Isla—I did warn you I was rubbish at relationships.'

'And you're using your parents as an excuse,' she said.

He winced. 'You don't pull your punches.'

'You're the one who set the ground rules,' she reminded him. 'Honesty.'

'You want honesty?' He leaned his forehead against hers. 'OK. I want to be with you. I want to make a go of this. The way I feel… I…' He blew out a breath. 'I'm never this inarticulate. Sorry. I'm making a mess of this. But I don't want to hurt you, and I don't want to end up hurt either.'

'Then you need to make a leap of faith. Is it really so hard to stay the night?'

'Last time I did that…' His voice faded. 'Actually, the last time I spent the night with anyone was with you. But the time before that—my girlfriend assumed that our relationship meant more to me than it did. And it got messy.'

'Spending the night,' she said, 'means both of us get

a little more sleep before work, the next day. But I guess you didn't bring a change of clothes or a toothbrush.'

'No. Can you be a little bit patient with me?' he asked.

'I can, but there's a string attached.'

He wasn't sure he wanted to know the answer, but he knew he had to ask the question. 'Which is?'

'As long as you promise to talk to me in future,' she said.

He remembered something that gave him a way out. 'I thought you liked brooding Regency rakes?'

'In period dramas on screen or in books, yes,' she said. 'In real life, they'd be a pain in the neck. I'd rather have openness and the truth, even if it hurts.' She gave him a wry smile. 'Because the alternative is leaving me to guess what's in your head. And I'm not a mind-reader. What I imagine can hurt me far more than the truth.'

'I'm sorry,' he said. 'I...have feelings for you.' There, it was out. The best he could say for now, anyway. He wasn't ready to say the L-word; he was still trying to come to terms with his feelings.

Odd. At work, he could always find the right words. Here, when it really mattered, he found himself silent. He couldn't even quote a song or poetry at her. His mind had gone completely blank. He felt numb and stupid and awkward.

She stroked his face. 'I have feelings for you, too, Harry. One of them's exasperation.'

He knew he deserved it. But he took a tiny risk and stole a kiss. 'I'm trying, Isla. This isn't easy for me.'

'I know.' She kissed him back. 'But we'll get there. We'll just have to work on it a bit harder. Together.'

She had more faith in him that than he did, he thought wryly.

* * *

Harry still hadn't quite managed to spend the whole night with Isla when she went back to the Western Isles to see her family for four days, the week before her birthday. She didn't ask him to go with her, and he wasn't sure if he was more relieved or disappointed.

He was shocked to discover just how much he missed her during those four days. Even though there was a team night out and a squash match to keep him busy on two of those evenings, he still missed her. The odd text and snatched phone call just weren't enough.

And if he put it all together, it was obvious. He was ready to move on. To take the next step. To take a risk. With her.

Surreptitiously, he checked out her off-duty for the week of her birthday and changed his own off-duty to match. He didn't want to take the next step in London; it would be better on neutral ground. If he took her away for her birthday, he'd be able to relax instead of panicking that it was all going to go wrong. He spent the evening researching, and found what he hoped would be the perfect place.

He knew which flight she was catching back to London, and met her at the airport with an armful of flowers.

'They're soft ones,' he said, 'because I remember what you said you'd do next time I bought you flowers.' Hit him over the head with them.

She laughed, clearly remembering. 'I meant if you gave me apology flowers instead of talking things through,' she said. 'These are different. They're romantic. Welcome-home flowers. I love them.'

He knew she wanted the words. And he was half-surprised that he was ready to say them. 'I missed you,' he said. 'A lot.'

'I missed you, too.'

'Did you have a good time?'

She nodded. 'It was lovely. It made me realise how much I miss the island. The sky and the mountains and the freshness of the air. And most of all, the sea.'

Then there was a fair chance that she'd really love what he'd arranged for her birthday. Though a nasty thought struck him. If she was homesick... 'Do you miss it enough to want to go back?'

'I've moved on,' she said softly, 'and they replaced me at the practice, so if I went back now...' She shrugged. 'I wouldn't have a place, really.'

'But you've retrained. You're an emergency nurse. I assume there are hospitals on the islands?'

'I could work in the emergency department in Benbecula, or in the GP acute department in Stornoway,' she said.

'But?'

She shook her head. 'Not right now. Maybe some time in the future.'

So she did want to go back. Then what was stopping her? He remembered what she'd told him about the way people had behaved towards her after the whole thing blew up with her fiancé's stepfather. 'Are people still giving you a hard time about Gillespie?'

'No, but I did see Stewart while I was there.'

He went cold. That night after their fight and he'd admitted to his feelings... She'd said she had feelings for him, too. But had seeing her ex again changed that? Maybe the surprise he'd planned for her birthday was a bad idea after all.

'He's engaged to another lass,' she said, 'someone we both went to school with, and I wish them both well.'

'And you're OK about that?' he asked softly.

She nodded. 'I've moved on. I've met someone else. Someone I really like.'

He smiled and kissed her. 'I like you, too.' More than liked, if he was honest about it, but he wasn't quite ready to say it yet. 'So it's your birthday on Monday.'

'Yes. I assume it's standard practice to bring in cake for everyone in the department?'

'And chocolate bars for those off duty,' he confirmed. 'And birthdays are always celebrated at the local pizza place with the team, so I'm afraid I can't take you out to dinner on your actual birthday.'

'Because otherwise people will work it out that we're an item.'

He knew that hurt her, but he still wasn't quite ready to go public. 'However,' he said, 'you're off duty two days later—that's when I'm taking you out to dinner.' He paused. 'And you'll need to pack.'

'Pack?' She looked surprised, then wary.

Did she think that he was asking her to stay at his place? 'For two days,' he said. 'It's part of your birthday present. You'll need casual stuff for walking, and something nice to dress up in. I'll pick you up at your place after your shift.'

It was good to be back in London. Isla had a feeling that Harry had missed her as much as she'd missed him—his lovemaking that evening was even more tender—but she noticed that he still didn't stay overnight.

Though he was planning to take her away for her birthday, the following week. But then a nasty thought struck her: were they sharing a room, or had he booked separate rooms?

On her birthday, she was touched to discover that banners and balloons had been put up in the staffroom, and the team had clubbed together to buy her some gorgeous earrings. She thoroughly enjoyed the team night out at the pizza place, especially as someone had arranged for a birthday cake with candles and everyone sang 'Happy birthday' to her.

Harry saw her home afterwards, and gave her a beautifully wrapped parcel. 'It's the first bit of your present,' he said. It was a beautiful bangle, inlaid with precious stones, and he'd clearly paid attention to the kind of things she liked. But again, he didn't stay the night. Not even on her birthday. And it hurt. Would he ever be ready to spend the night with her—to make a move towards a greater commitment?

Isla was rushed off her feet on the early shift on the Tuesday. Harry still hadn't told her where they were going, but after their shift he picked her up in his little red sports car and drove her down to the Dorset coast, down a tiny track to a lighthouse.

'We're staying here?' she asked, surprised. 'That's just lovely.'

'For two nights,' he said. 'I know you miss the sea and I thought you'd like it here.'

It was incredibly romantic; there was a four-poster bed against one wall, opposite picture windows that overlooking the sea. She walked over to the window and gazed out. 'Harry, this is so perfect. Thank you.'

And he'd booked only one room. She knew that for him spending the whole night together was a huge turning point. For the first time, she really started to hope that he could get past his fear of falling in love and they had a future.

'I got it right, then?' For a moment, he looked really vulnerable.

'More than right,' she said, kissing him. 'However did you find this place?'

'Just did a bit of research,' he said. 'Luckily, because it's midweek, they had a vacancy.'

Dinner was fabulous: locally caught fish, followed by local ice cream on Dorset apple cake. But better still was afterwards, when Harry carried her over the threshold to the four-poster bed. It felt almost like a honeymoon, Isla thought.

In the next morning, she woke in his arms. And, unlike their trip to Cornwall, Harry made love with her before breakfast.

The morning was bright; they went to Lyme Regis and walked along the famous harbour wall of the Cobb, then headed for the cliffs and looked among the loose stones for fossils. Harry was the first one to find an ammonite and presented it to Isla with a bow. Then they headed for the boulders; they were marvelling over the massive ammonites embedded in the rock bed when they heard a scream from the shallows.

A small girl was holding her foot up and crying, while her mother was clearly trying to calm her down and find out what had just happened.

'Maybe the poor kid's trodden on something sharp,' Harry suggested.

'Do you think we ought to go and offer to help?' Isla asked.

'Yes,' Harry said, and took her hand.

'We're medics,' he said to the little girl's mum, who

was sitting on the sand next to her daughter, looking at the little girl's foot. 'Can we help?'

'Abbie said she trod on something and it hurt—I can't see anything but I wondered if she'd trodden on some glass,' the mum said.

'Abbie, I'm Dr Harry,' he said to the little girl, 'and this is Nurse Isla. Can we look at your foot?'

The little girl was still crying, but nodded shyly.

'I can't see any glass or any blood like you'd get with a cut,' Harry said, 'but I think she might have stood on a weever fish. They bury themselves in the sand under shallow water; the spines on their back and gills are laced with venom, and it feels like a sting if you step on them.' He showed the woman the swollen and reddening spot on Abbie's foot. 'We'd better get her over to the lifeguards' hut. We need some tweezers so we can take the spine out, clean the area with soap and water and rinse it with fresh water, then put Abbie's foot in hot water so it'll "cook" the protein in the venom and stop it hurting. And hopefully they'll have some infant paracetamol.'

'I've got the paracetamol,' Abbie's mum said.

'Good. I'll carry her over for you,' he said.

'I'll go ahead and talk to them so they can put the kettle on and get the first aid kit out,' Isla said.

Harry carried Abbie to the hut where the lifeguards were working. Isla had already explained their theory, and the first aid kit was out already.

He set Abbie gently on the bed so he could crouch down and examine her foot again, this time with a torch illuminating the area. 'I can get one of the spines out, but there's another one near the joint of her big toe, so I'd like that one looked at in the nearest emergency department,' he said.

One of the lifeguards called the ambulance while Harry took out the weever fish spine he could see easily, and the other provided a deep bowl of hot water.

'Ow, it's hot!' Abbie said, crying again.

'I know, sweetheart, but you need to put your foot in to stop it hurting,' Harry said. 'If you can do that for me, I'll tell you a story.'

'All right,' Abbie said bravely.

He'd just finished telling her a long-drawn-out version of the Three Little Pigs—where he had everyone in the lifeguards' hut booming out the wolf's threat to huff and puff and blow the house down—when the ambulance arrived. Harry gave a quick rundown to the paramedics.

'Thank you so much for looking after us,' Abbie's mum said. 'And I'm so sorry we took up your time on your holiday.'

'It's fine,' he said with a smile. 'Hope Abbie feels better soon.'

He was so good with children, Isla thought. So why was he so adamant he didn't want children of his own? What had happened in his past? Had he dated someone with a child and it had all gone wrong? But she couldn't think of a way to ask him without it seeming like prying. She'd have to wait until he was ready to open up to her and talk about it. But Harry was stubborn. Would he ever be ready?

'Well, Dr Gardiner, I think you earned a pot of tea and a scone with jam and clotted cream,' she said lightly.

'Sounds good to me,' Harry said, and looped his arm round her shoulders.

They ended up spending the rest of the day at the coast, eating fish and chips on the cliff-top and watching the setting sun. The spectacular flares of red and orange faded to yellow at the horizon, and the colours were reflected across the sea.

'Definitely a selfie moment,' Harry said, and took a picture of them on his phone with the sunset behind them.

This was perfect, Isla thought. It couldn't have been a nicer day.

The next day, they went exploring again; they stopped to walk up the hill and view the famous natural limestone arch of Durdle Door, and discovered the enormous chalk-cut figure of the Cerne Giant looming across another hill. And just being together was so good.

Back in London, this time Harry stayed overnight at Isla's flat.

They'd definitely taken a step forward, she thought. And maybe, just maybe, this was going to work out.

CHAPTER TWELVE

OVER THE NEXT couple of months, Harry and Isla grew closer still. They both kept a change of clothes and toiletries at each other's flat, though they were careful not to arrive at work together when they were on the same shift, and they hadn't made a big deal of letting people know that they were an item.

But one morning Isla felt really rough when she got out of bed.

'Are you all right?' Harry asked.

'I feel a bit queasy,' Isla admitted. 'I think maybe I'm coming down with that bug that's hit the department.' Which probably explained why she seemed to have gone off coffee, the last few days.

'Maybe you ought to stay home and call in sick,' Harry said. 'If you've got the lurgy, you don't want to spread it to the rest of the team or the patients.'

Normally it took a lot more than a bug to stop Isla working her shift, but right at that moment she felt absolutely terrible. 'Yes, I think you're right,' she said.

Harry made her some toast and a mug of hot lemon and honey; he also brought a jug of iced water in to the bedroom and put it by her bedside. 'Can I get you anything else to make you comfortable? A book or a magazine?'

'I'll be fine. But thank you.' She smiled. 'You have a lovely bedside manner. Anyone would think you were a doctor.'

'Yeah, yeah.' He grinned back. 'Text me later to let me know how you're feeling, OK?'

'Yes—though I was thinking, maybe you'd better not come back here after work today. I don't want you to pick it up.'

'I've got the constitution of an ox,' he claimed. 'Look, I'll call you when I leave work and see how you're doing, and then you can tell me if you want me to pick up anything from the shops for you.' He kissed her forehead. 'For now, get some rest.'

Isla lay curled up in bed with a magazine for the rest of the morning. She was feeling considerably better by lunchtime, and she felt a bit guilty about being off sick when she was clearly fine. Or maybe she'd been lucky and had the super-mild version of the bug and it was over now. She texted Harry to say she felt better and was just going out to get a bit of fresh air. But, when she went to the corner shop to buy some milk, the woman in the queue in front of Isla was wearing some really strong perfume which made her feel queasy again; and the smell of greasy food wafting from the fast food place next door to the corner shop made her feel even worse.

When she got back home, it slammed into her. Nausea first thing, a heightened sense of smell, an aversion to coffee... If a patient had described those symptoms to her, she would've suggested doing a pregnancy test. But she couldn't be pregnant—could she?

They'd always been really careful to use condoms.

Although, the night of her birthday, they'd got carried away with the sheer romance of having a bedroom in a lighthouse, and maybe that night they hadn't been as careful then as they should've been.

She thought back. Her last period had been really light, and she knew that women sometimes had breakthrough bleeding during early pregnancy. Could she be pregnant?

It niggled at her for the next hour.

In the end, she went to the local supermarket and picked up a pregnancy test. This would prove once and for all that she was making a fuss about nothing.

She did the test and stared at the little window, willing the words 'not pregnant' to appear. Although she hoped that Harry was revising his views on the 'never settling down' question, she was pretty sure that his stance on never having children of his own hadn't changed. She knew he was dead set against it.

She kept staring at the window. Then, to her horror, the word 'pregnant' appeared. Followed by '3+'— meaning that she was more than three weeks pregnant.

What?

She couldn't be.

Maybe the test was faulty. Maybe there was a problem with the pixels or something in the area on the screen that should've said 'not', and that was why it was blank. Just as well there were two kits in the box.

She did the second one, just to reassure herself that the first one was a mistake.

Except the result was the same: Pregnant. More than three weeks.

Oh, no. She was going to have to tell Harry.

But how? How, when she knew that he didn't want children? When he was practically phobic about it?

She still hadn't found the words by the time he called her.

'I've just finished my shift now, so I'm on my way to see you,' he said. 'Do you want me to pick up anything from the shops?'

'No, thanks—it's fine.'

'How are you feeling?' he asked.

Panicky. 'Better,' she lied. 'But I think maybe it'd be best if you didn't come over, just in case I'm still incubating this bug.'

And that would give her time to work out how to tell him the news, wouldn't it?

Except she still hadn't come up with anything by the next morning. She felt even queasier than she had the previous morning and only just made it to the bathroom before she was sick.

Grimly, she washed her face and cleaned her teeth.

She definitely couldn't let Harry stay over—or stay with him—until she'd told him the news, because she didn't want him to work it out for himself. Which of course he would, if she dashed out of bed and threw up every morning.

She just hoped that none of her patients that day would be wearing particularly strong perfume or aftershave, and that she could either avoid the hospital canteen completely or they'd have totally bland foods on the menu with no smell.

Thankfully, she wasn't rostered on with Harry. But he caught up with her at her break. 'Are you sure you should be in? How are you feeling?' he asked, his dark eyes filled with concern.

'Fine,' she fibbed, and sipped her glass of water in the hope that it would stop her reacting to the smell of his coffee. 'How was your morning?'

'Rushed off my feet.' He grimaced. 'I had one mum bringing in a sick baby, but she had two more children with her under school age, both of them with rotten colds. Clearly she hadn't been able to get anyone to babysit them while she brought the baby in to us. It was total chaos, with both of the toddlers wanting their mum's attention, and she was trying to explain the baby's symptoms to me at the same time. I couldn't hear myself think.'

'Was the baby OK?'

'She had bronchiolitis,' he said. 'Classic intercostal recession. I sent her up to the children's ward. I took a sample of mucus from her nose, but I'm pretty sure it'll be RSV positive. It's the beginning of the RSV season,' he said with a sigh, 'where they'll have two bays of the children's ward full of babies on oxygen therapy, and every single member of staff up there will have the cold from hell.' He rolled his eyes. 'And people wonder why I never want to have kids.'

She flinched inwardly, knowing that he was just exaggerating a bit to make his morning sound dramatic—or was he? He was always brilliant with any sick children who came into the department, and at the wedding he'd been so good with his youngest brother. Yet he'd always been adamant that he didn't want kids of his own and he'd never really explained why. When she'd tried to ask him, he'd simply changed the subject.

So she really wasn't looking forward to telling him the news that, actually, he was going to be a dad. She had to find a way to soften the blow for him, but she had no idea how.

'Do you want to come over for dinner tonight?' he asked.

'I'm still feeling a bit fragile, so I think I'd better pass and have an early night with a hot water bottle,' she said. She knew she was being a coward, but she really needed to work out the right way to tell him. A way that wouldn't hurt him. Just... How?

Was it his imagination, Harry wondered a couple of days later, or was Isla trying to avoid him? Ever since she'd gone down with that bug, she'd been acting strangely. Had she changed her mind about their relationship? He'd been seriously thinking about it himself; he'd never felt like this about anyone else before in his life. And she made him feel that the world was a better place. Just being with her made his heart feel lighter. He'd started to think about asking her to move in with him, maybe even take the next step and get engaged. Take the risk he'd always avoided in the past, so sure it would go wrong because he'd seen it go wrong so often for both his parents.

But now Isla seemed to be going distant on him, he was having doubts about it again. Did he have it all wrong? Did she not feel the same as he did, any more? Or was he so messed up about the idea of commitment that he couldn't see straight?

By the end of the week he was really concerned. They hadn't spent any time together for more than a week, so something was definitely wrong. All he could do was persuade Isla to go somewhere quiet with him, and then maybe he could talk to her and find out what the problem was. And then he could solve it. He hoped.

They had a busy shift in Resus that morning, and Harry was about to suggest that they went for a break between patients when the paramedics brought in in a woman who'd been in an RTA.

'Mrs Paulette Freeman,' the paramedic said. 'A bicycle courier cut in front of her; she had to swerve to avoid him, and crashed into the car on her right-hand side, which made her air bag go off. She's thirty years old, and twelve weeks pregnant with her first baby. There haven't been any problems so far in the pregnancy, and when we examined her there was no sign of bleeding. Her blood group is A positive.'

Harry and Isla exchanged a glance of relief at the news about the blood group. At least there wouldn't be a risk to the fetus from rhesus antibodies.

'Can you remember, did you bang your head at all, Mrs Freeman?' Harry asked.

'No, but the airbag went straight into my stomach.' Mrs Freeman looked anxious. 'Is my baby all right? Maybe I shouldn't have worn my seat belt.'

'Seat belts really do reduce the risk of serious injury in pregnancy,' Harry reassured her, 'so you did the right thing. Now, I'm going to examine you—just let me know if any area feels a bit tender.'

'My stomach's a bit sore,' she said, 'but that's probably from the airbag. It doesn't matter about me. What about the baby?'

'The baby's pretty well cushioned in there but of course you're worried. My job now is to see how you both are,' Harry said. 'Try and relax for me.' He added quietly to Isla, 'Call the maternity department and get Theo Petrakis down here, please. I always play it supersafe with pregnant patients.' He turned back to Mrs Freeman. 'Is there someone we can call for you?'

'My husband,' she said.

'I'll do that. Can you tell me his number?' Isla asked, then wrote the number down as Mrs Freeman said it. 'I'll call him straight away and ask him to come in,' she said.

'I'm going to examine your stomach now, Mrs Freeman,' Harry said. 'Tell me if anything hurts.'

She was white-faced and tight-lipped, and didn't say a word. He couldn't feel any uterine contractions, but the uterus felt firmer than he'd like.

A pelvic examination showed no sign of bleeding, which he hoped was a good thing. But he was starting to get a bad feeling about this case.

'I'm just going to listen to the baby's heartbeat,' he said, and set up the Doppler probe. But instead of the nice fast clop-clop he was expecting to hear, there was silence. He couldn't pick up the baby's heartbeat.

'What's wrong?' Mrs Freeman asked. 'Why can't we hear the baby's heartbeat?'

'I'm sure there's nothing to worry about,' Harry reassured her. 'Often this particular machine doesn't work very well in the first trimester. I'll try the old-fashioned way—obviously you won't be able to hear it, but I will.' He picked up a horn-shaped Pinard stethoscope; but, to his dismay, he still couldn't hear anything.

Isla came back in. 'I've spoken to your husband, Mrs Freeman, and he's on his way in. Dr Gardiner, Mr Petrakis is on his way down right now.'

'Good. I just want to get the portable ultrasound. I'll be back in a tick,' Harry said, doing his best to sound calm and breezy.

Isla had clearly seen the Doppler and the Pinard next to the bed and obviously worked out that he hadn't been able to pick up the baby's heartbeat, because when he brought the machine back she was sitting next to the bed, holding Mrs Freeman's hand.

Harry's bad feeling suddenly got a whole lot worse.

He knew that pregnant women could lose a lot of blood before they started showing any sign of hypovolaemic shock. In a case like this, with blunt force trauma, there was a high risk of placental abruption—

where the placenta separated from the uterus before the baby was born—and the fetus was likely to suffer. Worst-case scenario, the baby wouldn't survive. Although there was no sign of bleeding, with a concealed placental abruption the blood remained in the uterus. It was the more severe form of abruption and if his fears were correct the baby had already died.

'I'm going to do an ultrasound now to see what's going on,' he said. 'It's very like the machine they used when they did your dating scan, Mrs Freeman. Can you bare your stomach again for me so I can put some gel on it? I'm afraid our gel down here tends to be a bit cold.'

'I don't care if it's like ice, as long as my baby's OK,' she said, and pulled the hem of her top up so he could smear the radio-conductive gel over her abdomen.

He ran the transceiver head over her abdomen and begged silently, oh, please let the baby be kicking away.

The ultrasound didn't show any sign of a blood clot, but it did show him the thing he'd been dreading: the baby wasn't moving and there was no heartbeat.

Oh, hell. He was going to have to deliver the worst possible news. This was the bit of his job he really, really hated.

Theo arrived just before Harry could open his mouth. 'You asked to see me, Dr Gardiner?'

'Yes. Thank you for coming. Excuse me a second,' Harry said to Mrs Freeman. 'I just want to have a quick word with Mr Petrakis, our senior obstetric consultant. I'll introduce you properly in a moment.'

He walked away and said to Theo in a low voice, 'I couldn't pick up the fetal heartbeat. I know that's common in the first trimester, but also there's no movement or heartbeat showing on the ultrasound. The mum's not bleeding and I couldn't see a clot, and there's no sign right at this moment of hypovolaemic shock—but, given that it was blunt trauma and what's happened to the fetus, I think we're looking at a concealed placental abruption.'

'Sounds like it,' Theo said. 'Poor woman. In that case we need to restore her blood volume before she goes into shock and we'll have to deliver the baby PV—it's the only way to stop the bleeding from the abruption. And I'll want to admit her to the ward for monitoring in case she goes into DIC.'

Harry went back over to Mrs Freeman with Theo and introduced the specialist to her. Theo looked at the ultrasound and from the expression in the consultant's eyes Harry could tell that his original diagnosis was indeed correct. They wouldn't have time to wait for her husband to arrive to break the news; they needed to treat her now, before she went into shock.

He sat down beside her on the opposite side from Isla and held her other hand. 'Mrs Freeman, I'm so sorry. There is no nice way to tell you this, but I'm afraid the accident caused what we call a placental abruption. Basically it means that the force of the accident made your placenta detach from the uterus.'

'What about my baby?'

'I'm so sorry,' he said. 'We still need to treat you, but I'm afraid there's nothing we can do for the baby.'

She stared at him in horror. 'My baby's dead?' she whispered.

'I'm so sorry,' he said again. If only he could make this right. But there was nothing that anyone could do.

Mrs Freeman was shaking. Fat tears were rolling down her cheeks, but she made no sound. What he was seeing was total desolation. And it wasn't fixable.

Isla had her arm round Mrs Freeman's shoulders, doing her best to comfort her.

Feeling helpless, Harry explained what they were going to do next and that they needed to keep her in for a little while to keep an eye on her.

Halfway through treatment her husband arrived and Harry had to break the bad news all over again.

'I'm so sorry, Mr Freeman,' he finished.

Mr Freeman looked dazed. 'Our baby's dead? And Paulette?'

'We're treating her now, but we want to keep her in for monitoring. Would you like to come and be with her?'

'Yes—I— Is she going to be all right?'

'She's going to be fine,' Harry reassured him. 'I'm just so sorry I can't give you better news.'

By the time Harry's shift finished, he was completely drained. The last thing he felt like doing was talking to Isla to find out what was wrong, but he knew it had to be done. Maybe he could arrange to see her tomorrow and they could sort it out then. When they'd both had time to recover from their rough day.

But when he saw her outside the staff kitchen, he could see that she'd been crying.

'Are you all right?' he asked softly, even though he knew it was a stupid question; it was obvious that she wasn't OK at all.

'Rough shift,' she said. 'You should know. You were there.'

'Yeah.' He closed his eyes for a moment. 'I hate breaking that kind of news to people. I hate seeing their dreams shatter like that.' He opened his eyes again. 'I don't know about you, but I can't face going anywhere and talking tonight. Shall we just get a pizza and go back to my place?'

'I...' She dragged in a breath. 'Harry, we really need to talk.'

He went cold. The way she was talking sounded horribly final. Just like the way he'd always broken the news to whoever he was dating that it wasn't really working and he'd rather they just stayed as friends.

Was Isla going to end it between them?

But surely not right now—not after the day they'd both had.

Not feeling up to talking, he asked, 'Can this wait until tomorrow?'

She shook her head. 'It's already been dragging on too long.'

He really didn't like the sound of that. He had a nasty feeling that he knew why she'd been distant, these last few days: because she was ending it.

'Is that café round the corner still open?' she asked.

He guessed that she meant the one where he'd taken her for a bacon sandwich, the morning after the night shift where the drunk had come on to her. 'We can take a look,' he said. 'Is that where you want to go?'

'It'll be a lot more private than the hospital canteen. It means we can talk.'

'OK.'

They walked to the café in silence. Harry could feel himself getting more and more tense, the nearer they got to the café; and, even though he was trying to prepare himself for being dumped, it just hurt too damn much. He didn't want it to end between them. He wanted to take it forward. Take the risk.

'Tea and a bacon sandwich?' he asked outside the door to the café.

She shook her head. 'Just a glass of water for me, thanks.'

'OK. If you find us a table, I'll sort out the drinks.' He ordered himself a mug of tea, to put off the moment that little bit longer.

When the waitress sorted out the drinks, Harry discovered that Isla had found them a quiet table out of the way. Good.

Well, he wasn't going to be weak and wait to be dumped. He was going to initiate the discussion and ask up front. 'So are you going to tell me what I've done wrong?' he asked as he sat down.

'Wrong? What do you mean, wrong?'

'It feels as if you've been avoiding me for the last few days,' he said. And he was aware how ironic it was that they'd had this conversation before—except, last time, he'd been the one doing the avoiding.

'That's because I have,' she said softly.

Pain lanced through him. He hadn't been imagining it, then. She was going to end it—and she'd been working out how to tell him, the last few days. While he, being a fool, had been thinking about moving their relationship on to the next step.

'So what did I do wrong?' he repeated.

'Nothing.'

He didn't get it. 'So why were you avoiding me?'

She took a deep breath. 'There isn't an easy way to say this.'

So she was definitely ending it—and he was shocked to realise how much it hurt. How much she meant to him and how empty his life was going to be without her.

* * *

This was one of the hardest things Isla had ever done. She hated the fact that her words were going to blow Harry's world apart. She was just about to make his worst nightmare come true.

But he'd clearly already worked out that something wasn't right.

Even though her timing wasn't brilliant—he was already feeling low after a rotten shift—she couldn't keep it from him any longer.

'I'm pregnant,' she said.

He looked at her, saying absolutely nothing—and she couldn't tell a thing from his expression. How he was feeling, what he was thinking…nothing.

'With our baby,' she clarified. Not that there could be any mistake. They'd both been faithful to each other.

Still he said nothing. He just stared at her as if he couldn't believe what he was hearing. He looked shocked to the core.

Well, what had she expected? That he'd throw his arms round her and tell her how thrilled he was?

He'd made it clear enough that he never wanted children, and she was telling him that he was going to be a father—exactly what he didn't want.

The fact that he'd said nothing at all made it very obvious that he hadn't changed his mind. He just didn't know how to tell her without hurting her.

So she was going to have to be brave and be the one to walk away.

'It's all right,' she said, even though it wasn't and it left her feeling bone-deep tired and unutterably sad. 'I know you don't want children. I'm not expecting anything from you, and I understand that it's the end between us.'

And it was clear what she needed to do next. This was Harry's patch. He'd lived in London since he was a student; he'd trained and worked in the same hospital for twelve years. She'd been in the emergency department at the London Victoria for only a few months. It was obvious which of the two of them would have to leave.

'I'm going home to Scotland,' she said. 'To the island. But I didn't want to leave without telling you why. I'm sorry, Harry.'

And she got up to leave.

CHAPTER THIRTEEN

SHOCK RADIATED THROUGH HARRY.

He couldn't believe what he was hearing.

Isla was pregnant?

With his baby?

Well, of *course* his baby—she wasn't the sort to have an affair. He knew that without having to ask.

But he couldn't quite process the idea of being a father. He couldn't say a word. It felt as if his mouth had been filled with glue. And someone had glued him to his seat, too, because Isla was walking away from him and he was still stuck here, watching her leave.

This had to be a nightmare. One of those hyper-real dreams where the situation was so close to real life that it could really be happening, but there was something out of kilter that would tell you it was all a figment of your imagination.

Like being stuck to your seat. Like there being no sound at all, even though they were in a café and there would usually be the hiss of steam from a coffee machine and the sound of a spoon clinking against a mug as sugar was stirred in, the low buzz of other people talking.

He'd wake up in a second. It'd be stupid o'clock in the morning, and he'd be in either his own bed or Isla's, spooned round her body. He'd hear her soft, regular breathing and he'd know that this was just a dream and all was right with the world.

Any second now.

Any second now.

But then the door closed behind her and the sound all seemed to rush back in—like the moment when a tube train arrived at the station, and all the noise echoed everywhere. Hissing steam, clinking spoons and mugs, the hum of conversation.

Oh, dear God.

This wasn't a nightmare.

Isla was pregnant, she was planning to leave London, and...

No, no, no.

He couldn't let her leave.

He needed to talk to her. Tell her how he felt about her. Ask her to stay. Beg her to stay. On his knees, if he had to.

He could do with someone tipping a bucket of ice-cold water over him to shock his brain back into working again, so he could find the right words to ask her to stay. Failing that, he'd just have to hope that he could muddle his way through it.

Ignoring the startled looks of the other customers in the café, he left his unfinished mug of tea where it was and rushed out after Isla.

He looked out either side of the door in the street. He thought he caught sight of her walking away and called out, 'Isla, wait!'

Either she hadn't heard him or the woman wasn't actually Isla. Inwardly praying that it was the former, he ran after her and finally caught up with her.

Thank God. It was her.

'Isla, wait,' he said again.

She stopped and stared at him. 'Why? You made it perfectly clear just now that you didn't want to know.'

'Did I, hell.'

'I told you the news and you didn't say a word.'

'You didn't exactly give me a chance!' he protested.

'I did,' she said. 'I sat there like a lemon, staring at you and waiting for you to say something.'

'I was too shocked to think straight, let alone for my mouth to work. I needed a few seconds for the news to sink in. And now it has. I think.'

She blinked back the tears. 'Harry, you've told me often enough that you don't want kids and you don't want to settle down. I'm not expecting you to change for me.'

'What if I want to change?' he asked.

She shook her head. 'I can't ask you to do that.'

'You're not asking me. I'm offering.'

'No. Don't make any sacrifices, because you'll regret it later. Anything you decide has to be because you really, really want it. You can't live your life to please other people.'

'I don't want you to leave,' he said. 'Stay.'

'If I go home to Scotland, at least I'll have my family round me to help with the baby. If I stay here, I'll be struggling on my own,' she pointed out. 'It makes sense to leave.'

'So you want to keep the baby?'

She dragged in a breath. 'You can actually ask me that after what happened at work today, when that poor woman lost a baby she clearly wanted very much?'

He winced. 'Sorry, that came out wrong. I don't mean that at all. Just—we didn't plan this, did we? Either of us. We haven't talked properly about what we want out of life. We've been taking this thing between us one step at a time.' He dragged a hand through his hair. 'I'm making a mess of this, but we need to talk about it, and I can't let you just walk away from me— and the street really isn't the right place to discuss this. Your place or mine?'

'I guess yours is nearer,' she said.

'Mine it is, then—and there's no pressure. We'll just talk things through, and then, if you want me to drive you back to yours afterwards, I will.' He blew out a breath. 'Just talk to me, Isla. You once said to me that you weren't a mind-reader. Neither am I. And I really need to know what's going on in your head.'

She looked at him, and for a nasty moment he thought she was going to refuse; but then she nodded.

They walked back to his place in uneasy silence. He tried letting his hand accidentally brush against hers, but she didn't let her fingers curl round his, so he gave up. Maybe she was right. Maybe they needed to do this with a clear head, not let the attraction between them get in the way and muddle things up.

'Can I get you a drink?' he asked once they were in his living room.

'No, thanks.'

Were they really reduced to cool politeness? But then he found himself lapsing into it, too. 'Please, have a seat.'

He noticed that she picked one of the chairs rather than the sofa, making it clear that she didn't want him right next to her. He pushed the hurt aside. OK. He could deal with this. He needed to give her a little bit of space. Clearly she was upset and worried, and all the hormonal changes of pregnancy weren't helping the situation one little bit.

Hoping that she wouldn't misinterpret where he sat, he chose a seat on the sofa opposite her. All he wanted to do was to hold her and tell her that everything was going to be all right. But how could he promise her that, when he didn't know that it would be anywhere near all right?

What a mess.

He didn't even know where to start. Emotionally, this was a total minefield and it was way outside his experience. So he fell back on the thing he knew he was good at. Being a doctor. Maybe that would be the best place to start. 'Are you all right?' he asked. 'I mean, are you having morning sickness or headaches?'

'It's not been brilliant,' she admitted.

'How long have you known?'

She took a deep breath. 'I did the test nearly a week ago.'

So she'd had a week to get used to the idea and work out how she felt about it, whereas he'd only had a few scant minutes—and it wasn't anywhere near enough. 'When you thought you had the bug that was going round?' he asked.

'Except it wasn't that.'

Now he was beginning to understand why she'd backed off from him—because she'd discovered she was pregnant and she'd been scared of his reaction. Because he'd told her often enough that he didn't want kids. He just hadn't told her why. And maybe it was time he explained. 'I'm sorry,' he said. 'You should've been able to tell me. And I feel bad that I'm not approachable enough for you to have said anything before.'

'We didn't exactly plan this, did we?' She bit her lip. 'And we were careful.'

Not careful enough. The only guaranteed form of

conception was abstinence. 'Do you know how pregnant you are?'

'The test said more than three weeks. My last period was very light, but I thought...' She shrugged. 'Well, obviously I was wrong.'

'Isla, I don't know what to say,' he admitted. 'I really wasn't expecting this.' He raked a hand through his hair. 'And, after a day like today...'

'I couldn't keep it to myself any longer,' she said. 'Not after today. Because what happened to that poor woman made me think, what if it had been me? I hadn't really let myself think too much about the baby and what options I had. But after sitting there, holding her hand while you told her the bad news, it became really clear to me what I wanted.'

To keep the baby. She'd already told him that. But what else? Did she want to bring up the baby on her own, or with him?

And what did he want?

He'd had no time to think about it, to weigh up the options. He'd always been so sure that he didn't want children. So very sure. But now he was going to be a dad, and he didn't have a clue what to say.

'I've been trying to work out for the last week how to tell you. I knew it was your worst nightmare,' she said, almost as if she could read his mind. But then she frowned. 'But what I really don't understand, Harry, is why you're so sure you don't want kids. You're so good with them at work—and at the wedding, you were great with little Evan. And when we went away, you were lovely with that little girl on the beach who stood on the weever fish—you told her a story to keep her mind off how much her foot hurt. You'd make such a great father. I don't understand why you'd cut yourself off from all that potential love. Is it because you have so many brothers and sisters, but you didn't grow up with most of them?'

'No.' He blew out a breath. Maybe if he told her the misery that had haunted him for years, she'd get it. 'Do you remember the little boy who'd eaten his grandfather's iron tablets?'

'Yes.' She looked puzzled. 'Why?'

'And you remember I told his grandmother that toddlers were unpredictable?'

'Yes.'

'And I know that's true, because I've walked in her shoes,' he said softly.

She stared at him. 'What, you had a toddler who accidentally ate iron tablets—one who died?'

'Not my toddler and not iron tablets and no death, but something bad happened, something that's haunted me ever since,' he said. 'I was eleven. Mum had just popped out to the shops and she asked me to keep an eye on my sisters. Maisie was five, Tasha was two, and Bibi was a baby. I thought it'd be all right. I put Maisie and Tasha in front of the telly—there was some cartoon on they both liked—and I was doing my homework at the dining room table. French, I remember. Then Bibi started crying. Maisie came and told me the baby was all stinky, so I knew I had to change her nappy— I couldn't just leave her crying until Mum got home. I thought the others would be fine in front of the telly while I took the baby upstairs and changed her.'

'What happened?' she asked softly.

'I forgot to close the stair gate,' he said. 'Tasha got bored with the telly and decided to come and find me. I had the baby in my arms, and I saw Tasha get to the top of the stairs. She was smiling and so pleased with herself. Then she wobbled and fell backwards. Right down the whole flight of stairs. Before I could get to her. Everything happened in slow motion—I could see it happening, but I couldn't do a thing about it. And then she was just lying there at the bottom of the stairs and she wasn't making a sound. I thought she was dead and it was all my fault.'

'This is your middle sister, yes? And she wasn't…?'

He shook his head. 'She survived.' Though she hadn't made a complete recovery.

'Harry, just about anyone would struggle to look after three children under five, and you were only eleven years old at the time,' Isla pointed out. 'You were doing your best. You were busy changing the baby. You weren't to know that your two-year-old sister would fall down the stairs.'

'I know—but if I'd closed the stair gate it wouldn't have happened.'

'Or she might have gone into the kitchen or the garden and hurt herself there instead,' Isla said. 'You're right about toddlers being unpredictable, and you can't blame yourself—plus it's so easy to see things differently with hindsight. It's not fair to blame yourself. What did your mum say?'

'She came home to find an ambulance outside our house with a flashing blue light,' Harry said, 'so she was pretty shocked—and her first words to me were that she'd trusted me to look after the girls while she went to get some bread and some milk, and why hadn't I kept a proper eye on them?'

Isla winced. 'That to me sounds like a panicky mum who isn't thinking straight.'

'She apologised later,' Harry said. 'She told me that it wasn't my fault.' He paused. 'But we both knew it was, and she never asked me to look after the girls again on my own after that.'

'I bet she was feeling just as guilty—she was the adult, and she'd left you in charge of three young children, when you were still only a child yourself,' Isla pointed out. 'And how far away were the shops?'

'A fifteen-minute walk,' Harry said. 'Not far—but it was long enough for me to nearly kill Tasha. I had bad dreams for months about it. I saw my little sister lying at the bottom of the stairs, her face white, and I couldn't see her breathing. I never wanted to go through fear like that again, and that was when I vowed that I'd never have kids of my own. I didn't want that responsibility—or to let another child down.'

Isla left her seat, came over to him and hugged him fiercely. 'You were a child yourself, Harry, and having that kind of a responsibility as a child is completely different from having it as an adult. And she was fine, wasn't she?'

That was the big question. 'The hospital said it was concussion and a broken arm.' He bit his lip. 'We thought she'd recovered just fine over the next few weeks. But over the months, Mum noticed that Tasha was always off in a dream world. When she got a bit older, if she was reading, you had to take the book out of her hands to get her to realise you'd been calling her.'

'Because she lost herself in the book?'

He shook his head. 'Mum talked to the health visitor about it. They thought she might have glue ear. But when the audiology department at the hospital tested her, they found out that actually, her hearing was damaged permanently.' This was the crunch bit. 'According to the audiogram, what was wrong was impact damage—so it had been caused by the fall. Because I didn't look after her properly, Tasha's on the border of being severely deaf, and for certain pitches she's profoundly deaf—she can't hear really deep voices.'

'Plenty of people cope with deafness,' Isla pointed out gently, 'and I get the impression from what you've told me about your sisters that they're all very independent.'

'They are,' he admitted. 'But don't you see? Her deafness was caused by the fall. It shouldn't have happened. And I feel bad that she's always had to struggle and work harder than everyone else. She was bright enough to pick things up from books, but half the time she couldn't actually hear what the teachers were saying. Even with hearing aids, it's difficult—when she's in noisy surroundings, it's hard to pick up what people are saying, especially if they have quiet voices or they're in her difficult range and she can't see their faces to lipread. She has to concentrate so much harder to pick up all the social stuff as well as cope with work.'

'Is that how she sees it?' Isla asked.

'Well—no. We fight about it,' Harry admitted. 'She refuses to be defined by her hearing. She says I'm overprotective and it drives her crazy.'

'Have you tried putting yourself in her shoes?' Isla asked softly.

'Yes. And I still blame myself. And I'll always remember how I felt, seeing her lying there on the floor, not moving. That choking feeling of panic.' He dragged in a breath. 'I see parents most weeks who are panicking as much as I did back then. Parents who are worried sick about a baby or a toddler with a virus or a severe allergic reaction. I think the fear's the same, however old or however experienced you are.' He paused. 'And I guess that's part of why I didn't want to get involved with anyone. I didn't want to risk things going wrong. I told myself that getting involved with someone, getting married and having kids…that wasn't for me.'

Isla swallowed hard. 'And then I came along.'

'And you changed everything,' he said. 'You made me see that things might be different to what I always thought they were. That, just because my parents had made mistakes, it didn't mean that I was necessarily going to repeat them.' He took a deep breath. 'So if I was wrong about that, maybe I'm wrong about other things, too. Like not wanting children.'

'So what are you saying?'

'I'm saying,' he said, 'that I need a little time to let it sink in and to come to terms with it. Right now, I'm still shocked and I feel as if someone's smacked me over the head with a frying pan. But give me a little time to think about it and get used to the idea. You've had a week, and I've only had a few minutes. I can't adjust that fast, Isla, no matter how much I want to. I'm only human.'

'I'm sorry. I'm being selfish.' Her eyes misted with tears.

She looked as if she was going to pull away from him, but he wrapped his arms round her and hauled her onto his lap. 'Isla. These last couple of weeks, I've been doing a lot of thinking myself. And this week I thought that you were avoiding me because you were working out how to dump me—'

'Dump you?' she interrupted.

'Dump me,' he repeated. 'I'd been thinking about us. About how I like being with you. About how my world's a better place when I wake up in your arms in the morning. About how you make me want to be brave and take the risk of a real grown-up relationship.' He paused. 'I had been thinking about asking you to move in with me.' He paused again. 'This is probably too little, too late. But I'm going to tell you anyway, because you can't read what I'm thinking. I was going to ask you to get engaged.' He swallowed hard. 'To take the really big risk and get married.'

'What? *You* want to get married?' She looked at him in utter shock.

'Yes.' He gave her a wry smile. 'I didn't believe it either, at first. But the thing is, I met someone. Someone I really like. Someone I really believe in and who seems to believe in me, too. Someone who told me that I was capable of really loving someone. She made me think about it properly for the first time ever.' He paused. 'And you were right. I am capable of loving someone. I love you, Isla McKenna. And, if you'll have me, I'd very much like to marry you.'

'Uh…' She stared at him. 'I think it's my turn to have the frying pan moment. Did you just ask me to marry you?'

'I did.'

'Me *and* our baby?' she checked.

'I believe you come as a package,' he said dryly.

'But—you—me—how?' she asked plaintively.

He stroked her face. 'Now I definitely know you're pregnant. The hormones have put a gag on all that strident Scottish common sense.'

'Have they, hell. Harry, you're allergic to marriage.'

'There's no immunoglobulin reaction, as far as I can tell,' he said, starting to relax and enjoy himself.

'You said you didn't want to settle down. Ever.'

'Tsk—are you so old-fashioned that you think it's only a woman's prerogative to change her mind?'

'Harry Gardiner, you're the most impossible—'

He judged that he'd teased her enough. So he stopped

her words by the simple act of kissing her. 'I love you, Isla,' he said when he broke the kiss. 'I might even have loved you from the first day I met you. But every day I've worked with you, or dated you, or woken with you in my arms, I've got to know you a little more and I've grown to love you a little more. And although I admit I'm absolutely terrified at the idea of being a dad—and I'm even more terrified by the idea that I might let our child down, the way I let my sister down—I know I'm going to make it work because you'll be at my side. And, with you by my side, I know I can do absolutely anything. Because I can talk to you, and you can make me see sense. And you can talk to me, knowing I'll always back you and take your part. We're a team, Isla. Not just at work.'

A tear spilled over and trickled down her cheek, and he kissed it away.

'Hormones,' she said.

He coughed. 'Wrong word. The one you're looking for has one syllable, three letters, and starts with the twenty-fifth letter of the alphabet. The middle letter's a vowel. And the last letter's often used as a plural. Got it?'

'You didn't actually ask me,' she pointed out. 'You said, if I'll have you, you'd like to marry me. Which isn't the same as asking me.'

'Yes, it is.'

She just looked at him.

He sighed, shifted her off his lap, and got down on one knee before her. 'If you're being picky about it, I also don't have a ring—and am I not supposed to present you with a ring if I do it the traditional way?'

'You said you'll back me. That's enough.' She flapped a dismissive hand. 'We don't need flashy gemstones.'

He laughed. 'Ah, the Scottish tartness is reasserting

itself. Good. Isla McKenna, I love you. And I'm still terrified out of my wits about being a dad, but I know I'll love our baby just as much as I love you. Will you marry me?'

She smiled. 'Yes.'

He coughed.

'What?' she asked.

'You haven't said it,' he reminded her. 'Three little words. And I've spent the last week in a bad place, thinking that you were going to walk out on me. I need a little TLC.'

'Ah, the three little words. Tender, loving care.'

'Three *smaller* words,' he said, giving her a pained look. 'Come on. I said it first.'

'I know. And I'm glad.' She smiled. 'I love you, too, Harry Gardiner. I think I did from the second you kissed me in the moonlight in Cornwall. And I admit that I, too, am just a little bit panicky about whether I'm going to be a good enough mum. But with you by my side, I think the answer's going to be yes. It's like you said. We're a team. Things might not always go smoothly, but we'll always have each other's back.'

'You'd better believe it,' he said softly.

EPILOGUE

Three months later

'WE SHOULD'VE ELOPED,' Harry said. 'How about I go and borrow a horse and a tricorn hat, kidnap you and carry you off to my lair?'

Isla laughed. 'Are the boys giving you a hard time?'

'Not just the boys. Five best men. *Five*. It's excessive. And then the girls accused me of sexism and demanded to know why they couldn't be best women. All of them.' He groaned. 'I can't possibly have eight best men and women on my wedding day!'

'As you're only going to get married once, none of them wants to miss out, so I don't think you have much choice,' Isla said. 'And I'm surprised your father hasn't tried to make it nine.'

'He did. He said I'd been his best man so I ought to let him be one of mine. I reminded him that he's already got a role as the father of the groom,' Harry said. 'But the others... They're supposed to let the oldest sibling boss them around, not the other way round. They're impossible!'

Isla laughed again, knowing that his grumbling was more for show than anything else. Since Harry had opened his heart to her, he'd also opened his heart to his brothers and sisters—and as a result he'd become much, much closer to his whole family. 'I love your brothers and sisters. They're so like you. Totally irrepressible.'

He groaned. 'So much for a quiet wedding. We really should've disappeared to Gretna Green.'

'Scotland? Hmm. I don't think that would've been quiet, either. And you do know my family's planning on teaching yours to party the Scots way tonight, don't you?'

'We definitely need to run away,' Harry said.

'I think it's a little too late for that. We're supposed to be in church in two hours. And you're not supposed to be here, much less talking to me through a closed door.'

'You're the one who insisted that it was bad luck to see me on our wedding day before you got to the church,' he reminded her. 'That's why I'm talking to you through a closed door. Are you quite sure we can't elope?'

'Harry, stop panicking,' she said. 'Go with the flow and let your siblings enjoy your wedding. Because you're only getting married once.'

He sighed. 'Our poor baby doesn't know what he or she has in store.'

'Oh, I think he or she does,' Isla corrected, 'and I think this is going to be the most loved baby in history.'

'And definitely by his—or her—dad.' Harry had been in tears at the scan, and had been a besotted father-to-be ever since.

'See you at church,' she said softly. 'And thank you for the beautiful necklace. It goes perfectly with my dress.'

'Well, you needed a "something new" to wear. It's traditional.' He coughed. 'It's also traditional to give your husband a kiss for a gift.'

'I will. At the altar,' she promised. 'I love you, Harry. And today's going to be fun. Really.'

And it was. Right from the moment Isla walked up the aisle on her father's arm, seeing the small church absolutely bursting at the seams with all their family and their friends from work, through to seeing the love in Harry's eyes as he turned to face her at the altar, through to everyone throwing dried rose petals over them both as they walked out of the church as man and wife.

The reception was even better. And Isla really enjoyed the best-men-and-women's speeches. Harry's brothers and sisters had clearly got together before the wedding and practised, because they all lined up on the stage behind the top table.

'The best man's speech is supposed to be short,' Evan said, starting them off, 'but we all wanted to be the best man and made Harry let us all do it, and we all want to say something so the speech won't be very short. It's funny, though. And I'm going to tell you a joke. What did the banana say to the monkey?'

The others all chorused, 'Nothing, bananas can't talk!' and did a little tap-dance with jazz hands, making everyone at the reception laugh.

Harry's siblings went in age order after that, with each of them telling a Harry story that made everyone laugh, though Isla noticed that Harry's middle sister seemed to have missed her slot.

But then, when Jack had finished speaking, Tasha took the microphone. 'My Harry story isn't a funny one. But it's about the bravest, best man I know. When I was two, I fell all the way down the stairs and I broke my arm. A few months later, we worked out that the fall had made me deaf in one ear, too. Harry's always blamed himself for what happened, but there's no way he could've rescued me when he was right in the middle of changing Bibi's nappy. We all think he's a superhero, but even he can't be in two places at once.'

Isla slipped her hand into Harry's, and squeezed his fingers.

'Without him, I wouldn't be a trainee audiologist, and I wouldn't be able to understand my patients as well as I do,' Tasha continued. 'And actually, I'm kind of glad it happened, because I know it was one of the reasons why he became a doctor—and the emergency department of the London Victoria wouldn't be the same without him.'

There were loud cheers of agreement from Harry and Isla's colleagues.

'And because he's an emergency doctor, that meant that he met Isla at work. We're all so glad he did, because she's the best thing to happen to him, and it's lovely to see my big brother get the happiness he never thought he deserved—but he really *does* deserve it.' She lifted her glass. 'So the best men and women all want you to raise your glasses now for a toast—to Harry and Isla, and may their life together be full of happiness.'

Harry stole a kiss from Isla as everyone chorused the toast. 'Yes. It's never going to be quiet, but it's going to be full of happiness,' he said with a smile. 'I love you. And our baby. And our chaotic, wonderful extended family.'

'Me, too.' Isla smiled back. 'I'm with you all the way. Always.'

* * * * *

THE PLAYBOY'S PROPOSAL

AMANDA BROWNING

CHAPTER ONE

KATHRYN TEMPLETON was wrapped in a pleasant haze, floating somewhere between sleeping and waking. The virtually silent engine and the gentle music issuing from the car's speakers had had her sinking more comfortably into her seat and closing her eyes some time ago. It was the sudden cessation of noise as the music was turned off which brought her eyes open with a start, and she turned puzzled green orbs towards the driver, her Titian hair swinging about her face as she did so.

'What's up?' Glancing ahead, she expected to see trouble in the form of an accident, but the road, winding through a Lakeland landscape clad in a late-winter fall of snow, was empty.

'We're almost there,' declared Drew Templeton, her cousin and the reason she was sitting here heading into the Cumbrian wilds, as if that explained everything.

As far as Kathryn was concerned, it left a lot to be desired. Sitting up, she glanced at him curiously. 'So what's turned you so serious all of a sudden?'

Drew's fingers tapped out a nervy tattoo on the steering wheel. 'Nothing, really,' he denied, then added, 'I thought I'd better warn you about Joel, that's all.'

Finely arched brows rose questioningly in a heart-shaped face. Drew had been fairly reticent about his employer. All she knew was that he had trouble with his computer, and, because she cared for her cousin, she had agreed to help. She ran a small but flourishing business sorting out problems with computer programs.

5

'What about him?' It seemed to her a fine time to start issuing warnings, when they were almost at journey's end, but she guessed Drew hadn't wanted to risk her running out on him. The rat. Not that she would have. 'OK, tell me the worst. Is he some sort of monster?' she teased lightly, and he gave her a sombre look.

'Not exactly. I think the best way to describe Joel Kendrick is as a wolf in wolf's clothing,' he declared seriously.

The description had her ears pricking up. Really? She had never met an honest-to-goodness real life wolf before. What would he be like? Handsome, of course, with sex appeal dripping from every pore, or how else would he attract women? How did he go about seducing them? What, she wondered, with a quickening of her heart, would it be like flirting with him? The thought sent a tiny tremor of anticipation along her spine. There was nothing she enjoyed more than a light-hearted flirtation with a handsome, like-minded man. The weekend, which had offered only some interesting work, now took on a different complexion entirely. Smiling to herself, Kathryn folded her arms and gave Drew her full attention.

'How interesting. Do tell me more!' she invited with barely suppressed enthusiasm.

Her cousin groaned, not at all surprised by her response. Kathryn was cheerful and vivacious, and generally saw life as an adventure. Instead of viewing Joel Kendrick as someone to be avoided, she was more likely to see only the challenge of flirting with him. Unfortunately, his employer wasn't like most men she met. It worried him that there was a real danger here, and he didn't want to see her hurt.

'Listen, Kathy, I'm being serious. Joel is my em-

ployer, and I like him, but I don't have to approve of
his attitude towards the opposite sex. He has a predatory
eye for beautiful women. When he sees one he wants,
he goes after her with single-minded intent. Oh, he
treats his women well, but he's only interested in an
affair. Marriage is quite out of the question. Which, in-
cidentally, is why you're here.'

Far from being put off, Kathryn felt her curiosity
sharpen. 'You mean, one of his women caused this
computer malfunction?'

'Apparently she took exception to his ending their
affair, and we think she slipped back into the house
whilst he was out and deleted everything she could lay
her hands on. Then the system crashed, and…. Well,
this isn't my field. God knows what else she did, but
according to Joel it's a mess.'

'I see,' Kathryn mused, silently praising the woman's
ingenuity. It certainly beat cutting his suits to shreds.
The woman had style.

Drew sighed and flicked on the indicator before turning off the main road. 'Joel called me and asked if I
knew anyone who could help. He doesn't want just anyone raking around in his business. I knew I could trust
you, but it wasn't until we were on our way that I realised taking you to Joel was like throwing you to the
wolf.'

'Because you think he might be interested in adding
me to his list of conquests?' Kathryn enquired teasingly,
and Drew turned troubled eyes on her.

'You certainly fit his criteria.'

She grinned. This was sounding very promising,
'You mean I'm breathing?' she taunted wryly.

'I mean, you're beautiful,' Drew corrected heavily,
and she quickly reached out and squeezed his arm.

'Thank you for the compliment,' she said warmly, and, unable to resist her patent affection, he grinned back at her.

'You're entirely welcome.'

Sitting back in her seat, Kathryn studied the starkly beautiful landscape. They were on a lakeside road, and the view was breathtaking. She liked winter. Everything seemed so sharp and clean. Eventually, though, her thoughts turned back to Joel Kendrick.

It was as well he wasn't looking for a wife, because he didn't sound her type at all. She was looking for that one man she would want to spend the rest of her life with. She knew that one day she would meet a man and fall in love with him in an instant, because love was like that. Whilst she waited, though, she wasn't averse to having some fun. So what if Drew's boss wasn't husband material? As a diversion he fitted the bill nicely. She was well and truly intrigued by the possibility of indulging in some fascinating exchanges with a man who must have flirtation down to a fine art. Really, Drew needn't worry about her being seduced by this latter-day Casanova. She had her head screwed on, and wasn't about to become Joel Kendrick's next conquest.

'So, Joel Kendrick is used to getting any woman he wants, is he?' she mused thoughtfully.

'Being handsome and rich has something to do with it. Women seem to fall for him in droves,' Drew added dryly.

'Ah, the pull of sex appeal.'

She knew its power. Had fallen under its spell once or twice in her search for love and Mr Right. She knew she was as susceptible as the next woman when it came to a hunky male, but that didn't mean she gave in to it.

She had had a grand total of two relationships in her twenty-six years. It was no hardship to keep her relationships platonic. Sex for sex's sake had never had an appeal.

'What does he do? I mean, he doesn't simply chase women all day, does he?'

'He's a business man, with engineering companies worldwide. He can be ruthless at times, but he's well respected in the City. He took over the original company when his father retired, and has taken it from strength to strength. He's a force to be reckoned with, but unfortunately it means he's used to getting his own way.'

So, he was a strong-willed man. Well, she was used to strong-willed men. Her father and brothers were such men, with a tendency to issue commands to the youngest child and only daughter because they loved her and wanted to protect her. She understood that, but never let them ride roughshod over her. Consequently, their battles had become legendary. She was, after all, her father's daughter, and equally strong-willed.

'Do you honestly think I'm likely to be interested in him?'

'I hope not,' Drew responded fervently. There was no knowing quite which way Kathryn would go, but a prudent man expected the worst. He pulled a face. 'Though it's been my experience that women can't seem to help themselves where he's concerned.'

She laughed wryly, easily following his line of thought. The trouble with Drew was that he knew her too well. 'Thanks for the vote of confidence. As it happens, I'm no push-over. Have you given thought to the possibility that *I* might not like *him*?' The law of probability said that there must be some women who were immune to his practised charm.

'No. You'd do something silly just for fun even if you didn't like him. Just don't get involved with him,' Drew commanded. 'Be kind to yourself, Kathy. He's not the sort of man you want to play around with.'

There was no doubting his concern, and she loved him for it, but she felt he was rather jumping the gun. OK, she was thinking of sharpening her claws a little, but she could always change her mind. 'I tell you what, I'll take it under advisement. For now, I think I'll just reserve judgement. After all, I haven't even met the man!'

A situation which was about to be remedied some fifteen minutes later, when Drew brought the car to a halt before a large stone-built house, with gables and an extra wing tacked on to one end of it.

'So, this is the wolf's lair?' Kathryn declared, tongue very firmly in cheek, as she climbed out of the car. It was beautiful.

Drew retrieved their luggage from the boot. 'Come and meet him. I hope you've got some garlic handy.'

'Silly, that's only good against vampires. What I need is a silver bullet, and I'm fresh out of those. I'll put them on my shopping list.'

'You may joke now,' Drew responded, seeing her determination to make light of the situation as a bad sign. 'I only hope you don't end up laughing on the other side of your face.'

Kathryn slipped an arm through his and squeezed gently. 'Don't worry, Drew. I can take care of myself.'

He looked at her doubtfully. 'Hmm. Famous last words. Oh, well, I've had my say. It's up to you now.'

The sound of footsteps came from inside as Kathryn

replied, 'I'm a big girl. I had my twenty-sixth birthday a month ago, remember.'

'I know; I was there. And, I'm happy to say, you were very well behaved. Perhaps you are getting some sense after all. Am I being overprotective?'

She smiled at him. 'Just a bit, but you're allowed.'

'It's just that with my flying off to Germany tomorrow I won't be here to protect you.'

Would her family ever stop protecting her? she wondered wryly. 'Stop worrying. I'll be fine. But if worse comes to worse, I'll let you say I told you so.'

The door opened before Drew could respond by telling her it didn't make him feel any better. Framed in the doorway, a cheerful woman in her sixties smiled warmly at them.

'Good afternoon, Mr Templeton. You made good time, then?' she greeted Drew, and nodded at Kathryn, stepping back so that they could enter.

'I thought it best not to keep him waiting, Agnes. Didn't want to make him testy,' Drew said, urging Kathryn inside ahead of him, where the warmth enveloped them both. 'Agnes is Joel's housekeeper, and all-round good egg. This is my cousin Kathryn. She's come to the rescue.'

The older woman looked at Kathryn more closely and her face fell comically. 'Oh dear,' she said faintly, and Kathryn frowned in ready concern.

'Is something wrong?'

'Not at all, my dear,' Agnes denied as she closed the front door. 'You're very welcome, I'm sure. It's just….you're very pretty.'

'Ah,' said Kathryn, seeing the light, and couldn't help laughing, though not unkindly. 'It's all right, Agnes. Drew has told me all about our furry friend.'

'Furry friend?' It was the housekeeper's turn to look puzzled.

Kathryn leant down towards the woman, who was a good half a head shorter. 'The wolf,' she whispered confidentially. 'Don't worry, I had a tetanus booster not long ago.'

'Just lead us to him, Agnes,' her cousin suggested, setting their bags at the foot of the stairs and removing his coat. He handed it to the housekeeper and Kathryn did the same. 'My cousin has a weird sense of humour. Don't try to understand her.'

Agnes, far from being put out, suddenly had a twinkle in her eye. 'Something tells me somebody might just have met his match. You're not at all what he was expecting. For one thing, he was expecting a man. You'll find him in the library, gnashing his teeth and cursing till the air is blue. I'll bring along some coffee in a few minutes. Unless you would prefer something else?'

Kathryn said coffee was fine, and Drew led the way to the back of the house, then along a passage to the west wing. As he opened the door, Kathryn felt her heart rate increase in sudden expectation, and smoothed the blue chenille jumper she wore with leggings down over her hips. As she followed her cousin inside, she heard a husky voice growl a greeting.

'It's about damn time you got here!' it said, and she grimaced. It sounded very much as if the wolf had a sore head.

She almost felt sorry for him. Almost. Stepping inside, she caught her first glimpse of the man she had heard so much about.

Joel Kendrick was certainly impressive. He stood by the fireplace, where a fire blazed welcomingly, a glass of what appeared to be whisky in his hand. He was a tall man, broad-shouldered and slim-hipped, and clearly at the peak of fitness. He wore jeans which hugged his long muscular legs, and a black sweater which outlined a powerfully masculine physique. He was somewhere in his mid-thirties, she guessed, with hair so dark it appeared blue where the light caught it. His face, even from the side, was most definitely handsome, but there was a ruggedness about it which prevented it from being too pretty.

There was no denying it; he was a very attractive man. In fact, he was the most attractive man she had seen in a long while. She could feel the aura of him even from where she stood, and rather unexpectedly it set her nerve-endings tingling like crazy. Even stationary he had a kind of dynamic magnetism which reached across the space separating them and touched her. At its basic level, it was the female responding to a prime example of the male of the species. Translated to the present day, it meant she could no more ignore him than she could stop breathing.

It wasn't at all what she'd been expecting, but she wasn't overly alarmed by it. On the contrary, it added a certain spice to the situation. It was time to make her presence felt.

'As we didn't have Scotty to beam us through the air in a split nanosecond, I think we did a pretty good job getting here so quickly,' she put in before Drew could utter a word, and instantly found herself staring into piercing blue eyes.

They were the sort of eyes which, in certain circumstances, would create havoc with a woman's senses, and when they locked with hers that was precisely what they did. Because something elemental connected them in the space of a heartbeat. The air seemed to sizzle and hum between them, as if it had taken a positive charge. It was pure chemistry, and a look was all it had taken to set off a chain reaction. The attraction was instant— and mutual.

Kathryn experienced a familiar curling sensation inside her. She acknowledged it with a shiver of excitement. Attraction, pure but not so simple. Just as she had supposed, the man had sex appeal oozing from every pore, and it had struck her on a primitive level. Her senses responded by setting every nerve in her body tingling. Given his visual attraction, she wasn't surprised to feel it, but she was surprised by its strength. The man had something, and whatever it was her senses liked it. Liked it a lot.

His eyes as they roved over her were like a lick of flame, and she wondered if it had been wise to wear leggings tucked into knee-length boots for the journey. It showed off altogether too much of her to his gaze. Not that she revealed her concern for an instant. Every instinct she possessed told her that he was not the sort of man you gave any sort of weapon to.

'And you are?' Joel Kendrick asked curiously, in a voice laced with a lethal brand of husky sensuality. Setting his glass aside, he slipped his hands into the pockets of his jeans, a move which tightened the material around his thighs and raised her temperature accordingly.

The man was pure dynamite, she acknowledged wryly, and all done without even trying. It was stunning. Nobody had had quite this effect on her before. How could she possibly ignore it? Did she want to? That imp of devilment which was always under indifferent control now decided to come to the surface, and, as Drew had feared, she didn't resist it.

'I'm the woman you've been waiting for,' she quipped back with a deliberate mix of seduction and mockery.

Amusement flickered in those devilish blue eyes. 'Is that so?' he drawled softly, giving her his full attention in a way that set up goosebumps on her flesh.

Caught between them, Drew rolled his eyes despairingly. 'Kathryn, cut it out!' he ordered.

'Shut up, Drew,' Joel commanded quietly, strolling towards her. 'This is just getting interesting.' Coming to a halt a mere foot away, he smiled lazily, an action that threatened to steal her breath away. 'So, I've been waiting for you, have I?'

She inclined her head, smiling sweetly, whilst her heart raced away at a mile a minute at his closeness. 'Impatiently, by the sounds of it.'

He shrugged that off without taking his eyes from her. 'My temper's been a bit frayed lately, but it's improving by leaps and bounds now.'

Kathryn laughed, a sultry sound that made something flare to life in the depths of his eyes. 'I have that effect on people.' She knew she was behaving outrageously, but she couldn't seem to help herself. 'In fact, they've been known to hug and kiss me on sight.'

He grinned, and there was definitely something wolfish about it. 'I can quite see why. I'm tempted to do the same.'

Oh, boy, he had the charisma to make a woman forget her principles just when she ought to be standing on them, she decided as she held up an admonitory hand to keep him at bay. 'I should wait until you've seen what I can do first.'

Joel laughed, sending a tingle down her spine and curling her toes. 'I'm impressed already.'

Drew, by this time, had steam coming out of his ears. He crossed over to them and took Kathryn by the arm. 'OK, that's enough!' he exclaimed, and she turned startled eyes on him, having quite forgotten he was there. 'When you've quite finished playing games, perhaps I should introduce you.'

A faint flush skimmed her cheeks, but it had nothing to do with his remonstration. She mouthed the word 'sorry' to him. It was partly true. She was sorry for upsetting him, but not for behaving as she had. It had been fun. It had been exciting. Her heart was still tripping madly, with no sign of slowing. Boy, the man was positively lethal. He had switched her senses on like a neon light. So that was what it felt like to flirt with the world's number one playboy! It could become addictive. Already she wanted more.

Drew, meanwhile, was making the promised introductions. 'Joel, this is my cousin, Kathryn Templeton. She's here to sort out your computer for you.'

Joel's eyes immediately narrowed on her thoughtfully. 'Ah, now I get it. That's what makes you the woman I've been waiting for.'

'Impatiently,' she added for good measure, laughing into his eyes.

He took a deep breath, which expanded his chest magnificently. 'Well, let's hope you're as good with bits and bytes as you are with words, Kathryn Templeton.'

Another laugh escaped her. 'With all modesty I can say I'm better.'

One eyebrow quirked lazily. 'All modesty? You don't believe in hiding your light under a bushel?'

She shrugged and exchanged a knowing look with her cousin. 'In my family you have to fight your corner or sink without trace. I don't intend to be the next *Titanic*.'

'Competitive, are they, your family?'

'Like you wouldn't believe. I have four older brothers,' she admitted, not to mention her father. She tucked her arm through Drew's. 'This side of the Templeton clan is protective and supportive without being combative, I'm happy to say.'

Joel rubbed his chin wryly. 'Which means he's probably warned you about the Big Bad Wolf.'

'Of course. He doesn't want to see me devoured like Red Riding Hood,' she responded brightly.

Joel looked amused. 'Something tells me if I tried it, I'd probably get indigestion.'

'I'm certainly too rich for some people's taste,' Kathryn agreed breezily.

'An acquired taste?'

'Absolutely.'

His expression revealing equal amounts of intrigue and appreciation, Joel Kendrick held out his hand. 'It's a pleasure to make your acquaintance, Kathryn Templeton,' he declared, his voice again carrying that husky sensuality which found its mark and set the nerves in her stomach quivering.

Nonetheless, she smiled back. 'Likewise, Mr Kendrick,' she returned smartly.

'Joel,' he prompted with a decided gleam in his eye as she took his hand.

'Joel,' she repeated obediently, a cool smile hovering about her lips.

What happened next rocked her belief in her ability to remain detached and in control. As their hands touched, she looked into those wickedly alluring, fathomless blue eyes and found herself drowning in them.

For an instant she lost her bearings entirely. Her nervous system went into overload and her breath got lodged in her throat, so that she forgot to breathe. The swiftness of her response to him was stunning. She had felt sexual attraction before, but never experienced quite this brand of magnetic potency. It drew her as nothing else had. Sensible thought was vanquished by a tidal wave of sensuality. In the flicker of a heartbeat she wanted him. Craved him like a hungry woman craved food, and her body swayed towards him, seeking appeasement. Seeking...

The sound of a polite cough gathered her scattered wits into a seething whole, and Kathryn careened back into the present with a gasp. She had an instant to see the answering passion in those blue eyes before the instinct of self-preservation took over and she swiftly hid her thoughts behind practised calm. She eased her hand away just as Agnes brought in a tray of coffee, and she turned to the woman, grateful for the breathing space.

Joel Kendrick had proved to be more than a little overwhelming close up. Always before she had had the ability to keep a cool head, but this man had changed that completely. It shook her, and sent a frisson of alarm through her system. Drew was right, this man was different. She had an inkling of what he could do to her, and it was distinctly unsettling.

'Can I help you with that, Agnes?' she asked in a voice that thankfully gave away nothing of her inner turmoil.

The housekeeper smiled at her. 'Thank you, my dear. If you'd just move that vase to one side... There.' She set the tray down whilst Kathryn found another spot for the vase. When she straightened up, she glanced at Drew. 'Have you eaten, Mr Templeton?'

'Not since this morning, Agnes,' Drew admitted.

It was a cue for Kathryn to shoot Joel a mocking look. She might be all of a twitter inside, but not for the world would she let anyone know it, least of all the cause. Keeping up the appearance of normality was suddenly very important. Having started out flirtatiously, she couldn't now back off without giving too much away.

'He said we couldn't spare the time. Food was weighed in the balance against your temper, and found wanting,' she taunted gently, not averse to saying what she thought. She was here to do him a favour. Her livelihood didn't rest upon his goodwill. Besides, she felt the need to goad him a little, because the best form of defence was often attack. Until she had had time to think, it seemed the most appropriate thing to do.

Joel's response was to raise an eyebrow, but he said nothing to her, merely turned to his housekeeper. 'You'd better bring dinner forward, Agnes. I'd hate to see such a beautiful woman fainting away.'

'Very good, Master Joel,' Agnes agreed. 'I've put Mr Templeton in his usual room, and I thought it best to put the young lady in the rose room.'

Joel's expression became wry, but he smiled fondly at the elderly woman. 'Quite right. The rose room does have some of the best views.'

'And it's on the other side of the house from you,' Agnes added pointedly, causing Kathryn to hastily smother a laugh. 'Now, if you'd give me a hand with the cases, Mr Templeton, I can get the food on the table sooner,' she declared in her motherly fashion, and bustled out again.

'*Master* Joel?' Kathryn asked in amusement, after Drew had obediently followed the other woman from the room. She had recovered her equilibrium, and felt more able to hold her own with him now that her pulse had steadied.

Joel pulled a wry face. 'Agnes used to be my nanny. She's been with my family for many years, and nobody wanted to see her go, so her position has changed several times. She was companion to my mother before becoming my housekeeper. She's more like one of the family now.'

Kathryn felt a curl of warmth grow inside her at his explanation. It showed, she was glad to notice, that there was a softer side to him. 'I like that.' Her grandfather, her mother's father, treated his servants as something below his notice. His only interest in their welfare was in how it would affect him.

'You approve?'

'I always approve of kindness. My grandfather would call it foolish sentimentality,' she admitted regretfully. 'You don't keep somebody on when they're past their usefulness.'

'Your grandfather, if you'll forgive me for saying so, is a fool.'

Kathryn smiled wryly. 'Blunt, but true. He's a cold man. I'll never understand how my grandmother came to marry him, but it's no mystery to me why she left. I'm very like her, so I'm told.'

Joel raised an eyebrow questioningly. 'Don't you know?'

'He won't have a picture of her in the house,' she explained evenly. 'She humiliated him, you see, by leaving. I used to think the reason he didn't like me was because I reminded him of her.' Childhood visits to her grandfather's house had been far from pleasant.

'But you don't think that now?'

She smiled and shook her head. 'The truth is it isn't in him to love or be loved.'

'Whereas you are eminently loveable,' he declared with a decidedly rakish gleam lighting up his eyes again.

Barely recovered from the last time, the nerves in Kathryn's stomach quivered in reaction, but she laughed and shot him an old-fashioned look. 'Do you think flattery is going to get you somewhere?' she asked, sounding far too breathless to her own ears, but thankfully Joel didn't appear to notice.

His grin was charmingly lopsided. 'A man has to live in hope.'

Kathryn groaned silently. Everything about him pleased her rioting senses. It was amazing she was still on her feet, considering her knees felt like jelly. Still she battled on. Tipping her head to one side, she eyed him thoughtfully. 'Are you really as good as they say you are?'

He placed a hand on his chest, whilst a smile flickered round the edges of his mouth. 'In all humility, I couldn't possibly say.'

Oh, Lord, just let me get through the next few minutes without turning into a gibbering idiot, she prayed silently, as the power of his charm hit her yet more devastatingly. 'Meaning, if I want to know, I'll have to find out for myself?'

His shrug was careless, but his eyes glittered invitingly. 'There's nothing to compare with first-hand knowledge. You might find it...interesting.'

She was sure she would. This was seduction on the grand scale, and, despite her floundering senses, she met it with a gurgling laugh. 'I'm sure it would be educational, but there's always the danger of the commodity being overpriced.'

'Trust me,' Joel urged throatily. 'I always do my very best to give value for money.'

'Hmm,' she murmured consideringly, whilst the nerves in her stomach fluttered around like demented butterflies. Oh, he was good. He was very good. All he'd done was utter a few innuendoes and she was quivering like a jelly because her mind had filled in the gaps with vivid pictures that definitely needed censoring.

'I've a feeling the woman who mashed your computer felt just a little short-changed,' she observed ironically, and Joel's smile vanished like magic. She blinked, surprised to find she had hit a nerve. So the man was vulnerable after all.

'She took the relationship too seriously,' he declared shortly, and Kathryn's heart lurched as she took in the message. She knew it wasn't specifically aimed at her, but it might as well have been. Her nerves steadied as she heeded the warning shot across her bows.

'Perhaps she didn't intend to. Perhaps she fell in love with you,' she suggested, and her lips parted on a soft gasp as her statement brought a chilly glitter to his eyes.

'I didn't ask her to,' he added grimly, and she laughed chidingly,

'Nobody asks to fall in love, they just do,' she argued, stating what most people accepted as universal, but Joel looked at her steadily.

'I don't, and I never intend to. I make no secret of it.'

Kathryn felt a chill wind brush past her and shivered faintly because he had sounded so adamant. 'How can you be so certain you'll never fall in love?' she asked curiously. It seemed to her a rash statement to make.

'Because in order for it to happen you have to believe in it, and I don't believe in love,' he told her firmly, but she saw the flaw in his argument immediately.

'You love Agnes,' she said softly, and his eyes narrowed.

'That's different. The kind of love we're talking about between a man and a woman doesn't exist.'

The flat statement, in direct opposition to her own belief, couldn't pass without argument. 'There are countless millions of people out there who would disagree with you. They can't all be wrong.'

He dismissed them, and her, with a shrug. 'If they want to believe in fairy tales, I won't stop them.'

Kathryn shook her head sadly. 'You know, beliefs like that are likely to get shot down in flames. It wouldn't surprise me if one day love hit you right between the eyes and proved you wrong.'

Joel laughed out loud, his good humour restored as quickly as it had departed. 'I won't be holding my breath. And don't you let those rose-coloured glasses of yours trip you up. I wouldn't want to see all that beauty spoilt.'

Kathryn smiled at him confidently. 'It won't be. You see, I happen to believe the man for me is out there somewhere. I just haven't met him yet.'

'And in the meantime?'

She laughed, her shrug a masterful touch. 'In the meantime, I enjoy searching, because there are interesting stops along the way.'

He stepped heart-stoppingly closer. 'Like coming here to sort out my computer?'

His closeness didn't make thinking easier. Still, she managed to find a chirpy reply. 'Exactly. If I hadn't said I'd help Drew, who knows when I would have met another Big Bad Wolf?'

'You're not afraid of me?'

'Should I be? Do you intend to devour me?' she challenged scoffingly, knowing she wasn't the least bit afraid of him.

The fires in his eyes sent out sparks. 'The idea becomes more enticing by the minute. Doesn't it?' he charged softly, the question heavy with meaning, and her breath caught as her stomach twisted with a powerful surge of desire.

Her lips trembled faintly, drawing his eyes. Crazy as it was, her flesh tingled as if he had actually touched her. Warning bells went off in her head. 'I think this is where I should protest that we have only just met.'

Reaching out, he drew a finger lightly across her lips, setting up a tingle she felt to her core. 'Maybe we have, but it took only a second for both of us to know we want each other.'

Without warning he had brought the unspoken out into the open and her brows rose. Instinct put her on the defensive. '*Do* we know it?' she charged mockingly, and he nodded.

'Oh, yes, and I give you fair warning. When I want something, I usually get it.'

Her throat closed over and she had to swallow hard to answer. 'It never does anyone any good to get everything they want,' she pointed out with creditable calmness.

His smile was pure seduction. 'Resist it if you want. It makes victory even sweeter.'

Her heart tripped. Like a big cat sensing its prey's vulnerability, he was trying to outflank her. She couldn't allow that to happen. 'Such confidence! You could lose, you know.'

'I could, but I'm going to do everything in my power to ensure that I don't.'

Kathryn gasped. 'Your arrogance is incredible!'

'My lovemaking is better,' he returned sexily, and sent her defences scattering to the four winds.

Wow! This man had all the weapons, and then some. Taking a steadying breath, Kathryn urged her fluttering heart to be still. Drew was right; this man was dangerous. If he could make her defences crumble without really trying, what would happen if and when he did try? It was more than time to beat a strategic retreat.

'I'll have to take your word on that. For the moment I'm more interested in freshening up before dinner. Agnes has put me in the rose room, isn't that right?' she said, with all the composure she could muster.

'This time I'll let you run away, but it won't always be so. Left at the top of the stairs and follow your nose. You can't miss it. No doubt Agnes will have fitted the steel door by now in an attempt to keep me out,' he added sardonically, and Kathryn left the room feeling as if she had been put through a wringer.

Events had taken an unexpected turn. This was not how she had foreseen the weekend going. Joel had turned her world on its head, and she found herself in a situation entirely new to her. Joel Kendrick wanted her and she wanted him. The problem was, she had never entered into a relationship that had no happy ending in sight. And that, if she responded to the way he could make her feel, was what she would have to do. He had made that very clear. From nowhere, she found herself with some serious decisions to make, and very little time to make them.

CHAPTER TWO

UPSTAIRS in her bedroom, Kathryn sank down onto the bed and gave her wobbly legs a much needed rest. She felt shattered and intoxicated in equal quantities. Nothing could have adequately prepared her for meeting Joel Kendrick. No advance warnings could have equipped her for the reality. She had thought to have some fun, and certainly hadn't expected to be attracted to him so strongly, or to have that attraction reciprocated.

What she felt went way beyond anything in her experience. She could honestly say she had never felt such an intense physical attraction. It was there between them like a living, breathing thing. What did she do about it? That was the question. She knew what Joel wanted, but what did *she* want?

To have an affair with Joel would no doubt be an incredible experience, but it would break her own rules, because if he were to be believed—and she had no reason to doubt him—there was no future in it. She might like to flirt, but she wasn't a fool. She never went further unless she thought there might be a future with the man.

Only, there was a part of her which said this time was special. That she would be a fool to turn it down. Yet if she took what was on offer, that would be doing what Drew had said, and throwing herself to the wolf. Would being part of his life for a brief time be worth it? Certainly she wouldn't know unless she tried it. But she was only here for two days. Two days wouldn't even amount to an affair. It would be, at best, a brief encounter. Surely she had more respect for herself than to give in to her passions for a mere forty-eight hours?

With a heavy sigh she fell back onto the bed, knowing the answer. Common sense said it had to be no. She mustn't allow herself more than a brief flirtation. At least she had an inkling of just how dangerous he could be to her if she wasn't careful. She was going to have to keep her wits about her, for she didn't doubt for a moment that he would take advantage of their mutual attraction. His reputation was proof enough. Pride dictated that she must not become his next conquest, no matter how strong the pull on her senses.

A soft knock on the door brought her up on her elbow.

'Who is it?'

'Drew,' the muffled voice responded, and she grimaced, knowing what was coming.

'Come in,' she invited, scrambling to the side of the bed and swinging her legs down.

Drew looked at her closely as he entered and shut the door, and she wondered what he expected to see.

'It's OK, you don't have to say it, I know,' she declared wryly, hoping to head him off at the pass. No such luck.

Her cousin came and sat beside her, concern heavy on his brow. 'What were you thinking of?' he challenged despairingly, and that brought a smile to her lips.

'It wasn't the sort of situation where thinking came into it,' she returned wryly. She had simply responded to the signals coming off Joel, and her own rioting senses.

'Kathy, this man could break your heart.'

Reaching for Drew's hand, she squeezed it reassuringly. 'Don't worry. I'm not going to let him. I have no intention of being seduced.'

'But you are attracted to him?' Drew persisted, and she shrugged fatalistically.

'I won't deny it. He's a very attractive man. But I'm not stupid, Drew. I know where to draw the line.'

He didn't look totally convinced, but grudgingly accepted what she said with a proviso. 'Just make sure Joel knows where the line is, too.'

Kathryn stood up and tugged him to his feet. 'Oh, I intend to. Now, get out of here and let me freshen up. I'm starving, and the smells wafting up are making my stomach rumble. Besides, if I'm quick, I could get a look at that computer before dinner. The sooner I start, the sooner I can be finished and on my way home.'

That clearly met with his approval, and he went without further comment, leaving Kathryn to sigh heavily. Then, because she was a practical person, not given to languishing on thoughts of what might have been, she gathered together her sponge bag and a change of clothes and went in search of the bathroom.

As it turned out, Kathryn didn't get an opportunity to look over Joel's computer until after dinner. When she went back downstairs, this time dressed in a long-sleeved holly-green dress made of soft wool, she met Agnes coming from the dining room.

'My, don't you look nice this evening, miss,' the housekeeper declared with a warm smile.

Kathryn smiled back. 'Thank you, Agnes. Something smells good.'

'Lancashire hotpot. Master Joel's favourite. The table's set, so it won't be more than a few minutes now.

If you go into the sitting room, you can help yourself to a drink before dinner,' Agnes suggested, pointing to a door on the other side of the hall.

Realising her hope of looking over the computer had to be abandoned, Kathryn obediently made her way to the sitting room. It was a pleasant room, with comfortable sofas and armchairs surrounding the brick fireplace where another fire blazed cheerfully. Drinks were set on a tray on the sideboard, and Kathryn helped herself to a small Martini. If she wanted to get some work done later, drinking too much now would be inadvisable.

She was studying a group of photos on the mantelpiece when a subtle shift of the air told her Joel had come into the room. She had never been so attuned to a man that she could sense his presence even at a distance. It was uncanny, and she didn't know quite what to make of it. Turning, she found him just inside the door, studying her with eyes that gleamed appreciatively. In response, her nerves took a tiny leap and set her pulse throbbing. He looked magnificent, and her heart did a crazy lurch as her own eyes ate him up. The white silk shirt and black trousers he now wore barely seemed to tame him. He moved, coming towards her with a lithe, pantherish grace that tightened her stomach with desire.

'You look good enough to eat,' he murmured, his gaze setting her nerves alight with such disconcerting ease it was a wonder she didn't melt on the spot.

'I thought hotpot was your favourite,' she countered, far too breathlessly for comfort, and he was smiling softly as he looked deeply into her eyes.

'When it comes to food, yes. However, the appetite you arouse will settle for nothing less than your presence in my bed.'

It was heady stuff on an empty stomach, and she groaned silently, aware that her body responded to every soft word with a will of its own. Still, she had made her decision and would stick to it.

'If you check with the management, I think you'll find I'm not on the menu,' she returned smoothly, watching the way his eyes crinkled at the corners when his smile deepened.

He bent towards her confidingly. 'Could you really watch me starve?' he taunted softly, and she raised an eyebrow quizzically.

'Somehow, I don't think you'd starve for long,' she quipped, and strangely enough it hurt to say it, which was odd, for she had always known she was not important to him. She was no more than a passing fancy because she was here.

'Ah, but sometimes hunger can only be satisfied by one thing—or one woman,' Joel insisted softly.

Kathryn took a steadying sip of her drink, fearing he was right. He had come out with all guns blazing this evening, and the attack on her defences were definitely weakening them. She needed the drink to strengthen her resolve.

'But hunger is such a contrary thing. Now it wants one thing; next time it wants something completely different,' she countered, but he shook his head.

'Not always. Sometimes it takes a very long time for hunger to be satisfied.'

'Just not for ever,' Kathryn shot back pointedly, and he acknowledged the hit with an inclination of his head.

'No, not for ever. Everything diminishes in time,' Joel agreed as he wandered over to the drinks tray and poured himself a small whisky. Sipping it, he looked at her over the glass.

'There is an exception, though I hesitate to mention it, knowing your opinion of love,' Kathryn reminded him, and he lowered the glass.

'Do you really think this love you believe in lasts for ever?' he asked curiously.

'It can do, but it has to be worked at. You can't ever take it for granted, but the more you feed it the more it grows,' she said with utter conviction, and that brought a tiny frown to his forehead.

'You can say that, even though your own grandparents' marriage failed?'

She sighed. He had to pick on the one failure to illustrate his case, but his argument was based on a false premise. 'The marriage failed because there was only love on one side. My mother has told me many times that my grandmother loved my grandfather; she just couldn't live with his coldness.' Left alone with her father, it hadn't been easy for her mother either. In the end it had driven Lucy Makepeace to find a place of her own to live as soon as she was old enough.

'What happened to your grandmother?' Joel asked conversationally, sliding one hand casually into the pocket of his trousers.

The question caught her off-guard, allowing the old sadness to show in her eyes as she frowned. 'I really don't know. There was a messy divorce and a bitter custody battle, which my grandfather won, and that was the last anyone ever saw of her,' she revealed with a faint shrug of her shoulders.

'You miss her?' Joel asked curiously, and Kathryn sighed heavily, because her feelings concerning the situation were more complex than a simple answer could convey.

'It's hard to miss someone you never knew. What I

miss is not having known her. The person she was. There is so much about her I want to know,' she said honestly, and her smile was deprecating. 'I guess I want to ask her why she never came to see my mother. I can't ask my grandfather because he never speaks of her. It's a mystery I don't know how to solve.'

'Have you never tried to trace her?'

Kathryn shook her head. 'I wouldn't know where to start,' she declared wistfully, then, because thinking of her grandmother always left her dissatisfied, she made a determined effort to lift her spirits. 'What about you? Are both your parents living?'

'Oh, yes. They're still going strong, and seem younger than ever, even though they celebrated their golden wedding last year. At present they're in Canada, visiting relatives. Then they're off to Hawaii,' Joel confirmed, and she tipped her head to one side thoughtfully.

'So they weren't the ones who made you so cynical about love. That means it has to be a woman,' she mused, watching him carefully. But, as she was coming to expect, he gave nothing away.

Instead one eyebrow lifted lazily. 'You think so?'

Kathryn laughed softly. 'It has to be, and you haven't denied it. What did she do? Leave you for another man?'

Joel shook his head. 'She couldn't, as she's nothing but a figment of your imagination.'

Her eyes narrowed as she tossed that around in her mind. 'Hmm, I see. That's very interesting. If it wasn't one woman, then it has to be all women. What do we fail to do that convinces you love doesn't exist?' She posed the question to herself, and almost immediately saw the answer. 'We don't see you as just a man, do we? All we see is a bank balance. An unending source of spending money. That's it, isn't it?' she charged him, convinced she was right.

In response, Joel drained his glass and set it aside. When he looked at her again, there was a dangerous glitter in his eyes. 'You're very perceptive.'

'That's because I have a similar problem. My father is a very wealthy man, and I'm his only daughter. Which makes me an heiress set to inherit a fortune, and a prime target. There are a lot of men out there who would like to get their hands on the money they think I'll get one day,' Kathryn returned with a grimace of distaste.

'And yet you still believe in fairy stories,' Joel remarked scornfully, and she tilted her chin upwards defiantly.

'That's because I know all men are not the same. Neither are all women.'

He came to her then, his hand reaching out to cup her chin. 'That hasn't been my experience. I prefer to believe in what I know exists: desire. Love is a fallacy; sexual attraction is real. You feel it. Right now your heart is beating just a little bit faster, isn't it? I can see that delicious pulse throbbing in your throat. It's urging me to kiss it. To know the feel and taste of you,' he whispered huskily, his eyes glowing with a fierce heat as they looked into hers.

Kathryn's heart lurched in response to the siren call of his desire. She wanted him to do it, too. Her flesh seemed to scream out for it, and it was incredibly painful to step back away from him, forcing his hand to drop to his side.

'I hardly think this is the time or the place for what you have in mind,' she told him sardonically, and he smiled faintly.

'Nevertheless, you felt it. You felt the hunger.'

Oh, boy, had she! Her whole body was still pulsating with it. 'Maybe I did, but right now I have a more urgent hunger that needs satisfying. I haven't eaten all day,' she protested, seeking to bring some order to the sensual chaos she felt whenever he was near.

Joel laughed wryly. 'Then we must deal with that one first. The other will be all the better for waiting.'

'What will be better?' Drew enquired idly as he strolled into the room, looking from one to the other questioningly.

Kathryn felt colour heat her cheeks, aware that if he had arrived a few minutes sooner he would have walked in on quite a different scenario, and she wouldn't have heard the last of it.

'Dinner,' she explained with feigned nonchalance. 'I was just saying I hadn't eaten all day. I'm starving.'

'Me, too,' Drew agreed, and as if to underline the fact his stomach rumbled audibly.

'Help yourself to a drink, Drew,' Joel invited with a laugh. 'I'll just go and see what's keeping Agnes.'

Drew followed the suggestion, but turned to his cousin the instant they were alone. 'Dinner?' he challenged with an old-fashioned look.

Kathryn stared him out, her chin raised. 'What else?' she countered, daring him to argue, but Drew, for once, wisely decided to hold his own counsel. She drained her glass and was tempted to refill it. Joel had won round one on points; she could only hope to do better in round two.

Dinner was every bit as delicious as it had promised to be. The meat and vegetables were cooked to perfection, and there was fresh crusty bread to go with it. The two men spent most of the meal discussing Drew's trip to Germany tomorrow, and Kathryn was happy to be left alone. She found herself watching Joel with fascination. Even talking business, he had an animation about him that held her rapt. She didn't bother to follow the thread of the conversation, for Drew's job was as much a mystery to her as hers was to him, merely sat and enjoyed the view.

'I'm sorry,' Joel apologised later as they sat over coffee. 'It was rude to exclude you, but there were certain matters I needed to touch base on with Drew before he leaves.'

Kathryn shrugged that off. She wasn't so vain she needed constant attention. 'No problem. I was far more interested in my food. Agnes is a wonderful cook.'

'I'll be sure to tell her you said so,' he responded, pushing his empty cup away. 'It's not too late. If you're not too tired, we can take a look at the computer now,' he declared with a glance at his watch.

Kathryn was never too tired to work on a computer. 'That's fine by me.' She nodded, and stood up. 'Are you coming, Drew?'

'I'll beg off, if you don't mind. Computers are a complete turn-off for me. Go ahead and enjoy yourselves,' he teased, though, unseen by his cousin, his smile faded as he watched them leave.

Joel's study was at the rear of the house and was set up with state-of-the-art equipment from the computer itself, to fax machines, printers and scanners. Everything he could possibly need was there, but he couldn't use it because of what one woman had done in anger.

'So, this is the scene of the crime,' Kathryn declared dryly, looking around her with interest. 'At least she didn't resort to smashing things. OK, let's see just what damage she did do.' Making herself comfortable at the desk, she switched the computer on, and the first thing that appeared was a message informing Joel he had mail.

'The Internet's working at least,' she observed wryly, hoping it was a good sign that things weren't too bad after all. 'Want to see what it is?'

Standing behind her, his hands resting on the back of her chair, Joel nodded. 'OK.'

Clicking on the box, Kathryn watched the screen unfold. The message itself was short and sweet, and originated from someone called Magda. 'That's her, I take it?' she enquired with lashings of irony, for the message was explicit about what Joel could do with certain parts of his anatomy.

'She has a volatile temper,' Joel said by way of confirmation.

That much was obvious. 'Her knowledge of human anatomy seems a little basic. Does she know you can't actually do that?' she taunted over her shoulder.

'Just get on with it, will you?' he growled irritably, and she bit back a smile. Right now he was more like a grouchy bear than a wolf.

Kathryn started hitting keys. 'I'd get on better if you weren't breathing over my shoulder,' she remarked. It was unsettling, not to say downright distracting. She could feel the heat of his body even through the chair, whilst her nose was assailed by the tangy scent of his cologne mixed with pure male essence. It sent messages to her brain that were totally out of place, even if they were undeniably tantalising.

Instead of moving away, Joel lowered his head until his mouth was next to her ear. 'Does my being this close bother you?' he asked in that sexy drawl which crawled over her flesh, starting up flash-fires which made concentrating on the job at hand extremely difficult.

Feeling too hot and far too bothered for comfort, she nevertheless denied it. 'Not at all.'

'Liar,' he taunted with a chuckle, and she closed her eyes momentarily as a powerful wave of desire swept through her system. She was glad she was sitting, because standing would have been an effort. He was playing hardball, and it didn't help that her senses were fighting on his side.

'Abuse me at your peril,' she warned him, her fingers flying over the keys whilst she struggled to appear cool, calm and collected. It was nothing short of amazing that she never hit a wrong one. 'I can probably do a lot worse to your hard drive than dear Magda did,' she added, then sat back with a tiny frown creasing her forehead.

'How does it look?' Joel asked seriously, and she folded her arms.

'It looks as if she was seriously miffed with you!' Kathryn exclaimed sardonically. From her very brief perusal it was hard to say just how extensive the damage was, but one thing had swiftly become apparent. Magda was no novice when it came to computers. She had known what she was doing.

'We'll take that as read, shall we?' Joel suggested tersely, and Kathryn obligingly subdued her amusement.

'OK, seriously. Have you any idea what's missing?'

'All the work I've been doing on several new projects.'

'Did you keep back-up files on disk?' One look at his face told her the answer to that.

'I made back-up files in the system, but I couldn't find them. I presume she deleted them, too.'

Kathryn sighed heavily. 'In future I suggest you copy sensitive material on disk and put them somewhere safe. At a guess, I'd say all your files are gone. The question is, was she mad enough to wipe them entirely, or did she just trash them? Which means we can retrieve them with a bit of work. Now, if she really wanted to be mean, she could have infected you with a virus.'

'I keep the anti-virus constantly updated,' Joel informed her, and she was relieved, because they could be darned tricky devils.

'Thank goodness for that. Still, I'll check that she didn't set a booby-trap before continuing. You realise there's every probability she wasn't actually physically here, don't you? She would have logged into your database from her own computer. At a guess, I'd say behind her undoubted feminine attractions dear Magda is a dedicated computer hacker,' she declared, looking up to find Joel frowning ferociously.

Catching her eye, he grimaced. 'I had no idea,' he admitted reluctantly.

The confession brought a mocking smile to her lips. 'Yes, well, her brain wasn't what you were interested in, was it?' she pointed out dulcetly.

Give him his due, Joel smiled ruefully, acknowledging the hit. 'We didn't do a lot of talking,' he confirmed, and she shook her head.

'Perhaps you ought to start vetting your women a little more closely. This is the twenty-first century. Women are not merely sex objects any longer. They have brains, and have even been known to use them.'

Straightening, he moved round her and propped a hip against the desk, folding his arms as if prepared to stay there for ever. 'I'm fully aware of that. I employ a good percentage of women in high-profile positions within my organisation.'

He rose a notch in her estimation. 'I'm glad to hear it.'

Joel tutted. 'Can we keep to the point? What I want to know from you is, can you repair the damage?'

Reproved, she folded her hands in her lap. 'Yes, I can. But it's going to take longer than I expected.'

His relief was palpable. 'Take all the time you need. It goes without saying I will pay you whatever you ask. I'm not going to quibble over the bill, because I need those files, and I need them yesterday.'

Kathryn smiled sweetly and pushed up her sleeves. 'Then you'd better let me get on with it. As soon as I've checked that there will be no nasty surprises, I'll be able to move along more quickly. Would you have Drew get my box of tricks for me?' she asked as she reached for the keypad once more.

'I'll get it. What does it look like?'

'It's a small black case. I left it on the dresser in my room,' she responded absently, her mind already running through the checks she would have to make. She didn't hear Joel leave the room, or come back a little later with the case, which he set on the desk beside her.

It was late when she finally closed down the computer and pushed back the chair with a groan as her body protested at having been fixed in one position so long. Yawning, she stretched, easing out the kinks.

'Well, what's the verdict?' A soft voice posed the question from the other side of the room, and she very nearly jumped out of her skin.

Her arms dropped, and, turning startled eyes in the direction the voice had come from, she discovered Joel sitting at his desk, a sheaf of papers in his hand. 'Have you been there all the time?' she charged in amazement, and he nodded.

'Pretty much. I went out for coffee once. Yours will be stone-cold by now,' he told her with some amusement, and Kathryn blinked, only now seeing the cup which had been set at her elbow.

'I didn't hear you,' she confessed, and he laughed softly.

'A herd of elephants could have stampeded through here and you wouldn't have heard them,' he retorted with wry humour.

Her grin was rueful because it was all too possible. 'I do tend to get a little wrapped up in my work.'

'Just a little,' he agreed.

They exchanged smiles, and in the blink of an eye the air seemed to thicken. Kathryn saw the look in his eyes change until its intensity scorched her and her eyes widened, her lips parting on a tiny gasp.

'Are you going to come over here, or am I going to have to come over there?' he asked her in a voice laden with so much passion she shivered.

Her body quickened, her senses silently screaming that either option would do. But there was still a sensible, sane portion of her brain in control, and she shook her head, albeit without any great deal of conviction.

'I think...' she began, only to stop when Joel set his papers down and rose to his feet.

'Don't think,' he ordered huskily, rounding the desk and coming towards her. 'I've been sitting here watching you chew on those luscious lips of yours for the past two hours and it's been driving me crazy,' he added with a groan.

Reaching out, he took her by the shoulders and lifted

her to her feet. Kathryn tried to protest, but her heart wasn't in it. Her hands rose to his chest to hold him off, but that was as far as they got. Instead of pushing him away, her fingers registered the heat of him and spread out like tiny fans to claim all of him they could. Swallowing hard, she stared up at him. Do something, her brain urged, and she did. Her eyelids closed as if weighted and his head descended. When his mouth claimed hers, a wave of such intense pleasure swept through her that her bones seemed to melt. At the brush of his tongue her lips parted, welcoming his possession.

In an instant the world spun away. There was only sensation. Somehow her arms were around his neck, her fingers gliding into silky hair and clinging tightly. From a long way off she heard Joel groan, felt his arms tighten, drawing her to his hard male body, and then his tongue was plundering her mouth with a devastating passion, and she met each thrust with her own, stoking a desire that set her blood sizzling in her veins and started up a throbbing ache deep within her.

It could have been one kiss; it could have been a dozen. Only the need for air finally forced them apart, and they stared at each other, hearts thumping, dragging gasping breaths through kiss-bruised lips.

Joel's eyes had darkened to a deep stormy blue. 'I think I got more than I bargained for,' he confessed thickly.

Kathryn knew that she certainly had. She had always known that this man could make her feel with more intensity than any other man she had ever met, but with that kiss she had entered a whole new realm of experience. Her response had been so quick, so intense, so all-encompassing. Nothing would ever compare to it. Nothing would ever come close.

'You shouldn't have done that.' She made the token protest in a whisper.

'You didn't stop me. You didn't want to,' Joel pointed out unnecessarily, for she knew how foolish she had been. It was too late to take back knowledge. From this point on she would always know what she was missing.

Kathryn pushed herself away from him with very shaky hands. 'Maybe so, but we both know it was a mistake,' she said as forcefully as she was able.

'If that was a mistake, I hope to make more of them,' Joel responded seductively, and the words trickled over her nerve-endings, setting them fluttering.

'Don't,' she protested, then closed her eyes and sighed heavily. 'OK, I admit I enjoyed it. But I'm here to work, not indulge in a…a…a liaison with you!' she continued, with more insistence this time, as her system began to settle down to something approximating normal.

His brows rose quizzically. 'Can't you do both?'

'I don't want to do both!' she lied, and they both knew it.

'Sure you do,' he countered chidingly, and she groaned, realising she was in a hole that would soon be too deep to get herself out of.

'I don't intend to get involved with you, Joel,' she insisted, notwithstanding.

'You can say that when not five minutes ago you went up in flames in my arms?' he charged, and she didn't thank him for reminding her.

Kathryn crossed her arms and raised her chin to a defiant tilt. 'I am saying it.'

Much to her dismay, he merely smiled. 'Now that, in my book, constitutes a challenge. It will give me great satisfaction—and you, too—to make you eat your words.'

Kathryn never had been a woman who knuckled under to attempted male domination—as her brothers could testify. She had a strength of will equal to any man, and if she said no, then no it had to be. 'I wouldn't attempt it if I were you,' she warned frostily, and Joel folded his own arms, mimicking her, and smiled again.

'What will you do to stop me? We've already established that when we get into clinches you fight on my side,' he taunted her, and her eyes narrowed.

'That won't be happening again.'

'You wish!' he shot back with a laugh, and she was very nearly tempted to stamp her foot in frustration. She resisted it, however.

'This is serving no purpose,' she returned, very much on her dignity. 'You do what you feel you have to do, but you won't be getting any co-operation from me.'

'Well, we'll just have to see about that, won't we? Now, why don't you slip off to bed? The rest will do you a power of good,' Joel suggested, and she took umbrage at his tone.

'Don't order me about. I'm not a child.'

The glint in his eye deepened. 'Don't I know it! You're very much a woman, Kathryn Templeton.'

How did he manage to turn the tables on her so easily? 'You are the most... Oh, I'm going to bed!' she exclaimed in frustration, needing to put some space between them so she could regain her equilibrium. 'Goodnight,' she said as she headed for the door.

'Goodnight, Kathryn,' he called after her, and the sound of her name on his lips was a seduction in itself. 'Sweet dreams.'

Her response to that was to close the door firmly

behind her and head for the stairs. She was pretty certain she would dream, but no way would it be sweet. Oh, no. The way things were going, her dreams were more than likely going to be hot and steamy in the extreme. As she mounted the stairs she was very much aware that, for a woman who had no intention of getting involved with a man, the prospect didn't disturb her the way it ought.

CHAPTER THREE

KATHRYN breakfasted alone the following morning, which suited her mood just fine. She had slept, but her dreams had been every bit as erotic as she had suspected they would be. It had been a frustrating night in every sense of the word, and as a consequence she felt less than at her best.

Drew had departed first thing to catch his flight to Germany, and that didn't help cheer her up any, but when Agnes informed her that Joel had insisted on driving him to the airport she breathed a sigh of relief. Putting off the moment of seeing him again seemed like a good idea with a man as perceptive as Joel Kendrick.

She was sipping at a second cup of coffee when she finally heard the car return, and instinctively braced herself. He came in not long afterwards, and, as before, she felt his presence like a charge in the air. She didn't turn around, though, and therefore jumped like a scalded cat when his hands descended on her shoulders and he bent to press a tingling kiss to the tender skin of her neck just below her ear.

'Good morning, Kathryn,' he greeted warmly, and released her before she could have the satisfaction of pulling away.

Annoyed that she hadn't anticipated the manoeuvre, she glowered at him as he poured himself some coffee, then pulled out the chair opposite her and sat down.

'Good morning,' she returned frostily, and his brows shot up above dancing eyes.

'Didn't you sleep well?' he asked, sounding concerned, but she knew that wasn't what he was thinking at all. He knew. Don't ask her how, but he knew.

'I never sleep well in strange beds,' she countered, not giving him the satisfaction of confirming that dreaming of him had made her so restless. 'But as it's only for two nights, I think I'll survive it.'

'Actually, it could turn out to be more. There's a weather front moving in, and they're promising us strong winds and some serious snowfall,' Joel enlightened her, resting his elbows on the table and sipping his coffee as if he hadn't a care in the world and hadn't just dropped a potential bombshell. Kathryn frowned sharply.

'What does that mean, exactly?' Surely she would be able to leave tomorrow? She had to. She was counting on it, she thought, a shade too desperately for comfort.

Joel disabused her in no uncertain terms. 'It means we could wake tomorrow to find ourselves snowed in for the duration. Something we've become used to up here.'

'You're not serious!' Kathryn gasped in dismay, only to see him nod.

'It was already beginning to snow as I drove home. But don't worry. If it does happen, you'll be perfectly safe here.'

Kathryn was not comforted. The definition of 'safe' depended on your point of view. It would not be safe being snowed in here with him, yet she couldn't leave until she had done the work she had promised. Whichever way you looked at it, she was trapped. She just had to hope and pray the snow held off long enough for her to get the work done and leave on time.

She sipped at her coffee, her free hand absently rubbing over the spot his lips had touched. Her skin still tingled with the charge which had ripped along her nervous system. It was incredibly stimulating, but it wasn't going to change her mind. She wouldn't get involved with him. Sighing, she glanced up, right into a pair of twinkling blue eyes.

'Incredible, isn't it?' Joel remarked as she jerked her hand away. 'I found it difficult to sleep last night myself, and I'm used to sleeping here. I kept remembering how it felt to have you in my arms. I wanted to feel it again. I had this fantasy of seeing you in my bed, your glorious hair spread out around you like a halo. It was incredibly erotic,' he added with husky sensuality, and with no effort at all Kathryn could imagine it, too.

Her body responded without conscious volition, her nipples hardening into highly sensitive nubs that cried out to be touched. The hardest part was knowing that she could have that, just for walking round the table and going to him. Making love with him would be an experience never to be forgotten. Yet, though she might remember it always, she doubted very much that he would. She would soon be replaced, and it was that knowledge which kept her in her seat.

'So, you believe in fantasies but not fairy tales?' she retorted, in an effort to alter the course of the conversation.

His smile acknowledged her hit. 'With a subtle difference. You can make your fantasies come true, but fairy stories will always be pure fiction.'

'Are you scared of commitment? Is that what it is?' she couldn't help asking curiously, but Joel shook his head.

'If and when I marry, the relationship will have my

full commitment, but I won't be dressing it up in the gloss of love and romance.'

'So you do intend to get married?' Kathryn asked at his unexpected response. She had imagined him as a confirmed bachelor.

'Of course. It is possible to have a good marriage based on mutual respect, Kathryn. People do it all the time.'

Which was true enough, but it sounded so...cold. Physical passion, however strong, could never replace love. True love survived long after passion was spent.

'I suppose so,' she agreed reluctantly. 'It just wouldn't be enough for me. But as it's a subject we are hardly likely ever to agree on, I'll take myself off to the study. There's a lot of work to do, and I want to get as much done as I can today,' she declared, setting her cup down and rising to her feet.

'I'll be along shortly,' Joel responded, which wasn't at all what she wanted.

'There's no need,' she countered hastily. 'If there's anything I need to talk to you about, I can come and find you.' The last thing she needed was to be shut up in the same room with him all day.

Joel smiled faintly, as if he guessed her reasoning. 'I'm sure you would, but I happen to have some work to do myself. I might as well get on with it, and at least I'll be on hand should the need arise,' he added sardonically, and she knew she was beaten.

'I'll see you in a bit, then,' she managed to say graciously, before quickly leaving the room.

Damn, she thought to herself, she didn't need this. Yet there was nothing she could do about it. It was his house and his study. She could hardly forbid him entry, however much she would have liked to. She would just have to grin and bear it.

Once in Joel's study, she made herself comfortable at the keypad and was quickly engrossed in her work. Retrieving the files was simple enough, but it was time-consuming. Fortunately the deleted files were dated, so it was easy enough to know which were the relevant files, and which had been Joel's intentional deletions. By midday, everything with a corresponding date was back in the main system.

With a feeling of satisfaction, Kathryn turned to where Joel sat at his desk, studying a batch of papers. She had been aware of his presence ever since he had come in, but he had said nothing to her, merely crossed to his desk and got down to business. Which had been a great relief. Now, though, she had to gain his attention.

As if sensing her gaze, Joel glanced up, one eyebrow lifting in silent query.

'I've retrieved everything for the date you think Magda got into the system. You'd better come and check if it's all there,' she invited, and Joel immediately rose to his feet and came to join her.

She had expected him to sit, but he chose to read the screen over her shoulder, one hand resting on the desk, taking his weight as he leaned closer. Kathryn was made very much aware of him. The musky scent of him assailed her nostrils, affording her senses a subtle pleasure.

'Let me just…' Joel began, reaching round her to take the mouse, and suddenly Kathryn found herself trapped between both his arms, with his torso pressing against her head and shoulders. Her breathing grew ragged as her heart slipped into a higher gear. She had an almost overwhelming urge to lean back against him and have those strong male arms enfold her. She might even have done it, except that the tone of Joel's voice altered, bringing her back to sanity.

'That's odd,' he murmured shortly, and she could tell from his tone that he was frowning.

She sat up straighter immediately, pushing all wanton thought aside. 'What is?'

'The files I've been working on aren't there,' he told her, and she frowned, too.

'Are you sure? What name are they under?' Joel told her and she took the mouse from him and started clicking. It only took a minute or two to confirm he was right. Those files were missing. 'I'll go back over my tracks. Perhaps she got in more than once, and those files have a different date. Give me some time to check it out.' Without waiting for his agreement, Kathryn started to hunt down the missing files.

Half an hour later she sat back with a grim expression on her face. Folding her arms, she turned to where Joel stood waiting by the window. He looked round at once, his shoulders tensing as he saw the serious set of her mouth.

'They're not there,' he stated shortly, and she nodded.

'They're gone, all right. Was the information on them vital?' It wasn't mere curiosity. She needed to know in order to think of what to do next.

Joel dragged a hand through his hair. 'They were highly confidential, concerning some new projects I'm working on. I used them all the time. She probably guessed that the files I used most often were current and wiped them totally,' he said in a voice that threatened retribution if he ever met up with the lady again.

Kathryn shivered. She wouldn't want to make an enemy of him. Unfortunately, what she had to say next wouldn't improve his mood, either. 'There is another possibility, and only you will know if it's feasible,' she ventured, and his eyes narrowed.

'And that is?'

Looking him squarely in the eye, because she had discovered it was better to deliver bad news without dressing it up, she gave him her worst case scenario. 'She may have copied the files onto disks, then deleted them permanently to make you think just what you have,' she said, and caught her breath when he seemed to freeze, a stunned look crossing his face.

'The devil!' he exclaimed through gritted teeth, and she could see his brain suddenly working like fury to follow that line of reasoning to its conclusion.

'It's possible, then?'

'More than possible,' Joel agreed wrathfully, and she winced.

Kathryn watched him, unblinking, then gave a tiny cough before posing her next question cautiously. 'Er…just how well did you know Magda? I hate to be the ghost at the feast, but was this an act of pure serendipity, or did she get to know you as part of another agenda, to get the information on your projects?' she asked, and could swear she heard his teeth grinding.

'I'm just beginning to wonder that myself,' he returned grimly, dragging his hand through his hair again as he paced back and forth across the room. Finally he came to a halt before her. 'OK, get your coat on. We're going for a walk. I need to think and I need fresh air to do it.'

Though she raised her brows in surprise, Kathryn didn't argue. The man had problems, and right now he didn't need her adding to them. Perhaps she might even be able to help. Without a word she quickly shut the computer down and hurried upstairs to change into jeans and a thick sweater. Tugging on her boots, she gathered up her coat and went down to find him pacing the hall impatiently. He had donned a thick, fleece-lined coat, pulled a woollen hat onto his head and wound a scarf around his neck. When he saw her slipping into her woollen coat, he tutted and strode to the closet, returning with several items in his hands.

'You'll freeze in just that coat,' he declared tersely, and proceeded to pull a cream woolly hat onto her head and, before she could protest, wound a matching scarf round her neck.

Feeling very much like a small child being dressed for the outdoors by an adult, Kathryn couldn't help grinning as she swayed back and forth under his ministrations. When he noticed it, he stood back and frowned.

'What's so funny?' he asked, and she giggled.

'I was just imagining you doing this to your own child. I bet you'd make a good father,' she pronounced just a little huskily.

Still frowning, Joel began pulling on a pair of gloves. 'You decided that on the basis of my putting a hat and scarf on you?'

Kathryn nodded. 'Because despite you being angry and upset, and having a million more important things to think about, you were still concerned about my well-being. It's called caring, in case you don't recognise it,' she added ironically, and he shot her a darkling look.

'Don't read anything into it. I just don't want you getting sick on me. Do you have gloves? Put them on then,' he ordered when she produced them from her pockets, magician fashion.

'Yes, Papa,' she returned demurely, and this time

when he looked at her his mood had lightened slightly, enough for a faint glimmer of amusement to appear in his eyes.

'Cut it out, or I'll do another fatherly thing and box your ears for you!'

Ducking her head to hide another grin, Kathryn subsided obediently and meekly followed him out of the front door. The cold hit her immediately, and she was instantly glad of the hat and scarf. It was snowing only fitfully at present, but the wind had picked up considerably, and she could well imagine that they were soon going to get the promised snowstorm.

Joel set out at a brisk pace down the hillside towards the lake. Kathryn had to hurry to keep up with him, but she made no complaint, for he was already deep in thought again. She could barely imagine what he must be thinking, but she knew it would not be pleasant. The ramifications of their suspicions were enough to set her own stomach churning. If someone had broken into her computer and stolen files, she knew she wouldn't just mourn their loss, she would feel violated, too, for a computer was a very personal thing. Right now Joel must be feeling betrayed. It was no wonder he had some serious thinking to do.

Which was why she said nothing when she began to struggle with the pace, merely put her head down and battled to keep up with him as he followed a barely visible path through the trees to the lake shore. There, without warning, he stopped. The move was so sudden she had no time to avoid him and careened into his back.

'Oh! Ouch! Sorry,' she apologised as she bounced off him and stumbled backwards.

One long arm snaked out and grabbed her before she

fell, steadying her. He noted the way her chest was heaving with her effort to keep pace with him, and frowned.

'You're out of shape.'

The comment, when she had been doing her best to be reasonable, stung, and she brushed his hand away. 'I'm in fine shape, thank you very much. You should have warned me we were in a race. Funnily enough, I assumed a walk meant just that!' she returned indignantly, and he had the grace to look a little shamefaced.

'Sorry,' he apologised in turn. 'I forgot you were there.'

Oh, this just got better and better! 'What an insult! You order my presence like some olde worlde potentate, after which I become instantly forgettable!' she gibed, and was a little surprised at how relieved she was to see him smile, however faintly.

'Now, that you could never be,' he said, then shook his head. 'Would you have kept on at the same pace until you collapsed from exhaustion?'

Her shoulders rose and fell. 'Like a faithful hound. I was banking on you being sorry when you realised what you'd done. I pictured you bent over my unconscious body, damning your selfishness.'

At that he shot her an old-fashioned look. 'Why didn't you just tell me I was walking too fast, hmm?'

She waved a hand airily. 'I wasn't really worried. I knew I'd get my second wind. By the way, I think I should point out that you'll never outrun the problem. But, if you're determined to walk your legs down to stumps, I'll keep you company.'

He gave her a strange look then, as if he didn't quite know what to make of her. 'The faithful hound?'

Kathryn smiled up at him. 'Something like that. Is

the air fresh enough for you to think clearly?' It felt cold enough to her to do physical damage to metal monkeys.

Joel glanced about him and took a deep lungful. 'It's certainly brisk,' he admitted, tongue-in-cheek. 'We'd better get moving or there's every possibility we'll freeze on the spot.'

No kidding, she thought wryly.

This time they set off at a more reasonable pace, which caused her no problems. Joel soon plunged back into thought, and Kathryn left him to it. She knew he would speak when he had something to say. For herself, now that she had caught her breath, she had ample opportunity to study the stark beauty of the lake in winter. It could have been alienating, but to her it had a kind of magical quality. In a frosty, mystical landscape like this it was easy to imagine oneself lost in the deep reaches of Middle Earth.

She was busy visualising conflicts of good and evil swaying back and forth over the lake when Joel's footsteps began to slow, and with a shake of her head she returned to the present. Crunch time. Turning to face the water, he shoved his hands into his pockets and stared out across the chilly expanse. Kathryn found a conveniently tumbled log, brushed off the snow and made herself comfortable on it, her gaze locked on his back as she waited. It wasn't long before Joel spoke.

'This is something I should have been expecting, but the last incident was so long ago I got sloppy. I failed to see it coming,' he explained, convolutedly, and her brows rose.

'You expected this?' she asked in surprise.

'Not this specifically, but something like it. Before we get to that, I'd better explain Magda's involvement.

I met her about a month ago. She backed her car into mine. At the time I suspected it was a deliberate accident to catch my attention, but that isn't unusual,' he revealed with a heavy dose of self-mockery.

Kathryn could easily picture the scene. Blonde beauty in severe distress over the shunt. Strong handsome type offers comfort, tells her not to worry her pretty little head about it, and…meeting achieved. 'Now you don't think it was that innocent?'

With a growl of disgust, Joel turned and looked at her. 'Not considering the timing. I'd forgotten, but now I realise we're coming up to the anniversary. This isn't about business at all. It's about one man getting revenge on another.'

'Revenge for what, exactly?' she queried carefully. The plot had thickened and she felt all at sea. Joel sighed heavily.

'For something I did wrong a long time ago. Gray, the man I believe is behind this, used to be my best friend, until I walked off with his girlfriend. What I didn't know was that he was in love with her. What he didn't know was that she threw herself at me, and, being stupid, I caught her instead of throwing her back. The long and the short of it is, she was out for what she could get. But it was no use my trying to tell him that. He refused to listen. All he knew was that I had stolen the woman he loved. Ever since then he's been doing his best to score points off me in whatever way he can. This little stunt is just the sort of thing he would do. I'd be willing to bet that somehow he persuaded Magda to do it for him.'

This had all the makings of an off-off-Broadway stage play. 'I see. The chickens have come home to roost with a vengeance this time. The big question is, can he make use of what's on the files?' She homed in on the important point, but Joel swiftly shook his head.

He came to sit beside her and propped his elbows on his knees. This close, Kathryn could see his breath freezing in the air as he spoke. 'No. We're not in the same line of business. My guess is Magda took the files because they were what I was working on, not because of what they contained. Gray will know the importance if he reads them.'

'And what will he do with them?'

Joel ran a hand around his neck tiredly. 'I have no idea. But I wouldn't put it past him to hold them over my head until he has exacted what he considers a fitting revenge.'

'Hmm, looks like he has you over a barrel. If you do whatever he asks, will he return the files?'

'I believe so. He just wants to make me suffer for a while,' Joel explained grimly. 'I have to hand it to him; he was clever. He knew me so well, he chose the one way of getting someone into my home without making me suspect anything.'

Kathryn shuffled her feet, which were beginning to feel the cold, and wisely chose not to comment. 'What are you going to do?' It didn't seem to her that allowing this man called Gray to get away with it was Joel's way, and he confirmed it in the next minute.

'Get the files back, of course,' he said grittily, and his strength of purpose was underlined by the hard set of his jaw.

Her brows rose. 'Fine words, but just how do you intend to go about it?' she asked curiously, and he turned those piercing blue eyes on her, capturing her gaze.

'*I'm* not going to do anything. *You* are,' he said

softly, taking her aback. The steadiness of his regard sent her a clear message, and her eyes rounded into saucers.

'You're not seriously suggesting…?' The remainder of the sentence tailed off into nothingness. Her teeth snapped together and she sat up straighter. 'I can't do that!'

He sat up, too. 'Of course you can. You told me you were better than Magda. What she did, you can do in reverse,' he argued firmly, and her eyes narrowed as he totally missed her point.

'I'm not saying I *can't* do it, I mean I *won't* do it,' she refused bluntly. Maybe in her early days at university she had enjoyed the thrill of hacking into different systems, but those days were long gone. She was a respectable businesswoman now. 'It's not ethical.'

'Ethics be damned!' Joel countered explosively. 'I'm not asking you to break into the system of a rival in order to steal. All I'm asking is for you to do what has been done to me. This isn't going to end up in court with your reputation in shreds. This is private, between the two of us, and will go no further whatever happens. Now, I believe we have time on our side. I'm betting Gray doesn't expect me to link it to him—at least not yet. So far as he knows, his tracks are still covered. Ordinarily I would be prepared to let Gray get away with it, but not in this case. I need those files back, and you're the only person who can get them for me.'

'Rubbish! There's any number of people out there who would be only too happy to do it for you,' Kathryn insisted, but Joel was having none of it. He caught her by the shoulders and forced her to face him.

'Maybe there are, but they aren't here and you are. You have to help me, Kathryn. Please. I need you.'

She'd been about to refuse yet again. Those three simple words kept her silent. Her heart seemed to give a crazy lurch and she bit her lip. Oh, damn. He had had to put it like that, hadn't he? He needed her help. He had even said please! How could she refuse him? She worried her lip some more, and caught the faint sound of a stifled groan. She blinked, and discovered that Joel's eyes were no longer looking at her own, but had dropped to her mouth and were locked there in fatal fascination.

'Do you have any idea what it does to me when you do that?' he asked in a low growl that set the fine hairs on her flesh rising.

Kathryn was very much aware that though her extremities were feeling the cold, parts of her were definitely warming up. 'You don't have to try and persuade me. I've already decided to help you, though it goes against the grain,' she admitted, finding it incredibly difficult to speak when he was looking at her like that.

A faint smile curled the edges of his lips and made her knees melt, so that she couldn't have moved away if she wanted to. 'Then I think I should thank you properly,' he declared thickly, drawing her towards him as he angled his head, the better to take her mouth.

In the back of her mind sanity urged she put up a fight, but Kathryn wasn't listening. Forgetting everything she had told herself not to do, she sighed and shivered with pleasure when his lips claimed hers, but it was a fleeting caress that was over much too soon. In dismay she blinked at him when he pulled back.

'Thank you, Kathryn,' he murmured softly, a dangerous light glimmering in the depths of his eyes.

'Is that it?' she asked, unable to hide her disappointment, then caught the tiny flash of triumph in those incredible blue orbs and knew that she had been successfully reeled in. 'Oh, you rat!' she exclaimed, and would have fought him then. He defeated her by the simple act of taking her mouth again.

Only this time it was completely different. He captured her lips with a passion that stole her breath away, and as she gasped he growled, and his tongue claimed her honeyed sweetness, plundering it remorselessly. Swept away on a tide of pleasure, she let her arms slide up around his neck and his arms enfolded her, drawing her as close as their bulky clothing would allow. In seconds they were lost to the world, exchanging kisses that aroused and tantalised, building a fire that threatened to rage out of control.

It was Joel who finally dragged his mouth away. Struggling for breath, he rested his forehead against hers, their frozen breaths mingling like wraiths around them.

'You must be some kind of witch,' he panted. 'There's a kind of magic in those lips of yours that make me want to keep coming back for more.' Framing her face with his gloved hands, he eased her head back so that he could look into her eyes. 'We're sitting on a log, with the snow falling around us, and I can barely keep my hands off you! I've got to be crazy!'

When it came to craziness, that made two of them. What was she thinking of? Why was it that every time he touched her every sane and sensible thought vanished? Who had put a spell on who? The question sent a wave of unease through her, and she couldn't say why. What she did know was that the breathing space had given her sanity the opportunity to recover. She placed her hands over his and prised them away.

'You have some pretty potent magic of your own,

but I guess you've had enough practice to get it down to a fine art,' she said dryly, wishing her pulse would settle down.

Joel dropped his hands and gave her a look of wry amusement. 'Ouch. You certainly know how to hit below the belt. I meant what I said, Kathryn. There's something extra special about you,' he insisted, and Kathryn sighed.

'I'm sure you mean it every time you say it.'

He frowned at her. Watching her get to her feet. 'That wasn't a very nice thing to say.'

She shoved her hands into her coat pockets and stamped her feet to get some feeling back into them. 'It isn't very nice to know you're just the latest in a long line.'

Joel got up too, and stood staring down at her with a faint frown still between his eyes. 'That is something I can do nothing about.'

'I know. Your past is a matter of public—very public—record. I'd rather avoid being just another statistic. It's a female thing. You wouldn't understand,' she told him mockingly.

'You're wrong; I do understand. You've always been different from the rest, that's why I find you so fascinating. I've never come across anyone quite like you before,' Joel countered. 'As to your being a statistic... You know I would never force you into anything, but I reserve the right to try and persuade you to change your mind.'

Kathryn didn't even have to think about it. She knew instinctively that Joel would never take what was not freely given. It was up to her to remain firm. The trouble with that was that he was so damned persuasive.

'Personally, I think I'm doing enough by agreeing to

track down those files of yours,' she returned dryly, and his expression became serious.

'It would be a debt I could never fully repay, and I wouldn't ask you to do it if it wasn't vitally important. The new projects are something my company could live without, but to allow this to happen once without doing something would be to invite it again. That I am not prepared to accept.'

Kathryn shook her head wonderingly. 'You know, for an unprincipled rogue, you have a surprising number of principles.'

At that he grinned. 'Even a rogue has his limits. Speaking of which, I've just reached my tolerance level for cold. The snow's getting heavier by the minute. It would be madness to stay here any longer. Let's go home.'

It was a suggestion she was happy to fall in with, for the weather was deteriorating drastically. In a reversal of roles, she was the one looked in thought on the way back, and it was all due to her companion. Like the best-laid schemes, hers was going wrong. Resisting Joel, she was beginning to realise, was going to be easier said than done.

CHAPTER FOUR

KATHRYN stirred and rolled onto her back with a sigh. As she lay there, wriggling her toes in the comfort of the duvet, she slowly became aware of the silence, and raised herself on her elbows, looking towards the window. Last night a blizzard had been howling around the house, making her start at every sudden bang and crash. Now it had stopped, leaving an almost eerie quietness. Throwing back the duvet, she climbed from the bed and went to the window, pulling aside the curtains only to gasp at the sight which met her eyes.

The whole world was white for as far as the eye could see. Thick drifts of snow lay everywhere, several feet deep, and it was still snowing with those thick flakes that said it had been doing so for some hours and had no intention of stopping any time soon. As Joel had predicted, they were snowed in.

She shivered, though the room was cosy and warm, due to the central heating. Kathryn had learned from Agnes that Joel had fires lit in some rooms because he preferred them to radiators. Thinking of Agnes only served to remind her that the other woman was no longer in the house, nor likely to be for the next few days, given the conditions. Apparently she always spent Saturday evening and Sunday in Kendal with friends, and as soon as they had returned from their walk Joel had insisted she go early, before it became hazardous to drive. After protesting, she had given in to his urging, and consequently Kathryn and Joel were alone in the house.

It was not an ideal situation, but Kathryn was determined to play it cool. So she had to stay here for a few extra days. That didn't mean anything was going to happen. Last night they had eaten the dinner Agnes had prepared for them and then spent the evening together quite comfortably, listening to the radio and talking. In fact, she couldn't remember when she had enjoyed an evening more. They had chatted about surprisingly disparate subjects, finding they had many things in common.

Leaning against the window frame, she allowed a tiny smile to tug at the corners of her mouth as she ran through the evening in her mind. She remembered being enthralled yet again by the animation on his face as he'd talked about his favourite subject. She wondered if he was aware that he laughed with his eyes when something really amused him. He wasn't at all the kind of man she had expected from his reputation. He had been relaxed and at ease, and the attempted seduction that Drew would have expected had never materialised.

In fact, she had enjoyed herself so much she had been loath to go to bed. It had only been when she'd found it impossible to stifle a jaw-breaking yawn that she had reluctantly taken herself off to her room. There she had tumbled into bed and been asleep almost as soon as her head had touched the pillow. Now it was morning, and she could feel an unexpected bubble of anticipation inside her. Crazy as it might sound, she was actually looking forward to seeing him again.

Which had to be the craziest feeling she had ever had, she berated herself as she pushed herself upright and reached for the robe that matched her long cream silk nightdress. It was early yet: not quite seven, according to her watch. She would just pop down to the kitchen and make herself some coffee. She would need the kick-start if she seriously intended to solve the matter of tracking down the missing files.

Barefoot, she padded quietly down the stairs and along the hall to the kitchen. Pushing the door open, she was brought up short with a gasp of surprise when she found the room already occupied. Joel stood at the counter, idly stirring a mug of coffee as he stared out at the snow. He turned at the sound of her entrance, the spoon slowing to a stop, and there was an arrested look on his face when he saw her standing there.

He was barefoot, too...and bare-legged. In fact she was pretty sure the towelling robe he wore, which gaped above the belt, allowing her a glimpse of silky dark chest hair, was the only thing he wore. It was a mind-blowing thought, and she suddenly found herself fighting an urge to go to him and discover for herself if that hair was as silky as it looked. Joel meanwhile allowed his eyes to travel the length of her and back again. It was like a caress, and Kathryn felt her body tighten in response.

Oh, God, she thought faintly. It was barely seven o'clock in the morning and the room was alive with that peculiar electricity they always generated whenever they came close to each other.

Joel cleared his throat. 'That has to be the sexiest number I've ever seen,' he declared gruffly, and the sound made her senses leap.

She laughed edgily. 'It covers me from top to toe,' she pointed out unnecessarily, and he grinned that wolf-ish grin which engendered various emotions in her, none of which was fear.

'I know. It's making my imagination work overtime in ways you can't imagine.'

Oh, Kathryn wasn't so sure about that. She could imagine all too clearly what he was thinking, and it didn't help to ease the curling sensation inside her.

'Are you coming or going?' Joel asked before she could form a rational response, and she wasn't too sure about that either. It was the effect he seemed to have on her.

'Ask me an easier one,' she quipped back wryly, knowing she was giving a lot away, but doubting that he had been unaware of it anyway.

In response, a gleam entered his eyes, and, abandoning his coffee, he prowled across the floor towards her. She tensed automatically, but all he did was take her hand and pull her a step or two into the room so that he could push the door closed behind her. Then, smiling faintly, he took a step closer and Kathryn backed up—only to meet the solid wood of the door. She was trapped, and they both knew it.

Joel placed his palms flat against the door, either side of her head, and his eyes glittered. 'Now what are you going to do?' he taunted softly.

Wise or not, Kathryn had never been one to back down from a challenge. Instead of doing the obvious thing, and demanding he let her go, she did what she had been secretly longing to do anyway. She reached up and slipped her hand inside the lapel of his robe and ran her palm caressingly over the taut skin of his chest. It was music to her ears to hear his breath hiss through his teeth as she took him by surprise, and her pulse-rate soared skywards.

'How was that for starters?' she goaded naughtily, and would have made good her escape by ducking under his arm. But he was one step ahead of her and foiled her by the simple act of taking that half-step which brought his body into full contact with hers. This time it was her breath that caught in her throat as she clearly felt the evidence of his arousal.

'Oh, no, you don't!' he said quickly. 'You don't get away with it that easily.'

Kathryn tipped her head up, eyes glittering with defiance and something far more potent. 'You started it,' she accused. It was impossible for her to move, with one hand trapped between their two bodies. Not that she really wanted to. Her senses were going crazy with the scent and feel of him. Beneath her hand she could feel the rhythmic thud of his racing heart, and it matched her own.

Joel's hands cupped her face, his fingers tangling in her hair. 'And I'm about to finish it,' he murmured sexily. 'You shouldn't have done that.'

'You shouldn't have dared me,' she shot back faintly, all the strength seeming to go out of her voice as her eyes locked on his mouth, so tantalisingly close to her own. Lord, how she wanted to feel it on her own, creating the magic that only he could conjure up.

'If you keep looking at me like that, I'm going to have to kiss you.' Joel issued the warning from low in his throat, and she raised heavy-lidded eyes to his.

'What's stopping you?' she whispered through a painfully tight throat, and he laughed softly.

'Damned if I know,' he admitted, and finally brought his mouth down on hers.

Her sigh of pleasure was lost as her lips parted to the insistent caress of his tongue. Her free hand clutched at the cloth on his back, holding on as their kisses stoked fires still smouldering from the last time. They went up like dry tinder, Joel's hands leaving her face to seek out the silk-covered curves of her back. She shivered with delight as his hands fastened on her hips and pulled her closer. Pressing herself against him, she struggled to free her other hand and slip it around his neck. At the same time she felt his hands gliding upwards, finding her waist, then his thumbs discovered the swell of her breasts and she stopped thinking. Her body surged, her breasts waiting achingly for his touch, and when it came she moaned at the exquisite pleasure. Joel's response was to press her back against the door and slip one powerful thigh between hers.

The jarring tones of the telephone broke them apart with all the finesse of a bucket of cold water, and it took them a moment to realise just what it was. Cursing under his breath, Joel dragged a hand through his hair and stalked to the phone which hung on the wall, barely managing to speak civilly.

Kathryn closed her eyes and pressed a hand to her bruised lips. This was all getting out of hand. She was supposed to be doing the sensible thing, not encouraging him. But when he got close things always got jumbled in her mind—when she was able to think at all. What on earth was the matter with her? Why couldn't she simply keep some distance between them?

She heard Joel replace the receiver and opened her eyes again. He was looking at her through smouldering eyes as he came back to her. Reaching out, he ran his hands slowly up and down her upper arms.

'That was my neighbour. He was checking up on us. I told him we were OK for food and heating. He uses his tractor to help clear the roads for the outlying houses. If the snow stops today, he'll be out to clear the lane. If not, it will be tomorrow at the earliest,' he explained concisely, then his eyes lowered to her mouth broodingly. 'Now, where were we...?' He made a move to close the distance between them, and Kathryn raised her hands quickly to keep him at bay.

'Oh, no. I don't think so,' she refused, having had time to cool her heated blood.

'Before Wilf rang you were more than ready to be swept upstairs to my bed,' Joel argued persuasively, and she couldn't deny it.

'Your friend has impeccable timing,' she returned calmly, although she was still far from calm on the inside.

'You mean he gave you time to change your mind,' Joel responded ironically, and to give him his due, however frustrated he was, he was far from being angry.

'It is a woman's privilege,' Kathryn added softly, fully aware that her behaviour had given him every reason to suppose she intended going to bed with him. Which she probably would have done, had the phone not rung. 'I'm sorry.'

Joel released her and stepped away. 'Don't be. I won't pretend I'm not disappointed, but there will be other times, and, as I told you before, I would never force a woman.' Turning round, he went back to where his mug of coffee stood cooling on the countertop. Lifting the coffee pot, he glanced at her over his shoulder. 'Coffee?'

'Thanks.' She nodded, attempting to pull herself together, when in truth all of her senses were still vitally aware of him. 'I guess you're what my mother would call a true gentleman. I, on the other hand, wasn't very ladylike. I shouldn't have taken that dare,' she added wryly as she crossed the room.

Turning, he held out a mug. 'Take my word for it,

Kathryn, when it comes to being a lady, you're hell on wheels. Which is why I will probably spend the next hour taking cold showers,' he observed with wry humour, smiling into her eyes, and it was in that instant, when she looked into those blue depths as she was taking the mug from him, that she made a startling discovery.

She had fallen in love with him.

It was the sort of revelation that made everything she had been feeling that much clearer, and, conversely, at the same time made everything unbelievably complicated. For there was nothing simple in falling for Joel Kendrick, except the manner of it. She had looked into his eyes and been lost. It was clear to her now that since the very first she had been fighting a losing battle. Unbeknownst to her, love had hit her like a bolt of lightning. Whilst she had thought herself flirting with a powerful attraction, deep in her heart had been hidden the fact that, as she had always expected it would be, she had fallen in love with him on sight.

'Is everything OK?' Joel's concerned voice broke into her jumbled thoughts and brought her back to the present.

Nerves jangling for quite another reason now, she stepped back from him, automatically cradling the mug for comfort. 'Everything's fine,' she insisted just a fraction too hastily, and caught his frown. 'I'm fine, really. Something just occurred to me, that's all,' she added, and that had to be the understatement to end all understatements.

'About the missing files?' he asked at once, and she quickly set his mind at rest.

'Oh, no. It was personal. Nothing to do with work at all.'

'Is it something you want to talk about?' he probed, taking his own mug and following her to the table, and her laugh carried the faintest edge of hysteria. This was the very last thing she would ever discuss with him.

'Not right now. It was nothing, really.' She refused his offer, and grimaced at the lie. Nothing? It was everything.

Sitting facing her, he didn't look convinced. 'You looked as if you'd seen a ghost,' he remarked, and that seemed very apt to Kathryn.

In a way she had seen a ghost. The ghost of all her hopes and dreams. She had always taken it for granted that the man she fell in love with would feel the same about her. Now she realised how naive she had been. It was entirely possible to fall for someone who didn't love you. Someone who would never love you, because he didn't believe in love in the first place.

Kathryn tucked a stray strand of hair behind her ear with fingers that carried a faint tremor and smiled crookedly. 'No. No ghost. You might say an unpalatable truth just reared up and bit me.' She attempted to make light of it, for one thing was patently clear: she mustn't ever let him know that she had fallen for him. Her wound might be self-inflicted, but it was her wound, and if she couldn't have his love, she certainly didn't want his pity.

Joel looked sympathetic. 'Truths have a habit of doing that,' he agreed wryly.

Didn't they just? Sighing, Kathryn took another sip of coffee. 'This weekend isn't turning out at all the way I expected,' she said with a wry shake of her head.

'What were you expecting?'

She laughed softly, though it was directed mostly at

herself. 'I certainly wasn't expecting you. You came as quite a surprise,' she declared honestly.

His smile was full of self-mockery. 'I wasn't prepared for you, either. Women don't usually go toe to toe with me.'

She quirked an eyebrow at him, not doubting it in the least. 'The way they apparently keep falling at your feet, you must be tripping over them all the time.'

Blue eyes glittered appreciatively. 'It can certainly be a hazard to my health. I have to do some fancy footwork to avoid them.'

It was amazing how heavy those light words hung in her heart. 'Do you avoid many?' she asked, with the scepticism he expected of her, and Joel shook his head reprovingly.

'If I'd had all the women I'm reputed to have had, I'd be a physical wreck by now.'

She forced herself to grin, amazed at how easy it was to keep up the appearance of insouciance. Which was as well, for it was necessary on her part. 'I'm happy to say you're in good physical condition.'

That had his eyes narrowing. 'I'm glad you like my body, because I'm rather partial to yours, too.'

Kathryn's heart flinched at the statement, which showed just how divergent their feelings were. His desire might be honest, but it hurt unbearably, and she struggled not to let it show. Her only defence was to be the light-hearted woman he expected. 'Have you always been this incorrigible?' she teased.

His teeth gleamed as his smile broadened. 'According to my mother, I was a perfect little angel, but then, she is biased.'

'Which means she knows you have more than a little bit of the devil in you.'

'If I hadn't, you wouldn't be attracted to me,' he pointed out roguishly, and she met the challenge honestly.

'True. I never did go much for angels. Who would choose a saint, when a sinner could be much more fun?' she returned with false brightness.

'So when are you going to go to bed with me and find out just how much "fun" I can be?' Joel charged outrageously, and Kathryn's nerves jumped as if they had touched a live wire.

'Oh, this year. Next year. Some time. Never...' Her throat closed over, and when she spoke the last word of the rhyme her voice was painfully husky.

A frown creased her brow, and her eyes dropped to her mug, although she barely registered it. It had hit her, with the childish rhyme she had begun so airily, that never was a long, long time. Opportunities were fleeting. These few days could be the only time she would ever have with Joel out of a whole lifetime. It was a prospect that made her feel so very, very cold inside. Their relationship had changed and so must her response to it. It was no longer a simple question of whether a brief affair would damage her self-respect or not. He had become more to her than that, and, consequently, this time had suddenly become precious.

'Kathryn?' Joel's hand touched hers, and she looked up with a start. 'You were miles away, and it didn't seem a very nice place to be,' he explained gently, with unexpected seriousness.

His touch was like a brand searing into her soul, and she eased her hand out from under his, because right now it hurt too much. 'I was just thinking how fleeting time was. Which isn't like me at all. It must be all this white silence. It's giving me the creeps,' she lied, covering her emotionalism with an exaggerated shudder.

'They call it cabin fever, but I imagine it takes longer than twelve hours to set in. For most people it should take days, if not weeks,' Joel observed ironically, and she smiled faintly.

'Well, that only goes to show I'm not like most people,' Kathryn riposted neatly, and saw those banked fires in his eyes set off a few sparks at her words.

'You certainly aren't,' he confirmed with a sensual growl, and her body responded with a shiver at remembered pleasure.

'You don't give up, do you?' she charged with an exasperated laugh, genuinely amused despite everything.

Joel leant forward across the table, holding her eyes with his. 'Well, now, that's because you haven't given me any of the signals that would tell me I should.'

Her brows rose, posting a challenge. 'I said no.'

'You didn't mean it, though,' he countered smoothly, and she had no comeback because he was right.

'If I didn't mean it, why did you stop?' she asked curiously, and Joel reached out to brush a finger tenderly over her lips.

'Because, as you said, I'm a gentleman, and you're not quite ready yet.'

The tantalising remark begged a response, and got it. 'Not quite ready for what?'

'For the next step,' he told her simply, and she shook her head in bemusement.

'But *you'll* know when I am, right?'

Joel's smile was chock-full to the brim with male confidence. 'My instinct hasn't failed me yet.'

She was damn sure she didn't like being thought of

as a sure thing. Even now she had a choice. He hadn't 'won' yet. 'There's always a first time. This could be it,' she pointed out coolly.

'Kathryn, sweetheart, there is no *if* any longer, only *when*. If you're honest, you'll admit it. Which is why I'm willing to play the game.'

God, the last thing she needed right now was to be reminded that this was all just a game to him. With a snort of disgust, Kathryn pushed her mug away and rose to her feet. 'You know something, Joel. Just when I think I'm actually beginning to like you, you go and say something so arrogant I could hit you.'

Laughing, he got to his feet, too. 'You already do like me, or you wouldn't get so mad.'

Kathryn sighed helplessly, because of course he was right. Damn it, she more than liked him; she loved him. 'There's probably a latent streak of insanity in my family and it's just manifesting itself,' she declared sardonically.

The message in the warmth of his gaze was unmistakable. 'Call it what you like. Just accept that we'll end up where we both want to be very soon now.'

He was probably right about that, too, but she wasn't about to say so. 'I think this is where I make a dignified retreat. I'm going to dress and get working on retrieving your precious files. At least the computer is always logical, and it doesn't answer back,' she sniped, but with the faintest hint of a smile curling the edges of her mouth. It was impossible to stay angry with him for long.

'How boring,' Joel returned as she headed for the door. She paused with her hand on the knob and glanced back at him.

'How restful,' she countered, and quickly pulled the

door to after her. She couldn't hear Joel laughing, but she guessed he probably was. Sighing, she headed for the stairs and went up to her room.

Safe inside, she felt the strength of purpose which had got her through those last minutes with him evaporate, leaving her feeling drained. She made no move to get dressed but instead curled herself up against the headboard, sweeping up a pillow to wrap her arms around as she took time out to ponder the discovery she had made. Had it really only been mere minutes ago? The knowledge filled her like an eternity.

She had fallen in love with Joel. It ought not to be a shock but it was, and she was still reeling from it. Although she had always known love would strike her like this, she hadn't expected it to strike her here and now, with this man. A man who, whilst he loved women, did not believe in the kind of love which had just dislodged her world from its foundations. There was no denying he felt a powerful attraction, one she felt too, but there was a subtle difference in what they felt. She had fallen in love with him. Never for a second did she doubt it. There was something extra where she was concerned. That indefinable something which put what she felt beyond the scope of any attraction she had felt before. That something was the magic ingredient which told her she had fallen in love.

Unfortunately, love wasn't part of Joel's equation. So far as he was concerned, what was on offer was a little harmless affair to pass away the time. Had her heart not been engaged, she would perhaps have seen it in that light, too. The strength of their mutual attraction might have made her revise her notion of what was acceptable. Now that her heart was ruling her emotions, they were no longer playing the same game. There was more at stake than her self-respect. To have a brief affair with a man you were physically attracted to was one thing. To have one with a man you had fallen in love with was quite a different proposition.

Deciding what she was going to do about it had consequences she couldn't ignore. Which was a cruel joke. What *could* she do about it? It wasn't as if she had multiple choices. There were, in fact, only two. To sleep with him, or not to sleep with him. To have something to remember, or nothing. Common sense said it would be less painful in the long run to call it quits now, but to do that would require more strength of will than she knew she possessed. It would be like cutting her heart out. How could she do that, when this was what she had been searching for her whole life? Maybe it hadn't turned out the way she'd expected. He didn't love her and never would, but that didn't change how *she* felt. She loved him, and the blunt fact was that this time would never come again.

From the moment of revelation it had been too late to walk away with her heart intact. It never would be again. She could go, but she would be leaving the greater part of herself behind. Somewhere down the road she would meet someone else and love him as much as she was able, but it would never be like this. It couldn't be, for she would never be heart-whole again. The irony was that meeting Joel had given her something precious, but she would be forever incomplete.

Could she hurt any more or any less if she denied herself this moment?

Put quite simply, Joel Kendrick was the love of her life. Any time with him, no matter how short, had to be worth it. She had to seize the moment and have no regrets.

At the back of her mind a voice insisted that the potential for disaster was great. But it was a small voice, and, as often happens to small voices, it went unheeded.

CHAPTER FIVE

THE snow stopped about midday, and not very long afterwards Kathryn, who was once again ensconced in the study, finally heard the sound of the tractor working down on the road. Her fingers stilled on the keys. It ought to have been music to her ears, but the message it conveyed was that she should be able to leave tomorrow, and it brought the act of parting from Joel too close for comfort. It was ridiculous, really, but after only yesterday wishing for the snow to stop so that she could leave, today she would have been only too happy for it to have gone on snowing indefinitely. The proverb was right when it said you had to be careful what you wished for because you would probably get it.

Sighing, she turned her attention back to the screen. This morning she had checked out Magda's database, just in case the woman had made copies of the files for herself, but she had been innocent of that. Now she was attempting to log into Gray's system. Which was proving to be something of a challenge. The man had state-of-the-art security installed. Of course, no program was fail-safe, but it made getting in as difficult as possible. Most hackers probably wouldn't waste the time, but she had a purpose, so kept plugging on.

'Lunch will be ready in fifteen minutes,' Joel declared, poking his head round the door and making her nearly jump out of her skin.

Pressing a hand to her throat, Kathryn turned and glared at him. 'Don't do that! Creeping up on a person can give them a heart attack!' Not to mention the way he looked. The chunky black sweater he wore along with his denims and boots gave him a rugged, outdoorsy look and was incredibly sexy. Her eyes ate him up, and, seeing it, he grinned.

'I'm glad you like what you see, sweetheart, because I do, too. The picture of you in those leggings that seem to make your legs go on for ever will keep me warm when I'm outside shovelling snow this afternoon.'

She quirked an eyebrow at him. 'A coat, hat and gloves will keep you warmer.'

'Only on the outside, darling. Only on the outside. Now, don't forget. Fifteen minutes. Don't make me come and get you,' he added, and departed with the threat hanging in the air.

He might have gone, but the memory of him lingered, keeping her warm on the inside, just as he had said she would do to him. It was difficult to concentrate after that, but somehow she managed it. Time lost all meaning, and she was progressing well when suddenly the door was thrust open again, and she looked round with a start.

'That's it,' Joel declared sternly. 'Come and eat now,' he ordered.

'But you gave me fifteen minutes!' she protested.

'That was half an hour ago. You need a break, Kathryn.'

'But I'm almost there,' she argued, pointing at the screen. 'Give me a few more minutes,' she begged, hating to leave now, with her goal in sight.

Joel's response was to grab the chair and pull it away from the desk, then bend down and scoop her up in his arms. 'Sorry, but you've run out of time,' he stated firmly, swinging round and striding from the room.

With a gasp of alarm Kathryn put her arms up around his neck. 'Brute! How dare you?' she wailed, but in truth the novelty of being carried in his arms smothered any real sense of annoyance she felt.

A whimsical smile curved her lips. My, but he was strong. He carried her easily, and she was no lightweight. Nobody had ever actually done something like this to her before, and it made her feel kind of soft and molten inside. Without volition her arms tightened their hold fractionally, and she allowed her gaze to study the strong cut of his jaw. He was a man of strength in more ways than one.

'Are you always this masterful?' she asked in a playful little voice, and he flickered her a glance as his lips twitched.

'Only with women who can't be trusted to do what's in their own best interests,' he responded as he pushed through the kitchen door. The aroma of hot tomato soup assailed her nostrils and her stomach rumbled.

'So you don't usually do this "Me Tarzan, You Jane" act?' she teased as he set her down on a chair.

He crossed to the cooker, where a saucepan sat with its contents gently bubbling. 'You seem to have brought out a latent protective instinct,' Joel returned wryly, ladling soup into waiting bowls and bringing them to the table. Placing one before her, he nodded at the spoon. 'Eat, Kathryn.'

'Another order?' she asked, though she did pick up the spoon. Smelling the soup had reminded her how hungry she was.

'A request,' he ameliorated, setting down his own bowl and taking the seat opposite her. But he didn't start eating himself until she had begun. 'Help yourself to bread.' He pushed over a plate with chunky slices of bread piled on it.

'There's enough here to feed a small army,' she remarked ironically, but took a chunk, ripping off a piece which she dunked and then popped into her mouth with a sigh of satisfaction. 'Mmm, delicious. I was ready for this.'

'Then why didn't you come when I told you?' Joel charged, and she shrugged and grinned.

'I forgot.'

'Do you often forget to eat?' he asked curiously, and Kathryn nodded.

'I get caught up in things, and the next thing I know, the day has gone. I look on it as an occupational hazard,' she admitted.

He watched her eat for a while, clearly amused by the way she was tucking in. When she reached for another slice of bread, he laughed. 'My child, you need looking after.'

Startled, she looked up, the spoon hovering at her mouth. 'Are you offering?' she asked, the question slipping out before she could think better of it. Her heart flinched anxiously as she expected a short, sharp response, but to her surprise Joel shrugged.

'Why not? Somebody's got to do it,' he declared evenly, and she set the spoon down in her bowl with a little plop.

Kathryn felt curiously giddy, and didn't quite know what to make of that unexpected reply. It would be so easy to read too much into it, and she couldn't afford to do that. Better to err on the side of caution, she decided, and treat it as a joke.

'Why, Joel Kendrick, that almost sounded like a commitment!' she exclaimed mockingly, whilst deep inside

her her heart waited in an agony of anticipation to know
just what he meant.

He smiled. 'Only in the short term. Whilst you're
here I'm going to make it my number one priority to
make sure you eat decently and on time.'

Hope died painfully, and she could only pray it didn't
show on her face. 'As I should be leaving tomorrow,
weather permitting, that hardly amounts to much.'

'I was hoping to persuade you to stay a little longer,'
he returned smoothly, and her heart lurched.

It was something to know that he didn't want her to
leave so soon, but it fell way short of what, in her heart
of hearts, she was hoping for. 'I can't. I have commitments. And whilst I can reschedule tomorrow's meetings with clients, it wouldn't be very professional of me
to cancel them indefinitely just for my own amusement,'
she refused, hoping to see disappointment on his face,
but his expression was bland.

'Then I'll just have to make the most of the time that
you are here.'

It was Kathryn who was disappointed, and she lowered her eyes to her soup, forcing herself to take another
spoonful although her appetite had quite vanished. His
remark was hardly encouraging to a woman who had,
however foolishly, fallen headlong in love with him.

'What are you thinking?' Joel asked after a while,
and she glanced up with a wry smile.

'I'm thinking that I must be crazy to even consider
getting involved with you,' she replied, telling the truth.

'So you are considering it?' He latched on to that
with a speculative gleam in his eye.

She met the look square-on. 'Like I said, I must be
crazy,' she said with a wry twist of her lips.

Reaching across the table, he took her hand. 'Sometimes crazy is the only way to be,' he said with soft persuasion, his thumb running caressingly over her skin.

Her eyes searched his for any sign of emotion, but she was fast coming to realise he only let her see what he wanted her to see. 'Have you ever done anything crazy, Joel? I mean personally, not in business. Have you ever knowingly walked out onto a rickety limb and trusted that it wouldn't break?' That was what she felt as if she was doing. It was scary but she would do it anyway, for a faint heart never won anything of value.

A frown creased his brow. 'That sounds like a loaded question. What exactly are you asking me, Kathryn?'

She could have retreated, but she chose not to. 'I guess I'm asking have you ever put yourself in someone else's hands and trusted them not to let you down?'

His frown deepened, and he released her hand, sitting back in his chair. 'If this is about you and me, I can only assure you that I would never hurt you.'

'Not knowingly, I agree. But has it ever occurred to you that you could? For instance, how do you know that I'm not in love with you right now?' she asked daringly, and her heart thudded sickeningly in her chest, then squeezed painfully when he laughed.

'Because I told you it would be a waste of time.'

Kathryn sat back in disbelief. Had he really said that? Of all the answers he could have given, that had to be the most unexpected. 'You think that's all it would take?' she asked incredulously. 'A word of warning from you, and a woman switches her heart off?'

He shrugged. 'It's as good a reason as any. Women tend to fall in and out of love at the drop of a hat anyway.'

This wasn't at all what *this* woman who had fallen in love with him wanted to hear. 'Your cynicism is frightening. I think it's just as well I'm not in love with you,' she lied, out of necessity. If she told him the truth, she was sure he would be kind, but it was possible to kill with kindness. 'I imagine you think one lethal cut is less painful than a thousand small ones when you end a relationship, too.'

'The pain, if there is any, should be over more quickly,' he responded blandly.

Thunderstruck, Kathryn stared at him in total silence. 'You're right, you'll certainly never fall in love if you believe that,' she declared at last.

He shrugged that off, too. 'I told you I wouldn't. I try not to inflict pain, but if I have, then I'm sure it passes the instant a new man comes along,' he told her mockingly, and it rankled.

'You do yourself a disservice. I don't think you'd be that easy to forget,' she retorted tartly, deeply hurt by his attitude. Women were no more fickle than men, and, for both sexes, the heart did not easily forget. 'Honestly, have you never regretted ending a relationship with even one woman?'

'Regrets are a waste of time and energy. I never allow myself to have them,' he answered simply, and a lump settled in her stomach at his ability to cut himself off from all emotion. It made her want to strike back and get some reaction from him.

'Have you heard of hubris? It's the sin of pride. I have this awful feeling that one day you're going to come down to earth with a bump. It will probably be painful, but at least you'll be back with the rest of us mortals.'

Laughing softly, Joel gathered up the dirty dishes. 'If it happens, I'll let you be the first to say I told you so,' he teased, carrying the crocks to the sink, where he quickly rinsed them and stacked them in the dishwasher. 'Right,' he said, turning back to her, 'I'm off outside to get started on the paths now the snow's stopped. You're welcome to join me.'

Kathryn stood up with a shake of her head. 'It's a job which uses more brawn than brain, and that's your department. I'll get back to the computer,' she refused with a sweet smile, and left him there, carrying back to the study a mental picture of him standing by the sink giving that laugh which always chased goosebumps up and down her spine.

Back in the study, Kathryn didn't immediately continue her search, for her thoughts were too full of what had passed between them in the kitchen. He had been cold to the point of being clinical in his determination to keep emotional ties out of his life. She frowned as something nagged away at the back of her mind. Finally it came to her, the contradiction in what he had just said. His opinion of her sex was far from flattering. Women were fickle, falling in and out of love, their emotions so shallow that any hurt they did feel would fade when the next man came along. It was strange reasoning for a man who had implied his faith in women was scant because they only saw him as a money machine.

At that point Kathryn's mind began whirling over past conversations. Joel had said once that no one woman had made him the way he was, yet she was beginning to think otherwise. He liked to give the impression that he couldn't be hurt. Nothing meant anything to him. Yet time and again he'd proved he wasn't a cold man. Inside there was a warm human being who could be kind and thoughtful in so many ways. So why did he give this impression that he wasn't? Because he had once been hurt very badly, and was determined not to be again?

Her eyes widened. That would explain the apparent contradictions. He *had* once trusted someone, and they *had* let him down. He had put up defences, as anyone would, and the wall he had erected to ward off hurt had become thicker and higher over the years, so that now very little dented it.

Which would explain a lot, but didn't exactly help her much. If she was correct, she was in love with a man determined not to love again. She didn't have trumpets to bring his walls crashing down. She only had her love for him, and if that didn't make a chink in his armour, then nothing would. She could not make him love her; she could only hope that he would want to be with her for longer than a few days. Of course, she could always hope for a miracle, but they were a scarce commodity these days. The unhappy truth was, nothing had changed, and his determination was such that in her heart she doubted that it ever would. Love didn't always find a way.

Sighing, she accepted that she had no answer to her own problem. Joel's, on the other hand, she could do something about. Brooding was pointless; better to concentrate on getting into Gray's database. Pushing all other thought to the far reaches of her mind until she could give them the time and care they needed, she forced herself to concentrate on the job at hand. Meeting yet another barrier, she was balked at every turn as she tried to circumvent it. Nothing worked until she had a brainwave. Following it up, the screen suddenly cleared and she was in.

She ran a search for the files and found them surprisingly easily. Gray obviously hadn't expected to be suspected, or that Joel would return the favour by having Kathryn follow Magda's example. All she had to do now was download them onto disks, wipe the files and any backups there were on the hard disk, and her job was done. Restoring them to Joel's computer was a cinch, and when she finally closed the system down, she did so with the satisfaction of a job well done.

Locking the disks in a drawer, she rose and stretched, then went off in search of Joel to tell him the good news. Collecting her coat and gloves from her room, she let herself out of the house and followed the sound of shovelling around the side of the building. Joel hadn't spotted her yet, and she paused, watching him work. He had slipped on a red plaid body warmer over his sweater, and the effect was exceedingly easy on the eyes. He wasn't the most handsome man she had ever met, but she suspected he would be the only one who could make her heart go bump just by the way he used a shovel! If that wasn't a sign she had it bad, then she didn't know what was.

She must have made some sound or movement, for he glanced up suddenly and caught her in the act. Straightening, he used the shovel as a prop and smiled quizzically.

'You look like the cat who ate the cream,' he remarked cheerfully. 'Does this mean you have good news?'

'Um-hm. Your files are back where they belong, and I've locked disk copies in your desk drawer. I don't suppose anything like this will happen again, but to be on the safe side I think you ought to have some security installed,' Kathryn suggested, and he nodded.

'Better late than never. Can you arrange it?'

'There are several programs on the market, or I could

devise one for you. Of course I'd have to send it on to you, with instructions for setting it up.'

Joel leant both arms on the shovel and crossed one foot over the other. 'Still intending to leave tomorrow?'

She would stay for ever if he asked, but he wouldn't. Not now, and probably never. 'I've done what I came to do,' she answered simply.

'What about the unfinished business between us?' he reminded her softly, and the words went right to her heart.

Kathryn lifted an eyebrow and smiled faintly. 'Maybe it would be better remaining that way—unfinished,' she suggested, and was mildly amused to see him straighten up.

Joel's reply was uncompromising. 'Not for me it wouldn't.'

His vehemence was good for her soul, but she didn't allow it to show. Folding her arms, she pretended to give the subject more thought. 'I don't know, a woman ought to keep her mystery. Perhaps I should leave you wondering about what you might be missing,' she proposed provocatively, and he growled low in his throat, rather like a peevish big cat. She laughed outright. 'Now, now. Little boys who throw tantrums are certain not to get their own way.'

Something dangerous flickered in his eyes as he tossed the shovel aside. 'But I'm not a little boy, as you are going to find out,' he promised, advancing on her with clear intent in his wicked grin.

Kathryn's heart leapt, and with a squeal she turned and ran, laughing helplessly at her inelegant efforts to escape over snow-covered ground. Seeing a path to her left, she headed for it.

'No, Kathryn!' Joel called out sharply, but she ignored him and in the next instant felt her legs fly out from under her. There was barely time for her to cry out in alarm before she hit the ground with enough force to knock the air out of her. Seconds later, Joel dropped to his knees at her side, his expression shocked and grim. 'Are you OK, sweetheart? Did you hit your head at all? Talk to me, Kathryn!' he ordered when she remained silent, his hands beginning to run over her, searching for possible injury.

'What happened?' Kathryn croaked out, now that she had her breath back, and Joel sat back on his heels, puffing out a relieved breath.

'Black ice is what happened. It's always under the snow on this path because it holds water. Are you sure you're OK?' he asked in concern, frowning as he helped her sit up.

Kathryn winced. 'Apart from having a bruise which will make it uncomfortable for me to sit down for a week, I'm fine,' she reassured him wryly, probing tender spots and wincing occasionally.

'I could always...' Joel began, but her head shot round, her eyes flashing a warning as she saw the gleam in his.

'No, you couldn't,' she declared firmly. 'No part of my anatomy needs kissing better, thank you very much.'

He didn't deny that that was what he'd been going to say. 'There's no need to snap my head off. I didn't make you fall over.'

Kathryn shot him an old-fashioned look. 'No, but you would have done if it had been to your advantage.'

Joel grinned. 'Whilst I might want you on your back, sweetheart, there's a more subtle way of going about it.'

There was something in the way he said 'sweetheart' that chased goosebumps up and down her spine. The man had everything. 'I've no doubt you know every art of seduction ever invented, and then some,' she returned mockingly, and he tutted.

'The way you say that makes me out to be some kind of modern-day Casanova,' he protested in hurt tones, and she gave him a look which told him he wasn't fooling her one bit.

'No, but you'd run him a close second,' she riposted, laughing softly as she probed another sore spot. Glancing up, she found him watching her with the strangest look in his eyes. 'What?' she asked in confusion, and Joel looked at her with a faint frown.

They were facing each other by now, and he reached out and cupped her cheek with infinite tenderness. 'I was just thinking how much I love your laugh,' he confided, and a frisson of excitement skittered along her nerves.

Suddenly she didn't feel like laughing. 'You pick your moment to tell me. We're sitting in a snowdrift, risking hypothermia,' she said in a breathless little voice.

His hand snaked round behind her neck and inexorably began to draw her closer. 'Are you cold?'

'Only on the outside,' Kathryn admitted huskily, and a smile curved the edges of his mouth upwards.

'Good, because I'm just going to have to kiss you,' Joel growled when they were no more than a breath apart.

Her hands fastened onto his body warmer as she leant towards him. 'What took you so long?' she demanded in little more than a whisper, and then his mouth took hers and the world spun away.

It was a deep, soul-searching kiss that seemed to be seeking an answer from her, though she doubted if he knew the question. She didn't either, so all she could do was respond to it with every ounce of the love she felt for him. It appeared to be what he wanted, for with a low moan he folded his arms around her and drew her across his knees, igniting the fire of their desire with the ever mounting passion of his kisses. Her eyes shut, caught up in the maelstrom, Kathryn responded blindly, and it was only when Joel lifted his head with a muffled curse that the world returned and she realised somewhere close by a bell was ringing insistently.

'It's the telephone again,' he explained, taking a steadying breath. 'I fitted up a speaker so I can hear it when I'm outside.' The ringing stopped, but he was still listening as he set her aside. A few seconds later, it rang again.

Shivering now that the heat of his body had been withdrawn, Kathryn scrambled to her feet. 'I had no idea your work was so important,' she remarked as he followed her up and headed for the house. She tagged along behind, more than a little peeved that he could so easily break off making love to her for the sake of his business.

'This is not about work.' He corrected her assumption without slowing his stride. 'That particular ring pattern is a signal I arranged because sometimes I ignore calls that might be work-related. I'm part of the local search and rescue team. Somebody could be in trouble, and if they are, in these conditions, time is everything.'

Kathryn immediately felt like a prize worm for being irritated, and at the same time felt her heart swell with pride that he should be part of such a worthwhile group. She admitted to being surprised, but, then again, knew she shouldn't be. She was beginning to learn that he was a man who gave of himself generously, it was only where his heart was concerned that he posted 'Keep Out' signs.

Entering the kitchen, Joel snatched the receiver off the wall phone. 'This is Joel. What's up?' He asked the question briskly, then listened intently with lowered head to whoever was on the other end of the line. 'I'll be there in twenty minutes,' he said finally, and hung up.

'Is it bad?' Kathryn asked when he turned and she could see the serious expression on his face.

'Three walkers were out on one of the crags. Two fell and could have God knows what sort of injuries. The third managed to reach a farm and sent out the alarm. Damn it, it doesn't seem to matter how many weather warnings are put out, some idiots always manage to ignore them and we have to go and pick up the pieces.'

Kathryn felt her heart clench in sudden anxiety as she realised just what rescuing the injured walkers would mean. 'Won't it be dangerous for you, too?' she asked unevenly, and he nodded, confirming her worst fears.

'Of course it will. No matter how well we know these hills, the weather is the enemy. However, we're committed to rescuing them. No way could we leave them there, unless the weather turns so bad we can't see our hands in front of our faces.'

'But…' She began to protest, only he stopped her by placing his hands on her shoulders.

'I'm sorry, Kathryn, but I don't have time to talk now. It will be getting dark soon, and we'll need all the light we can get.' With that he walked round her and out of the room. As she stood there, biting her lip, she heard him taking the stairs two at a time.

Her instinct was to tell him not to go, for she had this awful mental picture of him tumbling down a sheer cliff and breaking his neck. It made her blood run cold. Yet she knew, if she said it, it would change nothing. Joel would still go. So she held the words back, though her stomach was churning anxiously. When she heard Joel come back down the stairs, she went out to meet him. He was dressed in heavy-duty climbing gear and carried a backpack. Seeing her strained face, he smiled.

'Don't worry, I'll be fine. With any luck they won't be too hard to find, or too badly injured.'

'Be careful,' she advised, her smile a wobbly thing at best, and he bent and pressed a swift, hard kiss on her lips.

'I always am. I'll be back before you miss me,' he added, then turned on his heel and left her.

Kathryn pressed a hand to her lips, for they had an alarming tendency to tremble. She missed him already. She had no doubt he had done this many times before, but she hadn't been in love with him then. He was risking his life to save that of somebody who shouldn't have been out there in the first place, and that made her both angry and frightened. She had absolutely no control over the situation. All she could do was sit and wait, and pray that he came back in one piece.

It wasn't easy. She went upstairs and changed into dry clothes, then spent the next hour wandering aimlessly from room to room, constantly looking out of the window, hoping to see his four-by-four returning, though her brain knew it was far too soon for that. Finally she decided to be positive, and went back to the kitchen, searching the freezer for something to cook for dinner. He would be back by then, she told herself firmly, as she defrosted some meat and prepared vegetables for a casserole. Something hot and tasty to chase away the chills of the hillside.

When dusk fell, she went around lighting lamps and laying the table. The oven was sending out aromas that ought to have set her mouth watering, but as the minutes and then hours passed her confidence faltered. Where was he? What was happening? Turning off the oven, she paced back to the lounge and stood at the window, looking out, willing the flash of headlights to beam out through the darkness. But they didn't. Eventually she left her post and curled herself up on the couch, cuddling a cushion to her chest and watching the pictures come and go in the fire. When it died down, she built it up again, determined that Joel should return to a warm house.

Midnight came and went, and though she fought it her eyes grew heavy out of the sheer exhaustion of worry. Unable to fight it any longer, she stretched out on the couch, still clutching the cushion, and within no time at all sleep claimed her.

CHAPTER SIX

'KATHRYN?'

The soft sound of her name being gently repeated drew Kathryn from the depths of sleep. Rolling over, she stared blankly at the man who sat on the edge of the couch, one hand resting on the back cushion as he bent over her.

'Joel?' she murmured groggily, rubbing at her eyes. 'What time is it?'

He brushed a stray lock of hair away from her eyes, his gaze running over the lines of her face softened by sleep. 'A little before three. Why aren't you in bed?'

Memory returned with a rush. The emergency call. Her hours of anxious waiting. 'I wanted to wait up for you. How did it go?' Lord, she was so relieved to see him alive and well. Her eyes ate him up, noting the faint signs of weariness about his eyes. She wanted to throw her arms around him and hold him close, but was afraid of how much that would give away. All she could do was lie there and pretend she hadn't been worried to death.

'It went well. Lucky, our dog, found them without too much trouble, thank God.'

If Lucky were here, she would give her the hug she couldn't give Joel. 'And the walkers?'

'One has a broken leg, the other cracked ribs, but apart from the effects of exposure they're OK. They should consider themselves damned lucky.'

'I'm sure they do. Did you read them the Riot Act?'

Joel dragged a weary hand through his hair, 'Pat, our team leader, did that. Not that it will do much good. Some people never learn. We'll probably be out rescuing the same group next year. I don't know why I do it. It's a mug's game.'

This time Kathryn went with her instincts and sat up, slipping her arms around him in an all too brief hug. 'You do it because you'd never forgive yourself if they could have been saved and you'd done nothing.'

He eased her away, looking at her quizzically. 'Is that so?' he queried, running an exploring hand up and down her spine, setting her nerve-endings tingling.

She nodded. 'You're a good man, Joel Kendrick. You'll never get me to believe otherwise.'

'How can you be so sure? You barely know me,' he argued, and she sighed, using her fingers to comb back hair that fell forward over his forehead.

She couldn't tell him it was because her heart knew him. It wasn't what he wanted to hear. All she could do was shrug carelessly. 'I just know. Call it woman's intuition.' He smiled at that, and her eyes dropped to his lips. Before she could think better of it, she pressed her own lips to his in a swift kiss.

Their eyes locked, and all at once the temperature in the room rose by several degrees.

'What was that for?' Joel asked huskily, and she licked her lips, aware that by her action she had instigated a course of events that had only one ending.

'I just felt like it,' she returned, equally huskily.

'Hmm. Is there anything else you feel like doing?' The question was little more than a tantalising growl.

Her heart kicked. 'We-ell, I could think of several things, but you must be exhausted,' she responded, more than a little breathlessly.

His soft laugh shivered over her flesh. 'Sweetheart, right now I don't feel the least bit exhausted,' he confided, his roving hands finding the hem of her sweater and slipping underneath, searing her with the heat of his touch.

Kathryn closed her eyes and moaned softly as her own hands forayed over the breadth of his back and shoulders, delighting in their latent power. 'Aren't you hungry? I made dinner. It won't take a minute to heat up.'

His mouth found the line of her jaw and traced a path of kisses up to her ear. 'Kathryn, Kathryn. What I'm hungry for is already hot,' he sighed, nipping at her earlobe, making her gasp and shiver.

She rubbed her cheek against his. He needed a shave, but she didn't mind. The slight growth of beard only added to his maleness. A faint smile curved her lips as they brushed his ear. 'It will keep—unless you can't wait,' she teased, and he groaned, abandoning his exploration of her back to cup her face in his hands, looking at her with eyes that blazed with barely suppressed passion.

'I've waited long enough as it is. I'm a starving man with a hunger only you can satisfy.'

The confession was music to her ears. 'Then eat,' she invited huskily. 'Everything I have is yours.'

It was all the invitation Joel needed, and he brought his mouth down on hers, kissing her with an almost desperate passion, taking her lips, parting them, seeking out the honeyed depths of her mouth with his tongue. And Kathryn welcomed him wholeheartedly. She wanted this—needed it. Whatever he might feel for her, she loved him, and the only way she could ever show it was in the giving of her body. Tonight they would make love, and it would be precisely that for her.

Joel broke off the kiss long enough to throw some cushions onto the floor before the low burning fire, then he laid her down on the rug and joined her there, taking her in his arms once more. Like a forest fire in a tinder-dry wood, passion needed only the faintest spark to ignite, and within seconds it was blazing. Feverish kisses were soon not enough, and clothes were a barrier that drove Kathryn wild with impatience. She wanted to feel him, touch him, know him in every way there was, and what her hands could find beneath his sweater was not enough. With a grunt of annoyance, she tugged at the sweater, hauling it up, only to meet the barrier of his arms. But they were two minds with a single thought, and Joel moved, sitting up to pull the sweater over his head and throw it across the room.

Meanwhile Kathryn was removing her own sweater, and he took it from her, tossing it to join his own. She would have reached for the front clasp of her bra, but Joel stopped her. Swiftly straddling her hips, he pushed her hands to the floor beside her head before trailing his fingers down the tender inner flesh of her arms and across her chest, finally hovering at the shadowy cleavage between her achingly sensitive breasts. Instinctively her body arched, inviting him to release the clasp and touch her as she longed for him to do. Her lashes fluttered as at last he undid the fastening and peeled the lacy scrap aside. He touched her then, but it was gentle, almost worshipful, and she shifted beneath him, needing more. After what seemed an age, yet was mere seconds, his hands cupped her tumescent flesh, his thumbs finding her turgid nipples and caressing them into aching points.

A whimper of pleasure broke from her as she watched Joel lower his head and take first one nipple and then the other into his hot mouth and lave them with his tongue. Unable to lie there unmoving, Kathryn lifted her hands to the thick dark mass of his hair and clung on as delicious frissons of pleasure chased paths through her body, starting up a throbbing ache deep within her. Then he moved, his lips and hands tracing scorching paths down her body, meeting the barrier of her leggings only momentarily as he tugged them down, and then they were gone, along with the rest of her clothes.

'Beautiful,' he murmured, as he retraced the trail up her legs to the juncture of her thighs, parting them to seek out the hot, moist centre of her, tightening the coils of passion from which there could only be one outcome.

'No. Wait,' Kathryn protested faintly, wanting this to be a shared pleasure. But Joel had other ideas.

'This time is for you,' he insisted throatily, and continued working his magic on her until one last stroke sent her tumbling over the edge.

Heart racing, she lay with eyes closed as the shattered fragments of her senses reformed. Only when Joel came up beside her, one hand gently brushing damp hair from her face, did she open her eyes and look at him reproachfully.

'That wasn't fair,' she sighed, her desire momentarily appeased.

He smiled, his fingers tracing the ridge of her collarbone and its almost transparently silky skin. 'All is fair in love and war,' he argued, and that brought a spark to her eyes.

'Then it's my turn,' she declared, rising up so that he was forced to fall back, and in an instant Kathryn was straddling his body. Grinning dangerously, she met his gleaming blue gaze. 'Scared? You should be, because

I'm going to make you pay,' she promised as her hands ran forays over the taut planes of his powerful chest.

Joel's teeth flashed. 'Do your worst. I can take it,' he retorted, then his breath hissed in through his teeth as she found his flat male nipples and flicked them with her nails.

Smiling with satisfaction now that she had his attention, Kathryn dropped her gaze to his chest. It felt wonderful to touch him with such freedom, and she gloried in the way he responded to her, keeping nothing back. It was immensely arousing, and she felt her desire stir to life again as she set about tantalising him as he had her. Dipping her head she let her lips find his nipples, and her teeth nipped him, bringing a gasp of pleasure from deep in his throat, then her tongue traced lazy circles before flicking back and forth across the sensitised nubs.

Slowly, slowly she traced a moist pathway down over his flat stomach, feeling the tension grow inside him as she approached the waistband of his jeans. She rose then, her bottom lip caught between pearly teeth as she dealt with the clasp and zip, releasing the aroused male flesh that thrust against his shorts. It was no accident that her hand brushed him as she tugged his pants and jeans down together, and his body jerked up from the floor, a bitten-off curse remaining strangled in his throat. Then she tossed the clothes aside and he lay before her in all his naked male glory. There was no doubting his wanting of her, and she felt her own body start to throb with awakened desire.

It was no longer easy to keep her movements slow and tantalising. Her hands trembled faintly as she ran them over his thighs, getting closer but never quite reaching the place she instinctively knew he wanted her to. Finally she relented, and, as he had done to her, she caressed him, driving him inexorably towards the edge. Joel moaned aloud, and reached for her.

'No more!' he gritted out through clenched teeth as her head came up, and she looked at him, meeting the fiery blaze in his eyes. Knowing he could take no more, Joel clasped her hips, holding her to him as he sought to keep some measure of control.

'Joel.' His name was an ache of longing on her lips, and with it his immense control finally broke. He pulled her down, rolling over so that she was beneath him at last, and he claimed her with one powerful thrust. The presence of him inside her made her feel complete for the first time in her life, and Kathryn clung on, matching his thrusts, seeking an ending that suddenly overwhelmed her, sending her plummeting out into the vortex on a wave of incredible pleasure. Seconds later Joel joined her, climaxing with a groan that seemed to be drawn from the very depths of his being.

Clinging together, they rode out the stormy seas of passion until at last they washed up on the shore, replete and exhausted.

It was a long time later that Joel stirred and became aware that he still lay on top of her. Shifting to one side, yet seemingly unwilling to release her, he hauled her in to his side, settling her head on his shoulder. Then he closed his eyes, and within seconds was asleep. Poised on the edge of sleep herself, Kathryn sighed and laid her hand over his heart.

'I love you,' she whispered, needing to say it and safe in the knowledge that he could not hear her. Then, closing her eyes, she followed him into sleep.

*   *   *

She was jerked awake abruptly, hours later, and lay still with heart thumping as she tried to work out what was happening. Her back was warm, and she realised that some time during the night they had shifted; now Joel lay sleeping with his body cupped around hers, spoon-fashion. She became aware of other things. The room was warm, although the fire had gone out, which meant the central heating had kicked in. Just as well, as they were both lying as naked as the day they were born.

Her lips quirked, but an alien sound quickly wiped it away. It was the sound of a door closing, followed by the unmistakable sound of a car driving away. In a flash she realised that it could only be Agnes returning, and she was sure that in a few minutes or less she would be walking into the sitting-room, where the sight which would reach her eyes would be intensely embarrassing for all concerned.

Looking around desperately for something to cover them with, she caught sight of a throw folded over the arm of a chair. Footsteps crossed the hall as she reached for it and hastily shook it out over them. It didn't cover everything, but enough for modesty, which was just as well—for in the next instant the door was being opened and Agnes came in.

Their eyes met, one pair in surprise, the other in dismay. Yet though her cheeks were burning hot enough to start a fire, she didn't want Joel to wake up. He had had a busy night, what with one thing and another. So she held her finger to her lips to prevent Agnes from saying anything, and indicated that she would join her outside in a moment. At first she thought the other woman would not comply, but in the end she turned and quietly left the room again.

Kathryn eased herself away from Joel, freezing when he murmured something in his sleep, but he merely turned over and she scrambled to her feet, pausing only to drape the throw over him so that he didn't get cold. Dressing took some time, as her clothes were scattered about the room, but less than ten minutes after Agnes had arrived Kathryn left the room and went in search of her. She found her in the kitchen making tea.

Agnes paused long enough to give Kathryn a speaking look. 'I hope you know what you're doing,' she said forthrightly, though there was neither reproof nor dismay in her tone.

Kathryn combed her dishevelled hair with her fingers and folded her arms defensively. 'I think I do,' she responded, feeling uncomfortable at having been found in a compromising position.

Setting the pot of tea on the table, Agnes quickly produced cups and saucers, milk and sugar, then indicated Kathryn should take a seat. She joined her, but said nothing until two steaming cups had been poured out, then she sighed and looked Kathryn squarely in the eye.

'I love Master Joel, but I'm not blind. He plays with women. I've seen them come and go. Some, quite frankly, I was glad to see the back of, and others I thought might make him a good wife. A few of them even loved him, but the majority didn't. They used him, and one by one they changed him from the loving boy I remember. One in particular...' She broke off, biting her lip uncertainly, and Kathryn held her breath, because from the demeanour of the other woman it was obvious there was something she should know.

'What about her?' she probed carefully, and Agnes looked at her sombrely.

'I'm telling you this because I like you, and I can see

you're a good girl. He won't let himself fall in love with you because of that woman. I could see she was a flighty piece, but he was crazy about her. They were to be married until he discovered her with another man. One she was in love with but who didn't have Joel's money. The idea was that she would eventually get a divorce, and the pair of them would live on her settlement. As if that wasn't bad enough, when Joel broke it off, she got her revenge by telling him she had aborted his child. Was quite blatant about it,' Agnes revealed with a shudder of distaste.

Kathryn gasped, horrified. She had been right to suspect there was a woman behind Joel's attitude, but she could never have suspected this. 'Oh, dear God, how could she?' That was something she could never do.

'Easily, because she was a cold, evil woman. It sent him crazy for a while, and we all despaired of him. Then he sobered up, and when he did there was a wall around his heart inches thick, and it's getting thicker year by year. Love doesn't exist for him. He won't let anyone get close, and that will destroy the woman who loves him. He will be kind, and generous, but he will keep his heart locked away. I've seen it happen before, and I don't want to see it happen to you,' Agnes said gently, as if she knew Kathryn's secret.

'What makes you think it will?' she charged, trying to keep her voice steady, but it wavered tellingly.

Agnes sipped at her tea carefully, then looked at her over the top of the cup. 'Because you're here and he isn't. Your thoughts are for him, not yourself.'

Kathryn felt heat rise in her cheeks again, and knew how revealing that was. 'He had to go out onto the hills yesterday, for a rescue, and didn't get in until this morning. I thought he needed the sleep.' She explained away her actions, but Agnes was no fool, as was becoming clear.

'Maybe, but most of the others would have woken him and sent him out to deal with me and cover their blushes.'

Kathryn didn't want to be reminded of the others, and refused to think of those who would come after her. She was with him now. This was her time. 'I'm not like the others.'

Agnes reached out and patted her hand kindly. 'No, you're not. I only wish I could believe it would make a difference.' She sighed and shook her head sadly. 'I'm afraid Master Joel won't change.'

Kathryn stirred her tea for a second in silence, then sighed. 'You're right, I do love him,' she said honestly. 'But he'll never hear that from me. He must never know, and you must promise not to tell him either. You see, I don't expect him to love me. He's made that quite clear. So as far as he's concerned, this is just another affair. I know it's going to hurt when it's over, but it would hurt a lot more if he was to pity me. I believe I can take anything but that,' she added with a wince, and Agnes's expression changed to one of compassion.

'Don't get yourself into a fret. I'm no tattletale. Your secret is safe with me,' she promised. 'I wish there was something I could do, but it's gone too deep with him. I'll pray for you, though. Pray that he comes to his senses and sees what's staring him in the face. You'd be good for him. I can only hope he will come to see that, too.'

Silence fell then, for there was nothing more to say. By mutual consent they chatted about other things for a while, then Kathryn excused herself to go upstairs to shower and change—and pack for the journey home.

She looked in on Joel on the way, but he was still sleeping soundly, and she hadn't the heart to wake him, though she was sorely tempted to. Waking in his arms and making slow passionate love together would have been something to take away with her, but his need for sleep was greater, so she carefully closed the door again and continued on her way.

As she showered she did her best to remain positive, but she had no idea where they went from here. Last night had been magical, but how could it be repeated when they lived at opposite ends of the country? How could they continue an affair at a distance? She didn't believe it could be done, and steeled herself to the possibility that last night would quite likely be all there would ever be.

Painful fingers tightened around her heart. It was not enough. It was nowhere near enough. Yet, in all honesty, even a lifetime would fall short. Only an eternity would do, and that was out of the question because of an unknown woman who had all but destroyed him. But for her they might have had a future. She could only imagine how Joel must have felt, and she despised the woman for what she had done to him. Yet it was no use crying over spilt milk, for she could not change the past. All she could do was put on a brave face. If this was the end, then she would bear it somehow.

She was dressed once more and in the process of packing when a sound at the door caused her to straighten and turn. Joel stood in the doorway, the throw draped about him like a toga. With his hair in disarray and a night's growth of beard on his chin, he looked like an ancient Roman version of the morning after the night before. She couldn't help but smile at him, and her heart turned over at the rather endearing effect of his bare feet poking out of the bottom fringe. Her first instinct was to fling herself into his arms and stay there for ever. She resisted it—just—and made do with storing the memory of him in her heart.

'What are you doing?' he wanted to know as he sauntered casually into the room, a mild frown on his forehead.

'Baking a cake,' she riposted, as it must be obvious from the case and pile of clothes on the bed just what she was doing. Picking up a jumper, she folded it neatly and placed it in the case.

'Going somewhere?' he asked next, as she continued to pack.

Though it was the hardest thing she had ever had to do, she made herself respond lightly. Coming on heavy was absolutely the wrong thing to do. 'I have a train to catch, remember. Agnes says the roads are clear, so I'm going home as planned.'

'Agnes is back?' That clearly surprised him. Obviously he hadn't run into her yet. Kathryn felt sure the woman would have something pointed to say to him when he did.

Her lips twitched. 'Um-hm. You were unconscious at the time. She walked in on us. I just had time to cover us with your toga there. Which, by the way, is very fetching. Anyway, it could have been very embarrassing.' It had been embarrassing enough as it was. She picked up another jumper and was about to fold it when Joel caught her wrist, forcing her attention.

'Why didn't you wake me?' he asked a tad testily, and her brows rose.

'Because you needed the sleep. Although I have to admit it hasn't left you in a sweet mood,' she added, looking pointedly at where he held her.

'That's because I expected to find you beside me when I woke up,' he complained, and her shrug hid the fact that she had wanted to wake with him, too. It just hadn't been meant to be.

'As you can see, I had things to do,' she said matter-of-factly, making him frown even harder.

'Are you always this cool after you've spent the night with a man?' he demanded somewhat frostily himself, and she laughed softly, though it was the last thing she felt like doing. Howling better fitted the bill.

'I'm just being sensible. Besides, I thought you weren't enamoured of the clinging type. I'm sorry if I hurt you by leaving you downstairs, but I thought I was playing by the rules,' she replied dryly, and in a flash he had dropped her arm and stepped back, hitching up the toga, which showed a tendency to slip floorward.

'I wasn't hurt,' Joel denied curtly, and Kathryn shot him an old-fashioned look.

'It sure sounds as if you were,' she said, unable to resist taunting him, since he was behaving unreasonably so far as she could see.

'I was disappointed, not hurt. I wanted to make love to you again,' he corrected, his voice dropping an octave seductively, and she felt heat rise in her cheeks at the memory of what they had shared.

'I would have liked that, too,' she admitted huskily.

At her answer, heat dispelled the frost in his eyes, and he closed the gap between them, taking her by the shoulders. 'Then stay,' he urged huskily. 'Stay one more day and we can spend it in bed together. Last night was incredible, wasn't it?'

She drew in a shaky breath. 'Yes, it was,' she agreed honestly. 'You were right, your lovemaking is even more incredible than your arrogance.' She reminded him of what he had said to her mere days ago, and he smiled a crookedly attractive smile.

'If you want the truth, it surpassed even what I expected, and I want to feel that way again. Stay, Kathryn. Please.'

Lord, how she wanted to, but it wasn't possible, and she shook her head, her throat tight with emotion. 'I can't. I told you that. I have commitments.'

'To hell with your commitments!' Joel barked, then, lowering his head swiftly, he pressed a hard kiss on her lips that sent her blood racing through her veins. It was over far too soon and she was left staring up at him.

'If you do that again, you'll probably change my mind, but please don't. My work is important to me, as are my customers. I *have* to go home,' she argued unevenly, and looking down, he gave a resigned sigh.

'Damn, but you're a stubborn woman. You're going to make me wait, and I hate waiting.'

Her heart kicked, for she knew the wait would be longer than he thought. 'Does that mean you want to see me again?' she somehow managed to ask teasingly, whilst inside her stomach tied itself into a nervous knot.

'After last night, how could you think otherwise? This is not the end, Kathryn, but the beginning.'

'Maybe, but I don't know when I can get back here again,' she felt honour bound to point out, and his laugh came as quite a surprise.

'It's flattering to know you want to come to me, but it won't be necessary. I'm cutting my visit short. There are one or two things I have to do, but I'll be back in town at the end of the week. Have dinner with me Friday night.'

Her shock had to be written across her face. 'But…I thought you lived here?'

Joel shook his head. 'No such luck. I spend as much time as I can here, but my work keeps me in London most of the time,' he explained, and she realised that if she had been thinking clearly she would have worked that out for herself. Drew was based in London, so his boss must be, too.

'I see,' she groaned, feeling a fool.

'So, are you going to give me an answer any time soon, or do I have to wait in suspense?' Joel teased with a soft laugh, and when she blinked at him he gave her a tiny shake. 'Dinner. Friday night. Is it a date?'

About to give the swift *yes* her heart demanded, she bit it back in favour of a more flirtatious response. She couldn't let him see how relieved she was. 'I think Friday is free. I'll have to check my calendar.'

Joel's eyes glittered. 'It had better be. In fact, you can keep all your evenings free from now on. I'm not sharing you with anyone,' he declared, sending a thrill of excitement along her nervous system. They were the very words she wanted to hear.

Though she was more pleased by his reaction than she could ever admit, she knew she had to keep some measure of sanity, and she shook her head. 'I'm afraid you're just going to have to share me. I have dinner with my parents at least once a week.'

'That I will allow,' he conceded graciously, and she laughed and pushed herself away from him with a tiny thump on his chest.

'Generous of you. Now, go away and let me finish packing. My train leaves in a couple of hours and I daren't miss it.' She shooed him off, returning to her case and picking up another item with trembling fingers.

'You'll get there on time. I'll take you myself,' he promised, and she glanced at him over her shoulder.

'You don't have to do that,' she protested, though inside her nerves were fluttering like mad.

'Oh, but I do,' Joel insisted as he headed for the door. 'If I have to let you out of my sight for a week, I'm going to make damn sure you have something to remember me by.'

Kathryn stared after his departing back, wishing she could tell him that she would remember him always. It gladdened her heart to know that he didn't want this to be over between them too soon, but oh, how she wished that it didn't have to be over at all. But it was no use crying for the moon. She had to be grateful for what he could give her, and store the memories away so that they could warm her on those long empty nights that surely lay ahead.

CHAPTER SEVEN

A WEEK could seem endless when you were waiting for the weekend to arrive, but it was even longer when you were in love. An hour had never taken so long to pass, nor a day such an eternity. By the time Friday finally came round, Kathryn was a mass of fluttering nerves. Though it had only been a few days since she had seen Joel, and he had called her on the telephone every evening, she had missed him terribly. Eight o'clock seemed so far away. She didn't know how she was going to get through the day.

As is turned out, she had more distractions than she'd anticipated. Firstly somebody called with a problem that couldn't be handled over the phone, and she had to travel to deal with it. That took all morning, but she was home again in time for a late lunch of coffee and a slice of frozen pizza. Not exactly appetising, but Kathryn wasn't really hungry, and was only eating because she knew she'd better put something in her empty stomach.

She was just sitting down at the pine table set in the bay window which made up the dining area of her kitchen, overlooking her tiny garden when the doorbell rang. Answering its summons, she found Drew on her doorstep, a large florist's box in his hands, which he offered to her as he stepped inside.

'Why are you bringing me flowers?' she asked curiously, closing the door and following him back into the kitchen.

'I'm not. I met the delivery boy on the doorstep and offered to give them to you. Who is sending you flowers? Or do I need to ask?' he drawled, with a look that spoke volumes.

A faint pink wash stained her cheeks revealingly. 'I have been known to receive flowers before,' Kathryn countered, setting the box on the table and removing the lid.

'Not from that location, you haven't,' Drew asserted dryly, having noted the address of the high-class florist.

Kathryn wasn't listening to him; she was busy folding back the layers of tissue paper and revealing the exquisite blooms of a dozen long-stemmed red roses. The card lying on them simply said 'Joel', in a strong flourish, and her heart turned over in her chest. Her hand trembled as she picked up one bloom and inhaled the deliciously creamy scent. Her mind was buzzing crazily. Red roses. All the world and his wife knew what they were meant to mean, but she hastily told herself not to read too much into it. Yet they *were* red roses, and that had to mean he cared for her a little, didn't it?

'They are from Joel, I take it?' Drew sought confirmation, watching her cross the room and reach down from a cupboard a crystal vase which she proceeded to fill with water.

'Yes,' she answered simply, setting the vase on the table and looking at him steadily, daring him to stand in judgement.

Drew grimaced. 'Well, that explains why you've been avoiding me,' he declared with a sigh, and she frowned at him.

'I haven't been avoiding you,' she denied automatically although in retrospect that was precisely what she had been doing. With her emotions in a state of upheaval right now, the last thing she needed was to listen to Drew's well-meaning dissertation on why getting involved with Joel was not a good thing.

Drew looked at her askance. 'Leaving your answering machine on all the time smacks of avoidance to me. You haven't returned one of my calls, and that just isn't like you, Kathy.'

She started arranging the roses in the vase, and paused with a sigh. It wasn't like her, that was true. 'I'm sorry,' she apologised, and her cousin came across and slipped an arm around her shoulder, giving her a quick hug.

'Don't worry about it. I guess I don't need to ask how long this has been going on. Since I introduced you,' he said, with a nod to the flowers. 'How serious is it?'

'That kind of depends on your perspective, doesn't it?'

'I've got a pretty good idea what Joel's is, Kathy. Yours, I'm not so sure about.'

Kathryn toyed with a bloom, tracing the silky texture of the petals with her thumb. 'My perspective is very simple. I'm in love with him.'

Drew swore under his breath. 'Damn, I guessed as much. I could kill him!' he added angrily, and Kathryn laid a soothing hand on his arm.

'Joel had nothing to do with it. Not in the way you mean. He believes that, having told me not to fall for him, I won't. Right now, he thinks I feel the same way he does—that this is nothing more than another affair from which we'll both walk away unscathed at the end.'

'Only you won't,' Drew pointed out succinctly, and she didn't argue with him because she couldn't.

'Listen, Drew. I went into this with my eyes open,

and I have no intention of calling foul because my feelings will be hurt. I'm prepared for that.'

Drew pulled her close and sighed heavily. 'Kathy, I love you dearly, but you're a fool. Nobody is ever prepared for that kind of pain. Unfortunately, you're going to find that out the hard way. Just remember I'll be here for you whenever you need me.'

She rested her head on his shoulder. 'Don't tell the family. I don't want them to find out and start asking awkward questions.'

'OK, but they'll find out eventually. Joel is news wherever he goes, and if you're with him, you will be too,' he warned.

'I'll cross that bridge when I come to it,' she declared, easing herself away from him. 'Well, now that you're here, do you want some lunch? I'm having pizza,' she offered with a twinkle in her eye, for she knew how he loved it.

'Pepperoni?' he asked hopefully, and when she nodded he pulled out a chair and sat down. 'You've twisted my arm. Make mine a large slice,' he commanded, and Kathryn was laughing again as she headed for the freezer.

Though it had brightened her day, Kathryn had pushed Drew's visit to the back of her mind by the time eight o'clock came around that evening. The only man she could think of was Joel, and his imminent arrival. She had spent ages agonising over what to wear, nothing had seemed quite right for such a momentous occasion, but in the end she'd plumped for a simple emerald two-piece, consisting of a skirt and matching top with shoestring straps made out of some silky material.

Of course, then all she had to do was wait, and those

minutes until the doorbell rang seemed to stretch out interminably. When it did ring, her pulse leapt into a gallop, and she had to tell herself quite sternly to play it cool. So it was an outwardly calm Kathryn who opened the door to him, whilst on the inside she was a jumbled mass of nerves. The deep sense of joy it gave her just to see him there twisted her heart, and told her, had there been any doubt, that her feelings hadn't changed.

Joel looked magnificent in a black dinner suit and white silk shirt. With his hands casually tucked into his trouser pockets, he appeared suave and relaxed, not to mention extremely handsome, and the words of greeting she had planned to say were completely forgotten. All she could do was grip the door like grim death as her knees went weak, and say, 'Hello,' in a gruff little voice.

'Hello, yourself,' he returned, with one of those lazy smiles that turned her heart over. She smiled back, drinking him in, and lost track of the passage of time until he quirked an eyebrow at her and said, 'Much as I admire your front step, I'd much rather be inside with you.'

A comment which had her stepping aside to allow him in as a soft flush invaded her cheeks. Idiot, she berated herself silently. She had to pull herself together or her secret would be out of the bag in a flash. 'Oh! Of course. Come in,' she invited, and he did so with a soft laugh.

'I'm flattered you were lost for words. I don't imagine that happens often,' he teased, and she took her cue from that and hastened to recover lost ground.

'Actually, I was trying to decide whether you look more sexy in that suit or the fetching number you wore the other day,' she returned with a touch of irony, referring to the throw he had draped around himself. Closing the door, she sealed them into her compact hallway, which instantly shrank to half its size, heightening the atmosphere considerably.

'And your decision was?' he prompted.

Kathryn leant back against the door, folded her arms and tipped her head to one side consideringly. 'It was close. I'd hate to have to live on the difference,' she said wryly. 'You're looking extremely handsome tonight. Is that for something special?'

His teeth gleamed as he grinned at her manoeuvre. 'Fishing for compliments, sweetheart?'

She pouted prettily. 'You could at least have said I was special.'

Banked fires glowed in the depths of his eyes. 'Oh, you are that, Kathryn, darling. You are most certainly that. But, since you mention it, and now I come to look at you, you're looking pretty delectable yourself. That colour makes your hair gleam like burnished gold. It takes my breath away.'

'Good,' she declared with unabashed satisfaction, allowing her eyes to rove over him at their leisure in the low lighting. 'It's only fair. You've been doing that to me since I met you!'

'Now there's an admission. What else have I been doing to you?' he asked in that gloriously sexy undertone that skittered along her nerves, setting them at attention.

Her brows rose. 'Now who's fishing?'

He laughed. *Touché.*

Finally she lifted her eyes to his and held them, unable to resist adding achingly, 'It's been a long week.'

Joel's smile faded too, and as if her words were a

cue he had been waiting for he reached out for her. 'A hell of a long week,' he agreed with a groan, pulling her effortlessly into his arms and taking her lips in a long, deep, soul-searching kiss that she returned in equal measure and which left them breathless but temporarily satisfied when they finally broke apart. 'God, I needed that,' he said thickly, his breathing awry, resting his forehead against hers, and Kathryn linked her hands around his neck and sighed.

'I don't care if you want to know it or not, but I missed you,' she confessed, and Joel settled his hands on her hips, holding her to him so that she could feel the effect she had on him.

'I missed you, too,' he said, surprising her more than a little. 'I didn't expect to, but somehow you got under my skin last weekend and I found myself thinking of you when I should have been concentrating on my work. My secretary was expecting me to come down with flu or something.'

That he had been acting out of character because of her pleased her so much she just had to laugh. 'Poor darling,' she sympathised, but her heart had swelled just a little. Hope, she discovered, could find sustenance from many different sources.

Blue eyes narrowed dangerously, though they couldn't hide the glitter in his eyes. 'So, it amuses you to have me dangling on the end of your string, does it?'

If only he was, she thought wistfully, but this was all part of the game, and she was determined to keep up her side of it. 'It does give me a deliciously feminine sense of power,' she agreed.

'And what, exactly, do you intend to do with it?' came the softly seductive question, sending shivers down her spine.

Kathryn's smile was seduction itself as she toyed with his lapel. 'Well, now…that's for me to know and you to find out,' she said, glancing up at him through her lashes, and he growled low in his throat.

'Did anyone ever tell you you're a dreadful tease?'

Her smiled broadened into a grin. 'Hmm, often, but they didn't seem to mind.'

The declaration had his eyes narrowing. 'I don't think I like the sound of these other men you've twisted round your little finger,' Joel remarked darkly, at which Kathryn laughed huskily, delighted by this merest hint of jealousy.

'It all depends on who *they* are. It just so happens I'm talking about my brothers, so you really don't have to see them as a threat. I'm yours for as long as you want me,' she added lightly, though it was God's honest truth.

There was just the faintest hint of an odd look in his eye as he ran a finger down the bridge of her nose, as if his reaction had surprised him, too. The next second it was gone and he was smiling faintly. 'The way I feel right now, I'll want you for a long time.'

Knowing how he felt, it was all she could realistically hope for. 'Sounds good to me.'

'Your honesty is refreshing.'

Kathryn shrugged lightly. 'I try always to tell the truth, unless it could hurt somebody. Or when I'm trying to put one over on my brothers.'

A mock wary look entered Joel's eyes. 'Ah, your brothers. How many of them are there, did you say?'

'Four. And they're all big. Built like rugby players.' They had, in fact, all played rugby at university, and her eldest brother Nathaniel still did.

'You're just trying to scare me,' Joel charged, which made her laugh.

'Don't say you haven't been warned,' she said, and his eyes widened.

'Am I likely to meet them?'

Knowing her family, Kathryn grimaced inwardly. She wouldn't like to bet against it. 'Sooner than you think when they hear about you,' she said wryly, and that about said it all.

'Ah!'

'Precisely.'

Joel, contrary to her expectations, or maybe not quite that contrary, laughed out loud. 'It looks like I'm in for an interesting time.'

'I'll remind you you said that when you come back gnashing your teeth,' she returned dryly, though she was secretly pleased that he didn't seem bothered by the prospect. Most of the men she had dated had blanched at the thought.

'I get along with most men.'

She sent him a wry look. 'Ah, but you're not sleeping with their sister. It's a bit of knowledge I'd rather they found out later than sooner.' As soon as her father found out, the fat would be in the fire.

Joel placed a finger under her chin and tipped her head up. 'What do you think is going to happen? That they're going to chase me away? It isn't going to happen. Trust me.'

Her smile was unknowingly wistful. 'I do trust you, Joel. I just happen to know my brothers better than you do.'

'OK, I'll grant you that, but if what you say is true then they're my problem, not yours. Forget the Fearsome Four. Tonight I don't want any distractions.

I'm taking you to dinner, as planned, and later we'll go somewhere quiet where I promise you your brothers will be the last thing on your mind.'

He proved to be as good as his word. They dined at a small Italian restaurant, where Joel appeared to know the owners very well. Immediately they arrived the family flocked around their table, issuing greetings in their native tongue, before returning to their various jobs.

'You're very popular. Does that mean you bring all your women here? It would certainly give them a lot of patronage,' Kathryn observed ironically, once they had placed their order, taunted by a stab of jealousy.

Joel tutted reprovingly. 'You can sheathe your claws, sweetheart. This is my private retreat from the glare of the photographers' flashlights. Lorenzo is the son of an old family friend. I loaned him the money to set up his first restaurant. A loan he paid back in good order because he is a proud man.'

Kathryn could have kicked herself for allowing that tinge of jealousy to show through. It wouldn't be so bad if she didn't feel so vulnerable. 'I'm sorry, that was uncalled-for. No wonder you were virtually mobbed,' she apologised gracefully, and his smile was wry.

'Actually, sweetheart, I was mobbed because I've never brought a woman here before, except my mother, and the family wanted to get a good look at you. I should have expected it would cause a stir, but I wanted to take you somewhere where I could have you to myself. Lorenzo will make sure we're not disturbed.'

Kathryn tried not to read anything into that, but it was hard not to. Bringing her to a place he usually reserved for his own privacy was completely unexpected. At the very least it suggested she was different from all the others. Not that she expected it to bring a radical change of heart on his part. She had to be sensible and keep her feet well and truly on the ground or she would only be deepening the heartache that must come at the end of their affair. If she expected nothing, then everything he gave her was a bonus. Like being here tonight.

'Surely there were other restaurants you could have chosen?' she felt compelled to point out, hanging on the answer.

She wasn't disappointed. 'Undoubtedly. But I wanted to bring you here. I thought you would appreciate it the way I do.'

'Oh, I do. It's wonderful. I had no idea it was here. I'm glad the crowd haven't found it yet.' So many places she had gone to had been spoilt by their own popularity.

''Renzo offers two things I find invaluable. Good food in a friendly atmosphere. No smart talk or mobile phones.'

'Don't you use one?' she asked, for most businessmen found them a necessary tool of the trade.

'I do. But when I take a woman out I leave the mobile phone at home, so she can have my undivided attention,' Joel informed her in his lazy drawl, his eyes a sapphire caress.

And his undivided attention was what she got for the rest of the evening. They could have been the only two people in the room, and the food, whilst delicious, couldn't distract them from each other for long. It was late when they finally left. Kathryn had no idea where the time had gone. She settled into his car with a sigh of satisfaction and allowed her thoughts to drift as he set the car in motion. Happiness was a warm bubble inside her, and she felt that way simply by being with him. When the car stopped, she looked around her in surprise.

'Where are we?' she asked curiously. They were parked in a quiet tree-lined street of townhouses.

'My place,' Joel replied, releasing their seat belts. 'I thought we could have a nightcap here before I take you home.'

She looked into his eyes, and even in the darkness she could see the fire burning way down deep inside. Desire had been an unspoken thing between them all evening. The silent companion had been quietly building up, only recognised in a look or a touch, until now it was just below the surface, ready to explode out of control. Kathryn's stomach tightened, starting up that familiar ache inside her. She wanted him desperately.

At the same time her heart skipped, because he was giving her a choice. If she wanted to slow the pace of their relationship, he would take her home now. It was what she was coming to expect of him, but it wasn't what she wanted, for she had waited too long already.

'A nightcap sounds fine,' she agreed huskily, and very briefly he reached out and ran a finger over her lips. Then he was getting out of the car and coming round to help her out. Her heart was racing as they mounted the steps to the front door. In no time at all they were inside with the world shut out.

Without a word Joel tossed his keys onto a small table, then swept her up into his arms and carried her towards the stairs.

'I thought we were having a drink?' Kathryn challenged as her arms slipped around his neck and her lips found the angle of his jaw.

He didn't pause on his way to his bedroom. 'Kathryn, sweetheart, I'm like a man dying of thirst and you're the only thing that will keep me alive. I've kept my hands off you all night. Don't ask me to wait any longer.'

The passion in his voice turned her heart over, and emotions overflowed. 'I won't. Drink. Take all you need.' The spring of her love was never ending. There was more than enough for two.

Inside the bedroom, Joel lowered her to her feet and left her to switch on a lamp beside the bed. Shrugging out of his jacket, he tossed it and his tie aside before striding back to her. Kathryn went into his arms and sighed with satisfaction as his strong arms closed around her. When he bent and took her lips she met his kiss, returning it, sensing the need that he could barely control. It set her heart racing, and her fingers clutched at him, trying to pull him impossibly closer.

This was not like before. There was no slow loving, no languorous build up, for they had been apart too long and their need was too great. They gasped as each breathless kiss supplanted another, their hands dealing feverishly with clothes, discarding them in a staggered trail to the bed where, naked at last, they toppled onto the covers in a tangled mass of limbs. The feel of him against her, the unmistakable evidence of his powerful need thrusting against her belly, scattered Kathryn's senses. She moved against him with a moan, and one muscular male thigh pushed hers apart, allowing him to slip between them and enter her with one thrust.

Kathryn's body arched upwards in pleasure, and her legs rose, locking about his hips as she drew him deeper into her. Joel tried to slow down, she could feel the tension in his body, but the desire was too great, and with a groan he thrust into her again and again, setting up a rhythm she matched, driving them both towards the satisfaction they sought so desperately. It came with explosive force, causing them both to cry out and cling to each other as the waves of pleasure swept over them, drowning them, tossing them in the maelstrom until finally washing them up on calmer shores, where they lay unmoving as the world righted itself again.

At last Joel raised his head and looked down at her, a frown marring his brow as he brushed sweat-soaked strands of hair from her cheeks. 'Are you OK? Did I hurt you?' he asked, and there was genuine concern in his voice, for he had not been gentle.

Kathryn recognised his worry, but she hadn't wanted his gentleness. Only his wildest passion could have been enough. She smiled, lifting a tender hand to cup his cheek. 'You didn't hurt me. You couldn't,' she reassured him.

'You should have stopped me,' he insisted, the frown getting deeper, and she smoothed it away with her fingers.

'I didn't want you to stop. I wanted you just the way you were.'

Reluctantly reassured, Joel rolled off her onto his back and took her with him, settling her over his heart. 'I don't usually lose control like that,' he declared somewhat uneasily.

Kathryn locked that away in her heart, too. 'I'm glad you did. I liked it.'

'Hmm,' he sighed, and yawned. 'Damn, I can hardly keep my eyes open.'

'Go to sleep,' she urged, feeling her own eyelids growing heavy.

'You won't run off this time?'

She laughed softly. 'No. I'll be here when you wake. I promise.' She wasn't about to leave him. If it was up to her, she would never leave him, ever. Seconds later she heard the steady sound of his breathing and knew that he was asleep. Again, knowing that he could not possibly hear her, she pressed a soft kiss over his heart. 'I love you,' she murmured, just before sleep claimed her.

Hours later, Kathryn stirred, her hand automatically reaching out for the body which should have been there beside her. When her hand encountered only empty space her eyes shot open and she came up on her elbows. Blinking in the half-light of early morning, she discovered Joel sitting in a chair by the window. He must have been awake some time, for he had put on a knee-length silk robe.

Surprised, she pushed herself up against the pillows and realised that at some point he had pulled the bedspread over her. 'What are you doing over there?' she asked sleepily. 'Come back to bed,' she urged, holding out a hand to him.

'Are you on the pill?' he demanded tersely, causing her to gasp at his tone. There was nothing lover-like in it, and automatically she pulled the cover more closely around her protectively.

'No,' she said honestly, wondering what was wrong and where the conversation was leading. It wasn't at all what she had expected after the loving they had shared.

'Hell!' he swore abruptly, rising to his feet and pacing across the floor, dragging a hand through his hair, a clear sign of just how distracted he was.

Kathryn swallowed nervously, picking up on his unease. 'Joel, what's wrong?'

He swung round, and even in the dim light she could see how grim his expression was. 'I didn't use any pro-

tection last night. Or before. I wanted you too damned
much to think of it,' he told her tightly, and now she
did think she began to see where this was heading. She
hadn't thought of it either—because she'd been blinded
by love. But obviously the last thing he needed was for
her to have that sort of hold over him, if worse came
to worst.

'I see. Well, I doubt very much if anything will happen,' she returned levelly, keeping her composure with
an effort. It hurt to think how coolly he could look at
their relationship. She had only seen passion. Consequences had been far from her mind. Not so him, apparently.

Joel thrust his hands into his pockets and paced back
to her. 'It could. Even now you could be pregnant,' he
countered tautly, a nerve ticking away in his jaw.

'Of course I could be—but it's very early in my cycle
still, so the risk is small,' she pointed out, and could
have sworn she heard him grind his teeth.

'But if you *were*, what would you do?'

Put on the spot, all she could do was shrug helplessly.
'What every other woman would do, I suppose,' she
answered, and was astounded to see his face shut down.

'You'd get rid of it, then,' he pronounced coldly, and
her face registered her shock because that wasn't what
she had meant at all.

'No!' she denied quickly, sitting up to emphasise the
point. 'Of course I wouldn't do that!' Emotion tightened
her throat. 'How could you think I could do that? God,
I couldn't do that to my own child! What sort of woman
do you think I am?' she added angrily, coming to her
knees and only just remembering to take the bedcover
with her. Not for modesty, but because she was too
angry to sit there naked.

Her protest had obviously surprised him, and he stared at her through narrowed eyes. 'You wouldn't be the first,' he said tightly, and it was only then that she remembered what Agnes had told her, about his fiancée. The anger died out of her in a rush, and she swallowed hard.

'No, I wouldn't be the first, but I'm not like that. If I were pregnant, I'd keep my baby. I think most women would, given the choice,' she told him with soft insistence, and after staring at her for a moment he turned and walked back to the window, pulling aside the curtain to look out. Even from behind she could see the tension in him, the battle that was going on inside him. Tell me, she urged silently. Let me in. Let me in this much, please.

Whether he heard her or not, Joel dropped the curtain and turned to face her. His expression was so bleak it brought tears to block her throat, and she bit her lip hard.

'You probably think I'm making too much of it, but I have good reason.' He stopped there and took a deep breath, and she knew how hard it was for him to say this. To reveal so much of himself. 'I was engaged once, to a woman who I loved and who I thought loved me. In truth she only wanted my money. When she found out she was expecting my child, she got rid of it,' he told her in a toneless voice, and her heart wept, for beneath it all she could sense his pain, even if he wasn't aware of it. It had hurt then and it still did, which was why he was so troubled now.

'I'm so sorry,' Kathryn said gently, and he looked at her intently.

'I'm not going to allow that to happen again, Kathryn.'

She nodded and licked her lips, wondering if he was aware of all he had said. That he had loved once. She doubted it. Nor would she tell him. She would simply hold on to the thought of it, for what had once happened could happen again. 'That's understandable.'

Sighing, he returned to her, this time sitting down on the edge of the bed. 'I'm usually very careful about using protection, but you have the knack of driving every sane and sensible thought out of my mind. Now you could be pregnant, and, if you are, I want you to promise me that you won't get rid of it.'

Frowning to keep back emotional tears, Kathryn cupped her hand to his cheek and looked him squarely in the eye. 'I've already told you I would never do that, but, if it helps, I give you my word.'

Joel closed his eyes for a moment, and she could only imagine what sort of devil he must have been fighting with. 'You'd tell me if you were pregnant? We may be in the twenty-first century, but I believe a child should be brought up knowing both its parents.'

'I believe that, too,' Kathryn agreed, and, because she couldn't bear to sit there feeling his pain and doing nothing, she cast her arms around his neck and held him close. 'If it happens, I promise to tell you. I would never deny you your child,' she whispered, voice thick with suppressed emotion. Loving him, she could never think of doing that to him. Especially knowing what had happened before. When his arms lifted and encircled her, she closed her eyes tightly, emotions threatening to choke her.

'Thank you,' he said gruffly, and her soft laugh held the faint echo of a sob. 'I'm sorry if I hurt you, but I could only see history repeating itself. I should have known better. I know you're not like her. You're a good woman, Kathryn Templeton.'

Right then she would have given everything she possessed to have been able to tell him she loved him, that he could trust her, but it wasn't possible. All she could cling to was the fact that at least he had told her about his fiancée. It was something Agnes had said he never talked about. Maybe he had been driven to it by circumstances, but it was another tiny prop to shore up her heart.

Even as she held him, one tiny corner of her mind couldn't help wondering if she could be pregnant. As he had said, it was possible. A part of her hoped she was, for if she couldn't have him, at least she could have a part of him to love and care for. Yet it would change things. He hadn't mentioned marriage, and if he should suggest it could she go into it loving him as she did and knowing he would not allow himself to love her? That the marriage was only for the sake of the child? She honestly didn't know. She could only make that kind of decision if and when the time came.

'Now will you come back to bed?' she asked again, wanting to distract both Joel and herself from a subject that was too painful, and she felt the laugh rumble up from deep inside him.

'Are you sure you want me to?' he charged wryly, looking down at her.

'I don't have to get up for work, so I can catch up on my sleep later,' she told him impishly, and he grinned wolfishly.

'We aren't going to sleep?'

Kathryn held on to his robe as she allowed herself to sink back to the pillows. 'I'm not in the least bit tired. Are you?'

Joel followed her down, his lips hovering above hers. 'Now that you come to mention it…' he murmured, and kissed her.

Kathryn closed her eyes and kissed him back.

CHAPTER EIGHT

FOR Kathryn, the next few weeks passed in a blur. She was so happy she felt sure she wore a permanent smile on her face. They saw each other every day. Sometimes they went out, more often they stayed in, simply enjoying each other's company. To begin with Joel occasionally stayed over at her place, but as time went on more often than not they ended up at his house. Soon Kathryn took to leaving some clothes there, in case she had to go to an early meeting and there was no chance of going home first. Eventually, as more and more of her things ended up in his house, she was virtually living with him and only working from her own home.

Life was as close to idyllic as she could want it. The only small cloud on the horizon had been the recent discovery that she wasn't pregnant after all. When she'd told Joel, some emotion had flickered in his eyes. Relief? Regret? She couldn't be sure—it had gone too quickly for her to identify it. Nevertheless, their passion for each other had not diminished. In fact it had seemed to deepen, so that the more they made love, the stronger their need for each other became—although Joel never forgot to use protection. Her head knew he was right, but her heart wished it could have been otherwise, that he would one day want more from her. Even so, she kept telling him she loved him, although he was always asleep and never heard her.

Kathryn made a point of not looking ahead, but taking each day as it came. She knew she was living in a

133

false sense of security. It was only a matter of time before her family discovered who she was seeing, and she knew that when that happened the full weight of family censure would fall on her head. Because they loved her, and they would feel there was no future for her with Joel. His reputation spoke for itself. Sometimes she felt as if she was holding her breath, waiting for the axe to fall.

It fell, as often happens, when it was least expected.

The telephone rang one Tuesday when Kathryn was working on a particularly complicated program for one of her new customers. She answered its persistent ring with an irritated sigh at having forgotten to switch the answering machine on, thus preventing this kind of interruption.

'Kathryn Templeton. How can I help you?'

'I can think of several ways you can help me, sweetheart, but they'd probably get us arrested,' Joel's sexy tones came down the line and curled her toes. Her irritation vanished like mist in sunlight.

Relaxing back against her chair, she laughed. 'Hmm, sounds interesting. What did you have in mind?'

'If I told you, you'd never get any work done this afternoon, and neither would I, so I think I'll save it till later,' he replied seductively, and Kathryn gave a tiny shiver of anticipation.

'I'll look forward to it. So, why are you calling?'

'Does there have to be a reason? Maybe I just like the sound of your voice,' he told her softly, and her heart skipped a beat.

'Do you? Like the sound of my voice?' she asked throatily. 'Because I can't tell you what yours is doing to me right now.'

'Let me tell you something, Kathryn,' Joel returned

confidentially. 'Your voice… Well, I'll just say that in certain circumstances, when I think of it, it can be downright distracting.'

Kathryn chuckled. 'Good. I like the sound of you being distracted.'

'I had a feeling you'd say that.'

'I try not to disappoint you,' she teased, and grinned when she heard him groan.

'This conversation is going to play merry hell with my afternoon. I don't know how I'm going to concentrate,' he murmured, with more than a hint of laughter in his voice.

Kathryn twined the telephone cord round her fingers and smiled up at the ceiling. 'I'd suggest a cold shower, but remembering what happened the last time you tried it…' She left the sentence hanging, and knew he was recalling yesterday morning, when she had joined him in the shower and, rather than cooling off, their temperatures had soared. One thing had led to another, and he had been late for work when he'd left the house.

'You'll pay for that, sweetheart,' he promised, and she laughed softly.

'I thought I already had, and I enjoyed every minute of it. You never did tell me what your secretary said when you finally got to your office.'

'She asked if I was unwell. I told her it was just temporary insanity. It's you I have to thank for the majority of my staff giving me very strange looks,' Joel complained. 'They don't say anything, but I know they think you're having a very deleterious effect on me.'

Her brows rose. 'I don't see why. I'm hardly the first woman in your life, nor the last.' As ever, she made a joke of it, but it wasn't getting any easier to say. She was in way too deep to escape from this unscathed, but it was a price she was willing to pay.

'No,' he agreed. 'But you are the first one who's ever made me late for work. Do you realise I've had to re-arrange more meetings in the last few weeks than in the last ten years?'

It was some comfort to know their relationship was different enough from the others to raise comment. 'Are you sorry?'

'The hell of it is, I'm not,' he told her, in a strange tone of voice which made her wish she could see him and read his expression. Right now it seemed important to know what he was really thinking. It was extremely frustrating to be on the end of a telephone line. 'Frankly, I'd rather be with you than in some stuffy boardroom, and that's not like me at all. Sometimes I think you must be a witch.'

'What kind of witch? The kind who turns you into a mouldy old toad, or the kind who puts a spell on you to bind you to her for ever?' Oh, if there only were such a spell! She'd use it quick as winking.

'The second one, naturally,' Joel came back, and she could hear his amusement.

Her smile faded, because she would give anything to believe he really felt more for her than just desire. It was no joke to her, yet she forced her voice to be light. 'And are *you* bound to *me* forever?' Say yes, her heart begged silently. Say yes.

'Of course. I'm your devoted slave,' Joel responded laconically, and her heart ached with disappointment. 'There isn't anything I wouldn't do for you,' he added, and it was salt to the wound, for the one thing she wanted he would never do. He would never give her his heart.

'Be careful, I just might hold you to that,' she warned through a tight throat, but he didn't appear to notice and merely laughed.

'Do you think that will make me renege?'

'Most men would.'

'I'm not most men. Haven't you figured that out for yourself? I'm made of stronger stuff. Try me.'

'I don't know, you'd probably wriggle out of it somehow,' she goaded.

'Now you malign my honour. I'm going to have to demand that you put me to the test,' Joel retorted, sounding very much on his dignity, though she didn't miss the smile in his voice.

Her own smile returned. 'OK, I will, but I'll have to think of something worthy. I'll get back to you on it.'

'Make it as difficult as you like,' he offered, and she grinned.

'Oh, believe me, I will. Now, are you going to tell me why you really called. Because if not, I've got work to do,' she charged him.

'You're a hard woman.'

Kathryn laughed. 'I'm going to put the phone down now,' she threatened sweetly.

'OK, you win. Slip yourself into something sexy and meet me here at seven tonight. I have a surprise for you. Don't be late,' he warned, and before she could get her wits together to respond he had rung off, and she was left staring at the receiver.

She returned it to the rest with a faint little sigh. Joel could be the most aggravating man, but Lord, how she loved him! Now she would be wondering all afternoon just what the surprise was, and he would know it. But she would pay him back. He had given her the opportunity with that dare, and all she had to do was think up something really devilish. Having to fight four brothers all her life meant she had the best training to do it.

By seven that evening, Kathryn was riding up in the lift to the top floor of the modern office block that housed Joel's corporate headquarters. She had been here a few times before, and had been passed in with a smile and word of greeting by the security man on the door. The offices were empty as she walked the corridors to his office. His secretary had gone home long since, but the office door was ajar and she pushed it open quietly.

Joel was seated at a large desk, his head lowered as he studied some paperwork. As she watched he rolled his head to ease out the kinks before concentrating once more. A peculiar little lump lodged itself in her chest as she resisted the urge to go to him and simply hold him to take away the stresses and strains of the day. Yet she couldn't let it pass unremarked upon either.

'You work too hard,' she pronounced as she walked into the room, and Joel glanced up, a smile curving his lips and tweaking her heart. He closed the folder immediately and rose to come round and meet her.

'I have to make up the time I lost thinking of you during the day somehow,' he told her wryly, and pulled her into his arms. Kathryn raised her head to receive his kiss. It was languorous and deeply possessive, as if he were stamping his brand on her, and she wondered if he realised it. Not that it necessarily meant anything. He was probably the same way with all his women. Which reminded her unnecessarily that she only had him on a temporary basis.

A thought she resolutely blocked out as he raised his head and looked down at her, a possessive gleam in his eye. He allowed his gaze to rove over the discreet black dress she was wearing and nodded approvingly. 'Very nice.'

'Sexy enough?' she charged mockingly.

'You'd be sexy in a sack, but I've got to admit, less is definitely more,' he confided gruffly, referring to the fact that the dress showed very little bare flesh. 'My imagination can fill in the rest, and it's doing a grand job. Perhaps we ought to go home.'

'Oh, no!' Kathryn refused, placing her hands on his chest. 'Not before you give me the surprise you promised me.'

He sighed heavily. 'I suppose you're going to insist on it?'

'Absolutely. So give.'

Slipping an arm across her shoulders, he steered her to the door, switching off the light as he went. 'I just happen to have in my pocket tickets to the opening of the new Turner exhibition.'

Kathryn's head turned as if it were on a swivel. 'But I thought it was invitation only,' she exclaimed.

'It is, but I managed to wangle an invitation. However, we don't have to go if you'd rather not,' he teased, and she reached up quickly and kissed him.

'Thank you.' She adored Turner, and had been disappointed not to be able to go to the opening. She had said as much to Joel, and now he had conjured up tickets. Was it any wonder she loved him so much, when he did something thoughtful like that?

'Come along, we don't want to be late.' He urged her to the lift. 'You can thank me properly later.'

The exhibition was as wonderful as she had expected, and Kathryn wandered around on Joel's arm, a barely touched glass of white wine in her hand. She didn't notice the speculative looks she received from time to time, from people who recognised Joel and knew his reputation. Not until they literally bumped into an acquaintance of his who was clearly somewhat the worse for wear.

'Joel. Good to see you, old man,' he greeted effusively, with a public school accent, pumping Joel's hand as if he expected to get water out of it. 'What happened to the blonde I saw you with at Gstaad? Got to ask you, old chap. *Was* she more fun?' he queried with a loud laugh and a knowing wink.

Joel retrieved his hand with a faint grimace. 'You're drunk, Marcus, or you'd see I'm not alone,' he said with a haughtiness Kathryn had never heard before. Glancing up at him, she could see what the other man couldn't: a frostiness in his eyes which promised trouble.

'Oops, sorry. This the new filly?' Marcus carried on regardless, giving Kathryn the once over with a repulsive leer. 'She's a looker, but you always did manage to snap up the best ones.' He reached out a podgy hand towards Kathryn, but it was anyone's guess what he might have been going to do, for in flash Joel's hand had shot out and grasped the other man's wrist, holding it in a vice-like grip, preventing the move being completed.

'Keep your hands to yourself, Marcus,' he warned in a soft but deadly tone of voice that made the other man blink. 'You'd be well advised to go home and sleep this off.'

Kathryn thought it good advice as she glanced around uncomfortably. Thankfully, they were in a relatively quiet corner and the incident had gone unnoticed so far. Unfortunately, the man didn't take the hint.

'I'm not drunk, old chap, just well-lub-lubricated.' He grinned vacuously.

Joel's corresponding smile was grim. 'You're... lubricated...enough to insult this lady.'

Too far gone to exercise caution, Marcus snorted. 'Lady? When did you get to be so nice?' he charged as Kathryn's cheeks started to burn with embarrassed heat.

A nerve began to tick in Joel's jaw, so tight was he clenching it. 'Apologise, Marcus, or, so help me, I'll lay you out cold right here,' he threatened, and this time the message got through.

'OK, OK!' Marcus said hastily. 'I didn't realise I was stepping on your toes. I guess this one is special, eh?' He looked at Kathryn speculatively. 'I don't recall what I said, but I apologise if I upset you, Miss...?' He left that hanging, and Joel was quick to step in.

'Say goodnight, Marcus,' he urged, releasing the man's wrist. Marcus looked from one to the other, mumbled something which could have been goodnight, and hurried away.

Kathryn wasn't sorry to see him go. 'A friend of yours?' she asked sardonically, but Joel didn't smile.

'Not any longer,' he said coldly, and she glanced at him curiously as they strolled on.

'Would you really have hit him?' she couldn't help but ask.

'He was asking for it. People shouldn't drink if they can't hold their liquor,' Joel went on repressively, and Kathryn was left in a state of bemusement.

Nobody but her brothers had ever defended her so staunchly before, and they had a reason. She was their sister, and nobody was going to hurt her by word or by deed. She was nothing to Joel but a temporary lover, and yet he had come to her defence before she had even realised she was being offended. Her heart lurched. There was a name for that kind of response, and according to Joel the emotion didn't exist. It was a stunning thought. She wouldn't give it that name either, but could he *care* more for her than he was prepared to admit?

Now she came to think of it, there were many things he had said or done that, taken collectively, would seem to suggest that he more than cared for her. The trouble was, she had no way of knowing how much he had 'cared' for the other women he had had relationships with. So she had to be sensible and not get up false hopes, because even if he 'cared', that still didn't mean they had a future together.

Taking a breath to steady her pulse, she slipped her hand through Joel's arm. 'Well, thank you for defending me, though what he said didn't really bother me.'

'It bothered me,' Joel returned grittily, and that pleased her inordinately.

'Are you always this protective of your lady-friends?' she quipped lightly, though the answer held more importance for her than he would guess.

Joel paused before one large canvas and studied it so long she was sure he wasn't going to answer, but then he glanced down at her. 'I abhor men who speak of women like cattle. On the other hand, I don't think I've ever come so close to decking someone before. It would have given me great satisfaction to wipe the grin from his face.'

'I think he understood that eventually,' Kathryn murmured wryly.

'I didn't mean to embarrass you,' Joel apologised, running a gentle finger over her still flushed cheek.

She smiled up at him. 'You didn't embarrass me. I know it's probably old-fashioned, but it gave me a comfortable feeling, having a man come to my defence. I wouldn't want to give up my independence, but sometimes we women do appreciate the male protective instinct.'

Joel laughed, finally relaxing and losing that grim set to his mouth and eyes. 'You don't consider it too possessive, then.'

'It can be, in the wrong circumstances, but you don't come into that group. You protect women because it's what a man should do, simply because we cannot always defend ourselves. Speaking for myself, I like that in a man,' Kathryn responded honestly, then grinned at him. 'How's your ego doing?'

'Stroke it much more, and I'll be beating my chest like a gorilla. You certainly know how to make a man feel good,' Joel admitted, his eyes glinting with humour.

'Practice makes perfect. Not that I didn't mean what I said, but I have had to stroke a lot of male egos in my life.'

'Your brothers?'

Kathryn laughed. 'You got it,' she gurgled as they sauntered on again.

'Kathy?'

The sound of her name in an all too familiar voice had Kathryn tensing instantly. The moment she had been expecting any time these past weeks had arrived. Knowing who she would see, she pinned a determinedly cheery smile to her face as she turned.

'Hello, Nathaniel,' she greeted her brother, stepping forward to kiss his cheek.

'I thought it was you,' Nathaniel Templeton declared, returning the greeting. He was tall, sandy-haired, and built like a prop forward. 'I didn't expect to see you here.'

'Nor I you,' she said with a faint grimace. Joel had

turned, and she could sense him standing at her elbow, watching them. 'How are you?' she carried on, but her brother's attention had been caught by the man at her side. From the expression on his face, it was clear he recognised Joel, and didn't at all like finding his precious sister in the man's company. 'I suppose I'd better make the introductions. Joel, this is my brother Nathaniel. Nat, meet Joel Kendrick.'

Nathaniel reluctantly held out his hand. 'Kendrick,' he said curtly, which brought a faint smile to Joel's lips as he took the proffered hand.

'I'm pleased to meet you, Nathaniel. Kathryn's mentioned you several times. You play rugby, I believe?' he replied smoothly, with all the finesse she knew he was capable of. It would have disarmed a man made of less stern stuff than her brother.

'How long have you known my sister?' he demanded, point-blank, and Joel's brows rose as the gauntlet was well and truly thrown down.

'Several weeks now,' he informed him levelly, and Kathryn's heart sank at the look on her brother's face.

'I see.'

Joel smiled mockingly. 'Do you?'

Nathaniel chose not to respond to that, but instead turned to his sister. 'You've kept this very quiet.'

Her chin went up, and there was a warning light in her eye if he cared to note it. 'I happen to think a person's private life is precisely that—*private*.'

If she'd hoped that would rein him in, she was disappointed. Her brother ignored it and took her arm. 'Excuse us a moment,' he said to Joel, then drew her to one side. 'Are you crazy?' he demanded once they were out of earshot. 'Dad's going to blow a gasket when he finds out!'

Kathryn tugged her hand free, angry flags of colour burning her cheeks. 'Only if you tell him!' she whispered back angrily. 'This is none of your business, Nat, or Dad's.'

'Of course it is! That man's little better than a gigolo! What are you thinking of?'

That description of Joel turned her cheeks white with rage. 'Don't you ever call him that again, do you hear me?' she ordered, spitting mad, but Nathaniel had the hide of a rhinoceros.

'Are you sleeping with him?' he demanded to know next, and it made her so furious she was shaking with it.

'You have no right to ask that!'

'My God, you are!' he exclaimed in horrified disbelief.

Green eyes glittered with angry tears. She had known it was going to be like this! 'Whether I am or not is my business. Stay out of it.'

'You know I can't do that,' her brother said predictably, yet in a softer tone, his expression turning to one of concern. 'How can I simply close my eyes to this, when I know damn well you're making a terrible mistake?'

That was what she had always been afraid of. The cat was out of the bag, and her family cared for her too much to put it back again. She stiffened her spine and looked him in the eye.

'Then I guess you're going to have to do what you have to do. Don't expect me to thank you for it,' she told him stolidly, and, without another word, turned and walked away.

She walked past Joel, too, wanting to put some distance between herself and her brother, so didn't see the long, assessing look the two men exchanged before Joel came after her.

'Hey, where's the fire?' he teased lightly, though his eyes were watchful on her averted face.

Kathryn came to a standstill and sighed heavily. 'Sorry. I'm just…' She waved her hand for want of a word to describe exactly how she felt.

Placing his hands on her shoulders, Joel turned her to face him. 'What did he say to you?' he asked gently, tipping his head this way and that until he caught her eye, then holding her gaze resolutely. 'What did he say, Kathryn?'

'About what I expected,' she snapped. 'The game's up. As you know, he was appalled to see me with you. Quicker than you can say it, the whole family will know. You'll be able to hear the chorus of disapproval from the moon!'

'Hmm, I detected a definite frost in the air. I hope you told him to mind his own business?'

'I did, but I might as well have saved myself the trouble. He won't listen,' she replied glumly. A pall had come over the evening which had started so brightly.

'You're a grown woman, free to make your own choices.'

Kathryn laughed with scant humour. 'I'm his little sister and you're the Big Bad Wolf. If the roles were reversed, would you leave me in your clutches?' she asked him, and he frowned, then grimaced.

'Probably not,' he admitted wryly. 'So, what are you going to do?'

'Nothing. I'm certainly not about to give you up!' Kathryn declared forcefully, bringing a smile to his lips.

'You're not, eh?'

Tipping her head up, Kathryn smiled defiantly. 'Stubbornness runs in the family. Nobody can make me do anything I don't want to do. I knew what I was taking on by getting involved with you, Joel. I knew my family would cry foul. But I was prepared for that because I wanted to be with you.'

That confession brought a faint frown to his forehead. 'It isn't going to be easy, is it?'

Her smile grew rueful. 'I thought I'd have more time with you before the flak started to fly.'

'Perhaps we should call it quits, Kathryn. I'm not worth alienating your family over,' he told her with unfamiliar sombreness, and her heart lodged in her throat.

'Do you want me to go?' she challenged him, and after a significant pause Joel shook his head.

'I suppose I ought to do the decent thing, but I'm not ready to end this yet. I want you too damned much.'

Kathryn's lips curved into a wide smile. 'Then I'll stay.'

'It's as simple as that?'

'Of course. I'm a simple woman. I know what I want, and I'm willing to pay the price for it. My family will be upset, but it won't last.' How true that was. When this affair was over, and she was hurting as they would no doubt expect her to be, then they would be the first to rally round to comfort her.

Joel shook his head, as if he didn't understand her at all. 'You're an extraordinary woman.'

She laughed that off. 'I'm not extraordinary at all.' She was simply a woman who loved him. 'And don't imagine you're going to get off lightly. Pressure will be brought to bear. Just wait and see.'

'I think I can handle your family,' Joel said confidently, and she wasn't about to disabuse him. He would find out that the Templeton clan, separately and together, made a formidable fighting machine.

'Right,' she agreed dryly.

'I'm not about to give you up without a fight either.'

She laughed. 'That, I can safely say, you will get. It won't be pretty. In fact, it will get downright dirty. Do you think I'm worth it? You could cut and run to the next woman down the line, you know.' Though she made light of it, it was all too true. It would be oh, so easy for him to walk away.

'I could, but right now the only woman I can see is you. You're the only woman I want in my life, so I guess I'll just have to take my chances with your family.'

'I guess we're stuck with each other, then.'

'Looks like it,' Joel agreed.

Suddenly Kathryn wished they were somewhere else. Somewhere she could kiss him and not cause a minor scandal. 'I don't know about you, but I think I've had enough art for one evening.'

'I couldn't agree more,' Joel concurred, turning them towards the archway that would eventually take them to the entrance. 'Do you want to go somewhere for dinner?'

'To tell you the truth, I'd much rather go home. We can order something in if we're hungry,' Kathryn declared, and the look he gave her held a decided glint.

'Or, if we're not, I'm sure we can think of something to do to pass the time,' he drawled seductively, setting her nerves alight.

'Just what I was thinking myself,' she said with a grin.

Outside the gallery, Joel hailed a passing taxi and

gave the driver his address. She didn't argue. Wherever he was, was where she wanted to be. Maybe her time with Joel was going to be short, but one thing she did know: it was never going to be dull.

CHAPTER NINE

KATHRYN was in her kitchen preparing dinner on Thursday evening when she heard the front door shut with some force. Her eyes widened in surprise. She knew it was Joel, for she had arranged for him to come to her house tonight. She had had to travel for a consultation, and so had decided to cook dinner here for a change. Her surprise came from his being so early—almost an hour before he was expected—and, for another thing, he had not come straight through to find her and kiss her as he usually did.

Popping the salad she had been tossing back into the refrigerator, she wiped her hands on a towel and went off in search of him. Joel was in her sitting room in the process of pouring himself a drink. As she watched, he downed half of it in one go, giving every impression that he had really needed it. He studied the remaining half of the golden liquid broodingly.

'Bad day?' she queried consolingly, and he glanced round, for once not smiling when he saw her.

'A hell of a bad day,' he confirmed with a grimace, using his free hand to loosen his tie and unfasten the top buttons of his shirt. The jacket of his suit was draped haphazardly over a chair, looking for all the world as if it had been tossed there.

Kathryn went into the room and retrieved his jacket, laying it out properly so it didn't crease. 'Care to talk about it?' she offered, going to him and deftly removing the tie altogether.

150

'I'm just about all talked out,' he said tiredly, flexing his shoulders as if they were still tense.

'Difficult meeting?' she tried again, feeling as if she was attempting to get blood out of a stone.

His laugh was wry. 'Several difficult meetings,' he revealed with a heavy sigh. 'You warned me, so it's my own fault for not taking it seriously enough. You're quite within your rights to say I told you so.'

Light dawned. 'Oh, no!' she groaned.

'Oh, yes,' Joel confirmed sardonically, finishing his drink and setting the glass aside.

The meetings Joel had had, had been with her brothers. She had expected it—the only surprise being that they had waited until today.

She sought clarification with a sinking heart. 'Which ones?'

'All of them.' He grimaced, then shook his head and laughed. 'My God, they were good. They could grill for England.'

'Lord, I'm sorry,' Kathryn apologised, thinking she would have a word or two to say herself when she ran into the four of them again.

Joel, perversely, had started to relax. Taking her hand, he dropped down into a chair and pulled her onto his lap. 'Hell, don't be. They were there because they care about you, and that's something I approve of—though, given a choice, I'd rather not have been on the receiving end of it.'

'What did they say?' she asked curiously.

Unconsciously, Joel's hand began to run caressingly along her stocking-clad thigh. 'First they suggested I get out of your life. When I said I couldn't do that, they demanded to know what my intentions were. Which, as I told them, is my business. We circled around that for a while, then they told me what they would do to me if I should hurt you. The methods of my demise were inventive, to say the least.'

Kathryn had gone from dismay to seething by this time. 'Oh, I could strangle all of them!'

'Janet thought it was highly amusing,' he went on, referring to his secretary. 'She wasn't eavesdropping, but the walls are thin and voices were raised. She thinks it's long past time I got my comeuppance. I have to admit, the Templeton boys are just the men to do it, too.'

She frowned at him in perplexity, for, on the whole, he was taking this very well. 'How can you laugh about it?'

'Because they all wanted to grind my face into the dirt. I liked them,' Joel admitted, surprising her.

'Well, I hate them!' she snapped, so angry she could spit nails. Why couldn't they just leave well enough alone?

'No, you don't,' Joel corrected immediately. 'You love them as much as they love you.'

'Maybe I do,' she retorted in a disgruntled tone. 'I just wish they'd stop interfering in my life.' They had no idea what they were doing. OK, Joel had taken it well so far, but he had to draw the line somewhere, and what if they pushed him over it? How much longer would he consider their affair worth it with four angry men breathing fire down his neck? Damn them, they could ruin everything and bring about what they were trying to avoid.

'Trust me, it will never happen. You'll always be their little sister. They'll always look out for you. Try to protect you from the Big Bad Wolves of this world.'

'Whilst I accept that, they have to be made to understand that I don't need protecting from you,' Kathryn insisted, frowning heavily. There was a sinking feeling in her stomach that time was running out.

Joel cupped his hand about her cheek and turned her head until she was looking at him. 'Do you want to know what the really crazy thing is?' he asked with a self-mocking smile. 'I don't want to see you get hurt either.'

'Don't be silly.' She rushed to reassure him. 'You won't hurt me.'

Rather than smiling, Joel's expression was sober as he looked deeply into her eyes. 'Won't I? I'm beginning to wonder. For one thing, sweetheart, you're nowhere near as hard-boiled as you'd like me to believe.'

She tensed immediately, alarm signals going off in her head. 'What are you suggesting?' she asked uneasily. If he had somehow guessed her secret...

'Only that if everyone is doing their best to ensure you won't get hurt, then that means you can be. I'd hate to be the cause of it. Maybe your brothers are right. Maybe I should get out of your life,' he mused broodingly, and Kathryn's body felt a jolt of panic.

'Don't you dare walk out on me, Joel Kendrick. I'd never forgive you,' she declared hotly.

He frowned at her vehemence. 'I'm thinking of you, Kathryn. What would be best for you. I'm bad news.'

'Not to me you're not!' she insisted, and he smiled faintly.

'You shouldn't try and stop me doing the right thing. I haven't had such a noble feeling in years.'

She sniffed. 'Personally, I think nobility is highly overrated.' Especially if it meant she could lose him.

'All the same,' he went on with a sigh, 'I don't know

how long I can continue to keep you away from the press.'

Her brows rose. 'You mean you have something to do with the fact I haven't had my picture splashed across the tabloids?' She had been relieved to discover her presence in Joel's life wasn't news, but puzzled all the same. Now she knew why.

Blue eyes quartered her face, as if he was memorising it. 'I found I had a dislike of the idea of seeing you in print under some sensation-seeking banner. So far as I'm concerned, you're not for public consumption. I have no intention of sharing you with half the country, so I've simply been exercising more discretion.'

Kathryn's lips parted on a tiny gasp of surprise, even as her heart swelled with pleasure. There it was again, that caring he professed not to have any time for. He didn't want to see her hurt, and he didn't want her the subject of general gossip. That had to mean something, didn't it? Deep down inside, he had to care, didn't he? Lord, how she wished she knew for sure. Hiding her feelings was so unnatural. She wanted to reach out to him, show him how much she cared. It was getting harder to hold back all the time.

Swallowing a lump that blocked her throat, she smiled. 'Thank you. That was very thoughtful.'

'You're welcome, but it was entirely selfish. I don't want to share you. I want to keep you all to myself.'

That declaration warmed her heart, and Kathryn guarded it jealously as she combed her fingers through his hair, enjoying the silky texture. 'Well, I have no problem with that,' she said softly. 'I want you all to myself, too.'

Joel caught her hand and pressed a kiss to her palm.

'I've never known anyone like you. You make no demands. Isn't there anything you want?'

Her heart ached. She wanted so many things she couldn't name them all. But, in the long run, her happiness boiled down to one thing alone. Him. 'Well, now you come to mention it, I could do with your help opening a bottle of wine,' she said teasingly, loving the way laughter softened his face.

'Now, that is something I can do,' he declared, coming to his feet in one smooth movement with her still in his arms. Only in the kitchen did he lower her to the ground, tantalisingly allowing her body to slide down the length of his as he did so.

Kathryn looked up at him, her eyes twinkling. 'Hmm, your mood seems to have changed for the better,' she teased saucily, having felt his body respond to her as quickly as hers did to him.

'The things you do to me!' Joel grinned and gently pushed her away. 'I'd better see to the wine before you distract me too much.'

Laughing, she turned to the cooker. 'You can lay the table whilst you're about it. That should cool your ardour.'

'Don't you believe it, sweetheart,' he retorted as he retrieved the bottle from the refrigerator. 'Just being in the same room as you turns me on. I thought it would have lessened by now, but the more I see of you, the more I want. I'm addicted.'

She halted in the process of unwrapping some steak. 'Is that a good thing or a bad thing?'

'Oh, good. Definitely good. I usually get bored easily, but you're never boring, Kathryn. In fact, you're constantly surprising me.'

'I like keeping you on your toes. I wouldn't want our

relationship to grow stale,' she returned, concentrating on what she was cooking.

Joel set the opened bottle of wine on the table and came across to collect the cutlery. 'It will never get stale,' he told her, and she felt her smile fade. Without looking at him, she corrected him.

'Yes, it will. One day.'

He glanced sideways at her, frowning. 'Why do you say that?' he asked, and she did look at him now, her lips twisting wryly.

'Because my successor is out there somewhere, waiting to catch your eye,' she told him simply.

Joel stared at her, his frown deepening. Something flickered in the far reaches of his eyes, but she didn't know how to interpret it. Then he was turning away, setting places at the table.

'I wasn't thinking that far ahead,' he said uncomfortably, which was so unlike him she had to turn and watch him. 'I'm just happy that you're here now.'

'Are you?'

He glanced up. 'Of course. There isn't anyone else I want to be with right now.'

'But you can't rule out the possibility that that will change in the future?' she charged, being urged on by her feelings for him.

'No, I can't do that. Why are you asking me this now, Kathryn?' he probed, eyes narrowing on her face.

'I guess I just need to know where I stand.' She shrugged, smiling wryly.

Joel put down the cutlery and came across to her, taking her by the shoulders and giving her a gentle shake. 'We're together now, and I'm happy with that. I thought you were, too.'

'I am,' she insisted, quick to reassure him. 'I'm just

being fanciful. Forget I mentioned it. Let me get these steaks on, or we won't be eating until midnight.' She twisted out of his hold and busily set about collecting a frying pan and olive oil. She could sense Joel watching her, but she refused to turn around. Eventually he returned to the table.

Nothing more was said, and it was forgotten when they sat down to eat the meal she had prepared. She told him about her day, and he related more of his run-ins with her brothers, but in such a way that she was more amused than angry.

She was still laughing when the front doorbell rang. They were washing up, and she paused in the act of drying a plate. Surprised, she glanced up at the clock. It was almost ten o'clock.

'Who on earth can that be?' She frowned, setting the plate and tea towel aside, then heading for the door.

The man standing on her doorstep when she opened the door could have been one of her brothers, except for his greying hair.

'Dad!' Kathryn exclaimed in equal amounts of surprise and dismay. 'This is a surprise! What brings you here?' she added lamely, and wasn't surprised by the old-fashioned look he graced her with.

'Are you going to invite me in?' Victor Templeton prompted his daughter, and she stepped back, casting a weather eye towards the kitchen, but there was no sign of Joel.

'Of course. Come in.' She left him to close the door and led the way into the sitting room. There she turned, rather like a stag at bay, nervously rubbing her hands together. 'Er...sit down, won't you? Would you like a drink?'

Her father cut through all the polite inanities and

came right to the point. 'What's this I hear about you and that Kendrick fellow?'

Her back went up immediately at that, and her nervousness vanished as she folded her arms belligerently. 'His name is Joel, and what exactly did you want to know?' She hadn't been looking forward to this meeting with her father, but now that the moment was here she was prepared to do battle.

Red flags of colour stained his lined cheeks at her reply. 'So you are going out with him.'

'I'm sure Nat and the others have already told you so. What you really want to know is if I'm sleeping with him, and the answer to that is yes, I am,' she told him with a defiant lift of her chin.

Victor Templeton took in an angry breath. 'Don't get lippy with me, Kathryn. I'm still your father.'

Kathryn sighed at the unnecessary reminder. 'I know you are, and I love you, but you have no right to try to interfere in my life, Dad,' she told him, as she had told her brother.

'I wouldn't call concern interfering,' he argued, closing the distance between them, and she could see the concern written on his face.

'You mean you have no intention of trying to break us up?' she countered chidingly, and her father ground his teeth impotently, for, as they both knew, that was what he had intended.

He tried another tack. 'I know you, Kathryn. You would never go into a relationship unless you cared for the man, which does you credit, but in this case he's unworthy of you.'

'I disagree. He is worthy; you just don't know him. He's a good man, Dad,' she retorted, staunchly defensive.

'I know you think so, but he's what we used to call a philanderer, a playboy,' he returned forcefully. 'He's just toying with your affections. He won't marry you, you know.'

If he'd hoped to unsettle her with that, he failed. 'I'm fully aware of that,' she said evenly, and his eyes widened.

'Doesn't that bother you?'

Kathryn sighed again, then lowered her voice and motioned her father to do the same. 'I'd be lying if I said it didn't. Of course I want to marry him. I love him. I want to spend my life with him, have children with him. But I have to be practical. That isn't what he wants. I know this is just another affair to him, and maybe it does hurt to know that, but if that's all he can give, I'll take it.'

He father stared at her in consternation. 'Can you hear yourself? Don't you have any pride?'

Kathryn disliked disappointing him this way, but it was her life, her decision. She held his gaze stoically. 'Apparently not.'

'Does he love you?'

It was a calculatingly cruel question, and she felt it to her soul. Nevertheless, she answered honestly, for there was no point in lying. 'No. I think he cares about me, but no, he doesn't love me.' She didn't tell him that Joel didn't believe love existed.

'Damn it, that makes no sense! If he doesn't love you, Kathryn, why put yourself through this?' Victor asked in a softer, more cajoling tone.

'I told you. Because I love him, Dad, that's why.'

Her father raised his hands helplessly, then dropped them to his sides with a shake of his head. 'Does he know you love him?'

She shook her head. 'No.'

He dragged both hands through his hair in a gesture she recognised well. 'If I can't persuade you to see sense, just remember you know where we are when you need us.'

She had known he would say that in the end, and it brought a lump to her throat. 'Thanks for caring so much. I'm sorry if I've disappointed you.'

'You could never disappoint me, Kathryn. I realise this is your life, and I have to let you live it, but it isn't easy to let go, not when I can see you heading for disaster. Is he really worth it?'

'I think so,' she declared with a reassuring smile, which made him sigh and hold out his arms.

'Come and give me a hug, then,' he ordered gruffly, and, crossing the room, Kathryn slipped into his arms, feeling comforted, as she had when she was a child.

A noise at the doorway made them both turn in that direction. Joel stood there, his expression enquiring. He looked from her to her father and back again. Her heart lurched, as she wondered if he had overheard anything, despite their efforts to speak softly.

'Kathryn? Is everything all right?' he asked smoothly as he came into the room.

He was too bland, she decided. He had to have heard something. Easing away from her father, she took her cue from Joel and smiled and nodded. 'Perfectly. My father called round unexpectedly,' she explained, her eyes searching his. But he was giving nothing away.

He turned to her father with an easy smile and held out his hand. 'Good evening, Mr Templeton. I'm sure you know who I am,' he greeted, with more than a hint of irony.

'Your fame goes before you, Mr Kendrick,' Victor

Templeton returned with heavy meaning, nevertheless shaking the proffered hand.

Joel's smile broadened. 'Yes. I had the pleasure of meeting your sons earlier.'

'They're very protective of their sister,' her father confided unnecessarily. 'Woe betide anyone who does her harm.'

Joel inclined his head, then looked squarely at the older man. 'I have no intention of harming your daughter, sir.'

'That may be, young man, but the road to hell is paved with good intentions,' Victor pronounced portentously, and Joel winced.

'The trouble with having a reputation like mine is that nobody believes I could have good intentions,' he returned wryly, and Kathryn's father harrumphed.

'Probably because you've gone out of your way to prove the opposite. But I take your point and promise you this. By my family you will be judged by your actions now. My daughter believes you're a good man, don't prove her wrong,' Victor Templeton warned, before turning to his daughter and kissing her cheek. 'I'll say goodnight now, Kathryn. Remember what I said.' He gave Joel one last pointed look, then marched from the room.

'I'll see you out, Dad,' Kathryn said, following him to the door. There her father squeezed her arm comfortingly.

'I hope for your sake he does prove me wrong,' he said, before striding down the path to his car.

Kathryn closed the door with a sense of fatalism. If she was right, the cat was well and truly out of the bag, and there was nothing she could do about it. The ball was in Joel's court. She returned to the sitting room, feeling calmer than she had expected to. Joel was standing by the fireplace, head lowered, gaze fixed on the empty grate. He straightened as she entered, his hands slipping into his trouser pockets as he watched her consideringly.

Halting several feet away from him, she took the bull by the horns. 'How long had you been standing out there?' she asked, though in her mind it was a foregone conclusion.

'Long enough,' he said coolly, and she nodded wryly.

'You know, then.' It was a statement, not a question.

'That you love me? Yes,' he confirmed, without even the faintest flicker of emotion. They could have been discussing the weather for all the interest he showed.

Kathryn grimaced inwardly. Had she been hoping for a miraculous declaration of similar feelings, she would have been disappointed. She was too sensible for that, but his apparent indifference did hurt. He could at least have been angry, she thought irritably.

In response her chin went up a notch. 'You weren't meant to hear any of that. Do you make a habit of listening at keyholes?'

That did get a response. A nerve started ticking in his jaw. 'When you didn't come back I thought the caller might be one of your brothers and that you might need moral support. When I realised it was your father, I hesitated,' Joel confessed tightly, and she smiled grimly.

'And consequently heard more than you'd bargained for!' she jibed.

Blue eyes locked with green. 'Is it true? Did you mean it?'

She held his gaze unflinchingly. 'It isn't something I

would lie about. I do love you.' For all the good it does me.

It was Joel who looked away for a second, dragging a hand through his hair before sighing and looking at her again. 'You hid it well.'

Kathryn laughed. 'Well, I'm hardly going to wear my heart on my sleeve, am I? Not when I know you don't want to know,' she told him pointedly. 'And, as you still don't want to know, I suggest you just forget about it. I don't know about you, but I could do with some coffee. I'll set it filtering whilst we finish the washing up,' she went on matter-of-factly, turning on her heel and walking back to the kitchen.

It wasn't easy to act so blasé, but she had no choice. She was absolutely not going to have him pity her. No way would she be able to bear that.

Kathryn was spooning coffee into the filter when Joel caught up with her. Taking her by the shoulder, he spun her round so fast she dropped the packet. When she met his eyes they were no longer cool, but there was a blaze in their depths that set her heart tripping.

'How can you be so damned cool about it?' he demanded, with all the emotion she could have hoped for.

With a swift gesture she brushed his hand away. 'Because beating my breast and tearing my hair out would be a waste of time. I'm being ''cool'' because I have no choice,' she told him as she hunkered down to retrieve what she could of the coffee.

Joel instantly hauled her back up again. 'What do you mean, you have no choice?' he charged, taking the coffee packet from her and tossing it onto the counter top, where it spilled out again.

Ignoring the coffee, Kathryn turned to the sink, picked up the tea towel and began drying dishes. 'I have no choice because nothing has changed, has it?' she threw over her shoulder.

Impatiently Joel took the cloth and dish from her, set them aside with a clatter that made her wince for her crockery, and almost frog-marched her to a chair, where he exerted enough downward pressure to make her sit.

'Leave the blasted dishes alone!' he commanded, pulling out a chair and sitting so close she would have had difficulty rising had she wanted to. 'Get to the point, Kathryn.'

'Very well,' she agreed. 'You didn't love me before, did you?' she challenged, and he sat back, eyes narrowing.

'No,' he confirmed shortly.

Her heart was racing uncomfortably fast, but she persisted. 'And you don't love me now, do you?'

Joel's head went back, and there was the faintest of hesitations before he said what she had known he would. 'No, I don't.'

No more than she had expected, but difficult to take all the same. She had to swallow hard to continue. 'So nothing has changed. Life goes on. You just know something you didn't know before. But, hey, it isn't going to kill you,' she jibed.

Joel's eyes narrowed to angry slits. 'And just how in hell am I supposed to forget what you said?'

Kathryn raised her eyebrows at that. 'I should imagine it would be easy if it isn't important to you,' she told him evenly, and whatever he had been about to say got lost in the shuffle.

That nerve began to tick again as he stared at her. 'Damn it, Kathryn, I warned you not to fall for me!' he exclaimed angrily, shooting to his feet and striding to the back door, which he opened, then stared out into the night, taking in deep breaths of the cold air.

Kathryn watched him, scarcely knowing what to make of this remarkable display. He had never shown so much emotion before. 'Why are you so angry? This is my problem, not yours,' she said simply. 'I'm not asking you to love me back.' Even though I want you to, so very, very badly.

He turned and looked at her through stormy blue eyes. 'How could you do something so stupid as to fall in love with me, Kathryn? After all I said.'

She couldn't help but smile. 'I couldn't help it. I told you, people don't choose to fall in love, they just do. That's what happened to me.'

Joel shook his head. 'You're forcing me to hurt you.'

'I don't blame you for that. It was inevitable from the moment I realised how I felt about you. But you don't have to worry, I'm prepared to take the consequences.'

His fist hit the doorframe, making her jump. 'Well, I sure as hell am not!'

She wondered if he realised how revealing that statement was. 'Would it hurt you to hurt me?' she asked in a rather strained voice, for the answer was important.

'Of course it would!' he shot back instantly, but there was no 'of course' about it for her. He gave so little away she had to scrabble for crumbs.

Her smile was rueful. 'So you care for me a little, then?'

That brought him up short, and he blinked at her as the import of the question sank in. Then he frowned. 'I care for you a lot. That's why I don't want to see you hurt, Kathryn,' he told her huskily and her heart turned over. It meant so much to her to hear him say that.

A wistful smile curved her lips. 'I'm afraid that can't be avoided now. No matter what you do. You have to decide where we go from here. As I see it, you have two choices. End it now, or later.'

Joel stared at her sombrely, clearly deep in thought. For a while she didn't think he was going to answer at all. When he did speak, what he had to say was totally unexpected.

'There is a third option,' he said slowly, clearly churning over the ramifications in his mind. 'We could get married.'

Kathryn's heart crashed against the wall of her chest as if trying to get out. Marriage? The possibility had only presented itself to her as a sort of last resort, in case she'd been pregnant—but they both knew that wasn't the case. That he would consider it as an option now stunned her.

'You can't be serious!' she exclaimed breathlessly.

'Why not?' He shrugged. 'I always intended to get married one day.'

Kathryn shook her head to try and clear it. 'Are you seriously suggesting that you could marry me in order not to hurt me?' she asked carefully, because it was the craziest thing she had ever heard. Of all the reasons to get married, that had to be at the bottom of the list.

'Don't you want to marry me?' Joel countered. 'Don't you want to marry the man you say you love?'

Her lips parted on a tiny gasp. Of course she wanted to marry him, but not like this. It was too bizarre. 'You don't really want to marry me. You don't love me,' she pointed out shakily.

'I care for you more than any other woman I know. We have a lot in common. The more I think about it, marriage to you makes sense,' he told her firmly.

Kathryn shook her head dazedly several times and pressed a hand to her forehead. 'You are serious.'

He nodded decisively. 'Never more so.'

'But you don't believe in love,' she exclaimed in confusion.

'I don't have to love you to marry you. I've told you that before. What I can promise you, if you agree to marry me, is to make sure you never regret doing so. I will honour our vows and be faithful to them. Think about it, Kathryn. Wouldn't it solve everything?' Joel urged, coming to her and squatting down, taking her chilly hands in his.

She searched his eyes, and realised with a sense of awe that he was sincere. She could have him for always. All she had to do was say yes.

'You know this is crazy,' she whispered, and he grinned, twisting her heart.

'Sometimes crazy is the only way to be,' he reminded her.

Kathryn licked her lips. 'If I agree, don't expect me to hide how I feel. I couldn't do that. It's been hard enough up to now. If I marry you, it will be because I love you, and I will make sure you know it. Could you live with that?'

'So long as you don't expect it to change anything,' he agreed, laying down the parameters of their relationship. 'Well?' he prompted.

'Don't I have time to think about it?'

'How much time do you need? What will you know in an hour that you don't know now? Either you want to marry me or you don't.'

He was right, damn it. She was just procrastinating. He was offering her more than she could ever have expected. He cared about her; she believed that. One day that caring might turn to love, but it would mean taking a gamble on her part now, with no guarantee for the future. Could she do it?

Kathryn drew in a deep breath and took that leap of faith. 'Yes, I'll marry you, Joel,' she accepted, knowing there was no way back now. There was no shame in trying and failing. If all she ever had was what she had now, it would be enough. She would make it enough.

Something like relief flickered in his eyes for a moment, then was gone, and she told herself she must have been imagining things. What reason did he have for being relieved?

'I promise you, you won't regret it,' he told her again as he stood and pulled her into his arms, holding her close.

Kathryn held on tight. She hoped not. Oh, Lord, she surely hoped not, she prayed.

CHAPTER TEN

THERE were times the following day that Kathryn felt as if she was living in a dream. She kept pinching herself to see if she was awake. Nothing seemed quite real, even when Joel took her to a high-class jeweller's so she could pick out her engagement ring—a gorgeous solitaire diamond. Yet she could not doubt his commitment, for at the same time he insisted on buying matching wedding bands. All the same, she couldn't help feeling that she would wake up soon and discover it had all been a dream.

The feeling persisted until Saturday morning, then vanished when her mother telephoned whilst they were eating a late breakfast at her place.

'Kathryn, darling, I'm so happy for you. I forgive you for keeping me totally in the dark!' Lucy Templeton declared as soon as she heard her daughter's voice.

Kathryn's jaw dropped in surprise. 'Mother, I don't—'

'Is he handsome? Do you love him? Lord, what a stupid question. Of course you love him! Tell me all about him. I'm dying to know everything,' her mother went on with scarcely a pause for breath.

Slowly, Kathryn turned to look at Joel, who was watching her over the top of the newspaper. 'Yes, he is handsome, Mother. At least, I think so. And, yes, I love him very much,' she responded when she could get a word in.

'Have you set a date yet? Is it to be a church wedding?' Lucy bubbled with questions, but they only served to puzzle her daughter more.

'Nothing's set yet. Er…how did you find out about it?' Superstitiously, she had said nothing to anyone, not even her family. Now it appeared they knew.

'Why, the engagement notice is in all the papers. I've had calls from friends and family since first thing. It was a little odd not to have any details to tell them, for I was just as surprised to hear about your engagement myself. However, I waffled. Darling, you must bring him to lunch tomorrow. I'm dying to meet him in the flesh. Your father tells me he's very well respected in the City. Is he there? Can I talk to him?'

'Just a second.' Kathryn halted the flow and held out the receiver. 'My mother would like a word with you.'

Joel came and took it from her and she left him chatting to her mother whilst she checked out the newspaper. The notice was there all right. Kathryn Templeton was engaged to Joel Kendrick. The feeling of unreality vanished like morning mist. This was no dream; this was really happening. Joel had asked her to marry him and she had agreed. Now it was official.

'I'm afraid lunch is out of the question. Kathryn and I have somewhere to go in the morning. Could you make it dinner? And would it be all right if I brought a guest?'

Kathryn glanced round quickly when she heard that. She looked a question, but Joel shook his head. A minute or two later he put the phone down.

'A nice woman, your mother,' he pronounced, strolling back to the table.

'I think so,' Kathryn agreed, frowning. 'Where do we have to go tomorrow, and why didn't you tell me about the notice?'

Joel grinned unrepentantly. 'I thought it would be a nice surprise. Besides, it was the quickest way of telling the greatest number of people in the shortest space of time.'

It was certainly a surprise, she thought dryly. 'And tomorrow?'

'Ah, that's a surprise too,' he said mysteriously, and refused to be pumped for any information.

'I hate surprises!' Kathryn exclaimed at last, and Joel laughed.

'No, you don't. Anyway, even if you do, you'll like this one.'

'How can you be so sure?' she demanded grumpily. 'I could hate it.'

'Trust me?' he suggested, keeping frustratingly mum.

Her eyes narrowed on his averted profile. 'How can I trust a man who didn't even tell me he'd put the notice of our engagement in the papers?'

His head turned and blue eyes locked on hers. 'Because you love me,' he said simply, and that took the wind out of her sails completely.

'That was a low blow, Kendrick!' she accused, stabbing a finger at him. 'I don't think I love you after all.'

'You will, tomorrow,' Joel returned confidently, neatly folding the newspaper and setting it down on the table. His smile appeared briefly. 'Trust me,' he added, and Kathryn rolled her eyes.

'You are the most…grr!' she finished, flinging up her hands helplessly.

'So, where do you want to go for your honeymoon?' he asked next, making her frown.

'Why are you going to all this trouble, Joel? You can't possibly want all this fuss!' she challenged, not understanding him at all.

'Because both of us intend getting married only once, and in that case we're going to do it right.'

He stunned her with his answer. She had expected he would insist on the rather clinical atmosphere of a register office.

'But it's all so romantic, and...you don't love me,' she argued gruffly.

Joel's eyes fell away from hers, and he reached across to take her hand, locking his fingers with hers. 'I assumed you would want a white wedding. Am I wrong?' When he looked up at her again, he was frowning.

Kathryn instantly felt guilty. He was doing all this for her, because he thought it was what she wanted, and he wanted to make her happy. 'You're right, I do want a white wedding. I thought it was out of the question because our marriage...' She cut off the rest of the sentence, but Joel finished it for her.

'Isn't real? You're wrong, you know. It's going to be very real. Which is why we have to do it right. So, a white wedding it shall be, and then the honeymoon. If you ever tell me where you want to go,' he teased, and her heart swelled, because she loved him all the more for doing this when he didn't have to.

'Oh, I don't know,' Kathryn declared with a shrug, then grinned. 'Surprise me.'

'But you don't like surprises,' he reminded her, and she laughed aloud.

'I lied.'

'Hmm, I see I'm going to have my work cut out with you, sweetheart,' Joel growled, tugging at her hand until he had pulled her up from her chair and onto his lap.

Kathryn smiled down into his eyes. 'I never said I was going to make it easy,' she taunted softly.

He grinned back, his teeth flashing whitely. 'I wouldn't want it any other way.'

Cupping her free hand to his cheek, Kathryn dropped a kiss on his nose. 'I love you,' she said huskily.

Joel's expression was serious as he looked deeply into her eyes. 'I know you do, Kathryn. I won't forget it.'

'See you don't,' she cautioned as the telephone shrilled out once more. 'Something tells me this is going to go on all day,' she groaned as she stood up. 'Your turn.'

'What if it's one of your brothers?' Joel charged and she grinned at him.

'Don't worry, they won't be after your blood now. After all, you're going to make an honest woman of me. That has to be worth several hundred Brownie points.'

'Hmm,' Joel responded. 'That may be, but I was in the Boy Scouts.'

Kathryn started to laugh. 'I bet you looked really sweet in uniform. All gangly and knobbly-kneed.'

'I looked better in my birthday suit.' He grinned, lifting the receiver.

'Take it from me, darling, you still do.'

Joel was about to respond to that when the person at the other end of the line demanded his attention. His eyes promising retribution, he turned and gave his full attention to the caller. Kathryn smiled and began clearing the breakfast things. It was going to be all right. They would make the marriage work because they cared about each other. So what if he didn't love her? She had enough love for the two of them. Besides, one day... But that was only wishful thinking. Sighing, she carried the dishes to the sink and turned on the tap.

* * *

By half past ten the following morning they were in Joel's car, heading north out of the City.

'Where are we going?' Kathryn asked as Joel threaded his way through the Sunday morning traffic, which could sometimes be as heavy as a week day. 'Or is that a secret, too?'

'Cambridge,' he told her concisely, and her brows rose.

'Cambridge? Why Cambridge?' So far as she could recall, she had never been there in her life.

'You'll see when we get there,' he told her with infuriating lack of information.

'I'm surprised somebody hasn't strangled you before now,' Kathryn grumbled, though not really seriously. Folding her coat around her, she sat back to enjoy the ride. Joel cast her a sideways look and bit back a smile.

In a very short space of time they reached the beautiful Fenland town. Joel stopped once to study some directions he had been given, then drove on past the architectural wonders of the university colleges. Eventually they left the pale stone buildings behind and entered a residential area. Kathryn was no more the wiser as to why they were here when Joel pulled up before a well-kept bungalow that looked in no way remarkable from all the others around it.

'This is it?' she probed when Joel came round to open the door for her.

Taking her arm, he steered her up the path and rang the doorbell. 'Relax, I'm not selling you off to white slavers.'

She shot him a scowl. 'Yes, but who lives here?'

'Are you always this impatient?' he countered, and they could hear halting footsteps approaching.

The door was opened by an elderly woman who had

once been beautiful and who, approaching eighty, was still striking. Her hair had once been the colour of autumn leaves, and was sadly faded, but there was sharpness in her green eyes.

'Good morning, Mrs Makepeace,' Joel greeted her warmly. 'I'm Joel Kendrick. We spoke on the telephone. Thank you for agreeing to see me today. I've brought someone with me who very much wants to meet you. This is Kathryn,' he said simply, stepping aside and urging Kathryn forward.

Still puzzled, but winging it, Kathryn smiled at the old woman, who gasped and raised a visibly trembling hand to her lips. 'How do you do? Your name is Makepeace? How strange, my mother's maiden name was Makepeace, too.'

The old lady scrabbled for a handkerchief and dabbed it at her eyes. Even so she smiled through tears that constantly welled up. 'Not so very strange, my dear. Your mother is my little girl. My little Lucy,' she revealed in a voice choked with emotion.

As Kathryn stood there, stunned, Joel carefully took the elderly woman by the arm and gently urged her back into the house. 'I think you'd feel better sitting down, Mrs Makepeace,' he decided, helping her into the compact sitting room. 'Close the door, would you, Kathryn?' he said over his shoulder, and, like an automaton, she did so, trailing along in his wake.

At the sitting-room door, she clutched onto the doorframe as she watched Joel lower the woman into a chair. It was incredible. This woman was her grandmother?

'You're really my grandmother?' Kathryn sought confirmation, her thoughts whirling madly.

Mrs Makepeace looked at her, her tears giving way to an expression of uncertainty. 'Yes, dear. I am.'

Kathryn shook her head helplessly. 'But how…? I don't understand!'

The other woman caught hold of Joel's hand as he straightened up. 'This young man came to find me,' she explained in a voice that still quavered with emotion.

Kathryn stared at Joel in amazement. 'You did?'

He placed a comforting hand on the older woman's shoulder as he responded. 'You said you wanted to meet her,' he said simply, as if that explained everything.

'I did. I do!' she exclaimed, knocked sideways by the knowledge that he would do this for her. Then she smiled encouragingly at the elderly woman as emotions rose to block her own throat. 'I've always wanted to meet you. Ever since I was a little girl.' Crossing the floor, she dropped to her knees before her grandmother and, this close, she could see the likeness to her own mother. She gently took hold of a hand riddled with arthritis. 'Forgive me for being surprised. I never expected this, but I really am most awfully pleased to meet you at last.'

Joel looked from one to the other, smiling faintly at the bright Titian locks of the one, and the faded remnants of the same colour of the other. 'I'll leave you two alone to get acquainted,' he said gently. 'If you need me, I'll be in the kitchen making tea,' he added, though neither was listening to him, and he went out unnoticed.

Alice Makepeace let out a shaky sigh. 'I can't quite believe this is happening myself. When your young man contacted me and explained who you were, and that you wanted to meet me—well, it was like a dream come true. I never thought it could happen. I thought you must all hate me.'

'Oh, no, not at all. Nobody hates you.' Kathryn refuted that quickly.

The older woman shook her head. 'That's not true. George hates me.' She referred to her ex-husband. 'And maybe Lucy does, too. I wouldn't blame her.'

Kathryn was compelled to honesty. 'Grandfather never forgave you, that's true. We don't get on, really. It's because I look a lot like you.'

Her grandmother nodded agreement. 'You do. Very much.'

'But Mother doesn't hate you,' Kathryn insisted. 'She's never had anything but sympathy for your situation. What hurts her is that she doesn't understand why you never kept in touch with her. What happened? Will you tell me?'

Alice looked beyond Kathryn, her thoughts lost in the past and far from pleasant. 'George happened. I never wanted to lose my daughter, but George's family had never approved of me. They helped him when he sued for custody, and when he won they helped him make it difficult for me to see Lucy. There were always excuses, reasons why a planned visit had to be postponed. In the end I realised they would never let me see her.'

Kathryn was appalled. 'Why didn't you take him to court? You had your rights!'

Alice sighed. 'Yes, I had my rights, but in those days it wasn't so easy. I had no family to help me, and no resources. In the end, so much time had passed I decided that Lucy was probably better off without me. Later, when my situation changed, there were so many times when I wanted to contact her. I wrote her letters I never posted. Found out where she lived and went to school. But I was a coward. I thought she must surely hate me for leaving her, so I did nothing. I let my daughter go without a fight, and I'll never forgive myself for that.' Tears misted her eyes, and she looked away, pressing her hand to her lips.

Kathryn came to her feet quickly. Sinking onto the arm of the chair, she slipped her arm about the frail shoulders and hugged her. 'Please don't cry. You're not a coward. You'd just been hurt too much already. Mother knows that. She won't blame you, or hate you. Believe me. I know. She loves you. She always has.'

Alice Makepeace blinked up at her granddaughter hopefully. 'Do you really think so? I've missed her so much. If I could see her just once more, then all the pain would have been worth it. Do you think she would meet me, Kathryn?'

Kathryn smiled down into a face so much like her own. 'Of course she will. When I tell her that I've found you, she'll be on the telephone before you can blink.'

Her grandmother laughed, as Kathryn had wanted her to. 'How is she? Is she well? Is she happy?'

'Very well, very happy. You have four grandsons, too, you know.'

A light of interest entered those green eyes. 'Really? Tell me about them. Tell me about all of you,' she invited huskily, and with a laugh Kathryn drew up a chair and began to tell her all about the family she'd never known she had.

Almost an hour later Kathryn quietly entered the kitchen in search of the tea Joel had promised them. He was sitting at the small table reading a magazine he had found from somewhere. Her heart swelled with love for him for what he had done. Finding her grandmother for her. Crossing the room, she slipped her arms around his neck from behind and pressed a kiss to his cheek.

'Thank you,' she said huskily. 'You've made me very happy.'

Joel tossed the magazine onto the table and placed a hand over hers. 'That was my intention.'

'Well, it worked wonderfully,' she murmured with a decidedly watery smile. 'I don't know why you did it, but I'm glad you did.'

Joel eased her arms from over his head and drew her round onto his lap. 'I did it because I saw how important it was to you. It would make you happy, and making you happy suddenly seemed very important to me.'

Kathryn held her breath and searched his eyes. If she didn't know better, she could almost believe he loved her. It was the sort of thing a person would do for someone they loved.

She smiled bemusedly. 'I don't know how to thank you,' she confessed, and he quickly pressed a finger to her lips.

'Thanks aren't necessary. Seeing you happy is thanks enough. How is your grandmother?'

'She was very emotional, as you'd expect, but she handled it well. I think she could do with that tea now, and a rest to take it all in. It's a shock to the system to have your dreams come true like this.' She was still suffering aftershocks herself.

'It's all ready. We just have to boil the water again,' he responded, rising to his feet and settling her back on hers. 'Do you think she will be up to a trip to London today?' he asked as he switched on the kettle.

A light went on in Kathryn's mind and all became clear. 'She's the guest you're bringing to dinner?'

'It seemed the ideal solution, but if you think it would be too much…?'

Kathryn frowned uncertainly. 'I don't know. She's

not young any more. I'll ask her, but I have the feeling she would rather I paved the way first by telling my mother about her,' she ventured.

'You're probably right,' Joel conceded easily. The kettle boiled and he made the tea, carrying the tray through to the sitting room where Alice Makepeace sat with a bemused smile on her face.

As Kathryn had expected, when the suggestion was put to her that she come with them to meet her daughter she did not feel equal to the event. She needed time, and Kathryn understood that perfectly. She was still feeling the shock of surprise herself, and she was less than half this woman's age. Better to wait until her mother had been told, then the meeting could be planned, rather than thrust upon them.

They stayed with her grandmother for another couple of hours, listening to her reminisce. They weren't always comfortable memories, but they seemed to have a cathartic effect on the old lady. It was as if, by meeting Kathryn, a great weight had been lifted from her shoulders.

Eventually they had to leave, and Alice saw them to the door. There she caught Kathryn by the hand, and her eyes were twinkling. 'Your Joel must love you very much to have gone to so much trouble to find me for you,' she declared, winking at Joel, who grinned back.

'It's impossible not to love Kathryn,' he returned smoothly, and though she knew he was saying it solely for the old lady's benefit, colour dusted her cheeks.

'Now that we've found you, you must come to the wedding,' Kathryn invited, bending to kiss and hug the frail woman.

'I shall look forward to it,' Alice returned, smiling,

and it was with a full heart that Kathryn followed Joel to the car and allowed him to help her inside.

She waved until the bungalow was out of sight, then sat back with a sigh.

'Tired?' Joel asked, and she nodded.

'Emotionally more than physically. But I'm happy, too.' She turned her head against the seat-back to look at him. 'Thank you for lying,' she said softly, and he cast her a questioning look. 'About loving me.'

Joel turned his gaze back to the road. 'Ah,' he said shortly, and she smiled to herself.

'It was a kind thing to do, but then I've always known you were kind. I guess it's one of the reasons why I love you so much,' she went on with a soft laugh.

'Kathryn!' Joel exclaimed exasperatedly.

'I know, I know. You don't want to hear it. But you're going to have to. What you did today only makes me love you more.'

'That isn't what I meant,' he contested as they approached a crossroads. The traffic light was green as they went through it.

Kathryn was just about to respond when out of the corner of her eye she saw a car shooting the red lights on her left. Alarm shot through her. 'Look out!' she cried in terror, and then everything was a blur of light and noise as the two cars collided. Her head hit something hard and everything went dark.

When Kathryn returned to the world again, her nose told her where she was. That antiseptic smell could only be a hospital. One look confirmed she *was* in a hospital bed, but apart from having a raging thirst she seemed fine, and all of her limbs moved when she tested them. Her head ached when she attempted to raise it, and she recalled hitting it just before blacking out. Memory of the accident returned, and with it an intense anxiety to know if Joel was all right.

This time she raised her head despite the queasiness the thumping brought with it. 'Joel?' she called out, just this side of panicking. The room was empty, though it was designed for four, and she had no sense of him. Oh, God! she thought wildly. He couldn't be dead! 'Joel!' she cried more sharply, scrabbling for the buzzer, needing to know.

'Kathryn?'

The sound of his voice calling her name brought her head round, and she felt such a wave of relief tears sprang to her eyes. The next second he came striding in from the corridor. He was minus his jacket, and there was blood on his shirt, the evidence of a cut on his cheek that was covered by a dressing.

Joel came directly to her, sitting on the edge of the bed and swooping her into his arms. They closed so tightly about her her breathing was restricted, but she didn't care. He was alive and well, and relieved tears trailed down her cheeks as she clung to him.

'I thought I'd lost you,' she declared brokenly.

Joel's hand cupped the back of her head, pressing her into his neck. 'When I saw you lying crumpled in the seat beside me, I thought I'd lost you, too,' he confessed thickly. 'I've never been so terrified in my whole life.'

Kathryn closed her eyes, sending up a silent prayer of thanks. 'What happened?' she asked 'I remember the car hitting us, then everything went black.' She felt him shudder.

'Fortunately for us the other car only winged us and spun us around. That's how you came to hit your head.

We were incredibly lucky that traffic was light. Had there been more... The other driver was well over the limit, apparently,' Joel explained, and she could hear his underlying anger.

Easing away, Kathryn checked out as much of him as she could with her eyes. 'You were hurt, too.' She pointed to his cheek.

'Just a scratch. It bled a lot, but it's not deep. You were the one we were worried about. You've been out for a while now, and they're going to keep you in overnight to check for concussion. I telephoned your parents and they insisted on coming up. Don't be surprised if your family arrive mob-handed,' he added dryly, and she chuckled—then wished she hadn't when her head thumped.

'They're very protective,' she reminded him unnecessarily.

'Well, they're going to have to learn to take a back seat. It's my job to protect you now,' he declared uncompromisingly. 'Not that I did too good a job today. When I saw that car heading right for you...'

'Hush!' Kathryn interrupted, pressing her hand over his lips. 'Don't think about it.'

Joel kissed her palm before reaching up and pulling it away. 'I have to. You see, it gave me the jolt I needed to be honest with myself at last. In that split second, when I thought I might lose you, the truth reared up and bit me. I suddenly knew I couldn't lose you. It was totally unacceptable.'

Kathryn's throat closed over at the blazing depth of feeling she could see in his eyes. It almost seemed as if he was saying... Her heart quailed at the thought. What if she was wrong? She wanted to believe her ears and eyes weren't deceiving her, but dared not. To hope and have that hope crushed would be too much on top of everything else. She had to be certain before she dared believe that a miracle was happening.

'Did you hit your head, too? You're not making much sense, you know.' She tried to make light of it, but her heart was racing fit to burst and her voice wobbled dangerously.

The tenderness in his touch as he reached out and ran a finger gently along the fragile line of her jaw was almost her undoing. 'I've been a fool. Worse, I've been an arrogant fool. I thought I could command my heart not to feel, but it knew better. Whilst my head was telling me love doesn't exist, my heart was proving me wrong.'

Kathryn's heart seemed to swell inside her as joy burst its bounds. She wasn't mistaken. It was all right to hope and believe. 'Joel—'

His hand cut her off. 'No, let me finish. I have to say this and you deserve to hear it. When I was faced with the possibility of a future without you in it, I finally admitted to myself that I loved you. I've loved you for a long time, it seems. In fact, I can't remember not loving you. You walked into my life that day and changed it for ever. My heart knew it, but my head fought it. I'm sorry it's taken me so long to admit it.'

Though she felt like exploding with happiness, she responded cautiously. 'Are you sure? Please be absolutely sure, because my happiness depends on it.'

Joel cupped his hands gently about her face. 'I'm a man of my word and I won't renege. I told you once to put me to the test, and I guess this is the moment of truth. There is no doubt in my mind or my heart. I love you, Kathryn. I will always love you.'

Kathryn closed her eyes, drawing in a deep breath, a smile slowly spreading across her lips. When she looked at him again, her eyes blazed with love. 'I've longed to hear you say that, and thought I never would.'

'Do you trust me? Is my word enough?'

'Of course,' she sighed. 'I love you, and because I love you, I trust you.'

'In that case, there's one thing I have to ask you. Last time I did it, it was for all the wrong reasons. It was the easy option to ask you to marry me without admitting I loved you. Today I'm asking for no other reason than that I love you, and can't live without you. Will you marry me?' Joel asked in a voice made husky by emotion.

Her heart overflowed. 'Oh, yes,' she breathed happily.

'Thank God.' Joel's exclamation was heartfelt, and then he kissed her, carefully because of her head, but there was all the love in it that she could ever want.

'Did you really think I might say no this time?' Kathryn queried with a laugh.

Joel grimaced in self-mockery. 'Believe me, my hands were shaking almost as much as they were the evening I arrived to take you to dinner,' he confessed, and she looked at him in mild surprise.

'I didn't know that.'

His grin was shamefaced. 'I hid them in my pockets so you wouldn't see. I was so looking forward to seeing you again, I was very nearly a gibbering wreck. Something which had never happened to me since my very first date. That was the state you had me in.'

She would never have guessed. 'You hid it well.'

'So well that I hid the truth from myself.'

Kathryn rested her head on his shoulder, so completely happy it was almost like being slightly tipsy. 'Not any more, though.'

'No, not any more,' Joel agreed softly.

'When did you start to realise you loved me?' she wanted to know, and he laughed softly.

'You want your pound of flesh, don't you?' he drawled wryly. 'I guess it was when you described yourself as a faithful hound. Later I began to realise how jealous and possessive I felt about you. I wanted to see you happy, not hurt, and I was willing to take on your family to do it. The clincher was when you spoke of your successor waiting in the wings. I realised I didn't want anyone else. You were the only one for me.'

'So you asked me to marry you, and went off to find my grandmother for me. I'll have to start calling you my white knight.' Kathryn teased him with a full heart. She glanced up at him from the corner of her eye. 'Um—how long do you think we have before a nurse turns up to check on me?'

'Not too long, I should imagine,' he calculated wryly.

Her hand snaked up into his hair, tugging his head down. 'Then we'd better not waste any time. Kiss me again.'

'You know I could probably get thrown out of the hospital for this,' he warned, even as he complied.

'I'll risk it if you will,' she murmured seductively, and he gave that chuckle which melted her bones.

'Are you flirting with me, sweetheart?'

'If you can't tell, I'm not doing it right,' she breathed

against his lips. 'Come on, Big Bad Wolf, do your worst.'

Smiling male lips brushed hers. 'Wolves mate for life, you know.'

Kathryn nipped at his bottom lip with her small white teeth. 'Hmm, I like the sound of that.'

'Somehow I thought you might,' Joel growled, and finally, most satisfyingly, kissed her.

COMING SOON!

We really hope you enjoyed reading this book. If you're looking for more romance, be sure to head to the shops when new books are available on

Thursday
26th July

To see which titles are coming soon, please visit
millsandboon.co.uk

MILLS & BOON

LET'S TALK
Romance

For exclusive extracts, competitions
and special offers, find us online:

📘 facebook.com/millsandboon

📷 @millsandboonuk

🐦 @millsandboon

Or get in touch on 0844 844 1351*

For all the latest titles coming soon, visit
millsandboon.co.uk/nextmonth

Want even more
ROMANCE?

Join our bookclub today!